Rise of the Immortal

Path of the Ranger, Book 15

Pedro Urvi

COMMUNITY:
Mail: pedrourvi@hotmail.com
Facebook: https://www.facebook.com/PedroUrviAuthor/
My Website: http://pedrourvi.com
Twitter: https://twitter.com/PedroUrvi

Translation by:
Christy Cox

Edited by:
Mallory Brandon Bingham

DEDICATION

To my good friend Guiller.

Thank you for all your support since day one.

Content

MAP

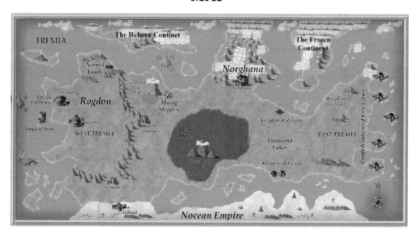

Chapter 1

Under cover of night, six riders were silently fording the river that separated the east from the west of the Kingdom of Norghana. They were crossing a shallow part in the reigning gloom of a starless night. Wrapped in their cloaks, hoods covering their heads and scarves over their mouth and nose, they traveled stealthily. Fall had just arrived and with it the snow, always present in the life of all Norghanians. The fields were already white, and heavy snow was falling on the riders and their surroundings.

If indiscrete eyes had been watching, they would have assumed them to be outlaws on their way to some night hit, which is why they were not using the not-too-distant bridge a little more to the south. But these riders were the opposite: they were Rangers, defenders of the realm.

The riders finished crossing the river and followed a northwesterly direction without a word. They crossed a white plain while the snowflakes fell by the thousands from the sky onto their clothing and mounts. The hooded cloaks protected them from the cold and the snow, although they were used to the harshness of the Norghanian weather, being experienced Rangers.

But tonight, they were not on any mission assigned by King Thoran, nor were they headed to fulfill their Ranger duties which their leader Gondabar used to ask of them. Tonight, they were marching for a very different reason, one of great transcendence for the Kingdom and most likely for all of Tremia.

They stopped beside three ancient oaks in the middle of the plain. No one said anything. They waited in silence under the heavy snow which seemed intent on burying them that night. But they did not appear nervous, although their somber faces and deep, thoughtful gazes indicated they were troubled.

All of a sudden from the north appeared a dozen riders. The six Rangers under the oaks did not stir and continued to wait. The dozen riders reached them and stopped a short distance away. Two of them came forward. Of the six Rangers, one advanced to welcome them.

"Cold is the night in the north," one of the riders greeted the

Ranger.

"It is colder still in the west," the Ranger replied.

"But the heart of the Norghanians of the West burns with strength, courage, and honor," the other rider said.

"And that is why the good men of the West will prevail," the waiting rider replied.

After this exchange, the three riders pushed back their hoods so their faces could be seen.

"Count Eriksen, I'm happy to see you," the Ranger said.

"And I am even happier to see my Lord, the King of the West," the Count replied.

"I'm only a Ranger, I have no title or possessions," Egil reminded him with a smile.

"You will always be our Lord and the true King who one day will sit on the throne of Norghana," Count Malason said as he greeted Egil with a small bow from the saddle.

Egil smiled and then greeted the two men with nods.

"I am truly happy to see both of you and find you in good health. Without you, the Western cause, Norghana's future, would be in serious danger."

"You attach too much importance to us. If not ourselves, other members of the Western League would still stand by you," Eriksen reminded Egil.

"Not to mention our kin," Malason added, "who are not here tonight, but who we're teaching properly so that one day they will take our place at the head of our houses as influential members in the coalition," Malason said.

"I expect nothing less. Blood unites us, and blood will save the West and the Realm," Egil said seriously.

"Your blood, that of the Olafstones," Eriksen stated.

"I'm not so sure about that..." Egil replied thoughtfully, his gaze lost in the dark horizon. The snow kept falling heavily and it did not seem the storm would be over soon.

"So it must be," Malason said. "The House of Olafstone is the legitimate heir to the throne. You must be King, Egil."

"We have to take the throne away from Thoran and Orten and their eastern allies who now make up the Court. Regardless of how long it takes, we will do it," Eriksen added.

Egil nodded, although he remained thoughtful.

"We will someday, or perhaps they themselves will call down doom on their own heads through their own acts. Both scenarios are plausible."

"I'd rather not wait for that to happen," Eriksen said.

"Better if we throw them out," added Malason.

"That's a risky proposition…" Egil told them. "We can't be the cause of another civil war. The cost of the first one was too high, and we'll still be paying for it in the years to come. Norghana will not be a strong, respected nation in Tremia for a long time because of what happened."

"Better to be weak than governed by ruthless tyrants," Malason said with such vigor that his horse became restless and he had to sooth it, patting its neck and haunches.

"Those two morons will drive Norghana to total ruin," Eriksen predicted.

Egil bowed his head and smiled.

"Yes, although I wouldn't bet that's what will happen. If it did, it would be our best chance to regain the throne."

The two western nobles exchanged confused glances.

"Must we wait until Thoran and Orten destroy the Kingdom?" Eriksen asked.

"That doesn't sound very promising," Malason added.

Egil shook his head.

"We must wait for a clear opportunity, for them to make a great mistake and lose power, or to get involved in a situation they aren't able to get out of. That's when we'll act. Until then, we wait. Fighting Thoran, his brother, and the Court Nobles openly and directly is suicide, and it would cause great loss and suffering to our people. Therefore, we will not pursue that course of action."

Malason and Eriksen looked at one another and bowed their heads. Their looks indicated that they were not at all happy with what they were hearing.

"You are our Lord and we follow you loyally, since the Western Blood wants us to," Eriksen said, accepting Egil's will.

"Only a fool attempts the same madness twice, having failed the first time," Egil instructed them. "We will wait for a chance to present itself. We'll prepare and be ready when the time of the West arrives. Don't despair. We need silence and tenacity. We must work in the shadows together. The day will come, I swear it."

"We trust and believe in our Lord, and we'll follow him to the end. For the West! For Norghana!" Eriksen cried in a firm and respectful tone.

"We'll do as our Lord wills. Our honor obliges us, and the blood of the West that runs through our veins and makes our Norghanian hearts beat unites us," Malason nodded, agreeing with and accepting the decision.

Egil took a deep breath.

"I'm glad to see I can count on your trust and loyalty. The day will come when both will be tested. I am sure you will pass the test and do the right thing, for the good of all Norghana."

"We will overcome any test of our honor," Eriksen promised.

"What else troubles you? Tell me," Egil invited them with a wave of his hand as he quieted his mount. The snow continued falling, and the horses' manes were as white as the landscape around them.

"Our Leader knows us well," Malason smiled. "Times are changing and the West is getting nervous."

"The new situation regarding the throne and the impending Royal Wedding have caused all kinds of rumors and concerns in the Western League, as well as the rest of the country," Eriksen explained.

Egil nodded repeatedly.

"The Royal Wedding is a given," he announced.

"Is the deal closed with the King of Irinel then?" Eriksen asked.

They're still tying up loose ends, but it will be. I believe the Wedding will be officially announced shortly," Egil told them.

"That's not good news for the West," Malason commented, shaking his head from side to side.

"If there's a wedding, it could lead to an heir, and that's not good for the West's interests. It would strengthen Thoran's position with the court and the nobles," Eriksen said.

"Very true," Egil agreed. "But on the other hand, an alliance with the Kingdom of Irinel strengthens the realm. Norghana will be stronger and recover faster from the sad state she's currently in."

"It's not good for us that there's a Queen, and least of all an heir," Malason said. "We already have enough trouble with the King and his brother as it is."

"We mustn't get ahead of events," Egil told them." There still hasn't been a wedding, and least of all an heir to the throne."

"But both things will occur if they're not prevented…" Eriksen commented, taking them for granted.

Egil was thoughtful for a moment.

"Does the League want to prevent the Royal Wedding?" he asked.

"There are some Western Nobles who see great danger in that wedding for our ambitions," Eriksen insisted.

"Has there been talk of an intervention?" Egil asked in a concerned tone.

"There has indeed, but not in a definite manner. It's only a feeling before the possibility of a Queen and a future heir which strengthen the King's hold on the throne, which would be terrible for us," Malason insisted.

"What do you two think?" Egil asked them.

Malason heaved a deep sigh.

"I believe we must intervene, one way or another. We cannot let Thoran dig his bloody claws into a throne that doesn't belong to him."

Egil looked at Eriksen and nodded at him so he would speak.

"I think the same," said the Western Noble. "We can't let Thoran strengthen his hold on the throne."

"I see…" Egil said and was thoughtful again.

"What does our Lord want us to do?" Malason asked.

"We'll obey our Lord and Leader's instructions," Eriksen promised.

"I want us to act with caution," Egil said. "We must think and plan any movement against the crown with extreme care. A lot is at stake, not only our lives and those of our people, but the Kingdom's future. The alliance with Irinel benefits Norghana, and at the same time is counterproductive to our interest in recovering the throne. On the other hand, we must think about Norghana first and then the West, not the other way round. Otherwise, we won't ever have a strong united Kingdom, which is what we all want."

"The Norghanians of the West have mixed feelings about that," Eriksen said.

"They're ruled by their love of the West rather than the Kingdom," Malason added.

"I know, and it's understandable, more so considering everything they've gone through with the war," Egil said. "Still, we must look to the future and what is best for Norghana, with a strong West leading her. We will not interfere, for now. We'll let the coming events happen and remain expectant and ready. The wedding might be thwarted without our intervention. There are so many interests against it that might come into play."

"The Zangrians?" Malason asked.

"The Noceans?" Eriksen cut in.

"Among others. We are not the only ones who would not benefit from this Royal Wedding. Every nation or kingdom that wishes for a weak Norghana would rather the wedding never took place."

"Might they intervene to prevent it?" Eriksen asked.

"Perhaps, indeed," Egil nodded, "and that's why we'll wait and see."

"Very well, Sire. We will wait," Malason promised.

"Now that we've talked about national politics, let's focus on the reason for this clandestine meeting," Egil said. "Have you gathered the information I asked for?"

"We have, my Lord," Malason replied as he stepped up to Egil and handed him a sealed scroll.

"It wasn't easy to get," Eriksen said. "It cost us a small fortune."

"I can imagine," Egil nodded as he put the scroll in his satchel.

"Why is it so important?" Malason asked him. "We've been using our agents and the gold of the West to get information we don't know the use of. Can you enlighten us …?"

"Yes, I can," Egil said. "It's important because Norghana is in serious danger, one of colossal proportions which we must face and defeat."

Both men showed their surprise; they had not been expecting Egil to say something like that.

"Are Thoran and his brother planning something against the West?" Malason asked.

"Are the Zangrians going to invade us? Or the Peoples of the Frozen Continent?" Eriksen added.

"I'm afraid it's something even worse," Egil said with a loud sigh that came straight from his heart. "You see, a new enemy we weren't counting on has awakened, one of immense power that seeks to bring death and destruction to our land. We have to stop it. If we don't, our beloved Kingdom, as well as neighboring nations and kingdoms, will be destroyed."

"We don't understand, my Lord…" Eriksen said as he looked blankly at Malason.

Egil nodded.

"For now, understand this. An ancient being, thousands of years old, a creature with immense power, is about to return. If it manages to do so, both our beloved realm and those adjacent will be razed to the ground."

Eriksen nodded.

"Is that the creature we're looking for?" Malason asked.

"It is, and we must destroy it," said Egil seriously.

"We'll find it and destroy it," Eriksen promised.

"It will not be easy, and there will be bloodshed," Egil warned them in a serious tone, his gaze stern. "We might not be able to stop it. It might cost us our lives."

"We will succeed," Malason said, convinced. "You have the West."

"Thank you. I'll need all the help we can get. Now go. Return to your domains, gather the Western League, and tell them what we've discussed. Make them understand. They must support us."

"Yes, Sire, we'll do that," Eriksen said.

Malason nodded. "So it will be." Then he looked at Egil's companions. "Greetings, Lasgol. Greetings, Snow Panthers," he said.

"Count Malason, Count Eriksen," Lasgol returned the greeting solemnly.

"Take good care of the King of the West," Eriksen told them.

"Always," Ingrid replied.

The Nobles of the West left with their guard and became lost in the distance as if the night has swallowed them.

Egil looked at the Panthers.

"Let's go back. We have to stop Dergha-Sho-Blaska."

Chapter 2

The Snow Panthers were standing in a line in the middle of the austere hall in the Rangers' Tower. They were looking at their leader sitting on the other side of his desk. If Gondabar's appearance had not been particularly good lately, what Egil had just told him had left him looking even worse.

"What you have just revealed to me does not fall short of any of the fantastic odes told in our folklore of fighting between ice gods and mythological beasts."

"I assure you, sir, that no matter how outrageous it may seem, it's the truth," Egil said, absolutely serious.

Gondabar looked at the six companions one by one, seeking their gazes with his own, which showed great trouble.

"You also believe everything Egil has told me is true?" he asked them.

"We do," Lasgol hastened to say, nodding.

"It's the truth. We can testify to it because we all lived through it together," Astrid joined in.

"The fact that you have all experienced a series of traumatic experiences doesn't make this... incredible story... true..."

"We know it sounds impossible, and that if we told others about it probably no-one would believe us, but even so, after talking about it we decided to come here to tell our leader," Nilsa said, stumbling on her own words, she was so nervous.

"It's not that I don't believe you... I trust you and your good judgment. You have always proven yourselves to have good judgment and have acted in defense of the realm with honor and courage. I don't doubt that for one instant. But the story is very hard to swallow," Gondabar said frankly.

"I already told them it would be better to keep quiet, that no one would believe us, but as usual they didn't pay any attention to me," Viggo said.

"The situation is serious. The Kingdom is in danger. That's why we decided to come and inform our leader," Ingrid said.

"As you should," Gondabar said with a nod.

"If we didn't inform you of what's going on and the catastrophe occurred, we'd be partly responsible," Lasgol said. "That's why we're here today."

"If we didn't come to our leader, if we didn't look for help in this dreadful business, we'd be committing a serious negligence," Egil said.

"It's our duty to report any great danger to the realm, one which we're sure is going to affect all Norghanians," Astrid said.

Gondabar's face darkened further. The group's insistence seemed to have him a bit confused.

"From what you've told me, I understand then, that this being… what's its name…?"

"Dergha-Sho-Blaska," Egil repeated.

"A complicated and strange name," Gondabar commented. "Am I to understand it's really a dragon?"

"Yes, sir," Egil confirmed.

"And that it's actually inside an orb at present?"

"That's right. We believe that inside the Orb is the dragon's spirit," Egil said.

"With part of its power," Astrid added.

Gondabar's gaze went to each of them in turn.

"And this dragon spirit and its power are going to reincarnate?"

"That's what we believe," Lasgol said.

"And when it does, it will raze Norghana," Ingrid added.

Gondabar heaved a deep sigh.

"Do you realize how unlikely and even ridiculous everything you're telling me sounds? And I want you to know that I say this with all the respect and affection I have for each of you. The more I listen, the more outrageous I find it."

"I told you he wouldn't believe us, not him nor anyone else," Viggo said, looking sour.

"Sir, it's the truth. If we don't act now, it *will* happen. Once it reincarnates it will be unstoppable," Lasgol insisted.

"Let me tell you to start with that so far, no matter how much legends and myth speak of them, both in Norghana and in other regions of Tremia, there is no irrefutable evidence of the existence of dragons, ever," Gondabar insisted in turn.

"There is a lot of literature and folklore about dragons, and very likely there's a true basis for it. Myths are often born of reality in most cases," Egil said.

"No reliable proof has ever been found of their existence, no matter how deeply the matter has been studied, and it has been done," Gondabar said, shaking his head.

"The fact that they don't exist now doesn't mean they didn't in the past," Egil added.

"Once again, that's only a belief, a hypothesis. It's never been proven, since nothing has ever been found to justify it."

"That's true, but now we do have evidence," said Astrid.

"A spirit in an orb? That's not evidence. And in any case, it would be evidence that the orb is some Object of Power, not of the existence of dragons. A lot more than that would be necessary to persuade me, and the rest of the leaders, that dragons exist in the first place. A lot more," Gondabar replied with a dismissive wave of his hand.

"Our leader is wise and wary. We understand his reluctance to believe that we've discovered the existence of a dragon," said Egil, "more so without conclusive evidence to present."

"Not only the existence," Gondabar interrupted. "There's no evidence that the Object of Power you found frozen in the Secret Shelter contains the soul of a dragon."

"We don't have evidence as such, other than what we've seen and heard," said Astrid. "But what we've experienced points to that being the case."

"You might believe so—you may even be convinced, I've no doubt, for whatever reasons—but I don't, and I'm not convinced. You haven't brought me anything to persuade me other than your story. Interesting, unbelievable, and troubling, but nothing more than a story."

"We believe that story," Lasgol insisted.

"Do you really think that this being, this dragon spirit, is going to reincarnate?" Gondabar asked them, pointing his finger at them. "Do you realize how crazy that sounds? It's not just that you want me to believe in the existence of dragons, you now want me to believe in reincarnation, which is as unbelievable as the former."

"Put that way... dragon spirits, reincarnation... our leader is quite right," said Viggo, folding his arms.

"We know it sounds crazy, but we're sure of what we're saying," Ingrid tried to persuade him.

"I know, and that worries me," Gondabar said.

"We can prove the existence of the Defenders of the True Blood my uncle Viggen Norling leads," said Astrid, "and also of Drugan Volskerian and his warlocks and Visionaries."

Gondabar nodded heavily. He was trying to process everything the Panthers had told him.

"It proves that there are a couple of orders, cults, or brotherhoods with sinister intentions. But you must know that there have always been and will always be such dark organizations. For some reason or another, men seek to find comfort in the grimmest beliefs, in following tricksters and fake prophets. A sect that believes in a powerful ancient dragon, who is waiting for it to reincarnate and bring the end of the known world, *that* I believe exists. I won't deny that, I believe it. Their message, on the other hand, their goal, I can't bring myself to believe, and the fact that you do troubles me greatly."

"We must stop both groups," Lasgol said. "They're extremely dangerous."

"We're simply asking for the Rangers' and the King's help to do so," Nilsa said.

Gondabar raised his hand and waved it negatively.

"I can't take this unlikely story to the King, least of all without any proof. He'd fly off the handle! He'd rage about me wasting his time and distracting him from his important duties with stories about dragons and other mythical beings."

"I don't see our beloved king swallowing our story either," Viggo said sarcastically.

"I won't bother the King with this unless you bring me solid proof."

"By then it might be too late," Lasgol said.

"If we can't count on the King's help, will we at least have the help of the Rangers?" Egil asked

Gondabar was silent, thinking.

"We'll do the following. I will charge you with a mission which must remain secret. The mission will be to find unquestionable evidence of this being, of this Dergha-Sho-Blaska. For that you'll have access to all the Rangers' resources and you may ask for support if you need it. You'll also find the two sects and their leaders, and bring them to me for questioning to see how much truth there is to their beliefs. In any case, I agree they are dangerous and must be stopped. You have permission to do that."

"Thank you, sir," Egil said, bowing respectfully.

"You will treat this mission as a secret and only report to me what you find. I don't want to start wild rumors among our people. That's all I can do for now. Do you agree?"

The Panthers looked at one another.

"We understand our leader's wariness and his good judgment," Egil said. "We'll get started at once and bring you credible, irrefutable evidence."

"All right then," Gondabar said. "One more thing…" he said suddenly, and once again looked at them one by one, as if trying to gauge that everything was okay in the Panthers' gazes, whether they were still sane. "I think I'm going to need Mother Specialist Sigrid's help with this. I'll consult with her," he announced.

"Does our leader believe there's something wrong with our heads?" Egil asked, guessing immediately why Gondabar wanted Sigrid's help.

The leader of the Rangers spread his hands.

"You're not like any other Rangers. You have all experienced things… things that others haven't. Your minds have been affected. We all know this."

"No matter how affected our minds are, and I'm not saying they aren't, we're definitely not crazy," Viggo assured him.

"Nor do I mean to imply that that is the case," Gondabar said. "You could also be possessed or under some spell or illusion. Sigrid's brother and Galdason will be able to help verify whether this is true or not."

"Wow… so much trust in the best Rangers of the realm…" Viggo said with marked bitterness in his tone.

"It's not lack of trust, it's prudence," Gondabar said. "I want to make sure there aren't any other factors at play in this plot, since you've come to me with an impossible-to-believe story."

"If our leader wants to make sure we're okay, we have no objections," said Ingrid.

"I do. A few," Viggo added.

"But you'll do whatever our leader asks of us," Ingrid told him with a glare.

"Of course," Viggo smiled.

"Go now and let me think of all this."

The Panthers took their leave of Gondabar with bows. They went down the tower stairs and outside. There were several Rangers chatting in front of the door, so they moved a little farther away to be out of earshot before standing in a circle.

"See what you've done? He thinks we're crazy!" Viggo said.

"We decided we had to tell him," Lasgol told him.

"You decided, don't include me in this. I told you this would happen."

"It wasn't that bad," said Egil.

"It wasn't?" Nilsa said. "I thought it went pretty badly."

"Very badly," Astrid said.

"If you think again, you'll see that on the one hand we've managed to plant the seed of doubt in Gondabar's mind, and on the other to get assigned the mission to capture Drugan and Viggen and bring proof of the existence of Dergha-Sho-Blaska. I think we've made some progress."

"It will allow us to keep searching without interference and with the Rangers' help," Lasgol said cheerfully.

"That's true, and that's good for us. The worst thing that could happen would be to be sent abroad again and lose the Orb's trail," Ingrid said.

"He's also going to examine our heads to see whether we're crazy," Viggo said bitterly.

"Or in case we're bewitched," Egil replied with a wink.

"The weirdo was born bewitched, and you're almost as much of a troublemaker as he is," Viggo said.

"What matters is that we did our duty. We've told Gondabar what we know and about the situation. It's his responsibility to take the matter into his hands," said Ingrid.

"We haven't told him everything we know," Nilsa said. "We haven't mentioned Camu or the Pearls…"

"It wasn't necessary and it would've only brought more confusion to the matter," Lasgol said.

"Gondabar has the bare facts he needs to act," Egil said. "That's what's important. He's made his move for now."

"By ordering us to investigate secretly?" Astrid asked.

"Irrefutable, my dear Assassin," he smiled.

"You do know that saying everything's irrefutable all the time is most repellent, don't you?" Viggo told Egil.

"I do," Egil said, unfazed. "That's why I do it."

Viggo put his hands to his head and swore to the heavens.

They all laughed at his exaggerated and dramatic reaction.

As they were laughing and teasing Viggo, a figure appeared and approached the group, coming from the stables. It was a tall, strong man, a true Norghanian of the mountains. He approached them with an awkward gait, unbalanced, as if his hips were not aligned. Lasgol noticed someone was approaching them and turned around. When he saw who it was his heart burst with joy.

"Gerd! What are you doing here?" he cried, taken aback by the sight of his friend.

The giant smiled from ear to ear.

"It was high time I joined up with the group again."

Chapter 3

"Gerd! Oh, I'm so happy to see you!" Nilsa cried, skipping as she ran to hug him with open arms. She reached him and threw her arms around his neck with such energy that Gerd had a hard time keeping his balance.

"I see you're as impulsive as ever, Nilsa!" he smiled.

"A little less clumsy, but as crazy as usual," said Viggo, coming toward Gerd as Nilsa hung from the giant's neck.

"And you're still as sarcastic as usual," Gerd said to Viggo.

"Give me a hug, big guy, before I stop being happy to see you and start teasing you," Viggo replied with a big smile.

Nilsa let go of Gerd's neck and he spread his arms to welcome his friend.

"Bear hug!" he said, closing his arms around Viggo.

"Oh no!" Viggo moaned, making a face.

Gerd started spinning with Viggo in his arms so he could not set his feet down.

"Let me down, you sawdust-filled head, you're not fit for this!" Viggo cried.

"I find him very fit," Ingrid said, chuckling.

"I'll say, look how he's spinning," Astrid joined her, also chuckling.

"If he can spin like that it means he's recuperated," Egil commented with a nod.

"Of course, I am!" Gerd cried, beaming.

"Put me down before there's an accident, you mountain of brainless muscles!"

Gerd did not pay any attention to Viggo and spun around once again with his friend trapped in his arms like a rag doll. When he finished his spin, he lost balance and took a funny sidestep. They nearly toppled over.

"I'm losing it!" Gerd warned.

Astrid moved swiftly like a gazelle and held Gerd fast so he would not completely lose his balance. A moment later Ingrid grabbed Viggo so he would not upset the giant even further. Nilsa also grabbed a hold of Gerd quickly.

"Are you okay?" Lasgol asked him once they were both steady.

"Yeah… I'm fine…" Gerd said as he recovered, although his face was bright red.

"Fine? You call that fine, you uncoordinated brute? We almost fell," Viggo scolded.

"I'm sorry…" Gerd started to apologize.

"Never mind him, he would've landed on all fours like a black cat," Ingrid said, patting Gerd on the back to cheer him.

"Black panther you mean," Viggo said, straining his neck and lifting his chin proudly.

"A baby black panther," Nilsa said, giggling.

They all smiled and the awkward moment was over.

"How are you, Gerd?" Egil asked as he gave him a hug.

"Well, they've let me come back. Mother Specialist Sigrid and Elder Annika think I'm well enough to return to my Ranger duties."

"Well, I'm not sure they're right," Viggo said. "Are you sure they've tested you enough?"

"I'm sure they've tested him more than enough," Ingrid said. "They wouldn't have let him come back if they didn't think he was well enough."

"I'm feeling quite recovered, although not entirely… I'm still not who I used to be…" Gerd admitted, and he started feeling embarrassed, as the color on his face proved.

"Don't worry, it's only a matter of time before you're in perfect shape again," Astrid said cheerfully.

"Sigrid and Annika think it will be good for me to be with you all and take part in your adventures. They say it'll help me recover faster."

"That makes all the sense in the world," said Egil. "Nothing compares to living the day-to-day life of a Ranger, and particularly the events we're used to experiencing, which are much more dangerous."

"A little danger and real action will be good for me, I'm sure," Gerd said.

"A little, he says, as if he didn't know us already," Viggo replied.

"Maybe he's forgotten after so long," Nilsa joked.

Gerd shook his head.

"I haven't forgotten in the least. I know all too well the kind of messes you get into and all the danger they entail."

"I'm thrilled you're back," said Nilsa as she clapped her hands hard and then hugged him again.

"We all are," Lasgol said, shaking his hand and then hugging him.

"Why didn't you warn us you were coming?" Ingrid asked.

"I wanted to surprise you," Gerd said, spreading his arms. "Surprise!"

"You're unbelievable!" Ingrid said while the rest of the group broke into laughter.

"It's a great joy to have you with us again," Egil said.

"The joy is all mine, you've no idea how much I've missed you!"

"Is Elder Engla recovered as well?" Astrid asked.

"If you are she must be too, right?" Viggo said.

"Well, not quite…. The Elder is having more trouble and her recovery is going a little slower than mine."

"Oh, wow… that's a pity," Lasgol said sadly.

"She's so strong and tough, I was sure she would've made it already," Viggo said.

"As you know, the problem is more mental than physical…. Her physical body has recovered well, but she's still struggling to recover mentally," Gerd explained.

"I'm sure she'll get there soon," Astrid said, wishfully.

"Edwina and Annika continue working on her recovery. I believe they'll manage to make her well soon."

"The Healer is still at the Shelter? Dolbarar will be missing her at the Camp no doubt," Lasgol commented.

"Yes, she's still there, and from what we've heard there have been several accidents among the contenders at the Camp, but nothing they couldn't handle. Dolbarar sent a letter to Sigrid assuring her they were doing well and that Edwina can continue looking after Engla. It seems that Master Sylvia, the new Master Ranger of the School of Nature, is a healing phenomenon and Dolbarar holds her in great esteem. Thanks to her, nothing serious has happened at the Camp."

"She must be skilled indeed if they don't need Edwina," Nilsa commented.

"Or maybe the new contenders are more intelligent and less brutal…" said Ingrid as a group of several Rangers who did not appear to be veterans and looked quite rough, arrived at the Tower. "No, never mind, I'm sure they're as brutal as ever."

"Then Master Sylvia must be very good," Astrid nodded.

"Are Ona and Camu well?" Gerd asked with a troubled look on his face as he looked around and did not see them.

"Yes, don't worry," Lasgol hastened to say. "But it's better that they don't wander around the castle and the city. They draw too much attention and people get nervous. The less attention Camu draws, the better for everyone."

"True," Gerd nodded. "I'm dying to see and hug them."

"I'm sure the bug will be delighted to get one of your bear hugs. See if you can hold him," Viggo said with irony.

Gerd frowned and bent his head.

"Why do you say that?"

"Never mind him, Gerd, it's just that Camu is quite a bit larger than the last time you saw him," Lasgol explained.

"Oh, well, I'll try anyway." He smiled.

"Are you sure they haven't told you to pace yourself?" Nilsa asked him with concern. "Don't you need to be careful?"

"Don't worry. I'll be careful, and I have permission to return to my post as a Ranger."

"In that case, welcome!" Ingrid said.

They all patted his back and shoulders and showed him their affection.

"What a great joy to see you all!" Gerd told them with moist eyes.

"The joy is ours to have you back," Lasgol told him, also moved.

"You have to tell me everything I've missed."

"Then we're going to be here for a long, long time..." Viggo told him.

"We find ourselves in a pretty complicated situation," Astrid said.

"Very bad?" Gerd asked.

"Quite bad, yes," Ingrid confirmed.

"We're knee-deep in a great mess," Viggo said.

"Well, good then, it seems I came back just in time," Gerd smiled.

"Yeah, well, wait until we tell you," Nilsa said and made a gesture shaking her hand.

"In any case, I'm thrilled to be back. Group hug?" he asked, spreading his arms.

The others smiled and joined Gerd in the group hug.

"No, no, no! Not that touchy-feely stuff," Viggo protested. "I refuse!"

"Come on, deep down you know you want to," Ingrid said, offering him her arm and winking at him.

"He had to come back…" he protested. "And we were doing so well without you," he muttered to Gerd.

"Stop that nonsense," Ingrid chided him.

"And don't be a pain in the neck," Nilsa chided him too as she took his other arm.

"All right…" Viggo said resignedly but without posing much resistance, and he joined the group hug.

The other Rangers who entered and exited the Tower stopped to watch the scene, which was as strange as it was unlikely. The Panthers' group hug surprised and puzzled everyone, but such was the respect they commanded that no one said anything or commented, simply watching in silence and then continuing with their duties.

One person, however, did dare come over and comment.

"I'm glad to see the largest Panther with the biggest heart among all the Rangers is back again," a voice said, walking past them with a dozen soldiers.

Gerd looked toward the source of the voice and could not believe his eyes.

"Val…. Valeria? … how? What's going on here?" he asked with eyes wide open when he recognized her and saw her with foreign soldiers.

"Your friends will explain everything. I'm glad to see you're well, Gerd. I was concerned when I didn't see you with the others," Valeria said, stopping.

"I, well, yes…" Gerd replied, looking at Valeria, unable to believe she was really there.

"Don't linger, go on your way and don't tempt your fate," Astrid warned Valeria in a threatening tone.

"I simply wanted to say 'hi' to Gerd. You look very well, stronger, more handsome," she told him and winked at him as she offered him a seductive smile.

"Don't let her hoodwink you," Viggo warned Gerd, "this blonde's still exercising her charms and games."

"I find you well too," Gerd replied. "And thank you."

Valeria gave him a nod and gave a slight smile to the rest of the

Panthers as she went on her way.

"You have to explain all of this to me..." Gerd said with a look of disbelief on his face.

"Huh! If you think this is surprising and strange, just wait until we tell you about the dragon," Viggo said.

"Dragon? A dragon?" Gerd's face was the picture of terror.

Viggo smiled and winked at him.

"Get ready, because what's coming will be fantastic," he said and looked at Egil, who smiled back and shook his head.

"Everything will be fine," Lasgol said in an attempt to calm Gerd's fears. "We'll tell you everything."

Chapter 4

The Panthers sat Gerd down on one of the beds of the large room they shared in the Tower and told him everything that had happened while the giant was recovering. As usual, they let Egil stick to the facts and the rest added their personal comments as the story unfolded.

Although the comments were varied and colorful, particularly Viggo's, Egil made sure he explained clearly the great problem they were up against. Gerd listened attentively, and his face became more and more ashen as they continued explaining the situation to him. By the time Egil finished his account, Gerd was so pale they thought he was going to faint. He took several deep breaths and seemed to recover a little. Then he asked a thousand questions until he was sure he had understood everything. His frightened look increased as they cleared up his doubts. The words "unbelievable" and "unthinkable" came out of his mouth at least a dozen times each. His friends assured him that everything they had told him was absolutely true, so he had no choice but to accept what they were telling him because he trusted his friends blindly. He was however, left deeply troubled.

"I'm not going to get over this fright and unease for days," he commented, snorting, his large hands on his thighs. "What a mess we're in."

"One of those we're so fond of," Viggo said ironically.

"You'll see, tomorrow you'll be completely over it," Nilsa said cheerfully.

"The thing is, you haven't lived through it all, so the uncertainty of the great danger we're up against affects you more than it normally would," Egil diagnosed. "But, as soon as you face the danger directly, all that unease will pass."

"I hope so…" the good giant snorted again.

"A good night's rest will do you good and make all your fears vanish," Ingrid said firmly.

"Exactly, by dawn you'll be as good as new," Astrid said cheerfully.

"And so that you have some good news, and not everything looks so bad, tomorrow I'll take you to see Ona and Camu," Lasgol said.

"I'll enjoy that."

"Tell the bug to show you his flying skill, you're going to love that. And make sure he lands beside you," Viggo said mischievously.

"That's something I'm dying to see with my own eyes," Gerd said, cheering up.

They continued chatting well into the night about inconsequential things, joking and enjoying being together again. It had been a long time, and if it had been hard for the rest of the group, for Gerd it had been sheer torture, physically, mentally, and emotionally. A good mood reigned among the Panthers, and they enjoyed it as they had not done so in a long time.

At last, they went to bed. Unfortunately, Gerd's fears were confirmed, and he barely slept at all that night. It was going to take him some time to process what had happened and the challenges that lay ahead.

As Lasgol had promised him, when they woke up the following morning, they went to see Ona and Camu. Of course, this was after a lavish breakfast in the Rangers' dining hall, which Gerd enjoyed as if he had not eaten in years. His excuse was that not sleeping much gave him a greater appetite than usual. So, with circles under his eyes and a full stomach, he went off with Lasgol.

Lasgol fetched Trotter at the stables and Gerd was given one of the horses kept there for the Rangers. They left the Royal Castle and began to cross the capital at a quiet pace. Gerd was enjoying being able to visit the great city.

"I've been at the Shelter for so long I forgot what a great city was like," he told Lasgol.

"It's only natural. It must seem strange to see so many people together," his friend replied as they went down the main street.

Gerd was looking right and left from the saddle.

"Not only strange, it's as if I can't see myself riding through these streets among so many people."

"Don't worry, you'll soon get used to it."

"I don't know, I've spent most of the time with four or five people at most. My time was spent between Engla, Edwina, Annika, Sigrid, and Enduald, or Galdason now and then. No-one else."

"Didn't you have any contact with the Specialist Contenders?"

"Barely. You know what it's like there. They were training and practicing day and night. The little free time they had, they spent either studying or sleeping. Besides, I think I have, well *we* have some kind of stigma... a nasty one..."

"And why's that?"

"You know what people are like. There are all kinds of rumors about us... about what happened to us there."

Lasgol nodded.

"I see. Don't worry. Here in the city, we're treated with great respect, and that's something I can't get used to, to be honest."

"The other Rangers?"

"Yeah, and the soldiers too. It seems the feats of the Royal Eagles are beginning to be known."

"Nothing's reached me at the Shelter. Besides, you know what the Mother Specialist is like... she only tells you the minimum amount necessary, and almost everything is secret."

"Well, here we have Viggo who goes around telling everyone how amazing he is and the wonders he's performed all throughout Tremia."

Gerd burst out laughing.

"Why am I not surprised," he smiled.

"He's going around chasing after bards and troubadours to have them write poems and songs about him."

"Our Viggo is becoming crazier and crazier," Gerd said, laughing.

"You can say that again, and sign it!" Lasgol said, also laughing. "I've missed you a lot, big guy," he admitted.

"And I've missed you," Gerd smiled.

"Now we'll have time to resume our chats."

"And hopefully they'll become routine," Gerd said.

"Irrefutable" said Lasgol, imitating Egil.

"Wow, everyone's so busy in the city. It's as if they're all in a great hurry..." Gerd commented as he watched the people go briskly by.

"That's on account of the Royal Wedding. Everyone's acting as if it's already been announced and is a fact."

"Haven't they announced it yet?"

Lasgol shook his head.

"We think it will happen soon, but if I've learned anything lately, it's that it's a lot more sensible to not expect or predict anything. As a rule, the opposite ends up happening—or what's worse, some catastrophe."

"Or both," Gerd said, looking horrified.

"That's right. So, I no longer make any predictions."

"Whatever happens, we'll find out sooner than later. After all, we're Rangers, and Gondabar will inform us of something so important that will surely affect us. I'm sure we'll have to intervene one way or another."

"Yeah, I suspect that myself. He'll definitely give us some job."

They left the capital and rode briskly to arrive at the Green Ogre Forest as quickly as they possibly could. It was a good way off, and they had to go fast if they wanted to make the most of the day. It was snowing lightly but there did not seem to be any storm brewing nearby, so the ride was quite pleasant. Norghanians liked snow, they were used to it, and seeing the fields and forests covered by a white cloak gave them a certain feeling of comfort. Gerd and Lasgol were no exception. Unfortunately, the winter storms, so common and dangerous, shattered that effect and brought everyone back to the reality of harsh winter.

They reached the forest and tethered the horses by a stream.

Trotter, wait here and rest, Lasgol transmitted to his faithful pony.

His friend shook his head up and down and nickered. Lasgol stroked his neck and whispered words of affection.

They entered the forest, whose trees were beginning to be covered in snow.

"Nothing like a good walk in the forest to stretch lazy legs and muscles," Gerd said.

"Indeed," Lasgol agreed, noticing that his friend walked in a funny way, as if both his legs were a bit crippled.

Gerd noticed Lasgol watching his funny walk.

"I'm still dealing with some side effects..." he said, looking embarrassed.

Lasgol made light of it, saying, "You can barely notice."

"You've always been a bad liar," Gerd said with a shy smile.

"I bet you'll finish recovering soon," Lasgol cheered him.

Gerd nodded. "I hope so too."

"Don't lose hope. With constant effort you can achieve anything in life, no matter how difficult it might seem. You just have to persevere."

"I am persevering, and doing my best. Let's hope the reward will be waiting at the end of the path."

"It will be, my friend, I haven't the slightest doubt," Lasgol said, putting his hand on his friend's shoulder.

They walked through the trees that protected them from the snow until they arrived at the clear area of the pond in the middle of the forest. There they saw a tent that could fit a dozen soldiers. In front of it was Eicewald. The Ice Mage was telling Camu how he should do an exercise.

"We have visitors," the Ice Mage announced when he saw Gerd and Lasgol coming.

"Camu, you've gotten so big!" Gerd cried when he saw the creature.

"Yup… he's grown a little," Lasgol said.

When Camu recognized Gerd, he ran to greet him. Ona, who was a little further away among some trees, also came running.

"And you've grown too, Ona!"

Very happy to see you, Camu messaged Gerd as the giant gave him a big hug.

"He spoke in my mind," Gerd said, eyes wide open in wonder.

"Camu is improving his skills. Now he can speak directly in other people's minds," Lasgol told him.

"Wow! That's shocking…"

Not shocking. I powerful.

"Yeah, I can see that. You've left me flabbergasted…"

Not have fear. You friend. I protect.

"Thanks, Camu, that's very comforting," said Gerd, giving him another hug.

You welcome. Gerd good, Camu messaged him, licking Gerd's face with his blue tongue.

"You are good indeed," Gerd said, moved.

"He's also developing new skills with Eicewald's help," Lasgol told Gerd.

Eicewald know much. Great mage, Camu messaged to everyone.

"Not really, I'm simply learned with too much experience on my shoulders," the Mage said, waving the matter aside.

"I'd say both—what Camu says and what Eicewald says," Lasgol told Gerd.

"I see," the giant smiled. "And Lasgol has been telling me, as we were coming, that you fly. That's really left me curious. It must be worth seeing."

I fly. I show.

Camu flashed silver and his ethereal wings appeared, created by his power. They shone as if they were made of silver threads so fine, they were translucent. Camu flapped them and Gerd was awed by how splendid and fascinating they were. He could not take his eyes off the silver wings.

"Awesome!" Gerd cried as he watched Camu, enthralled with his mouth wide open.

You wait here, I show fly, Camu messaged to Gerd, and with a leap forward he flapped his wings hard and rose, flying, toward the pond.

"Wow! That's amazing!" Gerd cried at the sight of Camu rising with his silver wings.

"It is," Eicewald smiled. "He's improved a lot and can now control his flight much better and with more confidence than when he first started."

Camu flew around the pond several times, flying confidently and with ease, maintaining a stable height, something he had not been able to do before.

"Spectacular! He does it so well!" Gerd was thrilled to see Camu flying.

Ona growled once.

"Well, his flight is improving a lot, but he still has a lot of trouble landing," Lasgol said.

"He does?"

"You'll see for yourself," Lasgol chuckled.

"All learning takes time. It's not advisable to accelerate the process. He'll learn in due course and with due practice," Eicewald explained.

Camu delighted Gerd by gliding past them several times and brushing his head, which made the giant, who was a lot taller than Lasgol and Eicewald, duck.

"Extraordinary!" he cried, holding his head and laughing.

To end his demonstration, Camu rose and then dropped to rise again just before touching the water of the pond. He came so close that he touched the water with his feet and almost crashed. Luckily, he avoided the blow, although not without some trouble.

"Careful, Camu, you're going to crash," Gerd said.

No crash. I great flyer.

Gerd looked at Lasgol, "I see he continues to be as confident as always."

"You mean stubborn," Lasgol replied.

I not stubborn. I champion.

Gerd burst out laughing and even Eicewald, who was always restrained, laughed. Lasgol put a hand to his forehead.

To finish his demonstration, Camu landed in front of Gerd. Lasgol and Eicewald stepped back unobtrusively. Camu did what he could, but he still had not mastered the whole process and ran over Gerd's leg.

"Oops!" the giant cried, trying to keep his balance. But he could not; he fell backward as Camu broke his landing, dragging his back all along the snow-covered ground.

"As you can see, there's margin for improvement," Lasgol said.

"Quite a bit, indeed," Gerd laughed.

Lasgol gave him a hand to help him up.

Gerd spent a good while playing with Ona and Camu. He was overjoyed to see them, just as the panther and the creature were happy to see him. They played around the pond, trying not to slip on the snow, which kept falling lightly.

"I'm going to catch you!" Gerd shouted, running after Camu and Ona.

You no catch, Camu messaged Gerd.

The giant stopped running and looked at Lasgol and Eicewald, who were sitting inside the tent sheltering from the snow. He waved at them and a great smile appeared on his face.

"It seems like Gerd is having a great time," Eicewald commented to Lasgol.

"And I hope he'll have a lot more. He's had a rough patch, and as you can see, he's still not fully recovered."

"I've noticed. His walk is a little unbalanced, as if he'd fallen from his horse and broken his back," Eicewald said as he watched Gerd running after Camu, who was running away bucking like a horse while Ona, a lot faster than both of them, waited up ahead.

"The truth is they're like children, the three of them," Lasgol smiled.

"And may they be like that for a long time," Eicewald said.

Chapter 5

The seven friends went to the Tower's dining hall for an early breakfast. The moment they walked in, the Rangers who were already eating immediately vacated a table close to the wall. It was as if the table belonged to the Panthers, which was not the case since the tables had no "owners" and all the Rangers had equal rights to sit wherever they wanted in the dining hall.

"It seems strange they would clear a table the moment we arrive," Gerd commented when he noticed.

"They'd better, they have to show respect to their betters," said Viggo out loud so the rest of the Rangers could hear him.

"Don't be a dumbass, no-one has to let us have anything," Ingrid chided. "See if you can learn a bit of humility and how to behave."

"My dear celestial blonde, let me assure you that humility is overrated," said Viggo, sitting down lightly. "And I know how to behave in any situation."

"The intelligence of some people is also overrated," Nilsa said, mockingly.

"Careful, redhead, don't trip as you always do when sitting on a long bench," Viggo replied ironically.

"You've no idea how much it cheers me to hear you arguing as usual," Gerd said with a huge smile on his face.

"What cheers you, is being in the canteen because you're going to fill that huge belly of yours," Viggo told him.

"Well, yes, that too," Gerd admitted, "but I stand by what I said first."

"It's wonderful that camaraderie and friendship have been maintained in the group with the passing of time," said Egil as he sat down, not without a certain amount of irony in his tone.

"Yes, nothing like your friends' good cheer to start the day out right," Lasgol joined in.

"If we weren't always fighting like cats and dogs, we'd be very bored, like those dullards over there," Viggo said, pointing at the table the Royal Rangers also "owned" when they came to the dining hall.

"Some of them are quite nice," Nilsa said at once as she greeted one of them with a nervous smile. The Royal Ranger returned the greeting with another smile that was definitely more self-assured.

"Aren't you mistaking nice with handsome?" Astrid said, eyeing the Royal Ranger.

"Maybe, I could be," Nilsa said, giggling.

"I love being back with all of you," Gerd told them, eyes bright with joy. "You've no idea how much I've missed you."

"We've missed you too, big guy," said Ingrid.

"Go fill those seven stomachs you have and stop being so sentimental or you'll bring a tear to my eyes, as you make me feel so sorry," Viggo said.

"Yeah sorry, says my little dimwit," Ingrid replied.

Nilsa pointed her finger at him. "Look, the sour one's touched," she said.

Lasgol and Egil laughed while Astrid hid a broad smile behind her hand.

They had a leisurely breakfast, enjoying their camaraderie and the fact that Gerd was with them again. As was expected, he had a second breakfast. The dining hall was busy, but little by little the Panthers were left alone. When there were only a couple veteran Rangers eating their breakfast at the other end of the room and out of hearing range, they started talking about important matters.

"Good, now that we're feeling relaxed, let's talk about our next moves," Ingrid said.

"We have permission from Gondabar to investigate, so that's what we're going to do, right?" said Nilsa.

"That's what we should do, yes," Astrid confirmed.

"Before they take away permission," Viggo said.

"Why do you say that?" Lasgol asked him.

"Because our dear King or his brother might decide to send us on another of their little missions at any moment."

"Oh, yeah... that's true." Lasgol realized Viggo was right. They were not free from being summoned by the King or his brother, and Gondabar would not be able to refuse if they did, even though he had tasked the Panthers with investigating the issue.

"The sooner we start, the sooner we'll finish," Astrid said.

"Haste isn't a good companion," Ingrid warned.

"What's the plan then? In general, I mean... I'm quite lost with everything you've told me…" said Gerd.

"We need to focus on one clear goal: we have to stop the dragon spirit from reincarnating," Egil told them.

"That doesn't sound so good…" said Gerd doubtfully.

"Don't worry, we'll do it one way or another," Lasgol said to Gerd.

"It's not going to be easy. To start with, we don't even know how or what it's going to reincarnate as…" Nilsa commented.

"Good point," said Viggo, "any idea how that's going to happen? What shape will it seek? What body will it take over?"

"Very true, and good questions we need to find answers to without a doubt," Egil nodded. "I've been reading and gathering information about the subject as much as I've been able to these days," he explained.

"You reading? How odd," Viggo grinned at him.

"Don't interrupt him, this is important," Ingrid chided Viggo and then turned to Egil. "Never mind what he says… finish telling us about your books and research."

Egil smiled and nodded.

"From what I've been able to understand so far in the tomes about reincarnation I've been reading, the soul or spirit of the person or being that reincarnates finds a new body, as a rule. It's important to understand that it passes into a body different from the one it previously had. There aren't many tomes of knowledge about this subject in particular, since it's a rare occurrence. But this seems to be the general belief. I say belief because this matter is subjective and not proven at all. The writings I've been able to examine and the information I've received are mostly the experiences and vagaries of those who have tried to study the subject, as well as those who have peculiar and esoteric ideas regarding reincarnation, since it's a subject that has to do with religious and contemplative matters."

"What does that mean?" Gerd asked, wrinkling his nose.

"Have you forgotten how convoluted Egil's speech is?" Viggo asked Gerd, slapping his back.

The giant shrugged.

"Maybe because I got very little…"

"What he means is that there's no real proof that a spirit can reincarnate in a different body," Ingrid explained, "In fact, it sounds completely unbelievable if you ask me."

"And that what's been written was done by the vagaries of fools, madmen, and fake prophets," added Viggo.

"Death and resurrection are matters that here in Norghana haven't been studied deeply. I got most of the information from the south of Tremia, where this matter has been researched more thoroughly."

"Here we believe that once you're dead, you travel to the realm of the Ice Gods to spend eternity beside them," Astrid said.

"Hopefully in peace and harmony and happy forever," added Nilsa.

"That sounds too good to be true," Viggo said with a face of incredulity.

"Well, that's what they teach us as children," Nilsa told him.

"I like that ending," said Gerd. "Resting happy and in peace for eternity,"

"I repeat, it sounds well and good, and when something sounds too good to be true it doesn't happen, you all know that," Viggo said, wagging his finger.

"Additionally, I have some new and important information from my contacts and collaborators which we must look into," Egil announced, thus ending the argument about the realm of the Ice Gods.

"You mean the nighttime encounter in the west the other day?" Ingrid asked.

"That's right," Egil confirmed, grinning.

"Is it about the Visionaries or about the Congregation of the Defenders of the True Blood?" Ingrid asked.

"Or about their leaders?" Astrid said.

"It's about both groups and their clandestine operations. I've got a couple of interesting leads we should follow. They might take us nowhere since these two groups hide well and are difficult to find— them, or their operations and secret dealings. But I think it's wise to follow up on them and investigate, they might lead us to Viggen Norling or Drugan Volskerian."

"Very well, let's get started," said Ingrid.

"Eicewald told me that when he has some time, he can instruct Camu and me in the art of magic. Although, he doesn't have much free time left, and I don't want to miss this opportunity..." Lasgol said.

Egil understood.

"It'll be best if we split into several groups for this task," he said. "Lasgol and Camu, keep training with Eicewald, you don't need to intervene for now."

"I myself have to go and get some more information," he explained.

"I'll come with you," Gerd volunteered.

The Panthers looked at the giant for a moment. Lasgol, as well as his friends, did not want Gerd to remain on the side like a cripple who could not take part in their day-to-day activities, but if he did get involved Lasgol was worried something might happen to him.

"Get ready, big guy, that means you're going to see some action," Viggo told Gerd.

"A little action will be great for me," he replied, smiling.

"For you and for all of us," Viggo said with a grin.

Chapter 6

Lasgol and Camu sat before Eicewald inside the tent set up by the pond in the Green Ogre Forest. Outside it was snowing lightly. Ona had taken refuge on a high branch in a nearby tree, although the snow barely bothered her because of her thick fur.

"Thank you for taking time to help us," Lasgol said to the Mage gratefully.

"It's always a pleasure for me to teach you. Unfortunately, my duties as First Ice Mage of the King are many and they keep me busy."

"That's why we appreciate it even more," Lasgol told him. He felt truly blessed that Eicewald had escaped his duties and was making time to teach them secretly.

I many thanks, Camu messaged him along with a feeling of gratitude, which reached not only Eicewald but Lasgol as well.

"I share the feeling," Lasgol said.

"No need to thank me. I'm happy to do it. Besides, I know that teaching you will be good, not only for the Kingdom but for me too."

"You really think so?" Lasgol asked.

"I'm convinced. I know you'll use everything you learn for the good of Norghana, I have no doubt of that. I also believe that in a not-too-distant future, I'll need your help, in the magical sense I mean, and I'm counting on it."

"Of course," Lasgol said. "It'd be the least we could do after all the time and effort you're investing in us. The opposite would be failing our honor. One should always be grateful and respectful."

I help always, Camu messaged.

"With pupils like you two, it's a pleasure to be a tutor."

"What have you prepared for us today?" Lasgol asked Eicewald.

I want learn more, Camu messaged, along with a feeling of joy and enthusiasm.

"That's the way I like it, a desire to learn is fundamental to achieve good results," The Ice Mage told them. "The good pupil is the one who keeps an open mind, a cheerful heart, and focused feelings on what will be learned."

I very cheerful and mind very open, Camu messaged.

Eicewald smiled, "As you should be."

"Me too, almost as much as Camu," Lasgol joked and half-smiled.

"Before we begin with a new principle of magic, I want you to show me the advances you've made on the Magic Creation Principle," the Mage said.

I show, Camu volunteered.

Lasgol nodded to the creature, letting him go first.

"What skill have you managed to develop during these days we've been apart, Camu?"

I develop Frozen Claw Slash.

"Sounds good. What type of skill is it?" the Mage asked.

Like Tail Whiplash but with claw, Camu messaged.

"Unless I'm mistaken, you have no claws," Eicewald said, pointing at Camu's feet, which ended in toes joined by cartilage which allowed him to cling to almost any surface despite his weight, which was beginning to be considerable.

Now yes, Camu messaged with a nod.

Eicewald looked at Lasgol, who nodded affirmatively.

"Show me," the Mage said to Camu.

"One moment," Lasgol said and left the tent. He came back a moment later with snowflakes on his head and shoulders, carrying a log as thick as a leg.

"For the demonstration," Eicewald guessed.

"Yes, we've been rehearsing with wood," Lasgol replied.

"Go ahead then."

Standing, Lasgol held the log horizontally between his hands. Camu stood on all fours and focused his attention on the log. A moment passed as Camu tried to make the new skill materialize. Lasgol continued holding the log tightly. All of a sudden, Camu's front legs emitted a silver flash that filled the tent. Camu moved his right front leg to hit the log Lasgol was holding. In an attack move, in pure Ona style, the end of his leg suddenly became what looked like a sharp claw of the purest ice. He hit the wood and cut the log in half, taking out a large piece that fell to the floor. Camu rested his leg back on the floor and Lasgol and Eicewald saw that it had become a sharp, icy claw, like that of a large cat only frozen.

"Very impressive," Eicewald said, nodding.

"Look at this," Lasgol said to the Mage, showing him both

broken edges of the log which were covered in ice.

"It not only cuts, but it freezes," Eicewald commented with interest.

"That's right," Lasgol confirmed.

Cut and freeze, Camu messaged.

"Very interesting," the Mage said as he watched the result, thoughtful. "The fact that the claw is ice indicates that, because you are a Creature of the Ice, you have an affinity for that element."

"I thought the same thing," Lasgol said.

"When you developed the skill, were you looking for it to have the ice effect?" Eicewald asked.

No. I only want have claw like Ona to attack.

"Very curious…" the Mage commented.

"He wanted to emulate Ona's attacks," Lasgol explained.

Ona strong, sharp claws. I no claws, Camu messaged regretfully.

"Well, it seems you have them now, and they freeze besides," Eicewald said in a tone of surprise.

"We still haven't tried with steel, but I believe he'll be able to cut through that too," Lasgol said.

"We'll have to try. We'll bring a steel shield and see if he's capable of cutting through it."

"I'll find one," said Lasgol.

I cut steel. I powerful, Camu messaged confidently.

"We'd better not take anything for granted. We'll test it out and make sure. Self-confidence is good, but we should always be cautious and not overestimate our skills," Eicewald instructed him.

I try, Camu messaged.

"But it does show that you're mastering the principle of magical creation. Keep it up, Camu, you're doing a good job."

I keep up.

"Wonderful. And how are you doing, Lasgol?" the Mage asked him with curiosity.

"I have to admit that the magical creation is harder for me than for Camu. I don't know if it's because I'm clumsier or because Camu has greater skill than I do."

"I don't believe it's a matter of clumsiness. Every magical being is different, both in the magic they can perform, and in their power and abilities to develop it. That's what makes us unique and special. That Camu is capable of developing a skill more easily than you is perfectly reasonable and expected. After all, Camu is a Magical Creature of the Ice."

"True…" Lasgol looked at Camu, whose claw was still active.

"We humans are, as a rule, arrogant and even vain regarding magic. We believe we're the most advanced beings regarding the power we have and the skills we can develop. But there are creatures in Tremia that are infinitely more powerful than humans. I think we might be standing here before one of them," Eicewald explained.

"Why are they more prone to magic?" Lasgol asked with interest.

Eicewald was thoughtful for a moment.

"It might be in their blood, because of the kind of creature they are. Perhaps it's because of their body, their organism. There are no certainties about this. What I can tell you is that we shouldn't take for granted that we, humans, are the most powerful and adept to magic."

Lasgol nodded. "I'll keep that in mind."

"You'll do well to do so, indeed," Eicewald smiled. "Now you go ahead, please."

"Very well. After trying hard I've managed to develop a new skill," Lasgol said. "I'm calling it Multiple Shot. It's a Martial Magic skill, and although it's been hard, I've noticed that visualizing what I hope to achieve, focusing my magic and knowing it's a Martial Magic skill, helps me develop it."

"That's the way to do it, well done."

"Thank you, I'll try to show you what it does. Let's go outside for a moment," Lasgol said and fetched his bow and quiver from the bottom of the tent. They went out under the falling snow and Lasgol stood, looking at the edge of the forest. He nocked his arrow, and without aiming looked at one of the trees in front of him. They were about fifty paces away.

Very exciting, Camu messaged.

Lasgol heaved a deep sigh. He was not sure he could call upon his skill since he had just created it a day ago and he still did not entirely master it. He concentrated, searched for his inner pool of energy, visualized in his mind what he wanted to achieve, and called on the *Multiple Shot* skill. Suddenly, a green flash ran down Lasgol's arms. The bow rose, and from it not one but three arrows shot out at great speed and buried themselves in three trees, the one Lasgol had indicated and the two on either side.

"Now I understand why the name is Multiple Shot," Eicewald

said, smiling.

"I'm still improving it, but the skill allows me to shoot three arrows at three different targets."

"That will give you a huge advantage when you're facing more than one adversary."

"That's the idea behind this skill, to let me finish off several opponents with a single shot."

"If you could use this skill repeatedly, you'd be unstoppable," Eicewald told him, nodding repeatedly.

"That's what I thought, and in fact, I've already tried it without results so far. Once the skill is activated, I'm unable to call upon it again. It's as if it had a cooling period during which it can't be used again. I'm not sure I'm explaining myself well…"

"You are, and I understand you perfectly. There are skills that require a lot of inner energy, some that demand a long summoning period, others that require you to have great power just to use them, and there are some which, once used, require a recharging time until they can be used again. Some powerful skills have all of these requirements."

"Like the enormous winter storms you conjure up."

"Exactly. They have all those prerequisites. And now that you've shown me your progress, it's time to keep learning," the Mage told them and waved them into the tent to get out of the snow.

"We're ready," Lasgol said as he went in, followed by Camu.

"It's time to teach you another fundamental principle of magic: the Magical Amplification Principle. This principle dictates the way in which we can expand, spread, lengthen, and amplify the skills we've already developed. At first, when they're created, skills have a limited use."

Lasgol and Camu stared at Eicewald with a puzzled look on their faces.

"Limited?" Lasgol asked.

"I'll explain. Let's take, for instance, a winter storm. It has a limited area of effect and a duration which is also limited. It can't affect a whole kingdom, for instance, and it can't last for a year either. I'm exaggerating so you can understand it more easily."

"I think now I do," Lasgol said.

I understand.

"But, thanks to the Principle of Magic Amplification, you can extend and amplify the effect of any spell. You can make it affect an area wider than only three paces around and last a lot longer than a few moments."

"Is its power also amplified?" Lasgol asked, raising an eyebrow.

Eicewald smiled.

"No, not with this principle. In order to do that you must understand the Principle of Magical Power. That's a lesson for some time in the future. For now, let's focus on the Amplification Principle."

Lasgol nodded.

I want amplify, Camu messaged.

"We all want to be able to amplify our skills. That's natural, since when they're created, they aren't at full capacity. To use a simile, let's say that when we create a magical skill it starts out as a baby. We have to transform it into a strong adult."

"By feeding it?" Lasgol said blankly.

"Something similar, yes. You must also understand that the skill that isn't amplified never grows. It won't grow by itself. It will always be a baby because it hasn't been nourished in order to grow."

"Understood. If we don't work to amplify a skill, it will remain the same as when it was created," Lasgol summarized.

"Exactly."

I feed, Camu promised.

"Very well. Now I only need to show you how it works, how to feed the skills in order to amplify them. It's not simple and requires effort."

"Like everything involving magic..." Lasgol commented.

"Yes, indeed. Everything that has to do with magic has a cost. That's why they say there's always a price to pay with magic, sometimes a very high one. We will continue tomorrow. I must return to the castle now."

Both Camu and Lasgol wanted so bad to continue learning, but Eicewald had obligations to attend.

Chapter 7

The training resumed next day. Eicewald was going to continue teaching them magical principles and concepts, something both Camu and Lasgol were grateful for. The Mage was a busy man—he had to lead the King's other Ice Magi after all—and the fact that he found or made time to teach them was something they truly appreciated.

They waited inside the tent since it was snowing again, heavily this time. They saw the Mage approach with a large tome under his arm. By the size of it, Lasgol knew they would have study material for several weeks.

"How are my pupils faring today?" Eicewald asked as he came into the tent.

I very wonderful, Camu messaged at once as he nodded, imitating his human friends.

"I'm almost as wonderful as he is," Lasgol replied with a smile, moving his head up and down like Camu.

Ona flopped down at the end of the tent and watched them with her feline eyes and a puzzled look, as if she realized they were doing something weird.

"I'm glad you're both doing so well. I've brought you reading material to educate your minds and not only your bodies," the Mage smiled.

"It looks pretty thick," Lasgol commented.

"It is, there's a lot of knowledge in it. It's called 'Basic Principles of Northeastern Magic' and it's written by the great Mage Coportius Urunguemus. He was a genius in his day and he helped write down much of the knowledge about Magic that was dispersed among the magi of the time."

"Well, if it's as complicated as the author's name, we're in big trouble," Lasgol smiled, scratching his head.

Name pretty, Camu messaged.

"I don't know about pretty..." said Lasgol, who was staring at the great tome. Just the sight of it made him so uneasy he felt nauseous.

"You'll have to study it. It'll help you better understand the explanations I provide and the lessons I'm trying to help you learn. Having a written text is handy when it comes to memorizing and remembering things."

I not need, Camu messaged, lifting his head and straining his short neck, clearly proud of himself.

"And why's that?" Eicewald asked him.

I great memory and lot understanding.

Lasgol's eyes opened wide.

"The thing is, he can't read," Lasgol explained. "Therefore, books aren't such a big help to him."

"Curious. You don't read because you can't, or because you haven't been taught?" Eicewald asked Camu.

Not know reason.

"Egil has tried to teach him on several occasions, but it seems Camu doesn't pay very much attention and gets bored easily, so they haven't made much progress."

"That makes more sense," the Mage said.

Read much boring.

"On the contrary, Camu. Reading is fascinating, wonderful. It fills you with the experiences of others. There are thousands of concepts and stories which are unbelievable, that you can only experience by reading them," Eicewald explained to Camu.

Not believe.

"Through books you can live a thousand different lives. You learn thousands of things and enjoy experiences you otherwise never would."

Maybe have to learn read... Camu admitted at last.

"It would be good for you, that way I wouldn't have to read out loud the whole time for you to know what the lessons are about," said Lasgol.

"Is that how you do it?"

"Yeah, I read, and he listens and memorizes what I read. He does have an excellent memory."

I very smart. Very, Camu assured them.

"Yeah, yeah... but you can't read for all that you're so intelligent," Lasgol said reproachfully.

I speak with Egil. He teach.

"That would be wonderful," said Lasgol.

"To be honest, the relationship between you two is amazing,"

Eicewald said as he looked at one, and then the other. "It should be studied because it's quite unique, and I believe that sometime in the future, it could be useful for when other similar relationships occur."

"Between a human and a Creature of the Ice?" Lasgol asked. He did not think their relationship was so special, for him it was natural.

"Between a magical human and a magical Creature of the Ice," Eicewald remarked. "I doubt it's common and it might be good to document it."

I very interesting. Lasgol less, Camu commented nonchalantly.

Ona growled twice.

"You're always so full of yourself," Lasgol said.

What mean that?

"You'll have to read about it and learn what it means. Oh, you can't read? What a pity," Lasgol said ironically.

Not funny.

"Oh, yes it is, very."

"I'm serious when I say that your relationship should be studied and recorded for posterity, because it is most curious. Unfortunately, I don't have the time to do it. I'll try to find someone who does have the time…"

"I don't think that would be possible with our duties. We can't take in strangers in the middle of dealing with realm matters," Lasgol said.

"True, that's very true. You don't even tell *me* everything you're involved in. And I don't mean that as a criticism—we all have secrets to keep in this life. There are private things that can't come out into the light."

"It's not for lack of trust, we trust you completely," Lasgol hastened to assure the Mage. The last thing he wanted was for Eicewald to feel uncomfortable around them. "It's a simple precaution because we never fully understand the situations we find ourselves involved in, and their repercussions. Because of this, we're cautious not to involve anyone else, not until we understand them completely and can make sure no one gets hurt."

Eicewald looked Lasgol straight in the eye as he explained himself.

"I understand. I know you do it out of good will, and because of that I don't mind. When you deem it necessary, you can come to me and tell me everything. I'll be more than willing to help you, as I've always done."

"We know, and we appreciate it very much. The King's Ice Mage has our complete trust," Lasgol said reassuringly. "And we appreciate everything you do to help us."

Eicewald nodded. "The fact that you're Rangers does complicate studying your relationship..." the Mage realized. "It's a pity. Perhaps in the future I'll be able to find a way to do it."

"Perhaps in a couple years it'll be easier," Lasgol smiled.

"Let's hope so. Now, let's see how much you've advanced in the Principle of Magical Amplification. I want to make sure the time you spend practicing without me is profitable."

I improve a lot, Camu messaged at once, along with a feeling of achievement.

"Is that so?" Eicewald asked with some doubt.

I show, Camu messaged confidently.

"Let's go outside the tent so you can show me," the Mage said.

They went outside into the snow, which although falling heavily, did not really bother them. The whole forest was covered in white, except for the large pond which had not frozen over yet.

While the snow fell on their heads, Camu stood at a distance of approximately three human paces from a solitary tree near the tent. Eicewald and Lasgol watched attentively.

I call magic, he warned. An instant later there was a silver flash in Camu's legs and he released a Frozen Claw Slash toward the tree, but because he was three paces away and had not leaned forward the slash would not reach the tree but fall short. Or that was the logical conclusion.

There was a crash and a section of the tree's bark and wood flew off to one side. Camu had reached the target with his slash, even at a distance that apparently did not allow for it.

I amplify skill. Reach farther, Camu messaged.

"That was excellent. You've amplified it, extended it, very well. Besides, you've done it with a new skill you haven't fully mastered, which is even more impressive."

I much impressive.

"Yes, you are. Well done. Obviously you've been following my instructions, forcing the skill to go a little further from what it initially allowed. Concentrating and sending more energy, forcing it to go a bit further."

I force. Amplify, Camu said confidently.

"That's the way to do it. I'm really impressed you've been able to do it so fast and so well."

I very happy.

"You should be, it's a great advance in a short time."

I practice amplify Magical Whiplash.

"With your tail?"

Yes, with tail. Not manage yet.

"I'm sure you'll get there. Keep trying."

I keep, tail not reach tree.

Ona moaned twice.

"You'll succeed if you concentrate and consistently practice. Practice is essential to reach the goals we set for ourselves. In order to reach the goal, you need to strive and practice daily until you achieve what you set out to do. It's not simple at all, but the reward is worth the effort. You'll see how fulfilling it is when you manage to amplify the skill, you'll feel exultant with the success you achieve."

I much exultant.

"That's the way to go. Keep working until you succeed."

I keep, Camu promised as the snowflakes continued falling on his silver scales and fell to the ground, unable to settle on or penetrate them.

"And what about you, Lasgol? Have you managed to make any progress?" the Mage asked, looking expectantly for a positive reply.

"I've advanced a little. But nothing as impressive as what Camu has achieved. I'm afraid that in my case, Magical Amplification is harder to develop."

"Did you encounter problems?"

"No, but I've noticed that it's a lot more difficult for me to make progress than it is for Camu. Compared to him I've done practically nothing."

"Show me an example, please," the Mage said.

"Very well. I've been trying to make my *Animal Presence* skill reach further. I've been practicing with Ona as a gauge."

"That's a good skill to work on, and the fact that Ona can help you should make it easier," Eicewald nodded, satisfied.

"I'll show you," Lasgol said.

Ona, stand where we started to practice, Lasgol transmitted to the snow panther.

Ona ran off and stood in front of Lasgol but at a considerable distance bordering the pond.

"That's the initial distance I've tried to start amplifying. I've done as you indicated, focusing on amplifying the distance and sending more energy as I tried to make it spread. For days I got no results."

"That's absolutely natural. Amplification is a skill that takes time and a lot of effort."

Lasgol nodded. "I understand, and I have been making efforts."

Ona, show Eicewald how far we've amplified the skill, Lasgol transmitted.

The panther took a couple steps back, moving further away.

"That's as far as you've been able to advance with the Amplification?" Eicewald asked.

"That's all I could do, yes," Lasgol said regretfully, bowing his head, a little embarrassed.

"I don't understand why you see it as a failure. It's a good achievement."

"It is?" Lasgol had expected to progress a lot more.

"It is," Eicewald nodded. "As I said, Amplification takes time. You're not going to do it in three or four days of practice. It will take you a lot more. Significant progress requires great effort and dedication. In fact, for the time you've been trying, you shouldn't even have made that much progress. It should have been much less."

"Really? Then it's good news."

"You young ones, you think you're going to achieve anything in the blink of an eye and almost without effort. Let me say, you're quite mistaken. In both life and magic, each success requires a lot of work, sacrifice, and effort. Determination and guts are also key factors."

"I nearly gave up, I was so frustrated..."

"Never give up, or you'll lose the little you've achieved," Eicewald said, wagging his finger. "Never give up. Never surrender. You should always keep striving, even if the results don't come as fast as you expected. If you keep working, they'll eventually arrive. If you give up, you'll only lose the little you've achieved."

"I understand. I will not yield," promised Lasgol, who had been touched by the Mage's words.

I never give up, Camu messaged.

"Very well, that pleases me greatly. Let nothing bad ever be said about my pupils," Eicewald said, smiling.

"The only thing is that so much practicing leaves us exhausted," said Lasgol.

Much exhausted.

"That's natural and to be expected," Eicewald said. "When you use magic, the body and mind are affected because they require great effort to use magic, even if you don't notice."

"Yes, we've already noticed that."

"Practice until you can't anymore, but not beyond. When your body tells you to rest, sleep. Pay attention to your body and its wisdom."

"We will."

"Now I'll teach you some lessons from the tome. I'll read out loud so Camu can memorize it. I'm sure it will greatly interest you."

They went back into the tent and the lessons continued. Lasgol and Camu enjoyed every explanation.

Chapter 8

Nilsa, Egil, and Gerd left the tower after breakfast. They were heading towards the gate in the wall that surrounded the Royal Castle when they saw a group of riders arriving. They realized at once it was the Royal Princess of Irinel, accompanied by Valeria and her retinue. Half a dozen Royal Guards and the Captain of the Guard were with them.

"We'd better stop and pretend," Nilsa said in a whisper.

"True, we don't need any unpleasant encounters…" Egil replied, also in a whisper.

Gerd looked at Egil, who nodded. The three stopped and bowed their heads, trying not to be noticed and recognized by the Princess. They did not want her to realize who there were. There was no risk for the giant, but there was for Nilsa and Egil. They could not hide either, because if they left in a hurry, they would draw a lot more attention to themselves. Besides, there was nowhere nearby to hide. The closest place was the Royal Stables, and they were too far for the group to get to them nonchalantly.

The retinue passed near them, so they tried to pretend even harder. Egil was looking at one of his notebooks he had taken out from under his cloak, where he always carried one to write down anything of interest. He was reading it with his chin tucked into his chest to hide his face. Nilsa could not hide her curly red hair—she drew attention from a league away, and more so for someone from Irinel, where redheads were common. She decided to pull her hood on to hide it while she also bowed her head and half-turned.

The Princess looked at them for an instant, squinting like someone analyzing her surroundings. Gerd was the only one looking at the riders directly. The Princess's eyes went from Gerd to his two companions. She pulled on the reins hard and stopped her horse. The whole retinue stopped at once.

"Do you really think you can hide that hair of yours, the color of fire typical of my country, from the Royal Princess?" she told Nilsa rudely.

Nilsa raised her eyes slowly until she met the Princess's furious glare.

"No…. of course I didn't…" she said, trying to defend herself, although she did not really know why. She glanced at Valeria, who smiled at her unobtrusively so the Princess would not notice.

"Well, you can't. And neither can that puny worm who is the mastermind of your group," Heulyn pointed a finger shaking with rage at Egil.

"Your Highness, I'd never try to hide from your pleasant Royal presence," Egil replied, raising his head and smiling, hoping she would not notice it was a completely false smile. Valeria looked at Egil and winked at him.

"Is the giant accompanying you some moron you use as a mastiff?"

Gerd threw his head back as if she had slapped him. He was not expecting to be referred to in such a derogatory manner.

"I'm no moron…" Gerd began to argue, looking annoyed.

"He's one of his Majesty King Thoran's Royal Eagles too," Valeria whispered to Princess Heulyn.

Egil patted Gerd's back to soothe him.

"Another? True, his face is as common as the others'," Heulyn said rudely.

"Norghanian faces tend to be pale and without much life. It has to do with the cold of the north," Egil said.

"Don't you dare address me directly without my express permission, or I'll dismount and cut your tongue out myself," Heulyn threatened him, enraged.

"I'm sure the Royal Eagles know how to behave before Royalty and be on their best behavior," Valeria said to the Princess as she glanced warningly at her old colleagues.

"Captain of the Guard, I don't want these disgusting personages crossing my path," she told Olson in a commanding tone, pointing an accusing finger at them.

"I beg your pardon, Royal Princess, do you mean *them*?" Olson asked, unable to understand why she meant the three Rangers.

"Yes, that rabble who soils me with their presence and whose heads I asked for on a platter and haven't been granted," she replied furiously.

The Captain of the Royal Guard was staring blankly at Nilsa, Gerd, and Egil, unable to understand what this was all about.

"They're King Thoran's Royal Eagles. They're the pride of the Rangers, appreciated by all, including the whole court and kingdom."

"I don't care who they are! To me they're cockroaches that must be squashed. I don't want to see them! Get them out of my sight!" she cried in rage.

The Captain looked at Nilsa, not knowing what to do.

"If you don't mind…" he began hesitantly.

"Of course, we'll get out of the way of the Royal Princess of Irinel, Captain," Egil said, making it absolutely clear he was addressing the Captain and not the Princess. He bowed elaborately.

"One day you'll pay for what you did to me. I'll never forget," she promised, threateningly shaking her fist. "I'll have your heads. It's only a matter of time."

Olson's eyes opened wide. The Princess's hatred of the Royal Eagles had taken him completely aback.

"Captain, Royal Retinue," Nilsa said with another elaborate bow.

Gerd joined in the bowing but said nothing.

They moved away so that it would look as if they were removing themselves from the Princess's presence.

"Royal Eagles," the Captain nodded at them.

The retinue continued on its way. As she passed by Valeria nodded at them without Heulyn seeing. They continued toward the Royal Castle. The Princess turned in her saddle to glare at them one last time with absolute hatred.

"Wow, she's really fond of us…" Gerd commented.

"We already told you about her," said Nilsa, pushing back her hood.

"Well yeah, but I wasn't expecting this. That woman hates our guts, even me, and I wasn't even with you."

"That's hatred by proxy," Egil said, smiling.

"Is she really going to have our heads?"

"Maybe she only means to hang us from a tree," said Nilsa. "It depends on the day, sometimes she wakes up in a better mood."

Gerd gave Nilsa a puzzled look.

"Are you being serious?"

"I'm afraid so," Egil said. "She speaks in earnest, and she will try, don't doubt it. She's spiteful and, according to her, we've committed an outrage against her person. She'll never forgive us."

"Well then, let me remind you that she's going to be our Queen.

That puts us in a treacherous position," Gerd told them.

"Well, as long as the King defends us, it seems we'll survive," said Nilsa.

"I don't trust the King at all, or that he will defend us."

"You're right there," said Egil. "Our monarch isn't exactly a man of his word, or even honorable."

"I don't see how you can be so calm about this. That woman wants us dead and she's going to be our Queen. Am I the only one who sees a problem with that?" Gerd raised his arms in frustration.

"Oh, we see it," Nilsa said.

"We must understand what plans the King has for the Princess. That's something we have to keep in mind. As long as she isn't the Queen, we're not in too much danger, but when she becomes our Queen we'll have a big problem, as Gerd says. Nilsa, do you think you could use your charisma and contacts in the castle and court to find out about the wedding plans?"

"Of course, I'll see what I can find out."

"My allies are nervous about this wedding. We must stay up to date in order to foresee and plan to avoid unnecessary conflict…"

"Like having our heads chopped off?" Gerd asked.

"Exactly like that, yes," Egil said, grinning. "Also, so my allies don't undertake any actions that aren't convenient for us without heeding my requests for peace."

"The West doesn't respect you as their leader?" Gerd whispered, looking around to make sure no one was listening.

Egil also looked around in case any treacherous ears were nearby.

"It's not that they don't respect me anymore, but there are different lines of thought among the Nobles of the West. There are some who are more impatient and don't want to wait and see what happens with the Princess but who want to take action immediately, before there's a royal wedding to complicate the West's options to the Crown."

"That might be dangerous…" Gerd commented, wrinkling his nose.

"That's why we must gather information that will help us plan and contain those possibilities. I don't want any unexpected events that might be potentially dangerous for our interests."

"I'll handle getting information. I'll be charming, more than usual," Nilsa smiled beguilingly as she headed to the main building of the Royal Castle.

"Perfect, see what you can find out," said Egil, "but don't overdo it. Don't appear too eager—we don't want anyone suspecting we're interested in the crown's movements."

Nilsa smiled innocently and sweetly, as if she had never so much as broken a plate in her life.

"How about this?"

"Perfect," Egil nodded.

"Very believable," Gerd nodded too, eagerly.

"I'll go and see what's going on," Nilsa said, waving goodbye to them as she left.

"You and I'd better go to town," Egil told Gerd. "I have several messages I need to send clandestinely."

"I guess your contacts will be in areas the City Guard doesn't frequent."

"Indeed, places where neither the Guards nor others we don't want to know what we're doing will be."

"I see, and I assume these will be pretty dangerous places," Gerd said, nodding.

"Irrefutable, my dear friend."

Gerd eyed him, raising an eyebrow.

"May I ask why you like this word 'irrefutable' so much? I don't even think you're using it right, and that puts me off, being you…"

Egil stared at Gerd with an amused look on his face.

"And what would be the fun in that? Since when have I used light rhetoric that can be understood with the least attention?"

Gerd shook his head, smiling.

"Yeah… it wouldn't be like you to be easily understood by those around you."

"Indeed, my dear friend. I must keep my precious friends' minds always alert and thinking."

"Well, my head might explode one day trying to decipher your comments," Gerd said, holding his head with both hands.

"You give yourself too little credit. That head of yours is well trained and instructed—it thinks very well," Egil replied and patted his friend's back, although being as big and strong as he was, he probably did not even notice.

"Well, you'd better try to take your degree of intellectual speech down a notch when I'm around so we can avoid trouble."

56

"You've always understood me the first time."

"Often not until the third time, or until I've been told what you meant."

Egil waved this off as untrue.

"Come on, we have a couple of important meetings I can't be late for."

"Your bodyguard will follow and protect you," Gerd said.

"So, I have nothing to fear," Egil said, smiling broadly, and they left the castle to go into the city.

Chapter 9

Nilsa was walking down the long corridor that led to the area that lodged the court nobles. She had not had any trouble getting there, since she knew the two Royal Guards who guarded the west wing she had come in through: Jurgen and Torlar, two veterans who had been serving at the castle for a number of years. She had casually greeted them, and they had returned the greeting without thinking twice about her being there.

She also knew the two other Royal Guards standing at the entrance of the corridor she was now walking along. They were Molwan and Tirwer, who greeted her. She exchanged a couple of courtesies with them. They were also veteran soldiers who enjoyed chatting with her. Besides, it was boring being on guard duty all day in the same spot, so any chance of friendly conversation was welcome. As a rule, soldiers were barked at by their superiors or the castle nobles. She knew this and also that they were always polite, so she was nice and friendly with them and they were always nice to her.

She smiled to herself. So far, she had been lucky. She was not always allowed to wander through the castle at her will, since she was a Ranger and they were usually in the Tower. With the exception, of course, of the Royal Rangers, who did have access to the castle and accompanied and guarded the King. Unfortunately, she was not a Royal Ranger. She wondered whether one day she would be—most likely not. She shrugged. She would have to see what life had in store for her. Her own life was always full of surprises, so she did not want to assume anything. Well, her life and that of her friends, who did nothing but get into trouble of the most varied, difficult-to-solve kind.

Thinking about it, it was not that she had been lucky. The fact that she knew the guards was because she had a nice, friendly personality and she made the effort to socialize and get to know both Royal Guards and Rangers. Not like that halfwit Viggo, who looked down on everyone. Ingrid knew only the officers she dealt with and was not interested in the rest, since she rarely had to speak to them. So, the fact that she was allowed to wander was due to her alone, and she ought to be proud of that. And as a matter of fact, she was.

The problem would come now. She wanted to get into the castle wing reserved to the Court, and she did not have access to it. But she had to get in, because that's where anything of interest went on. She could try and get information from a couple of Royal Rangers she believed were interested in her. It was risky, because trying to make a Royal Ranger talk was always dangerous and complicated. If she were found out and her interest in obtaining information was discovered, she would be in big trouble and end up in Gondabar's office, something she wanted to avoid at all cost.

What she was doing might be considered espionage, and in that case, she would end up tried and hanged. Gathering information, even for a Ranger on an official mission, was always complicated. There was a thin line that separated patriotism from high treason, and they were always balancing on that line. One slip and they would fall into high treason and it would all be over for them. Thoran and his brother were not the kind to forgive mistakes, not the Royal Eagles' or anyone else's.

She reached the end of the corridor that ended in a square room, an ante-chamber with three large double doors. One was always closed and the other two were guarded. She turned left and found two Royal Rangers in front of the door. Protecting the other door were two Royal Guards, and Nilsa checked them out of the corner of her eye. She did not know them and they looked forbidding. But luckily, she did know one of the Rangers.

She went over to greet him.

"Hi there, Johanes," she said, raising her hand and giving him her best smile.

"Nilsa, a pleasure to see you," Johanes greeted her back and smiled too.

Nilsa remembered that Johanes was always friendly with her, rather more than usual, so she suspected he was interested in her. Johanes was tall, strong, and quite handsome, with long blond hair and gray eyes. Nilsa was not immune to his charm—in fact, she was now looking at him with interest. He was more handsome than she remembered, not as much as others in the castle, but he came quite close.

"How's everything?" she asked to start the conversation and see whether he followed.

"Quite well. This month it's our turn to guard this entrance. You know, rotation and all…"

Nilsa nodded and smiled.

"No wonder you get bored, always doing the same work. Changing tasks every now and then is good to refresh the mind."

"Not the most daring of missions for a Ranger, but it's what we've got," said the other Royal Ranger.

"That's right," said Johanes, raising his eyebrows and looking resigned.

"Forgive me, I don't remember ever meeting you…" Nilsa said to the other Ranger.

"I'm Nilsum. It's a real pleasure to meet the famous Nilsa of the Royal Eagles," he said and bowed his head.

"I see you've heard of me," Nilsa smiled and giggled. She did this on purpose, knowing that boys liked it when she flirted or was very friendly. She needed to get through and a little flirting hurt no one, especially if it helped to reach her goals. She considered it as another weapon in her arsenal, not lethal, but one that opened doors in certain situations.

She smiled at the two Rangers and blinked her eyes. It was not always a good idea to kick a door down, Ingrid's preferred style, or slit the throat of the watch before they realized what was going on, Astrid's style. Hers was more refined and adequate for situations in the castle and the court, where Ingrid's and Astrid's ways would not be appropriate.

"How wouldn't I know of one of the heroes of the realm, famed not only for her skill with the bow, but for her splendid beauty?" Nilsum said and smiled beguilingly.

"You leave me speechless with your compliments," Nilsa said, smiling and putting her hands to her face to cover a non-existent blush as if she were really impressed, which she was not. Nilsa received all kinds of compliments from soldiers, Rangers, and even some noblemen of the Court, and she was quite used to them. Ignoring them without the compliment giver noticing was an art Nilsa mastered.

"You'll need more than a compliment for Nilsa to warm up to you," Johanes told Nilsum, with a look that said it was no easy task. "Her list of admirers grows daily, and still there's not one who's managed to woo her."

"Well, then, I hope our brave Royal Eagle will add me to that list as a fervent admirer of her beauty and friendliness."

Nilsa listened to them, very much aware of that skill of hers to wrap men around her little finger. It was also true that in the Royal Castle they were not too bright. Now that she thought about it, with the exception of her comrades the Snow Panthers, she did not know many intelligent men. Most were quite simple.

She had noticed that for a while now she had been attracting more attention. As if something had changed for some reason. She did not know whether she was physically more attractive or if her skill in flirting had improved with years of experience. It might be both.

"Absolutely, Nilsum, consider yourself listed. But I'm warning you, the list, as Johanes who is also on it has said, is quite long," Nilsa said, and she moved her hands as if she were throwing a scroll to the floor so it would unroll endlessly.

"We're screwed then," Johanes moaned, waving his hands as if everything were in vain.

"I say, that list sounds never-ending," Nilsum said, shaking his head exaggeratedly.

Nilsa could tell by the exaggerated, fake complaints of the two soldiers that they found her interesting. She had realized a long time ago that she had this effect on many men. She had always drawn the attention of men with her red mane of hair, her freckles, and her beauty, more of Irinel than of Norghana. Now that she knew she could dazzle men, she understood that she had an advantage to be used. After all, it was not her fault if men were a little foolish and were so easily seduced. Not all of them were like that, but a large number of men were. She decided to test her luck.

"You see," she said as she played with her long hair and put her head to one side, coquettishly, "I must get into the Court area, on an errand for Gondabar…"

"You're working for our leader at the Tower again?" Johansen asked her, surprised. "I thought that, being a Royal Eagle, you wouldn't have time for Gondabar's tasks."

"Not officially, I'm still a Royal Eagle and I must follow the King's designs. But every now and then, when I'm in between the King's missions, Gondabar seizes the chance to use my help in some delicate matters, and this is one of those."

"Then you're on a mission for Gondabar? Is it secret?" Nilsum wanted to know.

"I can't give you any details… you understand, don't you?" Nilsa said timidly as if she were a good girl who could not reveal something important that she had been entrusted with.

"Yes, of course. Our leader's missions are none of our business. We'd never dare to interfere, least of all to put you, Nilsa, in a spot for revealing information that doesn't concern us," Johanes said.

"Of course not," Nilsum joined in.

"You have no idea how much I appreciate the fact that there are true gentlemen among the Royal Rangers who are willing to look after a damsel like me," she said, smiling as if she really were a damsel in distress, which was not the case at all. Nilsa was playing with those two rangers to get past the door they were guarding and gain access to an area of the castle where she was not allowed to be. In order to do so she was going to dazzle and daze these two.

"Always at your service," Johanes said.

"My bow is at your request. You need only ask and I'll come at once."

Nilsa made as if she blushed and shook her red mane, showing off its crimson beauty.

"You're both most chivalrous. No doubt you'll let me through so I can proceed with my duty…" Nilsa said shyly.

Both Royal Rangers glanced at one another. There was doubt in their eyes.

"In order to come into this part of the castle, where the members of the Court are lodged as well as important visitors, you must have written permission. Those are King Thoran's orders ever since the arrival of the Royal Princess of Irinel and her retinue," Johanes told her.

"I know," Nilsa bowed her head. "I misplaced mine… I can be so clumsy sometimes… you know me…" she went on in a fake embarrassed tone with moist eyes.

"We can't let anyone through without permission," Nilsum said.

"But I've been in there hundreds of times, doing errands for Gondabar. This is just another…" Nilsa insisted.

"We know that… but now the orders are not to let anyone through," Johanes said.

"I wouldn't want to ask Gondabar for another pass… I'll be a laughing stock for my clumsiness…"

"It's a bit silly, yes. I can understand you. No one wants to appear foolish before their superiors…" Nilsum said.

"Raner Olsen, the new First Ranger, is very hard and inflexible with us, his Royal Rangers. If I were in your shoes and had to tell him I had lost my orders it would be horrible. I'd almost rather be sent straight to jail than be judged by his stern gaze."

"Yeah, our leader is tough as a rock, and even more so with us. He doesn't allow any mistakes."

"Then you do understand my situation…"

"Mind you, we wish we could help you, but…" Johanes said.

"We'd be severely punished if Ranger Olsen found out that we let you in without a pass," Nilsum said.

"Nothing will happen to you—it won't be more than a moment, in and out. And I'll owe you," she said and started playing with her hair again as she smiled beguilingly.

Both Royal Rangers exchanged glances.

"I guess if you're fast, the risk will be less…" Johanes said

"And everyone's seen you in there, there's no reason for them to suspect you don't have your pass…" said Nilsum.

"Exactly. I'll finish quickly and come back at once. No one will say anything to me. They never do. The members of the Court rarely deign to talk to the Rangers."

"Very true," said Nilsum. "They look down on us."

"All right, Nilsa. Go in and do your task as fast as you can. Don't get us in trouble," Johanes said pleadingly.

Nilsa looked at Nilsum, who nodded.

"You owe us one," he said and opened the door they were guarding.

"I'll pay you back, I promise," she said, smiling, and went in.

Nilsa snorted under her breath as the door shut behind her back. She had achieved her purpose and felt good with her small victory. Now she would have to be careful so no one would ask her what she was doing in there.

She arrived at a wide hall, very ornamented, which gave access to three corridors through domed entrances without doors. In this hall there were two Royal Rangers on watch duty who looked at her. Nilsa avoided eye contact and went past them quickly, as if she were in a hurry to get somewhere. She had used this ruse many times, and it was the most efficient way to avoid anyone who wanted to bother her when she wanted to be on her own.

The guards did not say anything to her. She was not surprised. They were there in case anything happened, not to control access to the area. As long as no one called them for some trouble or raised an alarm, those two were not going to move or take an interest in anything. They had to stay at their posts and do their duty, which was to watch and act if anything out of the ordinary happened.

Nilsa already knew the area, and she went along the right-hand corridor. It was deserted. Carved oak doors began to appear on both sides, and on each one of them there hung the coat of arms of some noble family of Norghana. These were the rooms of the members of the Court who resided in the castle. There were also distinguished guests whom the King, or his brother the Duke, invited every now and then.

Access to those rooms was forbidden. Only residents and those with a pass could be there. She was neither, so she should not even try. From what she had heard, the doors opened onto several large rooms where the nobles lived, alone or with company, and of course, with their personal guard. It was not a good idea to try and open any of those doors. The armed men watching them inside had hostile tendencies.

She kept going. Being in an area of the castle reserved only for nobles loyal to the King and their servants and bodyguards made Nilsa a little nervous, and nerves were what she did not need right then. She controlled herself and tried to quiet them as she always did. She had improved a lot since her days at the Camp and she could now almost extinguish them internally before they surfaced and got her into trouble. She was proud of the advances she had made, yet, every now and then, some nerve escaped her control and played tricks on her. It was going to be a while still before she managed to completely overcome them, but she was going to—that was one of her goals in life. She would stop being clumsy. She had already managed to become a Mage Hunter, which had been her main goal, and this encouraged her immensely. She would also manage to curb her nerves: it was just a matter of time and perseverance, which Nilsa had plenty of.

She took a deep breath while she passed carved doors with the coats of arms of the houses of Eastern Nobles. She did not know them all, but some were familiar. Of course, the houses of the Western Nobles did not have their rooms in this area but in another, more isolated one that was less luxurious. It was no secret that the King and his brother favored the Eastern Houses in everything, which was entirely understandable, since they had supported them in the civil war and had defeated the Western Houses.

Today Nilsa was not interested in the nobles of either side of the Kingdom of Norghana. Today she was interested in a very special guest, and she must reach the area where she was lodged, which was the most illustrious and ornamented part of the residential wing of the castle. She hurried up, and with long, fast strides she arrived where she was headed.

She saw Royal Guards posted at several corridor crossings and, just like before, she ignored them and went on as if she were late for some important meeting and she were going to be scolded. She even made herself look worried. She could not let herself be found out hanging about without permission. If she was caught, she would be in great trouble, the kind that puts a person in the dungeons, or worse.

She turned left at the end of another long corridor and saw several soldiers of the Princess's retinue posted before two doors. These had to be the rooms the Princess had been given. This made it difficult to get close and investigate, as she called it, although what she was really doing was spying for the Panthers.

She got as close as she could unobtrusively and confirmed they were Princess Heulyn's rooms. She went down another corridor to the right before reaching the Irinel guards so they would not suspect her. To her surprise, she heard voices coming from a room at the end of the corridor.

Nilsa went up to the double door of the room. She remembered that this was a library for the guests, smaller than the Royal Library. She stopped before the door and listened. The voices coming from inside were of a man and a woman. The woman was shouting and the man was muttering in a low voice.

She tried to understand what was going on. The voices became louder. Nilsa recognized at once that the woman's voice was Heulyn's. It took her longer to recognize the man's voice, more than anything else because he was apologizing and speaking very low. But it was none other than Ambassador Larsen.

The door was shut tight, but the Princess's shouts were so loud they could be heard through the wall. Nilsa looked down both sides of the long wide corridor and saw no one. Staying there, listening, could get her into serious trouble. On the other hand, there was no one around, and she was not doing anything that might be considered treason yet.

She bent down and untied the laces of her right boot, pretending she was retying them in case anyone appeared. While she pretended to tie her boot, she strained her ear and tilted her head to the door slightly.

"I said no! Are you deaf?" the Princess was shouting.

"Royal Princess… think again." The Ambassador was pleading with her, not shouting but having to speak loudly so the Princess could hear him in the midst of her own shouts.

Nilsa could not understand the next exchange, so she had to concentrate more intently to listen to what was said inside. She was finding this very interesting.

"You shouldn't spy on royalty, that's something that might cost you your life," a voice said from behind her.

Nilsa froze—she had been found out.

Chapter 10

Nilsa did not move, although she found it hard to maintain her balance from the fright she had; she had not heard anything, and she had keen hearing.

"I wasn't spying, I was lacing up my boot," she said even before identifying whoever had caught her eavesdropping.

"I see you're the same lousy liar," a feminine voice said in an amused tone.

Nilsa looked around in surprise.

"Val!"

"Hello, Nilsa," the Dark Ranger smiled at her.

"It's not what you think," she replied, raising a hand.

"Of course it is, and we both know it," Valeria said, smiling.

"I was really tying my laces..." Nilsa tried to keep pretending, but she realized her excuse was frail and that she would not manage to fool Valeria.

"Are you here on your own account, or has Egil sent you?

"I... well..."

"I see, Egil has sent you to gather information about the Princess of Irinel."

"I'm on an errand for Gondabar," Nilsa was still trying to pretend.

"In the area where Princess Heulyn's rooms are? That is indeed hard to believe. Gondabar might be the leader of the Rangers, but he has no interest or jurisdiction regarding the Princess of Irinel. That's a matter of state, and it only concerns King Thoran and his brother, Orten. The Rangers and their leaders have no say in these matters."

"The Rangers have always had a say in everything that has to do with the safety and well-being of the realm."

"So says the Path of the Ranger, yes. I know it well, I studied it for four years," Valeria smiled with irony.

"So there. We're where the realm needs us," Nilsa said, straightening up and stretching her back.

"Absolutely not in front of the door behind which the Princess of Irinel is discussing matters of importance."

"Well, it's been a pleasure seeing you, I'm leaving now," Nilsa said in a hurry, trying to get out of the situation no matter what it took.

"Not so fast," Valeria said, raising her hand. "I've caught you, and you know it. Tell me what Egil wants to know and I'll let you leave, otherwise I'll call the Princess's soldiers, who are just around the corner."

"You know I can't tell you anything," Nilsa said and spread her hands open.

"Tell your King I said no! Are you all deaf as well as stupid in this kingdom?" Princess Heulyn's voice was heard through walls and doors.

Nilsa and Valeria looked at the door. For a moment Nilsa thought it would burst open from the power of the shouting.

"Royal Princess... you must understand..." they could hear Ambassador Larsen say as he tried to placate the Princess's fury. But since she was shouting, he had to speak loudly, so they also heard him.

"Your lady sounds angry," Nilsa said to Valeria.

Valeria smiled.

"She rarely isn't."

"What are you doing with her? She's not the best kind of noble you could've found to serve, even if she is royalty."

"I'm touched by your concern," Valeria said ironically as she put her hands to her heart.

"Let me remind you that I never wished you any ill. What happened to you was the result of your own decisions," Nilsa replied, annoyed. Valeria had brought her own 'cliff to jump off' upon herself. They had had nothing to do with it. Every person must be responsible for their acts, especially when these are unforgivable.

"True, very true. My decisions were mine, and I must live with that. I must admit they weren't very good ones now that I can see them in retrospect, with the calm and cool that the passing of time grants me."

"Every person must carry their own acts and guilt," Nilsa said.

"And I carry them. That's what I do, every day of my life." Valeria heaved a deep sigh. "What's done is done. The mistakes made can rarely be amended. I accept my mistakes and I go on. I doubt I can be redeemed, and I'm not looking for it either."

"I'm glad you at least admit you did wrong." Nilsa felt that Valeria's words were sincere and she wanted to believe her. But she had already lied to them before, and she might be lying again. To trust once and be betrayed was one thing, to trust twice and be betrayed again was foolishness. Nilsa might be nervous, clumsy, and many other things, but she was no fool. She would not allow herself to be betrayed again.

"You've always had a good heart. I remember that you supported my banishment and were against my being sentenced to death. I appreciate that. I always will. But, don't think I regret everything I did. I regret the mistakes I made."

"I'm not sure I understand what you mean," Nilsa said, tilting her head and with a dubious look on her face.

"Let's say I regret how everything ended, the wrong decisions I made. Regarding you all, I do regret what happened, in case that eases your mind."

Nilsa sighed.

"It's a little, but it's something," she confirmed, although something told her that Valeria was not entirely regretful of her betrayal to the Rangers and to all of Norghana. She could not trust her. She must remain on her guard and not let herself be fooled. Valeria was not only beautiful, she was also intelligent and cunning. Better to be careful with her.

"As for the Princess and me, a misfortune unites us. One we share, and the reason why I'm serving her."

"And what would that misfortune be?" Nilsa asked with interest, since she could not think how Valeria might have entered the Princess of Irinel's service.

"I'll tell you while Heulyn knocks off Ambassador Larsen's head with her shouting," Valeria smiled as they heard the Princess's yelling. Larsen had gone quiet and was bearing the winter storm pouring out of the Princess's mouth.

"Well, you'd better hurry because I believe those doors are going to open and his head will just roll out."

Valeria burst out laughing. Hearing her laugh, recognizing the laughter of someone who had been a friend and which she had so often shared, touched Nilsa's heart. She realized she was softening and rejected the feelings of friendship and companionship—that was a thing of the past. Now Valeria was with the Princess of Irinel and the Panthers had not decided what to do with her when the time came. She remembered that Viggo wanted to eliminate her since she was still a danger to them all. He was right up to a point, although Nilsa resisted the idea of killing her.

Valeria sighed deeply.

"When you sentenced me to exile, I went through a difficult time. It was hard, a time filled with sorrow and pain. Hard for the exile and the loss of ideals that drove me, also pain for the loss of my father, for believing that I had lost everything, bitter for not having a place to call my own to drop dead. I must admit that I still haven't overcome everything that happened to me," Valeria explained with moist eyes.

"Where did you go?"

"I thought about going to Rogdon—that's a safe place to start a new life. The Rogdonians are narrow-minded, but they're not treacherous. They always hold to the truth. I should have gone there. It was a bad choice on my part. I let myself be driven by rage and I chose poorly."

"What kingdom did you choose?"

"One from which I knew I could hurt Norghana."

Nilsa saw it clearly.

"You went to Zangria."

"That's right. I went, and I regretted it. At first, I was accepted with open arms. I gave myself up to General Zorlten, an intelligent but evil man, more so than I could've imagined. I was given everything I asked for: a new post as a high-ranking officer beside the General, a good amount of gold, elegant clothes of good quality, all kinds of weapons, anything I needed."

"No one gives anything for free unless they're looking for something in return."

"Exactly. I was blinded by rage, for having been defeated, for having lost everything, and I thought the best place to be safe would be among the Zangrians. After all, the enemies of my enemy are my friends, right?"

"That's what they say, although I'm not sure it always turns out that way…"

"It does if you do what you're asked. If you don't, then you're their enemy, and then you have nowhere to go."

"You didn't do what they asked you to? I'm shocked…"

"I did at first. I gave them information about Thoran, Orten, and their Eastern Nobles. They wanted to know the location of their forces, how many soldiers they had and other relevant military information… but the requests soon began to change."

"More difficult to grant?"

"Yes. At first I thought I'd be able to, honestly. I thought I would be able to sell everything I knew of the enemy and not feel remorse. After all, I had attempted a regicide in Norghana and failed. I had paid with exile. My rage for everything that had happened to me, for the great failure and the terrible losses I suffered, slowly decreased. Every day the wounds healed a bit more."

"With the Zangrians your future would always be war, whether with the Norghanians or with Erenal," Nilsa said with a look that said it was not a good one.

"I knew that. I was aware of it. Then something happened. One morning it suddenly didn't hurt so much. The pain wasn't so bad. The lack of hope for losing everything wasn't the same. I felt a little better. The following day I was lighter. On the third morning, I was a bit more optimistic about my future."

"So, then you escaped from the Zangrians?"

"I couldn't. I was under close watch, and besides, although I had started to recover, I still had a long way before I was well," Valeria said, pointing her finger at her head. "I wasn't ready to run away in search of a new, bright future, at least not at that moment."

"I guess you were still processing and overcoming everything that had happened. It's a big trauma which in all likelihood will take you years to overcome," Nilsa said. She had often spoken with Egil about the subject of trauma and how to overcome it. It was something that had always interested her a lot. The fact that her father had died, leaving her with deep scars, had a lot to do with her interest. It was not simply a general interest. It was a deeply personal one.

"And that's when things got worse. General Zorlten wanted to start an invasion campaign before Thoran became strong again, and he needed to persuade the Zangrians and King Leonidas. In order to do that, he devised a coup that would reveal Thoran, showing his weakness. He wanted to finish off the leader of the King's famed Rangers he was so proud of."

"He wanted to kill Gondabar?"

"And whoever was with him."

"The treacherous games of politics between kingdoms never cease to surprise me, and they make me sick. They have no honor," Nilsa said angrily.

"Kingdoms have as much honor as those who rule them. Any ruler in a post of notoriety is a mark for the enemies of that kingdom. Gondabar is the leader of the Rangers, and with his death, General Zorlten would leave King Thoran in a weak state as a monarch."

"Did you refuse?"

"Not exactly. I accepted the mission. The Zangrian spies gathered information that Gondabar was going to visit the Camp. It's a visit he usually makes twice a year at least, if his health allows it, and on which he talks about important matters with Dolbarar and the Master Rangers. The Zangrians don't know where the Camp is located, at least not exactly, only an approximation. From the maps they showed me, it's quite wrong. They place it a lot more to the East than it really is."

"You didn't tell them where it is, did you?" Nilsa asked, horrified.

Valeria smiled and shook her head.

"I might have been a Dark Ranger, but I don't wish to cause more harm to the Rangers. I told them I did know where the Camp is and I would make sure Gondabar didn't get there alive."

"Only listening to you gives me the willies," Nilsa said, rubbing her arms hard.

"Don't worry. I set out on the mission with three Zangrian spies. I killed them on the way and fled."

"I guess the Zangrians didn't like that at all."

"You guess correctly, but by the time they were posed to react I had already crossed the Thousand Lakes and was entering the Kingdom of Erenal."

"That's a pleasant kingdom. I liked it a lot when we visited it with Egil, looking for a cure for the illness, well-poisoning of Dolbarar."

"It is, I like it too. The problem was that their spies knew about me: the Ranger who served with Zorlten. They caught me as soon as I arrived in the capital and took me to General Augustus, Commander in Chief of a company of infantry belonging to the army of Erenal. He was interested in me and my doings at once."

"If he took an interest and you liked the kingdom, why didn't you stay then?"

"Because Erenal was at war with the kingdom of Zangria.

They've been disputing the Thousand Lakes for generations. It's like a never-ending war, not at a grand scale, but always present. As soon as they found out I had been with the Zangrians, the Erenalians wanted to use me like they had."

"Information and murder?"

"Yes. They wanted all the information I had on the Zangrians and about General Zorlten. They devised a plan to bring him to the border with Erenal at the Thousand Lakes to kill him."

"They'd use you as bait."

"You grow smarter every day, apart from pretty, I had forgotten to comment how grown up and beautiful you've become," Valeria smiled and winked at Nilsa.

"Thanks, I'll take that as a compliment," Nilsa blushed a little. "Keep going, what happened?"

"I had no choice but to cooperate, but in the final part of the plan, when I was supposed to shoot at Zorlten, which they left in my hands to do, since I knew him and that would avoid him being fooled by a decoy. But I didn't kill him."

"You didn't release?" Nilsa said, surprised.

"Oh, I did release. He had it coming, and with a Fire Arrow at that. I'm not an Elemental Archer for nothing. But I didn't kill him. I hit him in the thigh and wounded him. The flames burnt half his leg and torso. His mount spooked and fled at a gallop, carrying off Zorlten."

"Let me guess, General Augustus and his company didn't take it all that well."

"No, they did not. I blamed it on the wind, which was blowing, but they didn't believe it. 'A Ranger rarely misses a shot, even we know that in Erenal' the General told me, and without more ado he threw me in the dungeons."

"Wow…"

"I spent quite a long time in the royal dungeons, and Augustus tried to make me collaborate with him on his plans to keep instigating Zangria. I was tired of serving others, of betraying everyone. I decided it was better for me to keep quiet and not accept any proposal of collaboration. I had a lot of time to think about my life, the mistakes I had made and what I wanted to do from then on."

"A long time in the dungeons must have been horrible," Nilsa said sympathetically.

"I wouldn't recommend it to anyone. The rats in Erenal are almost as big as those in Norghana," Valeria said, grinning. "But it was good for me. All that time in solitude in that grim cell helped me clear my head. I decided to go on with my life and make of it as much as I could. That's why I'm with the Princess of Irinel. From being a banished pariah, I've come to serve a Princess, and what's more, I'm serving the future queen of Norghana. I think I'm on a good path." Valeria smiled, and her eyes shone with the flash of a small victory.

"How did you get from a dungeon in Erenal to the Royal Palace of Irinel?"

"I'll tell you about that part some other day. It sounds like the Princess is already finishing with her shouting," said Valeria as she listened for a moment.

"She's a rude, unpleasant, loud whiner," Nilsa said, referring to the Princess.

"Better not let her hear you say that," Valeria said. "She doesn't take well to anyone opposing her, and least of all bad-mouthing her. She has a pretty big ego…"

"And thinks highly of herself," Nilsa added.

"True. There are relations that form unexpectedly between very different people, and   although they might begin abruptly, they sometimes bear fruit, as is our case," Valeria said, indicating the door with her thumb.

Nilsa wanted to know what was going on inside, why she'd heard so much shouting.

"Is it serious?" she asked Valeria, trying to elicit some information.

"You really want to know, don't you?" Valeria was not fooled and raised a blonde eyebrow.

"No… well… a little. After all, so much shouting… you know."

Valeria nodded repeatedly, smiling. She was not buying it.

"I can tell you what's going on in there. It's not a state secret," she said.

"Would you?" Nilsa narrowed her eyes at her doubtfully—was this a trick?

"Ambassador Larsen is trying to persuade the Princess to celebrate the wedding as soon as possible."

"Then there's certain to be a wedding?"

Valeria smiled.

"There will be one. That's why we've come all the way here, right?"

"Well… many times what appears to be and what actually happens differ greatly. This might be one of those times."

"Oh, don't you think Thoran and Heulyn make a great couple?"

Nilsa made a face.

"Does anyone think that?" she said with a look of disbelief on her face.

"Well, they both have strong tempers and they both like to command and shout. They're also both ambitious and love power. I'd say they're two peas in a pod."

Nilsa shook her head.

"They'll be at one another's throats on their second day of marriage."

"Well, from what I hear, that happens to most marriages anyway. Sooner or later, no matter how well they get along during the courtship."

"Marriage requires work and sacrifice, that's what my mother always says."

"Wise woman."

"Well, I don't believe she's that wise. But some things she does know. And why is the Princess arguing now?"

"Because she doesn't want to get married in winter. She hates this infernal weather. She doesn't take well to the cold. She wants a wedding with flowers and birds, hundreds of guests from the best noble houses, on a warm sunny day."

"That's not going to happen in winter," Nilsa nodded, understanding the Princess should want a pretty wedding.

All of a sudden, they heard a vase breaking against the wall.

"I'll marry in spring, or never!" the Princess shouted, and that was the end of the argument.

"You'd better get out of here so she doesn't see you. She's coming out," Valeria told Nilsa.

Nilsa nodded and left in a hurry. She had gathered some important information. The Royal Wedding would take place in the spring. Egil would want to know.

Chapter 11

Camu and Lasgol, accompanied by Ona, were enjoying another master lesson about magic that Eicewald was giving them in the tent at the Green Ogre Forest while outside sleet was falling.

"Today we'll begin the study of the Principle of Magical Power."

Very interested, Camu messaged almost at once.

"So am I," Lasgol said as he sat down before the Mage.

"In order to improve a skill's power, we need to overcharge it before we call upon it," Eicewald explained.

"How do we overcharge a skill?" Lasgol asked, tilting his head wondering.

Eicewald smiled.

"Very carefully, because it's dangerous."

I no fear, Camu messaged.

"I know you're brave, Camu, but courage might lead you to the grave if you don't combine it with common sense."

"Ufff, Camu doesn't have much of that," Lasgol commented, half-joking.

I sense and common much.

"I don't even think he knows what common sense is," Lasgol said, raising his arms in exasperation.

I know, yes, Camu messaged, but Lasgol and Eicewald were not very convinced.

"I'll demonstrate the concept of overcharge," the Mage told them.

Eicewald closed his eyes and concentrated. He spread his palms and an ice star began to take shape in the space between them. After a moment, the star was finished and hovered above the Mage's hands.

"I've created the ice star without overcharging the power, as a normal spell," he explained.

Lasgol and Camu nodded.

"Now, I'll do it again, but this time I'll increase the power. For this you'll need to draw a larger amount of magical energy before you conjure and send it to the spell. We're looking for it to cause an overcharge, since the spell itself doesn't need all that energy in order to be created."

Lasgol and Camu exchanged puzzled looks.

"I'm not sure we fully understand…" Lasgol admitted.

Eicewald nodded.

"An example is worth a thousand explanations," he told them and began to demonstrate the concept. He cast a spell with his eyes closed and there was a strange blinking white gleam that issued from his hands. An instant later there was a burst of energy that created a much bigger ice star.

Very big! I like! Camu messaged.

"I assume the size represents the star's power, which is bigger now."

"Indeed," Eicewald confirmed. "The first star, if thrown at a person, will burst upon impact and the shards of ice will kill or seriously wound them. This second star, if it burst, would kill all three of us."

"That doesn't sound good at all," Lasgol said, watching the star with fear as it hovered.

Eicewald pointed his finger at the star, and then with a wave he sent it outside the tent, through the entrance opening. He made it fly to the center of the pond, then snapped his fingers, and the star burst above the pond without harming anyone.

"You must be careful whenever you overcharged one of your skills, because there might be accidents that hurt you or the people around you."

Much accident? Camu asked.

"They're frequent when you use the overcharge. After all, you're trying to strengthen a spell, so it's more powerful, which isn't natural. Magic doesn't take well to the unnatural. Overcharging magic is always dangerous and it must be done very carefully. I can help you create layers of protection around you that will keep you from any magical harm."

"I think that would be very good for us," Lasgol nodded, sure they would have a few accidents.

I not need. I tough scales.

"Even if your scales protect you from physical harm, that doesn't mean they'll protect you from magical harm," Eicewald told him.

Not protect from all harm? Camu messaged, surprised.

"I'm afraid not. There are different types of harm, both physical and magical, and I doubt your scales will protect you from all of them."

I want try.

"We'll be deviating from the lesson…" Eicewald said.

I want know if magic harms, Camu insisted.

"I think it's a good experiment, since I'm also curious, and I don't want to assume anything that's not true and then end up disappointed," Lasgol said agreeing with Camu.

Eicewald thought for a moment.

"I think it's sensible to analyze it. Especially considering how sure Camu is of himself, which might become a problem."

"That's what I think. It could cost him dearly if what he believes isn't all true," Lasgol said, nodding repeatedly.

"You should always know your own limitations, especially when it comes to magic," the Mage told them.

"Well said. We know steel doesn't hurt him," Lasgol stated.

"Please, show me," Eicewald said.

Lasgol took out his knife and showed it to Camu.

Ready. Not scared.

Lasgol delivered a slash to Camu's right front leg. There was an almost metallic sound and the knife bounced off without inflicting any harm.

Not feel anything, Camu messaged.

"We can ascertain that he can bear cutting attacks. Let's see how he does against stinging attacks," said Eicewald.

Lasgol picked up his knife again, and after Camu's nod he delivered a stinging blow with the tip of his knife in the same place. Once again, the knife bounced off to one side.

Not feel anything.

Eicewald nodded.

"He's also immune to stinging attacks."

"Yes, his scales are impenetrable," Lasgol said.

"Let's try an elemental attack. For instance, ice, which I already feel won't affect him, given his origin."

Try, go ahead.

They did. Eicewald tried to hurt him with an ice beam, but it did not do anything to Camu.

No pain, Camu messaged conforming.

"Okay, let's try the opposite elemental, fire. I can't create powerful fire spells, but I can produce a basic flame which should be enough to know whether it burns his scales or not."

Go ahead, I no fear, Camu messaged, sure of himself.

Eicewald created a basic light flame and kept it for long time on Camu's leg. It did nothing to him. Fire could not penetrate his scales either.

"It would seem that our young Camu has very tough skin," Eicewald smiled.

I say. I powerful.

"Let's not get ahead of ourselves. We still have to see whether you can bear magical harm."

I sure bear.

"Let's see then." Eicewald began to cast a spell on Camu. All of a sudden, the creature was covered in a layer of frost.

"Let me know if you feel the cold," the Mage told Camu.

No feel.

Eicewald sent more power into the spell and the temperature dropped drastically.

"You should feel it now, because even for an ice creature the temperature is low."

Camu was covered in ice from head to tail.

Ona growled twice, unhappy.

No feel cold. No penetrate.

Eicewald stopped casting and looked at him, puzzled.

"That's weird, it should have affected him."

"Can he be immune to the cold?" Lasgol ventured.

"That might be it too. Let me think."

I very powerful. No-one harm.

"Don't start believing that, because it isn't true," Lasgol told him, worried Camu would believe he was indestructible, which Lasgol knew was not true.

Eicewald cast a new attack spell, and this time instead of basing it on Water Magic, to which Camu might be immune, he created a sphere of pure energy in his hand. He directed it with his finger, making it hover, and then shot it at Camu's right front leg. When the sphere contacted his scales there was a detonation of pure energy.

This time something different happened. When the sphere impacted on him, Camu's whole body flashed silver.

"Did you feel anything?" Eicewald asked him.

Not feel anything.

"I figured as much. It isn't at all usual. As a rule, the blast of pure energy should've hurt you, but you reacted and I believe you made a protective spell."

I not do magic on purpose.

"You might not have realized what you did, but I swear that's what it was."

"He defended himself without realizing it?" Lasgol asked, surprised.

"It looks that way. He must have an innate magical defense system," Eicewald said, looking at Camu speculatively.

"This is most impressive," Lasgol commented as he looked at Camu with great curiosity.

"I'm going to try a few more magical attacks to make sure," Eicewald said.

Go ahead. I ready.

Eicewald attacked Camu with several spells of pure energy. None managed to penetrate his innate defense. Every time he cast a spell on Camu, there was a silver flash that cancelled the attack.

"Truly fascinating," Eicewald said, taken aback. "It's as if he's instinctively canceling my magical attacks. I've never seen anything like this."

"Camu has always been different and special," Lasgol said.

I more than dragon, Camu messaged confidently, lifting his chin.

"Curiously, that's what I thought when I was experimenting," said Eicewald. "I only know, and only by reference, of one creature that has such power, a creature who isn't affected by magical or physical attacks..."

"A dragon," Lasgol guessed.

"Exactly, and a powerful one. An ancient creature with great power. Always on a basis of unproven knowledge since, as you know, there's no record of the existence of dragons."

"But Camu is just a baby in terms of a magical Creature of the Ice."

"Sure, and yet, he has the innate abilities of a thousand-year-old dragon, which is absolutely extraordinary."

Try more, Camu messaged them.

Eicewald and Lasgol spent the day trying all kinds of attacks on

Camu without managing to inflict any harm. Although it was true the attacks were restrained and launched with care just in case, they were beginning to see that Camu was an absolutely special creature. He was gifted with a powerful defense mechanism that allowed him to cancel both physical and magical attacks. They were left wondering whether if they really sought to hurt him if he would also bear it, but they did not want to risk it. Life circumstances would test him enough. Lasgol knew Camu was not invulnerable—something inside him told him so. Eicewald was of the same opinion, since there was no creature immune to all harm or invulnerable. The question was to determine what he was vulnerable to.

They did not make any other progress in the lessons about magical power, but they had established something Camu boasted about and which one day might easily become true.

Chapter 12

The following day they continued with the lesson about the Principle of Magical Power. Eicewald went over the concept with them and pointed it out in the tome he was carrying with him. Once the theory had been well explained, they moved on to the practice.

"Right, you try now, Lasgol. Let me first conjure up a protective cloak so you can't hurt yourself."

Lasgol nodded.

Eicewald cast a spell on Lasgol, and his body was covered with a protective ice layer. Over this the Mage created a second anti-magic cloak.

"I'm afraid it's not very comfortable," he apologized.

"Doesn't matter. I can move my arms, which I think is enough."

"Let's do it then," the Mage cheered him. "Remember my instructions."

Lasgol nodded and started to conjure. He decided to call upon a skill he used often and which always came in handy: *Cat-like Reflexes.* He thought he would be able to feel whether the skill had gotten more powerful, since it affected his whole body in a very direct way. He concentrated and sought his inner pool of energy. He found it. It was calm, large, and deep. He called on a large amount of energy, a lot more than was necessary to call up the skill. He prepared and summoned the skill. A green flash started to form around his body. Lasgol was encouraged—this was a good sign. Now all that was left was to finish the summons. At that moment there was a strange burst, like a flash but green and intermittent, as if it did not fully form. The skill did not activate. Lasgol knew he had failed. What he had not imagined was what happened next. There was an explosion of energy which reached Lasgol. It was so powerful he fell backward.

You well? Camu messaged him, concerned.

"Yeah … Eicewald's protection kept me safe from the explosion."

"It will hold for a few more attempts," the Mage assured him.

"You'd better try now, Camu…" Lasgol said. "My head is a little shaken."

I try.

"Be careful, you saw what happened to Lasgol," Eicewald cautioned.

I much careful.

"What skill are you going to suffuse with power?" Eicewald asked him.

Tail Whiplash

"Good choice. Okay, go ahead," Eicewald told him.

The creature shut his eyes and concentrated.

"Remember to gather enough energy," Eicewald said.

I know, he messaged back, and a moment later there was a silver flash which was also intermittent, like Lasgol's. There was an explosion of energy and Lasgol feared for his friend.

"Camu!" he cried.

But the magical explosion did not touch him. Instinctively and spontaneously, Camu's anti-magic defense mechanism activated. There was another swift silver flash and the explosion evaporated without harming him.

I well, Camu messaged them so they would be at ease.

"Your own magical defense has saved you," Eicewald said with admiration in his voice. "This is really impressive. You didn't activate it, did you?"

No, I not. No time.

"I assumed you couldn't have done it since it all happened in an instant."

"I wish I had that defense!" Lasgol said enviously.

"Me too," Eicewald smiled. "But I'm afraid it's something inherent to the type of creature Camu is. We humans don't have this ability."

"Do you think we might develop it?"

"I'm not sure. There's nothing impossible or unreachable in the world of magic, but the obstacles we would need to overcome might be too big in some cases. This is one of them, I fear."

"Yeah, it doesn't look easy at all to manage."

"But I don't want my words to limit or discourage you. If it's something you want, then try to do it. You never know what you can manage until you try with all your heart. You might be surprised."

"I just might."

I cheer, Camu messaged.

"For now, I'd better keep practicing the Principle of the Magic Power, because I haven't started out right at all."

Yes. Practice more, all, Camu messaged.

They got down to practicing and unfortunately did not manage to master the principle on the first day. Due to the constant failures and the fact that it was hard to keep trying after every failure, Lasgol guessed it would take them a long time to achieve it.

"Could you teach me some protective spell so I can continue practicing when you're not here, with less risk of hurting myself?" Lasgol asked Eicewald.

"Of course. You must create a skill that protects you from explosions of energy. It has to be something that covers your entire body, like I did with the cloak of ice, to which I added the anti-magic protection."

Lasgol wrinkled his nose.

"It sounds too complicated…"

You manage, Camu messaged encouragingly.

"You have to develop your own protective skill since it's unique to every person. My protective ice cloak spell isn't good for you. You won't be able to learn that one."

"I see. I must develop my own skill similar to that."

"Indeed. The shape the skill will take depends on your Gift and magical inclination."

"Let's try and see what I get."

"Perfect. You know you must use the Principle of Magical Creation."

Lasgol nodded. "I'll do that." He concentrated, remembering everything he had learned about magical creation, and started.

Camu was cheering him on, hopping about and doing his happy dance, which Ona joined. Unfortunately, no matter how much they cheered him on, Lasgol could not manage to create the skill. The magical world was as awesome as it was extremely frustrating. Nothing was easy. But Lasgol had realized this already, so he did not give up. He continued trying. It was something he needed. He was not trying to create a new skill just to have a new resource in his arsenal—it was something he needed so he would not hurt himself, and could continue improving his skills and magical development. It was imperative, since he would not always be able to count on Eicewald's help, who was already doing much more than he should to help him and Camu. Soon the King would summon his First Mage back and he would no longer be available to Lasgol and Camu. This was something they all knew would happen sooner rather than later.

As he was thinking about the new skill he needed, a green flash ran through his body. He was suddenly covered in braided creepers, tree branches, hard earth, and even pieces of rock. He did not know what he had done, but his body was totally covered by a tough cloak of foliage.

"Interesting creation," Eicewald said, looking at the cloak of branches and brush covering Lasgol.

You like forest, Camu messaged, laughing.

"I don't know…. This is what I've created," Lasgol shrugged.

Eicewald put his hand on the cloak of branches and leaves covering Lasgol's arm and cast a spell.

"Let me know whether it hurts," he told Lasgol.

A cone of ice left the Mage's hand and attacked Lasgol's arm.

"I feel nothing," Lasgol said.

"Interesting. I'm going to send more power."

Lasgol saw how his arm was beginning to freeze on the outside. But he did not feel any cold, even if his arm was turning into an icicle.

"How's that?" Eicewald said as he continued sending ice to Lasgol's arm.

"So far I feel nothing."

"That's great. You've developed a solid defense. I'll test it now," the Mage said, and with his other hand he conjured a second cone of ice.

Lasgol held out for a long time, but then suddenly he started feeling cold in his arm, a cold that reached his very soul.

"Now I do feel the ice," he told Eicewald.

At once the Mage withdrew his hands and stopped his spells.

"You've created a good defense. It will protect you from physical and magical attacks."

Very excellent, Camu messaged and he started to dance. Ona joined him.

"Wow, that's wonderful," Lasgol said as he stared at his unusual armor of branches, plants, earth, rock, leaves, and brush.

"But remember not to be overconfident. That defense will only protect you for a while, and you must send it more energy the moment you feel it becoming undone or that it stops being effective."

"I'll remember, because of what's at stake for me," Lasgol smiled.

What name it? Camu wanted to know.

Lasgol thought for a moment. "I'll call it Woodland Protection."

"I think that's a suitable name," Eicewald said.

"I'm going to check that it properly holds up to my failures with the Magical Power."

"Good idea," the Mage chuckled.

Lasgol tried to power up his *Cat-like Reflexes* skill with his *Woodland Protection* activated. There was another explosion of energy that struck his protective cloak. Lasgol suffered no harm, although the cloak was damaged in the torso area and pieces of it fell to the ground as twigs and earth.

"It held up," Lasgol said happily.

Very great, Camu messaged joyfully.

"Fix it by sending more energy into it," Eicewald told Lasgol.

He did so, and although it took him a while and a lot of energy to find out how to do it, Lasgol managed to repair his protection.

"Fixing your protection is difficult at first, but with use, it becomes easier and requires less energy to use."

"Great. I can see I'm going to have to practice a lot," Lasgol said, seeing they were still failing with the Principle of Magical Power.

"Don't worry, everything happens in due course. Keep working hard and you'll succeed in the end."

"Thank you, your advice and encouragement are well appreciated."

Much very, Camu messaged.

Lasgol and Eicewald smiled and good cheer reigned for the remaining practice session, although neither Lasgol nor Camu managed to master the principle.

Lasgol stopped to rest when night had already fallen, and a doubt came to his mind.

"Eicewald, I'd like you to explain to me what those magical words are that you murmur when you cast a spell."

The Mage nodded and smiled.

"It's an advanced concept, which for now we'd better leave aside since it's dangerous."

"Dangerous for whoever recites the words?"

"Indeed. The words I recite are known as Words of Power, and they help the spells to be more powerful. With them you can form Sentences of Power, which are even more powerful."

"What's the danger?"

"They can make the spells destabilize and cause you to lose control, and they can be harmful for whoever is casting or those around him or in the vicinity."

"Oh, I see... like what happens to us now with the overcharged energy."

"Worse, since in those cases the spell might be generated."

"Okay. Better not try yet," Lasgol half-smiled.

"That's an advanced subject, but you'll get to it. Give it time."

"Where do the words and sentences come from?"

"There are tomes that gather them and explain them. Just like magic has different origins which must be studied in order to use them, you have to study the words in order to understand them. It's a complex subject. It takes a long time to understand it."

"What language does it use?"

"That of Magic, and that's why it's so complex. It's like learning a language you've never heard, both ancient and complex."

"I see. I'd need to learn a new language then."

"A complex and arcane one, yes."

"I'll wait until I'm ready."

"When you are, come to me or go to any magic scholar to learn it."

"It'll take me a long time..."

"No one speaks a language in a week," the Mage smiled.

With this last explanation, they finished the day's lesson and returned to the capital. The path of Magic was arduous and dangerous.

Chapter 13

Egil and Gerd were wandering the streets of the capital at a relaxed pace, alert to the people they crossed with, or who walked by them. It was cold and the sky was overcast, announcing a new storm that would soon break out. The locals were tightening their winter coats, hurrying and looking up at the sky every couple of steps.

The Norghanians were used to the kingdom's icy weather in autumn and winter, but that did not mean they did not seek cover when storms bore upon them. It was one thing to be tough and a very different one to die frozen for showing off.

"I think the storm's going to catch up with us," Gerd told Egil.

"Yup, it's coming fast. We'd better hurry so it doesn't catch us in the open."

"Are we going very far?" Gerd asked as he hurried to follow Egil's new pace as he marched down the street.

"To the Craftsmen's Quadrant."

"That's not too far, if I remember correctly."

"You do," Egil turned to smile at the giant.

They went on along the streets of the city as the cold began to be more present. The wind was blowing with increasing force and was bringing the icy air of the mountains and blowing it through the streets and alleys. The buildings provided some shelter, but when a gust of freezing wind burst into a street it froze everyone walking along it.

They picked up their pace even more, because the sky over this part of the city was becoming a threatening black. There was a loud burst of thunder that sounded like a mountain splitting in two. Egil and Gerd stopped on the spot and looked up. A huge bolt of lightning zigzagged over their heads, crossing the north part of the city from side to side, indicating that the storm was upon them.

"We'd better run, my giant friend," Egil told Gerd.

"Running isn't what I do best right now," Gerd replied with a look of frustration on his face, but he started to run in the weird style he now had.

"I'm not the fastest of Norghanians either, a consequence of being small and fragile," Egil said to cheer him as he increased the pace and turned onto a street on his left.

"I'm neither small nor fragile. But my coordination is like that of a drunken penguin."

Egil burst out laughing.

"Don't worry, we're almost there," he told Gerd.

They went down another street as the storm bore down hard. The citizens of the capital ran to shelter in their homes, taverns, inns, or nearby businesses. The deafening thunder was followed by lethal lightning which crisscrossed the sky above. If the lightning fell inside the city there might be a tragedy, since they could kill several people or even knock down roofs and trees. The wind was already strong, and it carried freezing rain that soaked the very soul.

"We have to take cover somewhere, this is getting ugly," Gerd told Egil.

"We're nearly there," Egil said as he held down his hood with both hands so the wind would not blow it off. He went into a narrow alley that led to the back of some neglected stone buildings.

Gerd looked at the structures and could not tell whether they were houses or shops. Since they were the backs of the buildings and looked out onto a mysterious back alley, they were quite neglected. The storm was not blowing so hard in the alley since the buildings on both sides protected them, but the temperature was going down with gusts of rain that came from any direction without warning.

"There's no entrance to the building from this side!" Gerd shouted to Egil. The wind was so strong they could barely hear one another.

"Don't worry and follow me!"

Gerd wiped the freezing rain out of his eyes and saw Egil going down what looked to be some old steps. He followed as fast as he could. The strong wind was an added difficulty for the giant, and the increasingly slippery floor made matters even worse—it certainly was a challenge for his balance.

They went along to the back wall of a house and Egil followed it until he found a narrow passage between the adjoining houses. When they entered the alley, Gerd had the impression the houses were joined, but that turned out not to be the case. Egil went between the two houses to about halfway along the wall. There he stopped.

Gerd almost skidded on the muddy ground; they were between

the houses, and still the wind and cold were beating down on them. A new burst of thunder that seemed to rend the sky above them exploded right over their heads. Gerd was beginning to freeze, and they would pay dearly if they did not find shelter soon. This storm over the capital was one of the bad ones, the kind Norghanians feared, because if the wind did not kill you, the cold would.

Egil banged the wall with his fist. Gerd reached him and realized it was actually an old wooden door. There was a sound behind the door. It was tapping with a certain rhythm. Egil replied, knocking on the door with a different beat.

"You want me to knock down the door?" Gerd asked, motioning with his shoulder.

"That won't be necessary, my strong friend," Egil smiled.

With a *creak* and a shriek of old wood, the door opened.

"How many?" a shrill voice came from inside.

"There's two of us," replied Egil.

"Come in quickly, don't be seen."

Egil went in, followed by Gerd. He did not like this—he had the feeling they were entering the wolf's den through the back door.

"Thanks for seeing us at this unearthly moment," Egil said with a polite bow.

Gerd was squinting in the dark, trying to see something.

"Let's shut the door, to begin with," the same shrill voice said.

Gerd heard the door shutting and the scarce light that had been coming from outside went out. They were left in absolute darkness. They were in some kind of ground floor of an ancient house. He reached for his Ranger's axe and knife under his winter cloak and remained alert for any strange sound that might indicate danger. He knew where Egil was, just one step ahead of him. He also knew that the owner of the shrill voice was behind him, by the door.

"Don't move, there will be light presently," another voice said.

Gerd was not surprised to hear a second voice. He had to be alert to any kind of hostile movement. Egil was not saying anything, but Gerd could feel his presence in front of him. After so long at the Shelter, recovering, he had forgotten the risks that Egil's, plans always involved, and from what he was experiencing, this plan also entailed danger. He hoped Egil knew what he was doing—most assuredly he did. But sometimes situations became complicated for a variety of unexpected reasons. He was hoping this would not be one of those times.

"We'll be as still as statues," Egil replied.

Gerd understood his friend's words as an indication that he did not need to act, but instead keep calm and not move. He noticed it in his friend's tone. Nothing that would catch the attention of someone who did not know Egil, but Gerd identified it as a warning. That was something he could tell from the tone of his friend's voice without any trouble. It made him happy—he had not lost all his reflexes after all. He retained the knowledge and experiences lived with the Panthers, and that would always help him. Now more than ever since he was crippled, even if he did not want to fully admit it.

Then a light appeared at the end of the room. Gerd could see a tall man dressed in brown winter clothes holding an oil lamp in his hand. He looked like someone from the slums, where you would not usually find anyone smiling in the light of day at the market. He had a sinister look on a sharp face and a long nose, pointed like a throwing knife. He was armed with a sword, and a wide knife at his waist.

Behind the man there were three other thin men, somewhat shorter, who did not look very friendly either. Two were Norghanian, without a doubt, with their blond hair and light eyes. They wore their hair short though, which was uncommon in Norghana. The third one looked Rogdonian, with brown hair, brown eyes, and a dull-looking face featuring the square jaw of the inhabitants of the western kingdom. The three were quiet and focused, watching Egil and Gerd with great interest. They appeared to be waiting for orders.

Gerd checked them out quickly as well, including the one behind their back, who had a short blond beard and a scar on his right cheek and seemed used to being in dodgy situations. They were all wearing a white scarf tied around their wrist, which must identify them as belonging to some organization. Gerd guessed it was most likely criminal.

He wrinkled his nose. He had the feeling, by the good-quality clothes they were wearing and by how serious and confident they appeared, that these men were not mere scoundrels but something else. Gerd sensed danger, and he was not happy. He got ready to act swiftly, as he feared he would have to intervene, and not precisely in a peaceful way.

The one carrying the oil lamp, who seemed to be the leader, took a step forward with the lamp raised so there would be more light to see them better.

"How did you find us?" he asked Egil, ignoring Gerd.

"It wasn't easy or cheap, I must admit," Egil replied politely and smiled.

"Most of those who seek our services have good contacts and a lot of gold. Are you that kind of person?"

"I am," Egil confirmed. "My name's Egil, who do I have the pleasure of addressing?"

"No names. Names lead to dungeons or to hanging from a tree."

"Very well, no names. I understand I'm before the leader of the guild," Egil said.

"I'm one of the leaders of the guild, yes. You ask too many questions, I don't like that."

Egil nodded. He took out a sizeable bag of gold from the folds of his cloak and showed it to the man.

"Perhaps this'll put you at ease."

The tall man eyed it thoughtfully. He seemed to be pondering something, maybe whether to trust Egil or not.

"You know we could take that gold away from you if we wanted," the sinister character said, drawing a curved sword of the style used by the pirates of the north.

The three men behind him drew long knives and stepped forward. The one behind their backs, guarding the door, drew a short sword, also curved, and a long knife.

"It would be a real pity if you tried anything like that, since we'd be forced to defend ourselves, and that would create an unfortunate situation with bad consequences for all. But especially for you, I must add. I doubt that's what any of us would like, no one would benefit."

"You talk too much for such a small thing," the man who guarded the door said.

"Appearances can be deceiving, I can assure you," Egil boasted as he threw Gerd a look of warning out of the corner of his eye.

The leader of the group made a sign to the man at the door, who attempted to attack Egil from behind.

Gerd acted at once. He delivered a tremendous blow with his elbow to the man's head. The attacker fell to one side, senseless, behind Egil, who did not flinch.

The other three who were beside the leader prepared to attack.

Egil raised his hand.

"I only need information. I will pay handsomely for it," he said. "Confrontation is totally unnecessary, I promise."

Gerd took a step forward and stood beside Egil with his weapons drawn, ready to fight.

"Stand down," the leader ordered his minions.

The three looked at him. He gestured for them to step back.

"Tell your bodyguard not to try anything," the leader said, indicating Gerd.

"You heard the man," Egil told him.

Gerd nodded. He knew very well what he had to do. He had already been in many similar situations with Egil, who had a tendency to get into trouble. Could he not think of plans that would not put him in immediate danger? Although if they were not risky, they would probably not be so successful.

Egil glanced at him out of the corner of his eye, indicating he was expecting an answer.

"Don't worry," Gerd said to Egil, so he would know he was alert and ready in case he needed to intervene again. The three thin men behind the leader did not look like much, but they might know how to fight, and in such a small place as the ground floor room they were in, Gerd was at a disadvantage, being much larger and having trouble maintaining his balance. But regardless, if they tried anything he would make them pay. No-one would get close to touching a single hair of Egil's head while he was present.

"A guild of informers like yours ought to treat their potential customers better. The contrary's bad for business," Egil said reproachfully. "I understand you must make sure, since the information business is always dangerous and treacherous, but I don't think I've given you any reason for such a hostile welcome."

"The Guild of Collectors of the North is known for the excellent information it provides, but also for the safety measures it adopts. We don't like problems with the law or with those who intend to use us and betray us," the leader of the group explained.

"Being so wary in this type of business is only a sign of intelligence," Egil agreed.

"My contacts have informed me that you are Rangers, something you forgot to mention when you arranged for this meeting. I don't like that. It makes me uneasy, and I don't react well when I'm uneasy about my personal safety. You represent justice, and I don't want to end up hanging."

Egil raised both hands now.

"I swear this is a personal matter. It has nothing to do with the Rangers, and we most certainly aren't going to hand you over to the city guard."

"How do I know you're telling the truth? Why should I believe you?"

"You don't, but I can assure you that I want to do more business with the Guild of Collectors of the North and I have no intention of having you hanged. That would be against my own interests."

"You speak well for a Ranger."

"Thank you, I consider myself an educated person. I like to speak well, even if not everyone shares my interest," Egil commented as he threw an amused glance at Gerd.

The giant smiled for an instant and resumed his serious look. Egil was leading the situation and would end up making those men trust him. Gerd was sure. It was one of Egil's gifts, making people trust him.

"Are you of noble lineage?"

"I am, but my family, which I renounced when I entered the Rangers, no longer has any influence on me. Now all I have left of my former title is the knowledge I acquired living as a noble."

"That's good. Nobles only seek power and are capable of selling their children for it."

"That's absolutely true. As I was saying, I want the information you were asked to get. I understand you've got it and that's why we're all here, is that correct?" said Egil.

The leader moved the oil lamp up and down, shedding its light on Egil. He seemed to be studying him, checking whether he really was who he claimed to be and if his intentions were not treacherous.

"How do I know that as soon as I give you that information a dozen Rangers won't come in through that door and my days in this business will be over?"

"Because I have a second task for you and your organization," Egil replied. "One for which I'll pay splendidly."

The proposal seemed to leave the leader of the group undecided.

"How much gold are we talking about?"

"Double," Egil said, taking out another bag of gold with his right hand, which was twice as big as the one he was holding in his left hand.

The eyes of the four men opened wide, and on their faces, they could see the eagerness to grab those two bags of gold. Gerd prepared himself to face a possible frantic attack. Gold tended to make greedy men lose their heads, whether the gold was obtained legally or not. As a rule, in this type of environment, the way to get a hold of it was not usually legal, if at all.

"I think I'm beginning to like you," the leader told Egil.

"The feeling is mutual. Do you have the information I'm looking for?"

"I do," the leader nodded, reached his right hand into his belt, and took out a folded note.

"This information must be correct, otherwise I'll feel cheated, and in that case, I'll come for you with half a dozen Rangers, friends of mine, and you'll all end up in the Royal Dungeons," Egil warned him, shifting his tone to a dry, harsh one.

The leader eyed him, tilting his head.

"I see you're a resourceful man."

"I am. I have gold and I have Rangers, among other things. It wouldn't be a good idea for you to play me."

"Look who's threatening now," the leader said, somewhat surprised.

"It's not a threat. It's a second chance. If the information is good, I'll accept it. If you intend to fool me, I'm giving you a second chance to do the right thing," Egil threatened him calmly.

Gerd was listening closely and was a little surprised. He knew Egil could get serious, even harsh in some situations, but he had the feeling that now he was doing it with even more intensity. He felt a shiver, which he hid. Egil could be the best of friends, but Gerd was now realizing that he could also be the most fearsome enemy. He was becoming tougher with time as a result of the experiences he had been through.

"The information is good," the leader assured him. "The Guild of Collectors of the North doesn't trick customers. That's bad for business. Our reputation must be kept clean."

"Like any self-respecting guild. That's what I would think," Egil said, now smiling politely.

"Yeah, sure…"

"Shall we make the exchange?" Egil said, showing him the bag of gold.

The leader gave the note to one of his men, who handed it to Egil, who gave him the bag of gold he was holding in his left hand. He took the note and put it away.

The man handed the gold to his boss, who opened the bag at once and started counting the gold coins inside it.

Egil read the note.

"Satisfied?" the leader asked.

Egil nodded.

"I will be if the information is good."

"It is, I swear."

"Very well." Egil made a sign to Gerd and handed him a note of his own, indicating with a nod that he should hand it to the leader.

Gerd took a couple of slow steps toward the leader while his eyes sent warning messages to the three henchmen. If they tried anything stupid they would regret it. He handed the note to the leader of the guild and stepped back without turning his back to them.

The leader unfolded Egil's note and read it. Then he looked at him.

"You're getting into dangerous business," he warned Egil.

"Hazards of the job," Egil said smiling.

"That of a Ranger?"

"Yes."

"Well, this one's too big for you. From what I hear, this group is powerful and is gaining followers."

"I know. Hence my interest."

"I'll find the information you're asking for. Save that bag of gold."

"Saved," Egil confirmed as he put it under his cloak.

"Once I have the information I'll get in touch with you," the leader said.

"I'll be waiting."

"Go now," the leader told them.

Egil made a sign to Gerd and they went out into the alley. The storm was already passing, seeking some other place to fall upon.

"Everything fine?" Gerd asked Egil.

"Very fine, my dear friend."

"So now what?" the giant wanted to know.

"Now we're going to search in the city of Bilboson. Don't worry, you'll like it."

Gerd glanced at his friend and nodded, although he had a feeling they were going to get into more trouble. He sighed and followed Egil, who was already walking down the alley.

Chapter 14

Egil and Gerd arrived at the gates of the city of Bilboson on their horses at noon under an icy rain. The city was surrounded by a wall with three access gates which, as a rule, were open. At least in times of peace and when there were no outlaws in the vicinity.

"We're here at last. We'll be able to shelter from this winter deluge," Gerd said, the rain hammering on his upturned face.

"There's nothing like going out for a trip to make you want to reach shelter quickly," Egil commented.

"And Bilboson isn't far from the capital."

"Not too far, a few days' journey to the West, and with pretty good roads."

"But there's not a good forest to keep you out of the weather."

"True, but traveling through the forest and sheltering distracts us, and we have urgent business in the city."

They went into the city through the southern gate, which was watched by the city guard. They were not bothered and were let through.

"This city is one of the largest and most prosperous in the kingdom," Egil told Gerd.

"As I remember it's not exactly pretty…"

"That's because it's an important mining city and it's filled with forges, which work the metal that's taken out of the mines."

As they went along the main street of the city which crossed it from south to north, they could make out a dozen pillars of black smoke rising to the sky. They looked like great live fires in the northern part of town. But, unlike in fires, the pillars of smoke were steady—they neither increased nor diminished, nor changed place. This puzzled Gerd—fires varied and moved, these did not.

"Those aren't fires, are they?"

"No, they're not."

"Then I guess they're the forges," Gerd said, pointing at the smoke.

"Irrefutable, my dear friend."

"I knew you'd say that," Gerd smiled. The comment did not

bother him at all; on the contrary, he found it so "Egil" that it comforted him.

"Those are the big furnaces. They bring the coal and other minerals from the various large mines located north of the city."

As they rode toward the center of town, Gerd stared at the buildings and the people they passed by. The buildings were plain, functional, made of the black rock from the quarries common in Norghana, and were robust but ugly. They could barely make out any stately homes, nor was there a castle or any noble mansions in the city, or if there were, they were as ugly as the rest of the buildings.

"Thousands of people live off mining, practically everyone in this large city and the area around it," Egil explained.

"I'd rather have my farm and my clear skies a thousand times over."

"And I don't blame you. The air is a lot cleaner and the views more beautiful. But, this city produces great amounts of steel, which is necessary for the kingdom and its army."

"Weapons?"

"Weapons, armor, ships, and many other things that need the steel produced in this city."

"I see," Gerd said, nodding toward a group of people who must be returning from the forges. They were covered in soot and filth, the kind that stuck to your body when it got sweaty.

"This is a city where there's a lot of work and you can earn good gold, but this kind of work isn't for everyone," Egil commented in a whisper.

"I'm beginning to notice that."

They went on riding at a leisurely pace toward the center of town.

"Doesn't it smell funny? Or is it me?" Gerd said, wrinkling his nose in disgust.

"It's not you, it does smell funny."

"It's like the smell of something burning, but acrid, nasty..." Gerd shook his head, trying to get rid of the smell. "It's in my nose..."

"It's from the great forges. It's the smell of metal being worked, and it's not very pleasant. Here they melt large amounts of metal, and it's worked to leave it half-ready for the forges to give it shape."

"Breathing this every day can't be good."

"It's not. The people who work for many years in metallurgy get sick with respiratory problems, in particular those at the forges. It affects their lungs. It's from inhaling that toxic smoke."

"I'd rather work outdoors at the farm a thousand times over."

"You can earn a better salary in the city, they pay a lot more," Egil told him.

"It's no good to earn more money if you then get sick and can't enjoy it."

"I won't argue with that," Egil said, smiling.

All of a sudden, they found themselves before a great river that appeared to cut the city in two. A huge white bridge, narrow and somewhat askew, crossed it. It looked more like the work of a madman than a bridge. Or so it seemed to Gerd.

"And this river and strange bridge?" Gerd said in surprise.

"That's the river Bilbo, hence the name of the city."

"It's quite a wide river to be in the center of a city," Gerd commented.

"Indeed, it is. There are four large bridges that span it and join both sides of the city. The southern side is where the people live, and the northern one is where the forges and smithies are located. We could stay in the southern part, but what we're looking for is located in the northern side. So, we'll have to cross the bridge and head to the most contaminated area."

"This city is very unique."

"Yes, and that's why I like it so much," said Egil.

"So far I'm not falling in love with it…"

"Oh, that's because I haven't taken you for lunch yet."

"Is the food good here?"

Egil looked at Gerd as if he could not believe he could be asking him that.

"Good? It's fantastic. This city is known for two things: its forges, and its incomparable cuisine. Here you'll find fabulous dishes."

"You should've told me that before!"

"Would it have changed your perception of the city?"

"Absolutely!"

"Well, you'll soon be able to try the exquisite food they prepare here. It has no equal anywhere."

"You're making my mouth water. You'd better be true to your word after the high expectations you're creating."

"Don't worry, my giant friend. They'll be fulfilled."

They went across the White Bridge, which, as its name implied, was painted completely white. It was a snow-white, which contrasted with the black color of the northern side of the city, both in the sky and in the rooftops and parts of the front walls of the buildings.

"They must paint this bridge often, otherwise it wouldn't be so white," said Gerd as he looked at the snow-white structure in awe.

"They do indeed, that's one of the city's monuments. It was built by the craftsman Kalatra, a man of great renown in the kingdom. Although I must say that many citizens believe that this bridge causes more trouble than joy."

"Trouble?"

"Apparently it's slippery and some of its joints break easily."

"Well, who would think of building a twisted, narrow, and slippery bridge in a city where it snows almost all year round!"

"That's a good question. I guess Duke Landren thinks so, who's a third cousin of King Thoran and rules over the county and this city."

"Does he live in the city?"

"Yes, he does. He lives in that fortress," Egil turned in his saddle and pointed at a stone structure in the military style, with two high towers on the southern side, a little to their right.

"That's not a castle. It looks more like a fortress."

"It is. This city started as a military fort about three hundred years ago and was later made bigger. The city was built around the fort and on both sides of the river."

"You love all those things, history and cities…"

"And culture and traditions, yeah," Egil said, smiling.

Gerd nodded. They rode on, leaving the center of town behind, and headed to the northern area along what appeared to be the main avenue. It was wide and well cobbled. They began to see carts of different sizes crossing with them. They were drawn by oxen or mules, quite big and looking pretty robust, the kind used in the mines and quarries to move large amounts of rock. They were loaded and moving from left to right and vice-versa.

"Wow, this is most curious too," Gerd commented as it made them stop their mounts.

"Isn't it? They transport material, then carry mineral and raw material from the mines to the forges, where it's transformed into metal. Then they transport the metal to the smithies, where it's worked on and given shape."

A different cart passed them by toward the south with several wooden crates.

"And what's that carrying?"

"I'd say war axes, by the size of the crates. That's the finished product manufactured in the workshops. They'll be taken to the markets for sale, or if they're destined to nobles and lords of the kingdom, they'll be taken to finer workshops where weapons masters will give them the final touch. They usually work on the blades and the pommels. The works may vary—in general they're encrusted with precious stones, and the edge is usually engraved with words of special meaning and also the coat of arms of the house in question. In fact, if it's for a nobleman it will pass through several master craftsmen before it's finished. If it's for the army, it will probably go through a blacksmith for the finishing and sharpening, and that will be enough."

"I don't know how you can know so much. I'd never be able to fit so much knowledge in my head, never. In fact, I believe it would explode."

"It's a matter of reading a lot and paying attention when others who know about something explain it. It's not that difficult. And your head wouldn't explode, it's quite large," Egil smiled.

"That's what you say. I don't find it easy at all, and I'm sure it would explode."

Egil patted Gerd's shoulder from the saddle.

"You don't give yourself enough credit. You're worthy, and so is your head. Let's keep going."

The two friends rode on to the north until they arrived at a street filled with workshops of all kinds that had to do with metal work. The hammering came from left and right, and Gerd began to look to both sides blankly.

"Here they work hard on hammer and anvil," he commented, impressed, seeing about twenty workshops, smithies, and forges with three or four craftsmen and their assistants in each one working on the metal without pause.

"This is how the weapons the army and nobles need are made," Egil explained.

"Is this where we're going?"

"No, it's a little more to the east. I just wanted to show you the area. Then when you wield your short axe and knife, you'll know where they came from."

Gerd nodded. He found what he was seeing to be very peculiar—it was really a whole different world. All those smoking forges at the far end, the carts with material for the workshops and forges, all those craftsmen, blacksmiths, and experts in metal—he had never seen anything like it, and he could not begin to imagine this was how the weapons they and other Rangers, as well as the army used, were made.

"Come, we're close now," Egil called.

"Thanks for showing me all this. I didn't even know it existed."

"Isn't Norghana filled with peculiarities and other fantastic things to see?"

"I'll have to agree with you on that," Gerd nodded. He was truly impressed with everything he was witnessing.

Egil went down a street on his right and they followed it, moving away. They took the horses to the stables by the inn.

"Look after them well," Gerd told the two stable boys.

"We always look after the horses well, my lord," the brightest of the two replied. He had tousled blond hair and lively eyes and wore working clothes as dirty as his face and hair.

"I'm sure you do," Gerd said, who was not at all convinced. "These are Rangers' horses, they require extra care," he told them with a slight glare.

"Rangers' horses?" the other boy said blankly. From the looks of him he wasn't all there and was entirely covered with stable filth.

"Yes, our horses," Gerd said, jabbing his thumb at Egil and himself.

"You're Rangers?" the boy asked a moment later, when he managed to make the connection.

"Of course, they are," the bright boy said.

"Here, you have two extra coins. Make sure you look after them well," Egil told them, giving them a coin each with a wink.

"There won't be two better cared-for horses," the bright boy said.

"And when you finish working today, take a bath. You smell worse than horse manure," Gerd said.

"Yes, sir."

Gerd was not convinced they would indeed bathe, but he was sure they would take good care of their animals.

They headed to The Swift Axe Inn and went inside. It was quite crowded, with about a dozen people sitting at the tables enjoying the end of their meal. They could tell who were miners or worked at the forges because they were filthy from head to toe.

The innkeeper came to them at once.

"Welcome to my humble inn. I'm Unau, the innkeeper. I run this establishment."

"This is Gerd and I'm Egil, we need a room."

"Are you Rangers?"

"Well spotted, we are indeed," Egil confirmed.

"I thought so by the way you dress and those bows on your backs. Quite a few of your people come around."

"Do they?" Gerd asked, surprised.

"Yes, they do. The best axes in all Norghana are made here. Your people come to order them or pick them up once they're ready."

"Oh, I see."

"Rangers are always welcome at my inn. We appreciate the great service you do for the kingdom. Everyone knows you watch out for our safety, and we appreciate that. Because of it, I'll give you a room at half the price."

"Well, that's generous on your part," said Egil.

"It's the least I can do. Besides, if there are Rangers at the inn, I won't have any trouble. No one dares to cause trouble when there are Rangers near."

"We have that pacifying effect on people," Gerd said.

"That's right," the innkeeper said. "How long will you be staying?"

"A couple of nights, maybe three," said Egil.

"Very well, I'll prepare a room at once. Wait here and ask for whatever you want to eat and drink, it'll also be half-price for you two," he said and left them.

"I think that, given the situation, I'll ask for double the food," Gerd said, rubbing his hands with glee.

"You're impossible, my huge friend," Egil said, laughing.

They sat at a table with the wall behind them and asked for food and drink. They were brought bread with chorizo cooked in cider. The bread was still warm—it was white with a toasted crust and smelled recently baked.

"It smells so good!" Gerd cried as he put the bread to his nose.

"It will taste even better!" Egil smiled.

It took them the time of a sigh to devour it all. To their surprise they were brought four round pieces of bread, with a piece of veal sirloin with cured cheese on two of the pieces and several shreds of vegetables crowned with a fried quail's egg on the other two. It looked delicious, which was not common in the north, where quantity ruled over quality.

Gerd's eyes were shining, and he could not help himself. They were not very large, so he gulped his two pieces down at once.

Egil looked at him as he took a bite of the fried quail's egg.

"You're supposed to savor it, like this," he told Gerd.

"I do."

"No, you don't, you gulp it down. You don't enjoy the dish."

Gerd shrugged.

"I'm hungry, from the journey, you know."

The innkeeper brought them a beef steak with a side of sweet red peppers, and the moment he set it on the table, between Egil and Gerd, they realized it was enormous, even for Gerd, who had a healthy appetite. It smelled so good that even Egil's stomach grumbled in anticipation. The giant was drooling at the sight of the huge steak.

"This is what I call eating well!" he cried as he cut off a good piece of meat.

"The meat of this area and the way it's prepared is famous. No spices or other condiments, simply good meat, salt, and embers."

"This meat is pure butter in my mouth," Gerd said, ecstatic, as he swallowed a second bite.

"In many parts of Norghana meat is heavily spiced and sauced, which doesn't allow it to be fully appreciated. Here in Bilboson it's the opposite—inns and canteens have a good reputation for their excellent cuisine, and the grilled steak is very well-known and famous."

"We have to come here more often. This is to die for!"

"The yellow fat has a delicious taste, although it's not very healthy," said Egil.

"I'll tell you how it is in a moment," Gerd smiled at him as he cut off a piece of fat and put it in his mouth. He chewed on it and nodded repeatedly.

"D'you like it?"

"Scrumptious. A delicious taste," Gerd replied, smiling broadly.

I guessed as much," Egil said, picking a couple red peppers from the plate.

They went on enjoying the meat until there was only the bone left, which Gerd chewed on like he was a hound.

"Eat well, because we have a lot of work ahead of us in this city."

"Will we find trouble?"

Egil was thoughtful for a moment.

"It's likely, although I'll try and avoid it."

"In that case, let's see what there is for dessert. I think I saw a sheep's cheesecake pass by."

Egil rolled his eyes and chuckled.

"I'll order double for you."

Gerd was enjoying the food so much that he put aside the problems they might encounter and continued enjoying himself. He would face trouble afterward.

Chapter 15

On that cool rainy morning, Lasgol, Camu, and Ona joined Eicewald to continue with their magical training. Camu could not be more excited and was waiting for the next lesson with great expectation.

Much thrilled, he messaged to Eicewald as they sat inside the tent to shelter from the rain.

Ona, on the other hand, seemed less interested, and as usual she lay at the far end of the tent to watch.

"I'm glad you're thrilled, that's always good and cheers the tutor up, especially when he's teaching something that, as a rule, not everyone wants to learn. Teaching is a misunderstood art, easy to criticize, and hard to appreciate in all its difficulty."

"I share Camu's feeling," Lasgol said, "and we want to assure you that we fully appreciate how hard it is to teach us."

Eicewald smiled and nodded.

"I've brought some help today.   "

"A new tome of magic?" Lasgol asked.

"Something better. This is a Learning Crystal," the Mage told them, revealing the crystal he took out of his satchel. Lasgol and Camu stared at it for a moment with great curiosity. It did not look particularly special. It was a dull color, almost gray, and it did not shine or emit any light. It looked like a cheap, fake diamond.

"It doesn't look very special   ..." Lasgol commented.

Is a bit ugly, Camu added.

Eicewald gave a small guffaw.

"Don't be fooled by the look of the object, since looks are often deceiving. The same way that you shouldn't judge a book by its cover. It might be old, worn, and not even very attractive, but what's important is what's inside the book. The wrapping isn't important. It's the same with this crystal of such a humble appearance. I assure you, it possesses many interesting and valuable characteristics."

"Is it enchanted?" Lasgol asked.

"Indeed it is, and in the hands of a mage who knows how to use it, it can even conjure when required."

"Wow, I'm beginning to see why it's interesting," Lasgol smiled.

Eicewald held the crystal up so they could see it well.

"This crystal is used for Magical Teaching, and it has unique properties for that goal."

"Is it natural or manufactured?" Lasgol wanted to know as he stared at the crystal with his head to one side.

"Natural. It's found in a few mines in Tremia. One of them is here in Norghana, so we always have more than enough. In fact, we usually trade them with magi of other kingdoms who require them."

"You sell the crystals to other magi?" Lasgol was surprised.

"Rather than sell it, we exchange it for other components of value for us. The Ice Magi also need objects and materials we can't find here in Norghana."

"I had no idea the Ice Magi traded with other magi."

"Trade between magi has always been existing. It's not common knowledge among the people because it's usually done in secret. Also, because the Gift-less, or Talent-less, as Non-Magi are known in the magical community, aren't usually interested in these matters. And even if they accidentally come across some information about them, they dismiss it because it is of no interest to them."

"As Egil would say: fascinating. I'll have to tell him everything, I'm sure he'll   find it most interesting."

"I'm sure he'll find it fascinating," Eicewald smiled. "There are also intermediaries who specialize in obtaining special components, magical materials, plants—objects we Magi use. We call them Arcane Brokers."

"That will surely fascinate Egil. He uses many agents and traders to get information, I'm sure he would find magical matters useful too. *We* would find them useful," Lasgol added on second thought. They would surely need magical help.

"They facilitate that which is hard to find in the magical world. But I must warn you that in general they are not trustworthy and can even be dangerous."

"Dangerous? That doesn't sound good…" Lasgol wrinkled his nose.

"They are, since the goods they trade in are also dangerous and are in many cases very valuable."

"I think I know what you mean."

"They are dark characters of doubtful reputation, and you'd

better be careful when dealing with them. As a rule, it's better to contact magi directly. Although they might also play you, it's less likely because they have appearances to maintain."

"Understood. Dangerous characters to go to when you need something specific   you can't get through the magi."

"Exactly."

I not fear.

"I know, Camu, because you have a brave heart, but you shouldn't trust them," Eicewald told him.

Okay. Not trust.

"Very well. Now, I'll use the crystal to explain an important lesson regarding the world of magic you must know and always remember, since it might mean the difference between life and death in a confrontation with another magical being or person."

Instantly he had all of Camu's and Lasgol's attention. Ona yawned. She did not find any of this interesting.

"Go ahead," Lasgol said, and his voice shook a little with expectation.

"When it comes to studying a mage's level of magic and degree of power, there have always been different measuring scales to try and establish it, ever since the beginning of time. One of the main questions always on the mind of anyone with the Gift has been and continues to be knowing their own magical level, and especially that of their adversaries."

Adversaries?

"Enemies, rivals," Lasgol explained.

Oh. I understand.

"It's crucial to understand the degree of power you have in order to face obstacles in the path toward a goal, and to confront other magi and magical beings. Not understanding the power of each and of the enemy leads to death almost inexorably."

"I see. I wasn't aware there were degrees or levels among the magi…" Lasgol said blankly.

"It's not something Non-Magi know. It's kept secret, but I assure you they exist. Not only because they allow you to measure your strength against an enemy, but because even among allied magi, there is a hierarchy. For instance, not all Ice Magi have the same degree. When it comes to establishing who first mage is or who's at the lower levels, every mage is assessed and given a degree and level."

Like this. Want to know more.

"I'm glad you find it to your liking, Camu," Eicewald told him.

"How are the degrees and levels determined?" Lasgol asked, also intrigued.

"Initially, every group or brotherhood of magi, like the Ice Magi, had their own scale and manner of measuring. But people soon realized it would be necessary to create a wider and more accepted way of measuring all magi in general and not each specialization or family. Especially because each system was highly influenced by the type of magic used. Comparing an ice mage with a fire mage by using the criteria of the first group was totally inefficient and did not provide the correct level to the second group."

"I see, it would be like comparing my magic or Camu's with that of an Ice Mage using your own criteria, right?" Lasgol said.

"Exactly, my smart friend. A long time ago, a group of scholars and erudites of magic gathered to deal with this matter in Rilentor, the capital of the Kingdom of Rogdon. This gathering recognized the need to create only one measuring system that would serve for all those blessed with the Gift, whatever school of magic they belonged to or even if they belonged to none, as is your case," Eicewald said.

"Very interesting. Go on, please."

"In time, scholars managed to develop what is known in the Magical World as the Limer Method, which takes its name from the great magic erudite Raput Limer, one of its creators. This method allows us to measure the degree and level of the people with the Gift and place them within a scale created for this purpose."

"What's that scale like? What are the levels?" Lasgol's interest was growing, and the questions tumbled out of his mouth.

"The scale establishes a series of degrees and hierarchical levels. There are ten levels, and they establish the general power of a mage. Each grade is made up of ten other levels. In order to reach a higher level, you have to complete the ten levels of the grade you start with. It's like climbing a ladder."

I many grades and levels, Camu messaged proudly.

"That has to be measured for us in order to know," Eicewald said winking at Camu. The creature lifted his head, convinced he had many grades and levels.

"Then… if I understand correctly, there's a total of a hundred levels and every ten means a grade …" Lasgol muttered.

"That's correct, you understand perfectly,"

"In order to pass to the next level, you have to go up those ten levels as if it were a ladder of power.   "

"In a manner of speaking, yes," Eicewald nodded.

"Have you brought a tome where each grade's specifications are explained so we can study them?"

"Indeed," Eicewald said as he took a tome out of his satchel and put it gently on the floor. It was thick and quite large. The title left no doubt of what was inside it: *Simplified Limer Method*, by the great Erudite and Mage Raput Limer.

Very fat, much learn, Camu protested at the sight of the thick volume.

"And this is the simplified version, abbreviated," Eicewald said, chuckling.

"It's going to take us an eternity to learn all that..." Lasgol commented, also daunted by the tome's thickness   .

"Don't worry. That's why I've brought the Learning Crystal. It'll help you with this, although I recommend that you take your time to read the tome because it contains magical knowledge and concept explanations that will be very useful. Let me show you what the crystal can do."

Lasgol nodded repeatedly.

Eicewald placed the crystal on the open tome and, holding it with both hands, he began to conjure with his eyes shut, concentrated, intoning long sentences in an arcane language. A moment later he stopped uttering words and the crystal shone with a soft light. It rose from the Mage's hands and remained suspended in the air three hand spans above the open tome.

"Wow..." Lasgol could not help himself.

"Look at the crystal," the Mage told them.

The Learning Crystal started flipping the pages of the tome at great speed until it got to the first page. Lasgol had no clue what it was doing, but he had no doubt it was the crystal turning the pages, since Eicewald was sitting with his hands on his thighs seemingly not intervening.

All of a sudden, the crystal flashed white and, where the crystal was, above the book, there appeared an image. It was that of a boy, about ten years old, wearing a ragged tunic and looking shy, even cowered. On his torso there appeared some letters in gold and silver.

"Grade One: Neophyte Seidr," Eicewald read.

Lasgol understood what the boy signified—he represented the lowest grade. The crystal flashed white and the pages flipped by. At the same time the boy changed slightly, as if he were growing little older. As he did so, new letters appeared on his torso.

"Level two, level three, four..." Eicewald continued reading as the boy grew up. When he reached the tenth level the growing stopped and they saw a boy who was no longer a boy. He must be about fifteen, and he still looked a bit scared, although less so. He was wearing a slightly better tunic, albeit simple. The letters appeared on his torso.

"Grade Two: Apprentice Seidr," Eicewald read.

Lasgol realized that as he saw the image and the boy's change he also understood, without knowing exactly how, what each level represented and an idea of the effort and knowledge required to rise not only to the next level, but also to reach the higher grade. It was as he were partially living them, as if the crystal made him feel a part of what was required to pass every level and every grade.

"Impressive..." he muttered under his breath.

Much impressive, Camu messaged in agreement as he also felt what the crystal was sharing.

The crystal flashed white and the boy began to climb new levels. As he did, he continued to grow up, becoming a little older. The boy now looked like a twenty-year-old man with a somewhat more determined look on his face. There was no fear in his eyes, but there was not much confidence either. His tunic was of a better quality.

"Grade Three: Novice Seidr"

The crystal shone again and the young man evolved as he kept climbing levels. He was maturing, and when he stopped at level forty he looked about twenty-five. His expression was determined, confident of his power. He wore a simple robe and now carried a plain staff in his right hand.

"Grade Four: Mage Seidr"

Lasgol felt that at this Grade the mage they were seeing was one with power and confidence. He was thirty-five and his robe and staff were a little more elaborate, his gaze was one of confidence and knowledge.

The crystal showed them the next levels as Eicewald recited them.

At Grade Five, Adept Seidr, showed them a forty-year-old mage, more powerful and confident of his magic to confront enemies. He carried a fine staff, carved with runes and a more elaborate robe.

At Grade Six, Grand Mage Seidr, showed a fifty-year-old mage very sure of his power, serene, capable of defeating his enemies. The staff and robe were now accompanied by a magical necklace of power hanging around his neck. His hair was beginning to show some white.

At Grade Seven, Master Seidr, showed them a sixty-year-old mage with long white hair that fell down his shoulders, powerful and sure of himself. He was seeking arcane knowledge to keep growing.

At Grade Eight, Grand Master Seidr, the seventy-year-old mage looked like a scholar, someone with great knowledge and immensely powerful. His calm gaze made it obvious he was not looking for any conflict or to defeat enemies. The crystal went on showing the advancements.

At Grade Nine, Archmage Seidr, the mage must have been around eighty, thin with a wrinkled face, long white hair down to the middle of his back. He had the look of an Erudite and radiated power and knowledge. He was extremely capable. Yet he did not seek to eliminate rivals but to reach his full magical potential.

Finally, the crystal showed them the last grade—Ten.

"Grade Ten. Sage Seidr," Eicewald called out.

They saw an old man of about ninety, his face creased with wrinkles, his body worn with age, with long snow-white hair, but who radiated such power and knowledge that it was blinding. It was as if his aura of power were on the outside and visible. Lasgol and Camu had to close their eyes and blink hard in order to look at him. The magical power and knowledge of that old man were such that he could destroy all Norghana if he so wished. Lasgol and Camu had that impression because the crystal projected those feelings, and they were both afraid. But, this powerful mage was not looking for the destruction or annihilation of rivals or whole kingdoms—he was looking to gather even more knowledge and power to keep climbing.

"If the scale has a hundred levels and he's already got them all, why does he still want to go on?" Lasgol asked.

"Because at that level you only want to keep climbing. The mundane matters not. You look inward, not outward, and you seek to reach a grade that doesn't even exist on the scale. You seek to transcend the mundane."

"Become some kind of god?"

"Something like that, only that if you start as a human being, you never get to reach the divine."

I transcend one day, Camu messaged.

"Better not. You're already enough of a nuisance in the world as it is. I wouldn't want you to ascend to divinity," Lasgol replied, shaking his head.

Eicewald put a spell on the crystal and it stopped showing the image of the mage.

"That's the scale of power. I trust you have taken notice of it."

I notice everything.

"Oh yes, I felt it in myself, almost as if it were me climbing levels."

"That's why the Learning Crystal is so valuable," Eicewald told them. "Experiencing it is a lot more profound than seeing it or reading about it."

Me like experimenting.

"Let me say that this Limer scale I've shown you is used mainly by the magi of North, West, and Central Tremia. In the East and especially in the South they use other scales, different, although their function is about the same. That of the East has less grades and levels, and that of the South has approximately twice as many grades and levels."

"Understood," said Lasgol.

"Very well. Now, so that the lesson stays in your minds, we'll repeat the experience of the Limer scale."

"Oh, great!" Lasgol said. "How many times will we feel it?"

"Until it's well engrained," Eicewald replied with a smile.

Good. I like, Camu messaged excitedly.

They invested the rest of that day in learning the scale and what each grade and level represented, a ladder they would have to climb in order to become the great magi they wanted to be one day.

Chapter 16

Days later, as they continued learning about magic, Lasgol and Camu were full of questions, which Eicewald did his best to answer.

"Can all magi reach the highest grade?" Lasgol asked, more like thinking out loud.

I can, Camu said confidently.

"Theoretically, it should be possible," said Eicewald. "What varies is the level of effort and perseverance required."

"Then I'm not sure everyone can reach the highest grade," Lasgol said, thinking of himself and his own possibilities.

"It's natural to doubt your own possibilities," Eicewald told him. "There are several schools of thought regarding that. Some believe we can all reach the highest level, and others don't. Some believe only certain people with certain exceptional qualities can reach the highest grade."

"And what school of thought do you belong to, Eicewald?"

"I belong to the optimistic school. I've always believed that human potential is infinite and that therefore we can all reach the highest grade."

And Drakonian potential, Camu messaged, nodding.

"Indeed. I believe that magical creatures' potential is also infinite," Eicewald said.

"But not all of them reach the higher levels, do they?" Lasgol asked.

"No, they don't, since a person's potential or that of any other being," Eicewald replied, looking at Camu, "must be worked on. The most gifted magi with the highest potential will reach nothing if he or she doesn't work on that potential."

I work all, Camu messaged eagerly.

Eicewald put his hand on Camu's chest and stroked him.

"I know. I have no doubt you'll put all your effort into the task."

I much effort.

"I'm sure you'll go far," the Mage smiled at him.

"Then if we believe we all have the same potential, if we work without pause, we should all reach the same level. Is that it?" Lasgol reasoned.

"Yes and no. We all have the potential, and we all have to work hard to reach the higher levels. But those with the most potential, the most gifted, will rise a lot faster. The less gifted will need to make more of an effort to reach the same goal."

"I think I understand it now," Lasgol said.

"It's not that different from being a great craftsman. We can all be one, but those more gifted will become one much sooner and some, being naturals, will do so almost without effort."

I natural, Camu messaged firmly.

"Our young friend is full of confidence."

"Rather he's very stubborn and too optimistic for his own good."

"Being confident is always a good thing."

"Being too confident and failing because of it is not so good," Lasgol replied, staring at Camu, who ignored him as if the comment had nothing to do with him.

Eicewald nodded.

"Let's be confident and hope it leads us to higher planes."

"It will lead us there, I'm sure," Lasgol said. "Speaking of grades, and if it's not an indiscretion, Eicewald, what grade have you reached?"

Eicewald looked at Lasgol and Camu.

"It's no indiscretion coming from you," he smiled. "My present grade is eighth, the grade of Grand Master Seidr."

"Grade Eight? I thought you'd be at least ninth!" Lasgol said.

Me too. Eicewald powerful.

"Thank you both. I'm honored you two hold me in such great esteem, but no, and I still have a long way to go before I reach the last two grades. In fact, it was only recently that I reached Grade Eight, after much effort and many years of experience."

"That means it's going to be much harder than we imagined to reach those levels. It's going to take a long time," said Lasgol.

"It is. You must always keep that in mind. It takes a lot of work and great dedication, which is not always compatible with following other goals…"

Lasgol knew what Eicewald meant, since they had already talked about this. Being a Ranger was going to interfere with his progress in Magic. He would have to find a way to do both. It was going to delay him, he knew that, but he did not want to stop being a Ranger in order to be a Mage. Perhaps someday, but not now. His future was being a Ranger and staying with his friends.

"What level do you think we're at now?" Lasgol asked, pointing at himself and Camu.

The Mage looked at them for a moment and rubbed his chin.

"I could guess, but I'd rather know for sure."

"Is there a way to know?" Lasgol said.

"Yes, there is a way to establish the magical level, more than one in fact," Eicewald replied.

"Let's do it then! That way we'll know for sure and have no doubts."

I want know.

Ona growled twice—she was not interested.

"Very well," Eicewald nodded, and he bent over to search inside his mage's satchel which he usually carried on him. He took out the Learning Crystal.

"This will help us do the test which will tell us the level you're in," he explained.

"Go ahead. I'm half nervous and half intrigued," Lasgol admitted.

I very sure, Camu messaged.

"Yeah, when are you not..." Lasgol said, shaking his head.

"I'm sure everything'll go fine, don't worry," the Mage told them. He placed the Learning Crystal on the tip of his staff where the Jewel of Power was. He shut his eyes and cast a spell, holding the staff with one hand and the crystal with the other. He uttered several sentences of power and suddenly the measuring jewel lit up a deep white. They averted their eyes from the light, which formed a large ring around the staff. The ring remained suspended halfway up the staff.

Eicewald opened his eyes and addressed Lasgol.

"Place your hands on the staff. Don't worry, nothing will happen to you."

Lasgol did as he was told and placed his hand on the staff. All of a sudden, the ring leapt from the staff to Lasgol and remained suspended around his waist.

Very fantastic! Camu messaged excitedly.

Lasgol stared at the ring around his waist nervously. He had no idea what might happen or why the ring of light had surrounded him. He looked at Eicewald, who gave him a reassuring nod. Lasgol took a deep breath and relaxed.

"Now, in order to establish your level, you have to call upon two skills: one of those that activates most easily and one that's harder to summon. This way the crystal will determine your present level. It has to calibrate between a maximum and a minimum."

"I see. All right. Let me think for a moment." Lasgol pondered about which two skills to call upon. He had no doubt about the first one, but he had to think harder about the second one. Once he had decided, he nodded to the Mage.

"Good. Go ahead," Eicewald said. "You may begin."

Lasgol concentrated and sought his inner pool of magic. He found it in his chest and called on his *Animal Communication* skill. He sent a message to Camu.

Sending measuring test.

Camu messaged back, *Very wonderful.*

The skill of communicating with animals was by now so natural that he did not have to think about it in order to summon it. Just by wanting to send the message he was able to activate the skill. It was undoubtedly the easiest one and the one he used more often.

The light ring caught the skill and gave off a whitish gleam. It seemed to have managed to measure the skill. Lasgol concentrated and started to call upon his second skill: *True Shot.* He was not sure whether this was the one he found hardest to call of all, but it was certainly one of them. He picked his bow and nocked an arrow. He knew it would take him a moment, since it always did, and so he did not get nervous and went on calling upon it. After what seemed to him like an eternal moment the skill activated and there was a green flash. He released outwards and hit the rock he had been aiming at. The ring gave off a whitish gleam.

"Very good. Let's see now what the Crystal's verdict is," said Eicewald.

They waited for a moment and suddenly the ring started to move. It climbed to Lasgol's head and stopped.

"What's happening?" he asked the Mage.

"Don't worry, and don't move."

The ring began to move down to Lasgol's feet and then rose again very fast to his head and stopped. Then it stared flashing intensely.

Eicewald showed Lasgol his index finger. The ring he wore repeated the powerful flash, and Eicewald showed Lasgol two fingers.

Lasgol understood, the Mage was counting.

Two, Camu messaged, also realizing what it meant.

The ring shone fifty times in a row, while Lasgol and Eicewald counted each flash. At last, the ring stopped at fifty-three flashes.

Lasgol's eyes opened wide.

Eicewald smiled and patted him on the shoulder.

"You are level fifty-three, therefore, Grade Adept Seidr."

Lasgol stared at him in surprise.

"I thought it would be much less."

"I think you've improved a lot in the last couple of years," Eicewald told him.

"Well, that makes me very happy to be honest," Lasgol said, nodding repeatedly.

"Remember, you have to keep working on developing your power. Keep up the good work and you'll soon reach Grade Six."

"Am I too far back regarding where I ought to be by now?" Lasgol asked, concerned that his development might be behind.

"Not at all. Considering that you've had no formal magical training, that magic is not your main occupation, and that you have very little time to work on it, I find it amazing that you've reached this level at your age."

"You really believe that? I bet yours was much higher at my age."

"Not really, I was at level sixty at your age. So, you're not at all behind. In any case, remember, it doesn't mean you can't achieve much more if you want to."

"I can promise I'll try."

"I encourage you to do so. The fact that, given your circumstances, you've advanced so much and have such a good level is very promising."

"Thank you, that makes me feel a lot better."

"Let's see how Camu does," said Eicewald.

I lot of level, the creature said confidently.

"We'll see now," the Mage smiled.

They repeated the process with Camu, who chose Mental Communication as his first skill. It was the easiest one for him to call upon, as in Lasgol's case. Then as the most complicated one he chose Extended Invisibility Camouflage since he could not manage to extend it as far as he wanted and it was also hard for him to summon.

Once the second skill had been used—he made Eicewald and Lasgol invisible—they proceeded to measure his level.

The ring of power that surrounded Camu began to run up and down Camu's body from head to tail. It became spotted or narrower as it went along his body until it stopped around his head. At that moment it started flashing to indicate the magic level of the creature. Lasgol was watching, fascinated. He was sure the result would be even better than his own because Camu had more power than him.

The ring started to flash and they counted the flashes. To Lasgol's great surprise, there were only thirty-three. The ring stopped shining and faded away.

Very little! Camu messaged at once.

"It has placed him in Grade Three and one third. It seems too little, doesn't it?" Lasgol said, surprised and a little disappointed with the result.

Ring measure wrong. I powerful! Camu messaged, annoyed.

Eicewald tilted his head, eying Camu thoughtfully.

"It's odd that it's only indicated that level considering the magic Camu is capable of doing."

I more than dragon, Camu messaged stubbornly.

"Maybe the measuring was incorrect. This isn't normal—it's very well calibrated, I checked it myself. We use it in the Tower of the Ice Magi all the time and it's never given us any problem."

"I'd repeat the test just in case. Since Camu isn't a normal creature maybe the crystal didn't know how to measure his level."

Eicewald was thoughtful once again for a moment and examined the crystal carefully.

"I'm going to check that it's well calibrated."

He passed his hands over the crystal and cast a spell with his eyes shut.

Lasgol and Camu watched as the Mage worked. Once he finished his analysis, he turned back toward them.

"It appears to be perfect, but I think it's a good idea to repeat the test."

Camu and Lasgol nodded.

Eicewald repeated the test and the ring examined Camu, the same as it had before.

Once it finished, the ring started giving off flashes. Once again it stopped at thirty-three.

"Wow…" Lasgol said sadly.

Crystal broken! Camu messaged, indignant, moving his head from side to side, annoyed.

Eicewald narrowed his eyes, his gaze in the distance. He seemed to be looking for an explanation for such an unusual fact.

"I think I understand what's going on," he said after a while.

Crystal not work.

"No, the crystal works fine," Eicewald assured them.

"Then what's the matter?" Lasgol asked.

"What I believe is happening is that the crystal is measuring Camu's level, and is doing it correctly. The thing is, it's measuring him against his final potential, which is a lot greater than yours or mine," the Mage explained.

"Oh… I see…" Lasgol said.

I not understand, Camu messaged.

"The crystal, as a rule, measures human levels against a maximum potential which is usually similar."

Not understand still.

"In your case, Camu, your maximum potential is much greater than a human's and that's why the level it accorded to you is lower, since your highest level is a lot greater than mine or Lasgol's."

"It scaled it down so it's balanced," Lasgol nodded, understanding.

Then I more powerful than Eicewald and Lasgol?

"The crystal senses you will be, that your potential is greater. But, for all your potential, right now you've only reached Grade Three."

I more than Grade Three.

"I'm afraid not, taking into account your maximum potential," the Mage explained.

Since Camu did not seem to understand or want to assimilate this, Lasgol explained it in a way he would.

"You are so powerful that today you're only at Grade Three. Imagine what you'll be able to do when you reach Grades Eight or Nine."

Camu liked that idea.

I very powerful. Reach Grade Eight or Nine and all see I do amazing things.

Lasgol and Eicewald beamed.

"That's right, Camu," Lasgol said.

"It's going to be pretty amazing," Eicewald promised, chuckling.

Camu smiled and started doing his happy dance joyfully.

I very amazing. All see one day.

Lasgol slapped his forehead.

"We also have to consider that Camu is only a pup and he still has a lot of development ahead of him, both physical and mental, as well as magical," the Mage told Lasgol.

"I understand: in order to advance in magical grades, he'll have to grow up."

"That's what I believe too. He doesn't grow at the same pace we do, he does so much more slowly."

"Therefore, his magical development, in spite of his great potential, will take many years."

"It's most likely, but we can't tell since we don't know how a creature like Camu progresses."

I fast, you see, Camu messaged, dancing happily.

"Not sure it'll work like that," Lasgol tried to curb his enthusiasm.

I know. I powerful fast.

Eicewald and Lasgol looked at one another. The Mage shook his head and Lasgol understood. Camu was a creature that might grow to be a thousand years old, so he was still a baby. His power would grow with the passing years, but Lasgol would not see his full potential since he would be long dead, him and all the others. That is if Camu was indeed a creature who could live to a thousand years old, which Egil believed. They would have to wait and see what happened with Camu's growth, as well as his magical power.

Chapter 17

Egil and Gerd spent several days investigating the northern side of the city of Bilboson. They combed the entire area, building by building, shop by shop, searching for some suspicious trace that would allow them to access their prey, like the good Rangers they were. Unfortunately, they had not found what they were looking for, and they were beginning to get frustrated not getting any results as the days passed. No matter how thoroughly they searched, they found nothing to give them a clue to hold on to or go on.

One positive thing about spending more time than they had expected in the great city was that Gerd was enjoying himself immensely with Bilboson's fantastic food. He had already tried a dozen different places where the giant had tasted each and every dish he had been served. Every day they lunched and dined in a different place per Gerd's request, with the excuse of checking all the places the leaders of the Defenders or the Visionaries might eat or sleep in, so he had left no eatery unchecked. Egil had already told Gerd that if their search in the city took much longer, he was going to end up with a considerable belly.

They had also found out something that had caught Egil's attention in a positive way. It had nothing to do with his search, but it had fascinated him. All along the river Bilbo, on both sides, they were building avenues, parks with trees and beautiful fountains, decorating with greenery an otherwise neglected gray area. A long time ago, both sides of the river had been the ugliest areas of the city because the loads of mineral arrived by the river, and since they were unloaded at different points along the river, these had become the unloading docks.

They had even built a large library that held books and paintings of well-known artists, both from Norghana and other kingdoms. With the excuse of obtaining information about the Dragon Orb, Egil had visited it on several occasions and had come out without any new clues but thrilled all the same. Egil was fascinated by buildings like this one, filled with literature, art, and knowledge—he found them fantastic and could not understand why his friends did not see how amazing they were. By the third visit Gerd stayed outside, watching the river and the cargo ships that headed to unload further upriver.

It appeared that Duke Landren was trying to beautify the city, so gray and dirty from its main artery: the great river that crossed it from side to side. Perhaps there might be worthy nobles of the East after all, with a vision for something other than conquest and bloodshed. Still, Egil did not take comfort in the idea since, after all, Duke Landren was a direct rival for the Crown, being a third cousin of Thoran's. Besides, he was one of the King's main financial sources, since the city produced and traded in metal and weapons both inside and outside Norghana, and much of the benefit ended up in King Thoran's chests.

Gerd did appreciate the attempt to improve the city, which was covered in black soot from the many large forges, which spoiled all the buildings and the little green existing between the countless houses. He did not share Egil's enthusiasm for the large library as much and the art housed inside it, but he had to admit the new building was beautiful; in fact, he found it very modern for the kind of buildings that were erected in Norghana, which were all rocky and dull.

He had to admit to his friend that the whole area along both sides of the river looked beautiful with the parks, fountains, avenues, and trees. Egil commented that what had always been an industrial city was beginning to have a green heart, and that would make it into an even more beautiful city in the long run, if they kept developing green areas in the center and making them bigger.

Gerd found that harder to imagine, since the rest of the city was still quite ugly, especially the north side where the smoke pillars from the forges were still burning all day, contaminating the sky above the city. Forging produced a lot of contamination, more so if done in such a large amount as here. They would have to plant a lot of green if they wanted to counter the effect.

Since they were not getting results, they had abandoned the day search. Nothing of interest seemed to happen during the daylight hours, so they had concentrated on going out to investigate at night. Egil said that if you did the same thing without variation, you got the same results. So, they changed their focus in search of a better outcome. Night was riskier but also the time when most illegal activities took place. The night crowds of the city were picturesque and diverse, and they had already encountered thieves, smugglers, troublemakers, and other endless amounts of characters of ill repute that any city had.

What they had not been able to find was anything to do with Dergha-Sho-Blaska, the Dragon Orb that contained him, the Defenders of the True Blood, or the Visionaries. Egil was confident they would find something relevant in Bilboson, but Gerd was beginning to feel that perhaps he was wrong. Not all of Egil's plans were successful—some failed, and this might be one of those.

"Let's follow this street to its end," Egil whispered to Gerd.

Gerd looked up at the sky. It was overcast, so the night was black. It was not very cold: the storms had left and were giving them a respite with not-so-icy autumnal weather.

"Are you sure we'll find something? We've been in this city for days and we haven't found out anything of value."

Egil stopped and sheltered in the shadow of a doorway so as not to be seen in the night.

"The information the guild gave me is solid, we'll find something here."

Gerd got closer to Egil and they vanished in the doorway.

"You trust this guild a lot, what if they've given you false information?"

"Maybe. I'm not ruling that out, but I really don't think that's the case. They know who I am, and I don't mean only a Ranger. They know who my family is—they haven't given me false information."

"So, what information did they give you?"

Egil looked right and left but the street was deserted. The neighbors on both sides were sleeping peacefully, resting to face a new day when dawn came.

"I asked them to tell me where Viggen Norling had been seen together with his Defenders of the True Blood."

"And they've been seen here?"

"That's correct, in the north area of the city, the week before we arrived. That's the information they gave me."

Gerd scratched his chin.

"Well, it's not very accurate information—it doesn't tell you the exact place or whether they're still here."

"True. The information the guilds or agents gather is rarely exactly what one would desire. Life isn't so easy. The answers don't just fly into our hands."

"Yeah, I imagine."

"But this information is substantial. It tells us they were here, and if we find out the reason, we might be getting closer to our goal."

"The immortal dragon king..."

"That's right, we have to stop him. He can't be reincarnated. This is our main goal. We have to stop it any way we can."

"And what if he has already?"

"I have the feeling that's not going to be easy for him to achieve. From what I've read about this and other similar subjects, the process to reincarnate a spirit is complex and requires time to obtain everything necessary. Of course, what I've read doesn't speak of dragons specifically, and there's very little information that might be verifiable, if any. So, I can't make up a theory at this moment. In fact, the information I have might still be all false, merely derived from a colossal imagination."

"But if it's true, you think it won't be easy and that it'll take them time to achieve it, don't you?"

"Yeah, that's what I believe, although as I told you, all this is pure speculation since I have no true data to base my thoughts on."

"Well, that's enough for me. Let's keep searching and find the clue that'll take us to the dragon orb before the reincarnation."

"That's the spirit." Egil patted Gerd's shoulder and went down the street. The giant followed him at once.

They went along a street to the west and then down another to the east, always going north until they arrived at an area they still had not investigated during the night. It was not an area of taverns or shops but one of forges and workshops, so there was not much nocturnal movement. The night crowds gathered more to the south, in the areas of trading, eating, and drinking. They came to a square with a fountain and a large trough for the working mules. It was deserted at that time of night.

They stood on both corners of the square: Egil at the east and Gerd at the west. They crouched and hid: Gerd behind a loading cart that rested empty in front of a workshop, and Egil behind some large crates to transport material. The square was deserted. Two of the buildings, north and south, housed metal workshops and would not start work until dawn. Working on metal at night, with little light, was dangerous, and as a rule it was only done when there was an important order for some noble of the court.

Gerd stood in a position where he could see the square well and also two streets that led to it. He knew it was going to be a long night, since the previous nights they had also come out to investigate and had found nothing. Not having precise information about Viggen and his Defenders, they were forced to try and find them wherever they were hiding.

The night went by quietly. Gerd raised his head to see whether he could make out Egil, but his partner was well hidden and he could not see him. He changed his posture. His leg was going numb, and there was nothing worse than a numb leg when the alarm was called. You could get to your feet and in haste fall on your face. The leg was not going to respond because of the urgency. Besides, in his condition, the last thing he needed was a useless limb. He had enough trouble keeping his balance to add more to it.

A person appeared along one of the streets he was watching. There was little light and he could not see his face. The only thing he could make out was that he was dressed in forge working clothes, nothing out of the ordinary. He followed him with his eyes as the metal worker crossed the street and headed to a building at the end of the square. Most likely he was heading to start the fires for the morning-shift workers or to repair some boiler or tool that needed it.

Gerd did not think twice about him and relaxed. A furnace worker always crossed the city at night to arrive early at the forges or workshops, it was not out of the ordinary. He took up his position again to continue watching without leaning his weight on the numb leg. He got as comfortable as he could, huddling in his cloak, and kept watching. He remembered what Egil had told him about surveillance: *most are fruitless, but only one successful time would make all the effort worth it*. He cheered up thinking this—sooner or later they would find something.

Quite a while went by, and another figure appeared, crossing the street. Gerd strained his neck to see who it was. He watched him with narrowed eyes. It was another forge worker heading to his shift in his dirty clothes and with a long face. Gerd shrugged. It seemed they were not going to discover anything tonight either. He stretched his back as much as he could until there was a tiny *crack* and he felt somewhat better.

The night went by slowly and nothing of interest happened. A third figure appeared in the square coming from a street in the east that Egil was watching. Gerd could not see him well because it was too dark. He passed close to where his friend was hiding so if there was anything to worry about Egil would alert him. He stood watching Egil's position. He did not really think anything was going to happen, but a good Ranger was always on the alert, just in case.

All of a sudden, he heard a barn owl, only the way it hooted made it clear it was not a real one but Egil's warning. Something was up. Gerd crouched down and watched from behind the side of the cart where he was hiding. He made out Egil's arm, that signaled to him to get over to his position. Gerd crossed the square as fast as he could, half crouched so as not to be seen, as far as that was possible, to where Egil was hiding.

"What's up?" he asked Egil in a whisper when he reached him.

"That man looked suspicious to me," Egil replied, pointing at the figure who was walking away north along a lesser street.

Gerd narrowed his eyes and watched him walk away. He could not see his face, but from the back he could make out his forge working clothes.

"Him? He looks to me like a metal worker. Two more have already walked by."

"Yes, but I caught a singular detail on this one."

"What was that?" Gerd was looking at the figure as it walked away, not noticing anything odd or remarkable.

"His boots."

"Weren't they iron-toed metal worker's boots?"

"Irrefutable, my dear big guy."

Gerd smiled. "You couldn't help yourself, could you?"

"It's a word I like to say," Egil smiled and shrugged.

"Do we follow him?"

"Yes, there's enough distance by now. We can't let him see us."

"All right. Do you think he's one of the Defenders of the Blood?"

Egil made a face—he was not really sure.

"He might be a thief, or perhaps a scrap collector in search of debris. In any case, we'd better investigate, because he's an anomaly."

"Well then, let's get moving." Gerd began to follow the figure, hiding in the darkness provided by a high wall on the left of the street down which the man was going. Egil followed Gerd, hiding behind his friend's large body. Neither of them was as good as Astrid or Viggo at hiding in the shadows, but they managed. The fact that in that area there were no lamps or fires lighting the streets helped them. The working areas and the streets in between workshops and forges were pretty neglected and did not need night lights.

They followed the figure to the end of the street. When they got there, they found a large empty lot, and in the middle, the unmistakable buildings of a great forge and two metal-working workshops, also quite large. There was still black smoke, although very little, coming out of a tall chimney. The huge furnaces were out. The three buildings were rectangular and built of strong rock. Looking at the tall chimneys and at how black the walls and the roofs of the buildings were left no doubt about the kind of work that was done there.

The figure went into the forge by a side door. Gerd and Egil, who were watching at a crouch against the wall at the end of the street, exchanged looks.

"We have to find out what's going on in there," Egil told Gerd.

"It's a forge, I think you've made a mistake and he's no more than a worker coming to his shift. He might have to start the furnaces or something."

"Maybe, but I'll rest easier if we make sure."

"Whatever you say, but just to let you know, these nocturnal expeditions whet my appetite."

"Your appetite never rests," Egil chuckled.

"That's true," Gerd replied with a grin.

They went over carefully and in silence to the entrance the worker had gone in. They stood on both sides of the door with their backs to the wall and listened for any suspicious noise. An off-rhythm sound was coming from inside the forge.

"Offbeat hammering?" Gerd whispered.

"I'd say there are several hammers beating at different rhythms," Egil said after listening to the noise for a while.

Gerd nodded.

"Are we going in?"

"Very carefully," Egil warned him as he rearranged his bow and quiver on his shoulder so he could reach them quickly if needed.

Gerd did the same and reached for his knife and short axe,

making sure they were in their place.

Egil checked inside through the keyhole.

"There's light at the far end, at a lower level," he told Gerd. "I don't see any watchmen."

"Let's go inside," said Gerd.

Egil tried the door, expecting to find it locked, but it was open.

"That's odd..." Gerd muttered as they went inside.

"They're either not expecting anyone, or else they're not doing anything illicit," Egil reasoned.

They slowly entered the building and found that they were indeed in a large forge. From what they could see in the gloom, there were large amounts of material piled on one side, forming a mountain which they soon realized was mineral coal. Gerd touched it to make sure.

Before the mountain of coal, they saw sacks of other compounds and several piles of mineral with traces of metal in them. They went over to check, since there was only light at the far end and visibility was minimal. Indeed, mineral had been brought from the iron and copper mines and had been stored in several piles that looked like small mountains.

A little further in they saw three large furnaces, placed one behind the other. Each vertical oven was a colossal size, almost two floors tall by half a house wide. They had an opening at the front, like the square mouth of a steel-and-fire monster. These furnaces were where the metal was melted and purified.

On the sides they found the huge bellows the size of a house roof, which was used to blow air into the furnace for the coal to burn, also to keep the coals alive all day long, which was needed to keep the forge working.

Metal wagons with iron wheels rested on rails loaded with material. They formed a line that went from the huge piles of material to the furnaces. The workers dragged the wagons with the material to the great ovens.

What was most surprising was the size of that operation. The mountains of raw material, the huge furnaces, the amounts of metal that must be produced daily in that place had to be awesome, hence the pillars of smoke seen in the north part of the city.

"Let's go towards the light," Egil whispered to Gerd.

They went slowly and stealthily toward the light and the origin of the beating hammers they had heard from outside, which now sounded much clearer. Everything around them was in shadows, and only the light at the far end was discernible.

They reached the origin of the light and threw themselves on the floor. Before them they saw a lower level, as if it had been dug out in the ground to make a cellar. Only it was still being done. They saw a dozen men working on the strange cellar. They had excavated a large rectangle of about fifteen feet deep by twenty feet wide, taking out earth and stone. The workers were inside this area that could be reached by ladders.

At first it was difficult to see what those men were doing down there. But after watching them for a while they realized they were lining half the surface of the rectangle with metal sheets, creating two spaces. The left side was lined with dull metal, most likely steel, and the right side had another metal that looked like silver.

"What are they doing there?" Gerd asked in a whisper, a confused look on his face.

"I must admit, my giant friend, that I haven't the slightest idea. This is very puzzling," Egil replied in another whisper.

"You weren't expecting to find anything like this? You always have in mind, more or less, what we're going to find."

"Well, this time I can say with a certain amount of embarrassment, that I'm as puzzled as you."

"Well then we're screwed." Gerd put his hand to his forehead and shook his head.

At that moment they heard a noise behind their backs.

"Hey, what are you doing here?" an unpleasant voice asked behind them.

Egil and Gerd turned over on the floor to find four armed men with short swords and daggers who were glaring at them.

Egil looked at Gerd.

"We're in big trouble," he told him with wide eyes.

Chapter 18

Egil jumped to his feet with the speed and lightness of a grasshopper surprised by a snake, and he faced the four men.

"Forgive the intrusion, we got lost," he replied with an innocent look on his face. "We'll leave right away."

Gerd started to get to his feet; unlike Egil, he realized it would take him longer to do so than he would have liked because of his balance problems.

"Kill them!" the man who had spoken told his men.

"I assure you that violence is not at all necessary in this situation. We can talk about it calmly. We're not doing anything illegal," Egil said soothingly as he checked how Gerd was handling standing up.

"No talking! Kill them!" the man who seemed to be the leader of the group cried again.

Two of the men stepped forward to grab Egil, who stood up to them. The third one made to grab Gerd, who still had not recovered. He became unbalanced and had to bend down again to avoid falling.

Egil acted at once. He already had his weapons in his hands, and with a turn of his hip and an accurate throw he caught the one coming to knife Gerd with his short Ranger's axe full in the head. He hit him with the flat of the axe but with enough strength that it made a hollow *clonk*. The man dropped to the floor, unconscious before he could reach Gerd's back.

The sword of one of the two watchmen attacking Egil sought his neck with a sweeping blow, forewarned by a savage yell. Egil threw his head back enough to let the sword brush his face without touching him. The second watchman delivered a thrust straight to his heart. Egil turned sideways fast as a big cat and, being as thin as he was, the sword flew parallel to his chest while he held his breath and softened his ribcage.

"Come on, finish them!" the leader shouted.

Upon hearing the shouts, the workers who were at the lower level of the dug-out rectangle started climbing up the ladders, alerted by the fighting above. Things were getting complicated for Egil and Gerd.

Egil stepped backward quickly before his attackers delivered new thrusts and cuts, and with his right hand he took a phial out if his special belt. In the left hand he was holding his Ranger's knife, brandishing it before his face threateningly.

A dagger came directly toward his left eye. Egil blocked it with his knife, deflecting the arm that guided it to one side. Out of the corner of his eye he saw that the second watchman was also coming at him with a dagger. Egil threw the phial at his face. The sound of breaking glass was heard, and a purple gas surrounded the attacker's head.

"What's this?" he asked, confused, eyes wide open and taking two steps to one side in terror.

Egil took another step back to get out of range of the other watchman's sword.

"It's Violet Slumber, a special variation of Summer Slumber which I've developed myself," Egil said proudly. "I have the soul of an alchemist," he smiled.

"I'll kill you for throwing this filth at my face!"

Egil sidestepped again, more widely this time.

"I doubt it very much. I don't think you'll be able to do much of anything, no matter how hard you try."

The watchman took one step toward Egil and fell down on his face, senseless.

"But… what the…?" the other attacker cried, puzzled, and he lunged at Egil, intending to split him in two with a two-handed sword blow.

Right then Gerd, who was standing at last, turned and delivered a tremendous kick to the watchman, who flew backwards and fell to the level below with a cry of despair. The sound of the body hitting the ground two floors down was gruesome.

"I'm glad you've recovered your balance," Egil smiled at Gerd.

"Sorry, it's a little harder than before… and on this occasion, much harder. That was unfortunate…"

"There's nothing to be sorry for," said Egil.

"I'm going to kill you!" the leader yelled as he lunged at them, brandishing his sword.

"Do you mind…? Egil said to Gerd, pointing at the attacker.

Gerd turned to face him. He blocked the man's sword with his knife, and next he delivered a tremendous punch to the nose with the fist he was holding his axe in. The leader fell backward, unconscious, his nose broken.

"This one's not getting up in two or three days," said Gerd.

"I'd almost forgotten how strong you are. You nearly knocked his head off with that right punch."

"Luckily my physical strength wasn't affected by my other problems…"

"I'm glad that's the case. Be careful, don't go near the violet gas or you'll faint," Egil warned him.

"Don't worry. I still remember my Wildlife lessons. I can recognize Summer Slumber or something similar when I see it."

Egil smiled. "Fantastic."

"Who were these?" Gerd asked, kneeling beside the leader to check him.

Egil came over and also bent to inspect him. Then he checked and searched the others quickly.

"They're paid watchmen."

"They're not Defenders?" Gerd said, disappointed.

Egil shook his head, making a face.

"No, these don't belong to the Congregation of Defenders of the True Blood."

"Pity, I thought we'd found something."

"So did I."

"The ones from below are coming now," Gerd said, pointing at the group that had by now climbed up the ladders and were charging at them with swords and daggers in their hands.

"We'd better get ready. They're coming to get us… which doesn't make much sense if they're just workers…"

"They might be more than that," Gerd said with a shrug and prepared to stand up to them. He grasped his bow and nocked an arrow, and Egil did the same. Both friends raised their bows almost at the same time. Eleven men were running toward them, silently, their eyes on the two Rangers. They had no good intentions.

"I'm counting eleven, we're missing one," Gerd told Egil.

"Okay. One's fleeing to the back of the building," Egil said, locating him.

Without another word, they both calculated the minimum distance to be able to shoot twice. As soon as the first attackers were in range, they both released: Egil at the one on the left and Gerd at the one on the right.

Both attackers were hit in the torso and fell amid moans of pain. Egil and Gerd nocked again, pulled the string back to the tip of their nose, aimed, and released in unison at the last moment. Two other attackers fell down with arrows in their chests.

"There are seven left," Gerd told Egil.

"We have no time to release again," Egil warned, seeing the rest of the men running toward them, brandishing their weapons.

Gerd dropped his bow and grasped his knife and axe. Egil reached for his knife with his left hand while he took out another phial from his special ranger's belt. He threw the phial at the first assailant, who was almost upon them. The container broke against his arm and a green cloud enveloped the attacker and the man running beside him. They took three more steps, and before reaching Egil and Gerd they fell to the ground with much gagging, with their hands to their stomachs and looking as if their guts were going to spill from their mouths.

"Tell me what that was," Gerd said to Egil.

"Another of my alchemical concoctions. A beauty really. Green poisoning."

"Yeah, I can see how much you're enjoying yourself," Gerd said as he watched with horror how the two men kept vomiting and writhing on the ground with their hands to their stomachs.

Egil smiled and shrugged.

The next three attackers reached them. One went straight for Egil and the other two for Gerd. Egil leapt backwards to get out of range of the horizontal cut to his stomach delivered by his attacker.

Gerd blocked the sword of his first attacker with his short axe and delivered a powerful kick to his stomach. The man doubled up. Gerd was going to kill him off, but he saw the sword of the other attacker seeking his neck so he was forced to defend himself. He deflected the weapon with his knife, and before the man could react, he delivered a kick to his privates forcefully, in a learned movement.

"Viggo's teachings," Gerd told Egil, who was staring at him, not recognizing that low blow as one of those learned in their training. At the same time, he backed up, avoiding a frantic attack from his own opponent.

Gerd was unable to kill off the two he had left injured, since another man jumped on him with crossed thrusts of sword and dagger. Gerd stepped back to avoid being cut, and then he delivered an axe blow that caught his opponent's sword. The weapon fell to the ground. At once the man attacked with his dagger and tried to bury it in Gerd's face. Gerd blocked upwards with his knife and delivered a tremendous headbutt in the nose. The attacker dropped his dagger and put his hand to his nose. Gerd seized the chance to knock him out with a good blow to the temple.

Egil was defending himself from the attack of two men. His defense consisted in blocking or slipping away from the enemy weapons' range. Lasgol had taught him that technique—it worked well when what you wanted was not so much finishing your enemy as not being cut. Egil was distracting them until the arrival of the one who was really going to deal with them.

Gerd came running from behind and grabbed one of the men by his clothes and threw him against the other one. Both men fell down and rolled in the dirt on the ground. They tried to get back up, but Gerd grabbed one attacker he had already knocked out and threw him at the other two as if the man were a rag doll. The three fell over the edge to the bottom of the huge rectangular pit they had dug out. They fell all the way from above and, given the depth of the hole, they must have broken several bones, if not their backs.

"Thanks, my dear giant."

"You're welcome, it was my pleasure." Gerd looked around, and there was no one left standing. The danger seemed to have passed.

"You've certainly been working on your strength."

"Yeah, I have, a little, since I couldn't work on my balance."

"It shows," Egil said, nodding.

"And now what?" Gerd asked.

"Now we question this one," Egil said, pointing at one of the assailants, who was writhing in pain on the ground.

"Good." Gerd went over to the poor wretch and lifted him off the ground by the front of his shirt with both hands. He lifted him high so his feet were dangling about a handspan off the ground.

Egil checked him carefully: his clothes, his appearance, the weapons he was carrying that had fallen on the ground. He searched him while Gerd kept him in the air.

"This one's a Defender," Egil said, nodding.

"Well, well!" Gerd cried, pleased to have found one of them at last.

"I am... no-one," the man muttered.

"Put him down, please, Gerd. We'll have a chat with our friend the Defender in a civilized way."

"I have nothing to tell you," the man muttered.

Gerd let him down, and the man kept his balance with difficulty.

"We simply want to talk to you a little. We have some questions for you."

"I'll tell you nothing!"

Gerd punched him in the stomach and the man doubled up in pain.

"You'd better talk, or I'll throw you into the pit head first."

"I won't... say... impure blood."

"I believe he considers our blood to be impure. That's funny. Why do you say that?" Egil asked, appearing intrigued.

"You... aren't... of the true blood."

Egil and Gerd looked at one another. It was odd to be referred to like that.

"Aren't we?" Egil asked.

"No..."

"How do you know?" Egil asked the man, who was now sitting on the ground. Gerd was behind him and had his large hands on the man's shoulders, holding him down firmly.

"I know."

"I find it odd, since we don't know ourselves whether we are or not. Right, Gerd?"

"No, we don't. I feel quite true, so perhaps I am."

"No, you're not. The First Defender knows and has warned us against the Rangers of false blood who'll try to stop us."

"That must be us," said Gerd.

"Without a doubt. What has the First Defender told you?"

"I won't talk," the prisoner said, shaking his head hard.

"We only want to know what Viggen has told you about us," Egil told the man.

When he heard Viggen's name the man's eyes opened wide.

"That you'd try to stop our holy work."

"What is that work, and what has it got to do with this place? What are you doing here at this forge?" Egil asked.

"I can't reveal our purpose. I won't."

"Well then, I'll throw you down into the pit, and that's two floors down, free fall," Gerd threatened him, pressing his hands down on the man's shoulders.

"I... don't mind dying... it's for a holy cause..." he muttered painfully.

Gerd looked at Egil, raising an eyebrow. It did not look as if he was going to talk.

"Why are you lining that rectangular pit with steel and silver? What for? What are you after?"

"I ignore the goal. I only do what my lord has told me to."

"Did he tell you to build this pit at the forge? What for?" Egil insisted, wanting answers.

"I only follow the First Defender's designs."

"Egil, those two are starting to come to," Gerd warned with a wave at the two men Egil had knocked out with his concoction.

"Watch them, I'll deal with this one," Egil said.

Gerd went over to the other two Defenders, who were trying to stand.

"I need to know the purpose of this pit," Egil insisted, threatening the Defender with his knife.

"I won't tell you. I won't talk."

"In that case I'll be forced to use much more aggressive methods," Egil threatened him, narrowing his eyes.

The Defender jumped to his feet and headbutted Egil in the stomach, leaving him winded and bent double.

"Egil!" cried Gerd, turning around to help his friend.

The Defender Egil was questioning reached for his dagger, but instead of attacking Egil he ran off, reached the edge of the hole, turning to look at Egil and then at the pit. He shut his eyes and with both hands buried the dagger in his own heart. He fell in the pit and crashed at the bottom. He was dead at once.

"What the heck!" Gerd said, baffled. "Why did he take his own life? What madness!"

The other two intoxicated Defenders had recovered. They looked at Gerd and Egil and ran to the door of the forge like lightning.

"They're escaping!" Egil cried. He could not run, he still had not gotten his breath back.

"I'll go after them!" Gerd said and ran off.

Egil breathed deep several times before he fully recovered the air in his lungs. It had been an unexpected blow, and those had double repercussions: the impact and the surprise. He looked to see if there was anyone left alive. Those in the pit had managed to flee through the back door of the forge, with the exception of the wretch who had killed himself.

Egil was annoyed that there was no one left to question. While he was waiting for Gerd to come back, he inspected the bodies of the other workers and confirmed the fact that they were indeed Defenders as he had suspected.

He searched all the bodies for notes, instructions, something that might indicate what they were doing in there. All he found was some gold and scarves to cover the nose and mouth, most likely when they worked at the furnaces.

He looked at the forge and had the feeling that this was an operation of great magnitude. Viggen and his Defenders were managing one of the large forges, one with the capacity to produce a lot of steel. Were they preparing to make a great number of weapons? Were they going to start an armed rebellion? How? With what army? The Defenders seemed to have quite a few adepts from what Egil had witnessed, but not so many as to start a revolt. Perhaps they were planning on joining the Visionaries to their own group? But even if that was the case, and though the Visionaries had a large group of followers, they were not enough to take control of a whole region, least of all Norghana.

He looked at the piles of mineral and the loaded wagons ready to feed the great furnaces. If they produced steel it had to be for swords, knives, axes, and armor. But they were also lining that weird pit with steel. Egil could not guess what was going on there.

"I need more information..." he muttered under his breath.

Gerd came running with his strange gait. "I'm sorry... they got away..." he said regretfully as he tried to get his breath back.

"Don't worry. I doubt they could have given us any information. They just follow orders. They have no idea what's going on here."

"It makes me angry... before they wouldn't have been able to escape," Gerd said ruefully, his arms akimbo and bending forward.

"Life puts all kind of difficulties in our path: how we face and overcome them is in our hands. Don't worry, you're doing great."

"You say that because you're my friend."

"Irrefutable," Egil beamed at him.

Gerd could not help but smile. "You do like that word..."

"And you like hearing it," Egil continued smiling.

They waited for a few moments until Gerd was ready.

"Two got away."

"It's three. Remember the last one who arrived, the one in sandals instead of boots?" Egil told Gerd.

"That's right. They'll go and warn Viggen and his people that we're here. They might come with reinforcements—it might be dangerous."

"I don't think that's what'll happen."

"It's not? They'll come to recover the place, they've invested time excavating and lining that huge pit down there. Not to mention this whole forge they're working."

Egil nodded thoughtfully.

"Viggen is smart. He knows we've found him out. He won't come. He'll leave this place, get rid of it so we can't hunt him down. If he came and stood up to us and our comrades, he knows he could lose. He won't risk it, least of all knowing how important everything they're doing is to them."

"Yeah, those fools don't mind losing their lives, that's what puzzles me. You can't give away life like that. It's crazy."

"Absolutely true. But these people have fanatical ideologies. They'll do whatever their leaders order. Without caring whether they lose their life for it," Egil said. "It really is tragic."

"Not only tragic, it's terrible."

"I've never understood how a person can get to that. What's going on in a person's mind to make him act that way?" Egil commented sadly.

Chapter 19

Their magical instruction was moving forward at a good pace, or so Eicewald said to cheer them up. Lasgol was a little worried because he was still having difficulties, and although he understood that this was because of the intrinsic difficulty of improving his magical level, he could not help but feel that he was not the most gifted of those who had been blessed with the Talent. Camu, on the other hand, did seem more gifted with magic than him, something which made him truly happy.

"Now that we know the level of magical power we have, it's time to learn how to improve that power in order to reach new, higher levels, and with them new magical grades," Eicewald told them early that morning in the training tent.

"Wonderful! I'm so willing to learn!" Lasgol said eagerly.

I very ready, Camu messaged them.

"What else!" Eicewald smiled as he stroked Camu's crested head.

"Helping improve our level is something we're both very interested in," Lasgol said eagerly.

Eicewald told them to sit down. As usual, Lasgol and Eicewald sat facing one another while Camu lay down flanking both. Ona withdrew to the far end of the tent to rest.

"There are five main factors which affect your ability to go up levels. There really are a lot more, but that's too advanced to explain now. What I'm going to teach you are the five basic factors you must learn, memorize, and remember always."

We learn, Camu messaged confidently.

"The first factor that affects improving your magical level is known as the Magical Use."

Camu and Lasgol exchanged glances, not sure what that meant.

"You mean using our magic?" Lasgol asked, trying to understand.

"Indeed. What Magical Use means is that the use of our own magic helps improve it and rise in level. That is to say, the more you use magic, the more you master it."

"I'd always believed that using magic too much was a bad thing..." Lasgol commented, annoyed.

"That's a widely spread belief and something natural. That's because when we use our magic too much, we become exhausted as we use up our inner pool, which can lead to fainting and even death in extreme cases. But the truth is that the opposite happens—the more we use our magic, the easier it is to use, and that's because it stimulates the increase in magical level."

I use much. I camouflage much.

"Well, that's very good. The more you use your magic, the sooner you'll get to the next level and end up reaching a new grade. But you must always use it carefully so as not to exhaust your whole supply of energy, because then you'll faint from exhaustion, and that's bad, very bad."

I understand. Use magic. Not finish energy.

"That's right. You understand well," Eicewald said, smiling at him.

I very smart, Camu messaged, lifting his head high proudly.

Lasgol snorted and let out a long breath of air.

"The Magical Use is utilized by all schools of magic, magical tutors, and by any teacher of witchcraft or shaman who wants to teach a pupil. This is because it is the easiest way to improve. You simply have to use your magic, and gradually, little by little, you move up levels. It's like when soldiers train themselves by delivering slashes and thrusts with their swords. They always do it the same way, thousands of times, and this makes their slashes and thrusts improve over time. They become more accurate and powerful, raising their level of swordsmanship."

"Now I understand it clearly," said Lasgol. "If that's the case, by constantly repeating the same spell or skill, we'll reach the highest grade. Why do I feel like there's a 'but' coming?"

Yes, what but? messaged Camu, who also felt there was a catch.

Eicewald smiled.

"You really are smart. There is a 'but.' That 'but' is that advancement is painfully slow and tiresome. Repeating an exercise or a skill over and over helps you improve, but it does so slowly, and it's also repetitive and tiring."

"I can imagine that," said Lasgol.

Very boring,

"But, I promise there are advances. If there's no other way at hand, it will help you. You simply have to do hundreds of spells or summons and you'll gradually improve. I also advise you to use magic as much as you can in real life. That will help you without you realizing it, since without meaning to and without using such repetitive methods, you'll manage to improve."

People not like magic.

"That's true, Camu. When I say you should use magic as much as possible in real life, I also mean you must balance it with the unequivocal fact that most people fear magic and that watching you practice it might create conflict or, to say the least, uncomfortable situations."

"We need to find a balance between using magic as much as we can and not creating uncomfortable or conflictive situations to those around us," Lasgol said.

Be difficult.

"It is, but remember that always using magic helps you improve, so try to do it," Eicewald advised them.

"We'll try," Lasgol nodded, although he had serious doubts about how they were going to balance doing magic in the situations they often found themselves involved in.

Eicewald nodded once, eying his two pupils.

"The second factor that affects your magical level's development is Magical Creation."

Lasgol and Camu already knew the concept and had been working on it, so they cheered up and smiled.

"We know that one well," Lasgol said, encouraging the Mage to continue with the explanation.

"The Magical Creation I've already explained to you and which consists of creating new skills also influences your magical level."

"We're trying to create new skills: does that help us climb levels?" Lasgol asked, since they spent lots of time trying without much success. Perhaps the effort and time invested was not in vain.

"Only if the creation takes place," Eicewald said.

Not fair, Camu protested, looking unhappy.

"So then, if we don't manage to create a new skill or spell, we won't reach another level? All the time and effort are for nothing?"

"I wouldn't say they're 'for nothing,' since the more effort we make to improve in any facet of life, the farther it takes us. So, the effort isn't lost or useless. It helps us to be capable of creating a new skill more easily in the future. A blacksmith improves his craftsmanship with every blow of his hammer on the anvil. He won't always forge exceptional swords and armor, but on some occasions he will. Yet without those hammer strokes and hard work during years and years, he would never be able to create them."

"I see. It's just that's it's quite frustrating when you don't succeed… and seeing it doesn't help us progress our magical level either…"

"Think about it this way, Lasgol. The more you strive, the less it will cost you to create a new skill. At first the price for learning is high, but in the end the fruits of your learning are rich, since they will provide you with better creations and faster advancement in your progression as a mage."

Lasgol nodded and thought about Eicewald's words, which made all the sense in the world. Having a mentor like him, who explained concepts in such a clear way and with such good examples, was a luxury Lasgol appreciated from the bottom of his heart.

Work, win.

"That's right, Camu. Whoever works hard and with determination will reach their goals. Whoever doesn't will never amount to anything in life. Regardless of the area of study," Eicewald explained.

I much work.

"Absolutely."

"Being as determined as he is," Lasgol said, not using the word "stubborn," although that was what he was really thinking, "I bet he makes it."

"The third factor that affects the magical advance is Magical Amplification. This concept you also know already. Skills can be amplified, and when you do so it also influences the magical advancement. The more you successfully amplify your skills, the faster you'll reach the next level."

"That we understand," Lasgol said, seeing Camu nod.

Make sense. More amplification, more level.

"Very well explained, Camu," said Eicewald. "What you're really managing when you use the Principle of Magical Amplification is not only using your magic but increasing its power, so as a secondary effect you manage to improve the magical level."

"Do you manage to improve more or less than with Magical Use?" Lasgol said, curious.

"More. With Magical Use, the advance is in small, continuous steps. With Magical Amplification you obtain greater increases, but it's less constant since it's less common."

Understand, Camu messaged.

"Good. Let's continue then. The fourth factor is Magical Power. The more powerful your skills and spells are, the faster you'll reach the next level and grade."

"That's only natural," Lasgol said.

Much natural.

"Indeed. This factor is the easiest to grasp, since it's directly related. The more powerful your magic, the greater the magical level. It also works in the other direction, and it's important you understand this. When you reach a new level, the magic you've been using up until now generates skills and spells which are a little more powerful. When you reach a new grade, this leap is even greater and all the skills and spells are affected and become more powerful."

Much wonderful.

"It must be fantastic. I've never noticed anything…. Well, I haven't been aware of reaching new levels or grades," Lasgol admitted shyly.

"Yet I'm sure you've realized how your skills have become better with the passing of time."

"Yeah… that's true, I have felt some growth, although I'm not sure that's the right word…"

"You can think about it as growth, but the one who grows is you, at your magical level, and that shows in your skills. That's why you feel like they've grown, although what happens as a rule is that they become more powerful."

"I see…" Lasgol mused about what the Mage was telling him.

I grow soon, Camu messaged.

"Impatience isn't a good ally in the long journey of magical learning." Eicewald told him. "It's a lot more productive to be restrained and patient. Life is long, even more so in your case. You must take things calmly and go step by step."

Step by step boring,

"It is, but it is safe, and one of the main things you should always consider with magic is the danger it implies. I've already warned you that magic is dangerous—you must understand this and assimilate it. Haste usually ends in terrible results, not only for the hasty, but for those with them."

"We know of the dangers of magic. We won't be hasty," Lasgol promised.

Not run, Camu messaged, confirming.

"Very well, let's go on. The fifth factor that directly affects magical progress is Magical Learning. Every tome of magic you read, every manual of magic you study. Every magical parchment, rune of power, any magical text you analyze and understand, will help the magical fundaments and therefore help you in reaching a new level of power."

"It's fascinating," Lasgol said to Eicewald.

Much fascinating.

"It's for this reason that many magi, myself included, spend so much time studying magical tomes of all kinds. Not only for the knowledge we gain, but because, at the same time, it helps us progress in levels to reach a new grade."

"But only if you learn, right? It's no good to study without understanding or processing and retaining the information you're learning," Lasgol guessed.

"Indeed. Advancement and progress up the ladder of power can only be achieved if you manage to succeed. Attempts and failures give no rewards in magic. It's similar to what happens in life. You might try to be successful, but if you aren't, there's no end prize," Eicewald said, smiling gently.

"Magic is quite tough…" Lasgol replied.

"Like life itself," Eicewald said with great gentleness.

Magic only for strong, Camu messaged like a proclamation.

"One must be strong, yes, in spirit and mind, in order to go far in the world of magic. There are no shortcuts and there is no easy way. Whatever you manage will be the consequence of working hard and for a long time. I'd like to be able to tell you there's another way, but it's not like that. Those who tried to fool magic and took shortcuts ended up badly. Never try that. It's better to pay a known price than end up losing your life because the price was too high."

"We'll keep that in mind," Lasgol promised. It was clear that no tricks or cheating would do with magic. They would have to work hard and pay the price in effort and sweat. Not in tears because of trying to cheat.

"As you see, all the magical principles and concepts are interrelated. So, working and making the effort to improve in any of them always produces a reward, no matter how small it might seem," Eicewald said, opening his arms.

"I see, and I understand," Lasgol nodded.

"Remember, Camu, there are no sure things with magic. Never expect great rewards, and appreciate the smallest one you get."

I appreciate. Not worry.

"Very well."

The three worked on the factors, and Eicewald continued passing on his knowledge to Lasgol and Camu as they tried to memorize each and every one of the Mage's words. The path of magic was arduous and dangerous, but also filled with great reward.

Chapter 20

Eicewald opened the tome he had brought to use as a studying tool with Camu and Lasgol. It was not a very striking tome, with old, moth-eaten covers. Lasgol noticed they must have been golden but were now so weathered that you could barely make out the color they had once been. They were now a grayish brown with worn-off sheen in some parts.

The Mage leafed through it carefully. The yellowed pages were filled with writing and drawings. Lasgol wondered whether handling the tome so carefully was due to it being of great value or because it was so old. Or in case it had some spell which Eicewald did not want to deactivate or trigger by mistake. As the matter worried him, he asked the Mage.

"Both," Eicewald confirmed. "I see you're paying close attention. This tome is precious—there aren't many copies, and this one is the original in fact. It was very costly to get, not only in gold but in time and effort."

I feel magic, Camu messaged.

"Indeed. This tome is enchanted with several spells. Some are for protection and others help with comprehension, since its content is as valuable as it is difficult to understand for the non-adept."

I want see magic, Camu messaged.

"Don't worry, my restless creature, you'll see it," Eicewald said with a big smile.

"I also want to see how the spells work, in case we come across a similar tome and want to study it," Lasgol said.

"In that case, I'll show you one of the protective spells, since they're usually dangerous for those who don't know about them. You should always pay attention if you find an arcane tome of this kind. Many are protected, and they might even kill whoever tries to manipulate them. As a rule, only the mage who cast the spell or one with knowledge can handle it without danger."

"Yes, please. That knowledge will be quite useful," Lasgol said.

Eicewald closed the tome and left it on the floor of the tent. He started to conjure using his hands, moving them in circles over the book.

"I've created a protection that allows you to open the book and that contains the magic of its protective spell."

Can open?

"Better use a stick," Eicewald advised them.

Lasgol went outside and came back with a long thin branch which he stripped of leaves.

"That will do," Eicewald smiled. "Go ahead, lift the cover of the book with the stick."

Lasgol penetrated the protective dome over the book with the stick and carefully lifted the cover to open the book. There was a bright purple flash, followed by flames. The stick caught fire but the flames were contained inside the dome Eicewald had created. Lasgol took the burning stick outside and, after staring at it for a moment with a look of surprise, he threw it far into the snow, where it went out.

Much fun, Camu messaged excitedly, and he started to flex his legs and wag his long tail, hitting Ona, who growled at him.

"I didn't find it funny at all, rather the opposite," Lasgol protested. "If it hadn't been for the dome I would've burned whole!"

"Indeed, my clever pupil."

"I see the danger these magic tomes pose. I doubt I'll ever get close to one of them without being extra careful."

"As you should. You must be cautious with all magic tomes, especially those with knowledge or spells."

I cancel magic, Camu messaged.

"Could you do that?" Eicewald said with a look of genuine surprise on his face.

I can.

"The spell is activated when you try to open the book, and it seemed to me almost instantaneous. Are you sure you'd have time to cancel it?" Lasgol asked.

As usual, Camu was sure he could.

I sure can, he messaged nonchalantly.

"Let's see," Eicewald said.

The Mage conjured again over the book.

"The protections are activated. I've left the protective dome just in case," he told Camu.

I not need. You see.

Lasgol took out his Ranger's knife and tried once again to open the tome with it. Carefully he put the tip under the cover to lift it a bit. There were two simultaneous flashes: that of the protective spell on the tome, in purple, and one Camu produced in silver. The expected burst of fire did not take place.

"That's impressive," Eicewald said as he looked at the tome and then at Camu, gaping.

I tell. I know.

"There were two simultaneous flashes, one a spell and one canceling it. I agree with Eicewald, it was impressive."

I much impressive, Camu said, smiling, and he resumed his leg flexing and tail wagging joyfully.

"This skill of yours is very powerful," Eicewald told him in a serious tone. "Really powerful. Can you cancel any type of magic?"

Not know. Not try always for Lasgol.

Eicewald looked at Lasgol blankly.

"What does he mean? I didn't understand."

"He means that when he was younger, he canceled all magic almost instantaneously. He had to learn to control it so he wouldn't interfere with my skills or those of the magi we deal with," Lasgol explained.

I control.

"Well, that's an extraordinary skill you should continue to work on. There's nothing worse for a mage or anyone with the Gift than being unable to cast a spell or summon their skills. It gives you an enormous advantage when confronting a magical enemy or in dangerous situations," Eicewald said as he kept going over the implications of having such a skill in his head.

I work cancel magic, Camu messaged firmly.

"If you need any help, I'm more than willing. I'm really intrigued by that skill," Eicewald admitted.

"Why is it so interesting?" Lasgol asked him.

"Because I've never heard of any mage or magical creature that has it. Because it's unique and so useful in combat, it makes anyone who has it extraordinary."

"We had no idea it was so special," Lasgol said.

"I can assure you it is. You're still young and lack experience, more so in magical matters. That kind of skill can disarm any mage— that's why it's so special. That's why I'm recommending you develop it, and to do so in secret."

I develop. I powerful.

"Let's try one more time, changing the spell. We'll open the book at the middle," Eicewald said, watching Camu with bright eyes.

Lasgol did so using his knife. The moment he opened it so there was another purple flash and at the same instant another silver light from Camu, which stopped the spell.

"Well done, Camu!" the Mage congratulated him.

I attention.

"If you're not paying attention, can you still cancel the spell?" Eicewald asked.

Not think. I have be prepared.

"I see. That's natural, all magic has its limitations, and such a powerful skill must have several."

I search.

"That's right, try to find the limitations of your skill. It will be very useful."

"Yeah, we need to find out what conditions we can use it in and when it doesn't work," said Lasgol.

"Very well. Now I'll cast a spell to deactivate the protection spells so we can use the tome," Eicewald said.

The Mage placed his hands on the protective dome and withdrew it. Then he conjured again and the tome flashed with an intermittent whitish gleam for a long moment. Then it went out.

"I hope I can do that someday," Lasgol said, although it was more wishful thinking out loud.

"I'm sure you will, someday," Eicewald said encouragingly.

"I really hope so," Lasgol nodded.

"Well, for that we must study the principles of magic in this tome. So, let's get started," Eicewald said with a big smile as he opened the book, which was now harmless.

Lasgol nodded eagerly, anxious to start learning.

Several days later they met again to study the tome. Lasgol had a doubt, which he asked the Mage about as soon as they entered the tent.

"This is a tome of knowledge, but there are also tomes of spells, aren't there?"

"There are, and they are precious since they not only contain the theory, but the practice of magic as well."

"Is that how magi learn spells?"

"Some do it that way, yes, and the societies of magi, such as the Ice Magi, have tomes of spells that gather all the spells we have and use. It's fundamental to keep them all together in order to teach the young who join our ranks."

"Very interesting, I guessed it would be something like that. Could I use one of those books of spells to learn them?"

"You could, of course, but the fact that you may study them doesn't necessarily mean you'd learn them."

Lasgol looked at Eicewald, puzzled.

"Why not?"

"There are multiple factors that affect the ability to learn spells," the Mage explained. "The first is that they must be spells of a type of magic you're aligned with."

"Why? Isn't magic universal? Can't anyone with the Gift use it?"

Magic all? Camu messaged, suddenly interested.

"It is. But it's necessary to have a certain affinity with a specific type of magic in order to learn it and use it. For instance, I highly doubt you could use Blood Magic, or Curses or Death Magic, the magic the sorcerers of the Nocean Empire use in the South."

"Because I have no inclination to those types of magic?"

"Indeed. I don't either, and if I wanted to, it would take me a lot of time and effort to learn since my inclination is to elemental magic, that of the four elements: water, earth, fire, and air."

"And you've specialized in the water element, leaving the others aside," Lasgol added, wanting to understand.

"Exactly. I could study and learn the other three types of elemental magic if I wanted to, because I'm already aligned with Elemental Magic. But if I wanted to study Illusion Magic or Enchantment Magic, it would be hard for me. I could do it, yes, but it would take me a long time. Too long," the Mage smiled.

Too long bad, Camu messaged. He was not the most patient being, the creature liked having immediate success at whatever he tried.

"I see," Lasgol nodded and motioned the Mage to continue.

"Another important factor is the grade of magic you've reached. Depending on the full levels you have you'll be able, or not, to memorize and execute the spell or enchantment in the tome."

Much grade good.

"Exactly, Camu. As everything in life, the more expertise you have in something, the easier it is to learn new things related to that topic."

"Could we try with one of those books of spells someday?" Lasgol said.

"Absolutely. I'll bring you an arcane book and we'll experiment," the Mage promised.

I want experiment! Camu messaged, excited about the possibility.

"Yeah, me too," Lasgol joined him.

"Well then, so it will be," Eicewald said.

Chapter 21

Ingrid and Viggo arrived at the city of Denmik at mid-afternoon. This was the most important city in the south of Norghana because of its strategic location near the border of the Kingdom of Zangria and its easy access to the endless Masig prairies, a place frequented by spies of several kingdoms, including the Norghanians.

They stopped beside the road about half a league from the city walls with their access gate, and watched it from a distance.

The city was infamous for this reason, since no one trusted anyone in it. Any stranger was arrested by the city guard and questioned the moment they set foot in the city. It was ruled by Count Esvelk, who was a fierce ally of King Thoran and his brother Orten. The King had given him the county and city when he had come to power, with the order to control the spies and foreign agents who wandered through it.

Information was almost as important a weapon as swords and axes, and sometimes even more so. King Thoran knew this and wanted to control its flow. Esvelk was in charge of watching and questioning whoever he found suspicious in his city and, as it was said, he did this like a rabid watch dog. It also did not help his fame that his methods were not at all elegant or subtle. It was said that the screams at the questionings done in the castle dungeons at the top of the city could be heard throughout it.

The spies and agents of other kingdoms were well aware of what went on in there. But even so, they came because the benefits of getting important information were greater than the risk of undergoing the Count's interrogation or of being found stabbed in the back behind some ill-reputed establishment. This was the vision of kings, princes, and nobles who did not care much about losing spies or agents.

"This city's going to be fun," Viggo commented and smiled lightly.

"I highly doubt it. This city's dangerous. It's always been dangerous, and even more so now," Ingrid said.

"That's what I mean," Viggo replied, smiling.

"We'd better split," Ingrid said in the tone that meant they should be focusing on what they had to do. "It's possible there are watchmen stationed throughout the city. We can't let them see us together, in case we're recognized."

Viggo nodded, "This city has a reputation for having a thousand eyes that never shut."

"All the more reason," Ingrid nodded. "I don't want Drugan and his followers to know we've arrived."

"It's more than likely some of those eyes are the Visionaries," Viggo agreed, "or that they've paid certain agents to watch for them."

"You think that might be the case? That they'd use third parties to watch us for them?"

"Egil thinks so. We talked about this and he said it was a real possibility. Just as Egil uses contacts, informers, and agents, Drugan and his sect might be doing it as well."

"I don't like any part of this world of informers, spies, and double betrayals. Everyone should do their job and not have others doing it for them and complicating situations that might be solved directly," Ingrid said with a grimace of disgust.

"That's because you like to dive straight into the core of the matter. Unfortunately, very few people function as directly as you do and so the situations become complicated."

"And we're all wasting time instead of finding a solution."

"They're wasting their time making things complicated because they want to win, and they know that a direct confrontation decreases their possibilities of victory."

"Has Egil also told you that?" Ingrid asked, surprised by the reasoning.

"That's from my own crop," Viggo replied with a grin.

"Since when have you started making assumptions and reasoning things out?"

"Since always. The thing is that most of the time they don't come out as well as just now," Viggo replied with a shrug.

"Keep trying. Practice brings improvement in all facets of life," she said encouragingly.

"Don't worry, I'm going to keep using this," he said, tapping his head with his finger.

"I'll be alert to progress."

Viggo could not tell whether Ingrid was being sarcastic or not.

The truth was she was never sarcastic—she preferred actual truths, even if they hurt whoever was before her.

"I'll wait until nightfall to go in. I'd rather act at night, I'm better then," he said with a wink.

Ingrid ignored the insinuation and maintained her firm tone, her mind focused on the task at hand.

"We'll meet at the great fountain north of the main square."

"Victory Square?"

"Yes. That'll be our meeting point," Ingrid said seriously. "You do know which one it is, don't you?"

"I have it marked on the map," Viggo said, taking it out of his traveling rucksack and unfolding it. He studied it to locate the square.

"Look for the square in the center of town. The fountain is a bit more to the north. It's a fountain with the statues of three white roaring, standing bears, life-size."

"It shouldn't be hard to find if it has three large bears standing on their hind legs."

"It's not, but don't get distracted. The city is known for its social establishments where information is exchanged."

"Social establishments? What do you mean?" Viggo asked innocently as if he had no idea what Ingrid was referring to.

"Yeah, you go ahead and play innocent. You know perfectly well what I mean. Don't you go anywhere near those places. We focus on what we have to do and that's it."

"Of course," Viggo raised his hands in a gesture of innocence before the implied accusation.

"Good. Meanwhile, I'll go and see what I can find out. A Ranger out alone passing through shouldn't draw too much attention."

"Let's hope not," Viggo said.

"I'm sure I won't draw attention, but you on the other hand…"

"Me? They won't even see me go in."

"I find it hard to believe you'll avoid confrontation."

"There's a time to fight and a time for subtlety. They both get results. Today it's time for the latter."

Ingrid stared at Viggo with wide eyes.

"You surprise me again. You even seem to be developing some common sense."

Viggo smiled and nodded.

"Little by little, the fruit ripens and the taste becomes sweeter and tastier."

"Don't compare yourself with fruit and don't get all poetic on me, you're confusing me. You haven't been drinking Nocean wine behind my back, have you?"

Viggo shook his head.

"Not at all. My head is clear, as it should be in order to face a mission. I know you don't need my good wishes, but good luck and be careful," he said.

"The fact that I don't need them doesn't mean I don't appreciate them," she replied with a softer look in her eyes than was usual in her.

Viggo bent toward her in his saddle.

"Then you won't mind if we part with a kiss of good luck."

Ingrid looked at him for an instant, then she agreed. She bent in her saddle toward him and kissed him.

For a moment the two Rangers enjoyed their love, the part they did not show openly in public, but it was not for lack of feeling. In fact, with each new day the peculiar relationship between them, which might mislead others, solidified a little more. They both felt better and better in their relationship, and even if it wasn't a very orthodox one, they liked it and it was working well for them.

They realized that the unlikelihood of them falling in love and developing a prosperous relationship was becoming a solid reality. This they could appreciate better when they were alone as they were now. Inside the group they each had their own defined dynamic and their own way of interacting with the others.

"Just don't do one of your tricks," Ingrid said, and she left before Viggo could deny the statement.

Ingrid spurred her horse and headed into the city. She had always found the name curious: Denmik. She wondered whether the city was called that in honor of someone named Den. Or perhaps Den-de-mik. Or maybe it was not a person or deity but a place. She would have to ask Egil when they returned, once they had finished their operation.

Egil had decided to call these small missions 'operations.' First, because they were not Rangers' missions ordered by Gondabar or King Thoran but their own. And secondly because they were not very long or complex tasks. Ingrid thought it was adequate, there would not be any confusion this way.

She arrived at the gates of the city and noticed that, although they were controlled by soldiers, they let people through without any trouble. They simply asked for their name and origin, as well as their reason for visiting the city, something quite normal in many cities. They were not at war and it did not look as if the soldiers were looking for anyone in particular that day. What she did notice was an officer who wrote some things down as certain people went through. She had the impression that perhaps they were writing down the names of people of interest to follow them.

Being a Ranger, they ought to let her through in any case, but she preferred not to draw attention. Perhaps some Visionary or Defender of the Blood was watching the access to the city. She needed to avoid altercations and act naturally. She was a passing Ranger, and that's what she told the soldiers at the gate, who greeted her respectfully and did not ask further questions. When she went in, she checked the officer and noticed that he had not written anything down, she liked that—it meant she would be left in peace.

Egil had told them to take extreme precautions, and that's what they had to do. Now everyone was aware of who was who, both the Panthers and their enemies, and the enemy would be on the alert. Catching them was going to be difficult. They were going to hide, and the Panthers were going to have a hard time drawing them out of their lairs. Besides, if they found them, they would come out with teeth and claws up front, so it would also be dangerous.

Besides, although Ingrid preferred to face them openly if they found them, Egil had warned her that what they were after was information, not fighting. They needed to know the next move planned by the immortal dragon and his followers. Only then could they stop him before any step was taken.

Facing up to some Defenders and Visionaries who did not have this information was useless and would warn their leaders, something that would not suit them, not before having a plan to finish them off. They needed to know what they were plotting, that was crucial. Without knowing, they would not be able to stop them. Egil had insisted on this and made it clear to the whole group.

Ingrid wandered the streets of the city, famous for its trade and the number of people from different origins that came to it. Most were either rich tradesmen from other kingdoms or messengers, emissaries, and the like—all spies most likely, working for foreign interests. There would also be Norghanian spies and informers spying for King Thoran, his brother, and his nobles. On second thought, there would also be those informing the Western league.

She remembered the conversation with Gondabar and how, even if they had not fully persuaded him of the real danger of the thousand-year-old dragon reincarnating, they had been able to arouse his interest and concern enough to give them permission to continue investigating. Ingrid knew they needed to find irrefutable evidence to convince their leader of what was happening. She was sure, just like Egil, Lasgol, and the others, that they were not mistaken, that the danger was real and that they had to eliminate the threat—not only for Norghana, but for all Tremia.

On the other hand, she also wanted to persuade him, the leader of the Rangers, of such danger, since otherwise they, the Snow Panthers, would simply be a handful of lunatics going after a demented goal, and if there was something Ingrid did not want to appear as, it was insane.

So, in order to find convincing evidence and obtain Gondabar's support, and even that of the King himself, she had made this her personal goal.

She was aware that she did not need to persuade them, that with what they had already found they could operate, especially with Egil's contacts, but she did not feel completely confident. Ingrid needed to do what was correct and get the support of the Rangers' leadership and the King. This is how she had been brought up and how she felt.

As she went along the streets filled with such a variety of people, she wondered whether she was too square-minded and honorable, as Viggo had told her on many occasions. Perhaps she was, but even so, she believed in hierarchy, in the institutions, and for her they were sacred. The only way to maintain order in a world that was as brutal and ruthless as the one they were living in was by having iron-clad, unbreakable institutions and hierarchy. Otherwise, everything would crumble and chaos would reign. Ingrid did not want to see that happen.

She sighed. She could not tolerate that, and she would fight with all her being to prevent it. She had to admit that she often found it very hard to see how Norghana, the country she loved so much, had such an immoral and useless king. Still, she knew it was better than letting the monarchy and army be destroyed, since that would cause a civil war, the end of the nation, and would ultimately open the door for other kingdoms to conquer Norghana—and they would, without a doubt.

Serving despot kings without honor was a tragedy and it gnawed at her guts, but it was better than suffering destruction and conquest at the hands of other foreign kings. One day Egil would be king, of this she was certain. Everyone in their group was. It was the fair thing and what must be. Egil would find a way. Until that day came, they would have to do everything in their power to protect the realm and save it from the dangers that threatened it, even if they had to swallow their pride so often. The alternative was simply not an option.

She wandered around the southern part of the city slowly, watching, picking up the atmosphere. Everything seemed quiet. She did not feel any tension or nervousness in the streets, and that made her feel more at ease. Cities had a way of transmitting what their inhabitants felt, and Ingrid liked to know. This way one could avoid getting into complicated situations without warning.

The next thing she did was head for the tower fort of the city watch. This was a military building, quite large, which was in the center of the southern part of the city. It was not as robust or impressive as the Count's castle, but it served as the city guard's fort, and the underground dungeons were usually full.

She left her horse by the trough in front of the fort and introduced herself.

"Specialist Ranger Ingrid Stenberg reporting," she said to the three guards standing at the door of the tower. She said it in a loud tone so that the whole street could hear her.

"Welcome to Denmik, Specialist Ranger," the officer at the gate saluted her as he came out of the door to greet her.

"Thank you, Officer," she said, looking straight into his eyes.

"Are you on a King's mission?" the officer asked her. It was not simple curiosity; if that were the case, he was required to provide Ingrid with all the help she might need.

Ingrid shook her head.

"I'm just passing through," she raised her voice so that everyone would know she was not there for anything important.

"Can the city guard of Denmik offer you anything?"

"Water and some food is all I need. I'll be on my way east at once," she lied, still loud enough for anyone to hear.

"Very well, we'll make sure to give you what you need."

Ingrid looked over her shoulder out of the corner of her eye and could make out at least three characters spying on her. Their interest in her was obvious—they were staring at her blatantly. They might be hiding their interest for information with looks that might be mistaken for desire, but Ingrid knew her cold Norghanian beauty did not arouse much interest in the south. These people were interested in what she might be doing there.

She hoped her little theatrical act would work. That way she would have no trouble moving around the city. A Ranger passing through did not awake enough interest to be followed. Not even in this singular city.

She went into the fortress with the officer and waited until they brought her the supplies she had asked for. Since she was not in a hurry, she ate in the canteen with the watch guards and no one bothered her. Soldiers respected the Rangers very much—they respected and feared them. They also envied them, but luckily respect and fear almost always trumped envy so there were usually no altercations.

Ingrid waited a good while before leaving the fort, and when she did, she made sure she had not attracted any interest. She did not see anyone watching her. Her little ruse appeared to have been effective. She could now go into the city and take a look at the interesting areas.

Afterwards she would meet Viggo and they would begin their night hunt.

Chapter 22

Viggo entered the city through one of the side gates. He made sure he went in at a moment when the three guards stationed there were busy, and the moment came—two of them were asleep from exhaustion and boredom, and the third one was trying to pierce with his spear a small rodent that was running around.

They did not notice that Viggo had slipped through under cover of the gloom and the shadows of the surrounding buildings. He always experienced a feeling of triumph when he slipped past a guard or watch without being seen. And more so if this happened in a city, since his forte were the forests and mountains and the city presented added difficulties he had to avoid.

He blended into the dark, always flat against the rocky wall of one of the buildings, and kept moving. Every time he had to melt into the shadows he did so with gusto, because that was where he felt better, stalking, ready to act if necessary. His friends thought he liked drawing attention to himself, but they were wrong. What Viggo really loved was passing close to his enemies, like a ghost, before killing them.

He smiled as he went on, moving away from the entrance and going deeper into the city. It was true that he also liked to stand out, to be recognized, for bards and troubadours to sing his epic feats in taverns and courts and to have odes created after his fame to cheer soldiers and warriors. Not only would he be the best Norghanian Assassin, he could be that and make the whole realm know, even nearby realms. He did not see why it could not be like that. A little notoriety might represent a little more danger, but he did not fear the risk.

He was not too worried about the operation he had to carry out in the city. He did not think it would pose a great difficulty, although things always tended to get complicated. But even so, he did not believe they would get so complicated as to trouble him. What did cheer him about this incursion was being able to spend more time alone with Ingrid. It was something he was always thankful for. So, he was feeling happy, and every now and then a smile appeared on his face. In fact, he was delighted—he could enjoy spending time with Ingrid and, more than likely, deal with danger. What else could he ask for in life?

"A lot of gold," he muttered under his breath as an afterthought, and he ran on in the dark of a secondary alley.

One day he would have a pile of gold and live like a king. He would buy himself a duchy with a large walled castle and at least three tall, round towers. Of course, the duchy would come with a lot of land, servants, farmers, cattle raisers, and in general many peasants who would love him for his generosity and charisma. He would be an old-fashioned lord but a generous one that was loved by his people. Yes, he would have that someday. Besides, by then he would already be famous and feared throughout Tremia so he would live as quietly as a Mountain Troll in his winter cave.

He went on deeper into the city like an evil spirit, hiding in the darkness, passing by people without them noticing. In time he would have everything; he had other plans besides being a Ranger. Unlike some of his friends, one day he would leave the Rangers and become rich and famous. Ingrid did not see it so clearly but he thought it was better than to die serving the Kingdom on some crazy mission for the ridiculous pay they were given. He did not see anything wrong with having higher expectations than being a Ranger.

Protecting the realm and the poor and helpless in Norghana was all very well, but one could aspire to more. Maybe others did not, but he, Viggo Kron, certainly did. Those who came from the most absolute poverty, from living in stinky sewers in the city slums like him, understood. Those raised in good families with hot food on the table and a good roof over their heads every day of their lives did not understand as well. They were happy with much less. Those who had suffered greatly wanted to go further.

He went into an even darker street and headed to the meeting point. He had memorized the map of the city and handled himself pretty well. Egil had taught them how to memorize city maps. He had a curious system which consisted of dividing the city into squares and identifying the main street in each one. Although it had been a bit difficult for Viggo to learn how to do this, he had to admit it was a useful method, especially on night incursions where there was no chance of taking out the map to check it in the dark. Besides, a good Ranger Assassin never stopped to consult, it was too dangerous. An

Assassin watched and acted and never got distracted.

Thinking about the know-it-all, he realized he did expect Egil to become King of Norghana one day; he could use their friendship to obtain a duchy. That was the least he could do after Viggo helped him gain the throne, was it not? Besides, Viggo was sure Egil would be king someday and that he was going to help him achieve it. It was only a matter of time, of waiting for the right opportunity to appear. Egil was very intelligent and was waiting for the right moment, even if it seemed he was not too interested in the throne. Viggo knew he was, however. Egil watched constantly, he never missed anything. The moment would come and Egil would seize it. And in that moment, he would need his friends, and he would need an exceptional Assassin like Viggo, and Viggo would be there.

He and his friends would help him, and once Egil was king Viggo would ask him for his duchy. Unfortunately, knowing Egil and his honorable, straight side, he would most likely not give him a duchy because of all that nonsense of not having favorites among friends. Viggo did not believe in that kind of thing, if he could get something out of his friendship with Egil he did not see why he should not. After all, he had to put up with the wise guy and his convoluted blabber, not to speak of his plans, which although successful, were always filled with unexpected obstacles to overcome. Thinking again, he should be charging Egil for having to put up with him already. When Viggo saw him again he was going to ask him for a salary per season, and if he did not pay then let the rest put up with him.

He took a right turn into a better lit street. He stopped and looked for the shadows to continue moving unseen. By the time he had crossed the whole street he had already convinced himself that Egil would definitely not give him a duchy.

"I'm surrounded by people with good intentions, but they're not roguish enough. Thank goodness I'm a lot smarter than all of them. Smart from living on a dark, slum street of a dangerous city, like this one," he said to himself.

He continued along the city in the middle of the night. He saw a couple of thugs he did not like and decided to take a detour and see whether they followed him. It was practically impossible that they had seen him, but just in case. If what they said about this city was true—and Viggo believed the stories—there were many dangerous spies here. Spies were smart and hard to fool, so even though Viggo was very self-confident, he preferred not to take unnecessary risks. One thing did not rule out the other. To be the best, one had to behave like the best, and arrogance and blind trust were inadmissible. Viggo knew this and never made mistakes.

He arrived at the square and looked around from his hiding place behind a barrel full of rain water in front of a house that looked on the entrance to the square. He listened. There was barely any noise, and this made him feel easier.

The square was deserted with the exception of a cloaked and hooded figure waiting beside the great stone fountain. Viggo recognized his beloved at once. One glance was all he needed—he was sure he would recognize her even if she were disguised as a lady at court or a soldier of the Royal Guard. He would recognize her wherever she hid.

He approached Ingrid quickly, revealing himself as little as possible.

"Everything in order?" he asked her when he was beside her.

Ingrid nodded, "Everything's in order."

"Shall we proceed with the plan?"

"Yes. I've seen a couple suspicious characters but I don't think they pose too much of a threat. I gave them the slip a while back."

Viggo nodded. He was not completely sure Ingrid had given them the slip; there were skilled informers here, and even though she was an excellent fighter she was not as experienced at evading watchers. He hoped she was not wrong, or else they could be in trouble.

"It's the third house on the north street. I've marked it with the sign of the fox," Ingrid told him.

"Good. I'll find it without a problem."

"D'you want me to intervene? I can go in from the ground floor while you go in through the back or the second floor."

"I'm tempted, I'd love to assault a house with you."

"Then let's do it," Ingrid said, looking eager to act.

"The thing is, it's not the best option… it's much better to use a more subtle approach. If you go into the house knocking down the door, they'll realize we're attacking and pull back and even get away. That's not what we want. We want to catch them by surprise."

Ingrid thought for a moment.

"Yeah, perhaps that's not the best choice. They might escape or

165

put up more resistance than necessary."

Viggo nodded. "It's better to use a stealthier approach, that of an Assassin, and reach the target without them realizing and having time to react."

Ingrid realized he was right and resigned herself to not enter by force.

"Fine, we'll do it your way. I'll be nearby for the extraction."

"Good. I'll let you know when I've rendered the target useless."

They looked at one another briefly, hoping nothing bad would happen to the other.

"Be careful and don't be overconfident," Ingrid whispered

"I'm good, not foolish. I won't be overconfident."

Ingrid drew him to her and kissed him hard.

"Go, and come back without a single scratch."

Viggo smiled.

"Not even a graze," he promised.

An instant later they parted and each one headed to take their positions.

Viggo watched the house for a while. He had identified it easily— the sign of the fox was unmistakable on the stone wall. Ingrid had used a piece of white chalk. Once the mission was over it would be easily erased and there would be no sign left that anything had ever happened there.

The house had three floors and was pretty large. It had a main door and six windows, two on each floor opening onto the facade. There were no lights on in the two lower floors, but there was light in the third floor. It was not in a room that looked out on the front but further in. Viggo calculated the length of the house: it went from the street they were on to the one at the back. He calculated three rooms per floor—it was a large house.

He could not see any guards or watchmen posted in the vicinity, so he would not have any trouble accessing the building. This concerned him a little—it was too easy for someone like him. The target was a Visionary deputy who had to have an escort and a watch. Maybe they were hidden inside the house. That was a possibility.

He decided not to take any risks and find out. He slipped through the shadows and reached the side of the house. There was a narrow gap between this one and the next house on the left. It was not even a passage but a simple piece of land that had not been built on. A separation between the two houses.

Viggo went into this gap and started climbing the side of the house carefully and in silence. Because the house was made of rock and had been built quite hastily, there were holes between the rocks that allowed him to find footholds. With amazing skill and agility, Viggo climbed the wall without being seen. He flattened his body against the wall as he went up so no unwelcome eyes might see him.

He reached a window on the second floor, stood on the ledge, and looked inside. He did not see anything suspicious. The room was in shadows and he could only make out some light at the back of the house. He took out his throwing knife and, careful not to make any sound, proceeded to open the window. It was locked from the inside, but this was no problem for Viggo. Using his knife skillfully, he opened the window with barely any noise.

An instant later he was inside the house. He stood still until his eyes became used to the little light inside. He listened attentively in case he heard footsteps in his direction. Nothing. He was in a bedroom. He went to the door, which was shut, and opened it a crack. He peeked out into the corridor with his left eye. The doorway where he stood was in shadows, but at the other end of the corridor there was light.

He left the room and, crouching by the left wall of the corridor, Viggo moved toward the light. Where there was light, there were people—that was a fact. As he moved forward in the corridor, he passed two pairs of doors. He stopped in front of one pair of doors and listened for anyone inside. He did not hear anything and the rooms were dark because there was no light under the door, so they were either empty or their occupants were sleeping and were doing so silently without snoring.

He continued moving forward. He could not check all the rooms of the house one by one, it would take him too long and it might alert his prey. He was there to hunt and he was not going to let his target get away, so he would not risk encountering anyone in one of those rooms. Although Viggo was used to dispatching his enemies swiftly and in silence in most cases, he might be so unlucky as to make an unexpected noise and be discovered approaching his target.

If he was discovered, there would be fighting and the prey would escape. Or try to, but Ingrid was posted outside the house, and if the target ran away, she would catch him outside. That was the good thing about working with a partner, if one person did not manage to catch the target the other person still had a chance to do so. Besides, Ingrid would make sure he would not escape even if she had to riddle him with arrows. Although that was not a good idea, since they needed the target alive in order to get information out of him.

He went on along the corridor and reached the back side of the building on the second floor where there was light. He realized that the light was coming from some stairs that accessed both the lower and upper levels. There was also light that came out of a door that was ajar and which had to correspond to the back room that looked out on the back street.

Viggo stopped to listen. There were voices coming from the room and also from the floor below. He counted five different voices, maybe six. Things were getting interesting. He took out his two long knives, and to not take any risks he also took out his paralyzing poison and soaked the blades with it. If for any reason someone escaped after being cut, something that rarely happened with Viggo, the victim would not run very far.

He smiled. He was the best Assassin, and he was the best because he did not overestimate himself. He had learned that as a child. No matter how good you were at something, you should never overestimate your skills because there would always be someone better, or circumstances might deal you a bad hand. Both had happened to him before joining the Rangers, and he had had a terrible experience. So, he never thought too highly of his abilities, no matter how good he was now.

He had two options: go into the room, or go downstairs. It took him a second to decide that it was better to clean out this room before going downstairs. Better not to leave enemies behind who might surprise you from the back. He would deal with the ground level once he finished with this one.

He glanced quickly into the room and saw two men—Visionaries. They were standing by the window, looking out as if they were watching the street. Viggo had already guessed there would be a watch, so he was not surprised.

The attack needed to be swift and hard so the Visionaries would not raise any alarm. He prepared and waited for the right moment. An Assassin's patience had to be unparallel, because success depended on it in many situations. Haakon had taught him this at the

Camp, and he remembered it well. Luckily, Viggo had a lot of patience, and he never lost it when things became difficult. It was one of his best qualities in his opinion; that, and the fact that he had an innate skill for anything to do with killing someone.

The two Visionaries started to talk and Viggo knew the time had come to act. He went into the room like a bolt of lightning without making the slightest sound. He lunged at the two men watching out the window. They had their short swords with dragon-head pommels in their scabbards at their belts. Viggo would not give them the chance to use them.

He hit the Visionary on the left on the back of his head, a dull blow with the butt of his knife. The man fell to the floor at once. The other one began to turn toward Viggo. He never finished the movement. With another dull blow, this time on the temple, he left the Visionary senseless as he fell to the floor beside his comrade.

Viggo checked the room for any other danger. It was a study with several shelves with books and a large table at the far end with an elegant chair. There was no one else there. He did not want to take any unnecessary risk, so he tied up and gagged both men with gags and ropes he carried ready with him. He did not expect them to wake up for a good while, but it was better to be safe than sorry. There was nothing worse than an enemy coming to and raising the alarm right in the middle of a stealthy incursion.

He left the room, closing the door behind him, and started going down the stairs, making sure that every step he took on the wooden stairs did not make the feared sound of a creaking step. Walking with the lightness of a gazelle was not easy, but Viggo handled it calmly with concentration.

He reached the end of the stairs and checked the corridor on the ground floor. It was deserted and covered in shadow. There did not appear to be anyone there. The room on his right, which was immediately below the one he had just left the two watchmen in, was lit up, the door ajar. Viggo guessed there would be guards here too, so he prepared to act.

He approached the door and took a peek inside. To his surprise, he found the room empty, which puzzled him. Why leave a light on in an empty room? The answer came to his mind in a moment: it was a trap.

He turned around and found two Visionaries with their short

swords in hand lunging at him. They had come out of the two nearest rooms in the corridor. Before they took their last step to attack him, Viggo outdid them and rolled over his head, landing at their feet.

The sword with the dragon-head pommel of the one nearest to him on the right swept a side-blow above Viggo's head. The sword of the one on his left came down, seeking to split his head in two.

Viggo lifted his arm and blocked the sword coming down on him with his knife. Next, he stood up as fast as a snake attacks, and buried his knife in the Visionary's neck. The other one was raising his sword to strike again, but Viggo kicked him in the face. The man received the full blow and took two steps backwards in the corridor.

Before he could react and sound the alarm, Viggo threw his knife at him with great force and it buried in his heart. The Visionary put his hands to the knife and fell on his knees. Viggo slid forward and finished him off so he would not cry out. Both men were left on the floor, dead. They had not made any noise, but a fight was a fight, and the sound of steel on steel could travel for leagues. In a house like that it was more than possible it had been heard. He would have to be even more cautious.

The target was on the third floor.

It was time to go and get him.

The problem was, it was very possible they would be waiting for him.

Chapter 23

Viggo was about to go upstairs when he noticed movement at the end of the corridor on the other side of the house. It was dark so he was unable to see who it was, but he was sure he had detected movement in the entrance hall.

He decided to go and check it out. He did not like leaving loose ends. If he went upstairs, whoever was below might follow and attack him from behind when he least expected it. That would not be good for his health. He ran down the corridor as silent and stealthy as a leopard. He wanted to surprise whoever he had heard without giving them a chance to react.

He reached the end of the corridor and saw that it opened onto a hall with a large cupboard and a chair that faced the entrance door. There he found a Visionary who was watching out of a window in the dark. He was glad they had not followed Ingrid's suggestion, since that Visionary would have seen them as they arrived.

The watchman was looking toward the street and had not noticed Viggo's presence behind him. This puzzled him. He looked around to see whether there was any other Visionary lurking in the shadows, but he saw no one else. He decided to attack the man from behind, finish him off in a heartbeat and move on. He took the first step and his ankle brushed against something. Almost without thinking, Viggo stopped on the spot and stood very still.

He looked down and saw what his leg had brushed. It was a thin cord, which meant a trap had been set and that the Visionary was the bait. He smiled to himself—very clever. Carefully, he withdrew his leg slowly and then stepped over the cord without activating the trap.

He went for the Visionary, who turned to him with his short sword unsheathed. He tried to attack Viggo, but it was already too late. Viggo lunged at the watchman and knocked him down, then he buried his knife in the man's heart as they were falling. The man died with nothing but a deep last breath.

Suddenly, from inside the cupboard in the hall came two Visionaries who lunged at Viggo. The attack caught him by surprise—he had not been expecting that.

"Die! Our all-powerful lord demands it!" cried one.

"Death to the unworthy!" cried the other.

Viggo reacted quickly, leaping to one side and rolling in order to avoid the first two blows that sought his body and make time to get back on his feet. The movement had to be quick and well balanced, but this was no problem for Viggo, in fact, it was his specialty.

Once he was standing again, he blocked one sword with his knife in his right hand and deflected the other with his other knife. Before they could attack him again, Viggo delivered a tremendous kick to the stomach of one of the Visionaries and another kick to the supporting leg of the other. The first man doubled up in pain, and Viggo killed him with a powerful stab. The second one, unbalanced, stumbled, and by the time he had recovered Viggo had already jumped on him like a hungry tiger and knocked him down on the floor. He finished him off with a stab to the heart.

He got to his feet and looked all around in case there were any other surprises. He had to admit they had caught him by surprise, and he had not liked it at all. He was not a fan of this kind of unpleasant surprise. He snorted. His reflexes and skill had saved him. Well, that and the fact that the Visionaries were not great fighters. They were clumsy and blinded by their beliefs, so they were not great rivals. But they did pose a problem in large numbers or when they attacked from behind.

If he had suspected before that the target knew that Viggo was inside his house and after him, Viggo was now sure. The incursion had not been as silent as he would have liked. But that was life—things did not always turn out as one expected them to. Often things went sideways no matter how hard you tried to do your job well. As Egil used to say, 'the enemy also thinks, and sometimes is more intelligent and has more resources than we'd like.'

Viggo went up by the front stairs, not the ones at the back, to the third floor. He went up slowly, on the alert. They would be waiting for him upstairs, without a doubt. He started along the corridor toward the room at the back with the light on. It had to be the target's study, and he would most likely be there. Or it might be another trap. Whatever it was, Viggo was not going to let himself be so easily surprised again.

He went by one door and heard a sound behind it. He stopped. The door burst open and a Visionary appeared with his sword in his hand.

"The immortal dragon will have your heart!"

Viggo turned sideways at once and the Visionary's thrust brushed parallel to his torso without touching him. He stretched his arm and buried his knife into the man's neck with a dull blow. The Visionary died on the floor a moment later.

He continued walking. This operation was going pretty wrong, something Viggo hated. He took every step with all his senses alert. He was approaching the room at the end of the corridor where the light was coming from. One of Drugan's deputies was waiting for him, it was for this deputy they had come for and they would not leave without him.

Another door opened suddenly on his left.

A Visionary came out of a darkened bedroom and leapt onto him. "Our lord will reincarnate and be invincible!" he cried.

Viggo stepped back swiftly and the Visionary completely failed in the attack. He was left in the middle of the corridor, stumbling, and he did not fall down by a hair's breath. Viggo did not let him recover. He kicked him on the back of the knee and the attacker half fell to his knees when his leg gave out. A moment later Viggo had grabbed his hair, pulled it back, and slit his throat in the blink of an eye.

"Not happening," Viggo whispered into the man's ear as he fell dead to the floor.

He continued down the corridor and rapidly arrived at the room the Visionary's deputy was in. The door was open; the light was coming from inside, but there was no sound.

Viggo stopped by the door, his back against the wall on the right of it. He waited a moment, listening. He was sure this was a trap. If he burst into attack, he would most certainly land in the middle of an ambush, an ambush that would be almost impossible to escape from alive. Viggo knew he was an exceptional Assassin, but even the most skilled Assassin could be killed in a good ambush.

He continued to listen. One of the things he had learned at the Shelter while he was getting his Specialties was to perceive different breathing patterns. This was a complicated discipline but very useful for an Assassin. He concentrated, shut his eyes, and listened attentively. He was trying to detect how many people were in the room and their location based on their breathing.

It was not at all easy, but it was efficient. Viggo knew that no man

173

or woman could stop breathing, no matter how hard they wanted to hide their presence from an enemy. Or, in any case, they could not do so for a long period of time. So, he listened, just like Engla had taught him. As he thought about her, he sent her good wishes for a prompt recovery so she could go on teaching others like she had done with him and Astrid. And also, because he wanted to fight her again, once she was recuperated, and defeat her.

He concentrated and focused his hearing. Viggo did not have Lasgol's advantage with his *Owl's Hearing* skill, but he was able to distinguish close breathing, particularly beside an open door. It did not take him long to locate three different breathings. The clearest was just on the other side of the wall, in the same position he was in, no doubt with a weapon in hand waiting for him to cross the threshold.

The second breathing was a little further back, diagonal with the door. Based on its distance from the door and the fact that it was diagonal to it, it was surely an archer that would release the moment he walked in. He would have a short bow, spear, or throwing knife most likely. The Visionaries carried short swords, so it had to be a throwing knife.

Finally, he detected a weak breathing, which he had not even noticed at first. It was coming from the back of the room, and that was why he had not heard it initially. He could barely hear it. It had to be the deputy. Viggo wondered whether it would be Vingar or Xoltran, the warlocks who accompanied and served Drugan. Whichever it was would give him trouble—serious trouble, since both were good fighters.

The moment to act had come. He had already analyzed the situation; he knew it was a trap and that most likely a warlock was waiting inside to kill him with two of his minions. Still, he was not at all worried, guessing what the enemy had planned always made him feel good. It was like hunting the one who wanted to hunt him. Besides, he was the best Assassin in Norghana and he had to prove himself.

He took out one of the poisons he carried in his Assassin's belt and poured it on the blades of both his knives and his throwing knife. He got ready to storm the room. He backed up silently a couple paces in the corridor and took a run to the open door. An instant before bursting in he took a big leap and crossed the threshold through the top, as if he had been shot from a crossbow.

As he flew through the air into the room, he saw the Visionary waiting by the door deliver a two-handed blow with his sword at about half height, intending to cut him in two at the waist. The edge of the sword passed below Viggo's body as he started to fall back to the floor and ended his leap rolling over his head. The Visionary waiting by the window, at a diagonal from the door, threw a knife at him, which buried itself into the cupboard at the back, a handspan from Viggo's head.

"Good try, but not good enough!" Viggo smiled.

"Death to the heretic!" cried the third man, standing behind a desk covered with scrolls.

Viggo moved with lightning speed and attacked the Visionary who was looking to deliver another thrust with his short sword. He deflected it with the knife in his left hand as he buried the one in his right into the man's heart. The Visionary moaned in pain and fell to his knees. He died on the floor.

With a sideways move, Viggo avoided a second knife the other Visionary threw at him.

"You should practice more often," Viggo said sarcastically.

The Visionary drew his short sword and lifted it above his head as he started running at Viggo. By the time he reached the Assassin, the Visionary was already dead. He collapsed on the floor with Viggo's throwing knife buried deep in his heart.

The Visionary cried out as he died and fell down.

"See? That's a good throw, I've practiced it a lot," said Viggo with a wink.

The warlock came out from behind the desk with a long sword with a dragon head on the pommel. It was not Vingar or Xoltran, which intrigued Viggo. He was wearing a cloak with a dull silver hood, but the hood was down so Viggo could clearly see the warlock's features. He looked Norghanian, with blue eyes, long blond hair, and a strong chin. He looked like a Norghanian warrior but without the usual brutality, since he was thin and not very tall, in his mid-thirties. He seemed to trust his skill, because there was no fear in his eyes.

"You're new," said Viggo casually while he retrieved his throwing knife.

"My name is Zirken, and I've been in the service of my lord and master for a long time."

"Pleased to meet you, I'm Viggo," he smiled as if this were a casual, friendly meeting. He saluted and stood before the warlock, four paces away. He let his arms fall to his sides so his knives were along his thighs, in a non-aggressive attitude but ready to act as soon as necessary.

"I know who you are...who you all are and what you seek."

"Great, that makes things a lot easier. I like to be recognized wherever I go."

"Perhaps because you're a fool. Only someone full of himself is stupid enough to announce it," Zirken replied.

"Well, it looks like we have a philosopher Visionary. This gets better by the day. And here I was thinking you were all a bunch of fanatic lunatics with no sense of humor," Viggo said.

"I serve my lord and our cause. I'm not a fanatic or a lunatic. I'm not a thinker and least of all a philosopher. But I am learned, unlike you, who I can tell has come from the most ignoble sewers."

Viggo's face showed surprise.

"Besides being philosophical, you're a seer. This is most entertaining."

"There's not much to see, it's written on your face," the warlock said.

"A great honor. The sewers where I grew up are the stinkiest in Norghana. But I got out of them and made good friends. One of them, learned like you, wants to have a friendly chat with you."

"I will reveal nothing. My lord's plans will be carried out successfully. A new era will begin in Tremia, one where the all-powerful lord will rule like the immortal god he is," the warlock said.

"Yeah, yeah, I know the drill. All Tremia will burn, he'll make slaves of all men who aren't of the true blood, and a bunch of other nonsense. I've heard it all before, your preachers are very insistent."

"You can mock all you want, but it's what will happen. The preachers only tell what will happen because everyone must know what will come when the all-powerful lord is reborn and rules over the earth."

"I don't think that's going to happen," Viggo said, shaking his head.

"Dergha-Sho-Blaska, the Immortal Dragon, he who sleeps when he should have died, has awakened. We'll provide him with a body where his spirit will be reborn. The all-powerful lord will rise, immortal, and rule over men."

"I don't think that'll happen. You haven't realized it yet, but I can assure you that's not going to happen."

"Who's going to stop it? You and your fellow Rangers?" Zirken asked with incredulity and certain sarcasm.

"Of course. That's why I'm here."

"You won't be able to stop him. The forces against you are too powerful. You'll fail."

"This isn't the first time we've faced powerful forces, and I'm afraid it won't be the last, but here we are," Viggo replied with a shrug.

"This time you face an immortal dragon that has awakened and will rise to rule over the world. No-one can stand against that. You can only accept fate and serve the new all-powerful lord."

"I'm very good at killing vermin too, be they centuries old or not. So, tell me where he is so we can end this pleasant chat," Viggo said with a grin.

"I will tell you nothing about my lord. Our fate is written in fire. We are the servants of the all-powerful, and we will help him become the owner of the whole world. The age of man is coming to its end," he said, opening his arms.

Viggo snorted in exasperation.

"You're really stubborn with that little message about the end of the world. Where the heck is the Dragon Orb? It's a simple question. Answer it!"

"I'll die before revealing his whereabouts to whoever wants to destroy my lord."

"Didn't you say he's immortal and all powerful? What are you afraid of?" Vigo taunted him to see if he could learn anything.

"He will be as soon as he is reborn and rises."

"So, he isn't yet. You'd better tell me where he is, or you'll end up like the rest of these fanatic lunatics," he said, waving his knives at the two dead Visionaries on the floor.

"I'll serve my lord to the death. You'll gain nothing from me," said Zirken, and he rushed forward, brandishing his sword as he murmured some arcane spell under his breath.

Viggo reacted and got ready to fight. Drugan's warlocks knew how to fight with weapons and magic. They were very dangerous. He had already experienced that. This new enemy would also mean trouble, so he would have to be wary.

Zirken delivered a thrust, which Viggo deflected with his right knife. He countered with his left knife and went straight for the warlock's heart. Zirken opened his mouth and roared. The sound was followed by a wave of power that deflected Viggo's arm outward, as if he had been hit with a shovel.

"Ouch!" he cried, pulling his arm back and retreating to make sure it was not broken.

Zirken delivered a combination of slashes to the neck, followed by a thrust to the heart with his long sword. Viggo blocked and deflected the attacks skillfully. The warlock was skilled with the sword, but he was better with his knives.

"I see my lord Drugan warned me for a reason. You are dangerous, talented fighters."

"He did not warn you enough. You're going to die here unless you tell me where that little dragon of yours is."

"The only one who's going to die here today is you," Zirken said, pointing at Viggo's heart with his sword.

Viggo attacked with lightning speed. Zirken defended himself from the cuts and knife thrusts with expert movements. He was a good swordsman. He finished with another roar, opening his mouth wide and stretching his neck, directing the roar at his rival. An invisible force hit Viggo with tremendous force. He flew backward and hit the cupboard at the back of the room. He fell to the floor, stunned.

"We of the true blood have an ancestral power which men like you can't begin to understand," the warlock said, coming toward him slowly.

"You're nothing... but a warlock... with some tricks... up your sleeve," Viggo muttered, trying to get back to his feet.

"It's no trick. It's dragon power, because we're his descendants among men. His blood runs through our veins."

"Even you... can't believe... that nonsense..." Viggo replied, already standing and ready to keep fighting. His head and back hurt from the blow, but he did not think he had broken anything, or at least he hoped not.

"I believe it, of course, because it's the truth. You sacrilegious, ignorant fools don't understand, but it's all the same. The future is written in fire and can't be changed. My lord will rule and we, his blood descendants, his faithful servants, will rule with him."

"I'd rather be a king myself and not serve another," Viggo replied, lunging at Zirken as he was coming to catch him by surprise before he could use his magic. The attack made the warlock stop to defend himself with the sword. Viggo finished his combination of knife cuts and thrusts, which were all deflected, with a kick in the stomach of the Visionary deputy.

"Argh…" Zirken was left breathless from the kick and stepped back to get out of Viggo's range of action and not be cut with his knives. Viggo seized the moment and attacked again with fury. Zirken's defense began to falter and he found himself in danger. With a nimble movement he leapt over the desk and took shelter behind it.

Viggo took two steps back and then ran, leaped, and flew over the table, but Zirken was already expecting that and under cover of the desk he opened his mouth and released his magic. A roar came out, upward, just at the peak of Viggo's leap, and the forceful wave hit him and threw him off hard. He crashed in the center of the room with a hard blow.

"Blasted… roar…" he moaned, sore all over.

"The moment has come to finish you off and continue my lord's work," Zirken said and rose from behind the desk.

Viggo was dragging himself along the floor like a black adder toward the open door.

"Don't you dare flee, you vermin!" Zirken shouted at him and came after him.

Viggo reached the door and went out.

Zirken ran after him. When he was halfway across the room, Viggo's head appeared at the door.

"Peekaboo, little warlock," he taunted.

Zirken stopped his advance and opened his mouth. A roar came out seeking Viggo's mocking face.

Viggo heard the roar and sheltered behind the wall. The force of the roar hit the wall and part of it went out the open door, but it did not touch Viggo.

"Don't hide, you coward!"

Viggo appeared again just for an instant and lashed out with his right arm before hiding again.

The warlock opened his mouth to use his magic but could not.

He cried out as he looked at his torso. Viggo's throwing knife was buried to the hilt just above his heart.

"Who said I was hiding?" Viggo said as he poked his head in, smiling. "By the way, it's poisoned. I poured some more poison on the blade, so you won't feel your legs soon. Sorry for the bad news."

With a look of horror, Zirken understood the situation. He released another roar, which Viggo avoided by hiding behind the wall.

"These walls are well-made, they're solid," he commented. "That's lucky. Well, for me—for you not so much."

"You can mock all you want, since the final victory will be ours. You won't be able to stop it."

"That remains to be seen," Viggo replied.

One of Zirken's legs began to fail as he went to the window and opened it.

"Only those of true blood will enjoy the time that is coming."

"I wouldn't do that if I were you, you'll break your back," Viggo warned him from the door, seeing the warlock was going to jump down to the street.

"See you never," the warlock said and jumped.

Viggo ran to the window and heard a tremendous roar, followed by a muffled moan. He reached the window and looked out. Zirken was getting to his feet; he had survived the jump. Viggo could not believe his eyes—he did not seem to have broken anything when he should have broken both legs and arms. It had to have been because of his magic; somehow, he had used his roar to break the blow of the fall.

"Wow… that was smart…" Viggo said under his breath.

Zirken looked at Viggo with a triumphant smile and prepared to escape.

An Earth Arrow hit his torso. It burst into smoke, dirt, and stunning and blinding compounds that left him completely numb. A figure approached the warlock at a run.

Ingrid knocked him out with a right hook.

Chapter 24

A few days later, as promised, Eicewald brought them a tome of spells. He called it a Basic Magic Grimoire.

Lasgol and Camu focused all of their attention on the tome at once—they were fascinated with the book, and being able to learn spells would be very useful. Creating skills was so hard and took such a long time and so much effort that learning them from a book almost seemed like cheating.

"This tome contains basic spells and enchantments that any person with the Gift can learn. They're easy and functional, the kind of spells known as basic or neutral magic, which don't require any specific inclination or affinity to any type of magic. It also doesn't require whoever uses it to have reached an advanced level of magic. That's why it'll be good for us. We use it as a rule with all Ice Magi when they begin their journey in the magical world."

"Oh, I like that!" said Lasgol, cheered by what he was hearing.

I learn everything, Camu messaged with his usual optimism and infinite self-confidence.

"On the other hand, the spells aren't very powerful, but for experimenting and learning I can promise they're very efficient."

I want powerful spells, Camu messaged, annoyed.

"And I want you to have a bigger head," Lasgol replied.

Camu looked at him blankly and blinked twice.

My head good size.

Lasgol put his hand to his forehead.

"Ice Gods give me patience!" he muttered under his breath.

Eicewald could not hold back a chuckle.

"I believe that, for this exercise, these spells are most appropriate," he told Camu as he opened the tome.

Okay, he messaged, along with a certain disappointment.

Lasgol, on the other hand, was eager. "Let's get started."

"Good. This spell is both basic and useful," Eicewald said, pointing his finger at the tome.

Lasgol looked at the two pages of the book, filled with words written with elaborate handwriting and two drawings in color: one on each page, which represented the use of the spell. The drawings had gold and silver hues and the titles at the top of both pages did too. They caught the eye at once with their faint glow.

"It's beautiful..." Lasgol commented, gaping without realizing.

"The artwork is finely done. It's not an original, but it is a pretty accurate copy."

"Those colors, gold and silver... how they draw the eye..." Lasgol muttered.

"It's the color of magic. It's always been represented with gold and silver hues."

"Aren't there any more colors in magic?" Lasgol asked, puzzled. His own magic flashed green.

"There are of course, but basic magic, elemental, is always represented in those two colors. This has been the case since the beginning of the time of humans and their magic. There's no exception, or at least I don't know of one. I've never seen it in any tome of knowledge. There must be a reason why it's always represented in these two colors, but I don't know what it is."

I much silver, Camu messaged.

"What do you mean by that, Camu?" Lasgol asked him, not fully understanding.

My magic be silver.

"That's most peculiar..." Eicewald commented. "I have noticed that you shine silver when you use your magic, and there must be a reason for it..."

"I think I've also seen him do it in gold once or twice, but faintly," Lasgol added, "but I honestly don't remember when."

"Interesting. It could be significant," said Eicewald.

"Lately it's always been silver when he uses his magic," Lasgol said, scratching his head, trying to remember.

"There's no clear theory about this, so we magi can only speculate. It's believed, or rather certain magi believe, that the two most powerful types of magic, and the base for all other types of magic, are the silver and gold. That's why they're commonly used to represent spells of magical knowledge. But as I said, there's nothing written anywhere to confirm it. They're magi beliefs."

"No one knows what type of magic they are?" Lasgol asked.

"No, but perhaps someday someone will find out. A scholar, or yourselves," Eicewald replied, smiling.

"Us?" Lasgol wondered, uncertain.

We find out. We smart, Camu messaged immediately.

"I can attest to that, both of you," Eicewald nodded.

"What language is this spell written in? I can't understand it," Lasgol said, worried because he could not read the text.

"It's an ancient one, known as the Arcane Language. The magi created this secret language so that what they wrote down in their tomes would only be understood by themselves or other magi."

"Wow… and there's only one Arcane Language?" Lasgol wondered, since in all of Tremia there were many different languages.

"When a secret language began to be used to hide magic, there were different ones created for that purpose in far-away corners of the continent. The different groups of magi started using their own language, developed by each group. This way each magic society had its own secret language to hide their spells and magical language."

Very smart.

"Seems like a good way to hide what they knew, yes," Lasgol nodded. "Egil has told me something about this. He's also into societies, not magical ones but secret groups that didn't want their knowledge or deals discovered. They invented their own secret languages to communicate between them."

Eicewald nodded.

"It's a widely spread practice, that of hiding information within secret languages, in many areas, not all of them honorable."

"Yes, criminal organizations also use them, we know that, such as guilds of thieves or assassins."

Bad people.

"That's right. In the case of magic, with time, people recognized the need to cooperate, especially when it came to research. That's what the secret language was created for: the Arcane Language which magi could use for collaborations and yet remain secret. Its use slowly became standardized among scholars of magic. Not entirely, of course, and several variants of this one appeared."

"Different variants depending on the groups that use it?"

"Indeed. But although there are still many variants of the language, in general it's easy to understand."

"Well, I don't understand a word…" Lasgol said ruefully as he kept trying to read the language unsuccessfully.

"That's because you haven't been instructed until now," Eicewald said, smiling.

Then you're going to teach me the Arcane Language?" Lasgol was interested, and simply thinking about the look on Egil's face when he found out Lasgol was learning a magical secret language cheered him very much.

"It would take too long to teach you the language of the magi. Unfortunately, time is a precious thing we don't have much of."

"Oh...." Lasgol was disappointed.

"That's why we'll use a shortcut," Eicewald said with a wink.

I like shortcuts, Camu messaged happily.

"There are tools, objects and even spells, that allow you to read an arcane language written in a grimoire. To make this task easy for you, I've brought this tool," Eicewald said as he took out a kind of lens on a ribbon.

Lasgol and Camu stared at the object, which was not particularly pretty and looked rather rudimentary.

"I'll show you how it's used," he said and wound the ribbon around his forehead and tied it at the back of his head. Then he placed the hanging lens in front of his right eye.

Eicewald handsome now, Camu messaged, making a joke.

The Mage let out a guffaw.

"Indeed, I'm sure I look quite handsome right now."

"It gives you a serious look, as if you belonged to the nobility," Lasgol joked too.

"Me? Nobility? The Ice Gods forbid!" the Mage joked back. He used the lens. "Now you can read," he told them.

Lasgol nodded, "May I try?"

"Of course." The Mage loosened the ribbon and handed it to Lasgol, who put it around his forehead, tying it behind his head like Eicewald had done. He placed the lens in front of his right eye. He looked at the book and at first it felt strange—everything was blurred, but the next instant he was able to read a sentence that had been totally incomprehensible a moment before.

"In order to cast this spell, you must imagine the creation of..." he read out loud.

"Very good, that's what the text says," Eicewald confirmed.

Much good.

"I can read and understand it perfectly. This lens is enchanted," Lasgol guessed.

"It has a spell on it," Eicewald said, smiling, pleased. "It's a useful tool used by those unlearned in the magical language."

We little instructed? Camu messaged, a tad annoyed.

"I'm afraid so, Camu," Lasgol told him.

I want instructed magic, Camu messaged.

"Well for that you'll need to work," the mage told him kindly.

"Now that I can read it, what do I do to learn the spell and use it?" Lasgol asked.

"I see impatience is getting the better of you," Eicewald said with a look that meant that was not so good.

"A little, yes, sorry…" Lasgol apologized and shrugged.

"Don't worry. It's natural that you're eager to learn. What you have to do is follow what's written in the tome, in detail and with all your attention on it. You have to visualize the spell in your mind. The instructions will help, as well as the magic of the tome itself."

"The tome has magic?" Lasgol asked, pouring over it. "I mean, does it have magic besides the spells written in it?"

"Indeed, in order to facilitate the interpretation of what's written, as well as to help with memorizing the spell."

"Do I need to memorize it?" Lasgol asked, although he was beginning to see that this was how it worked.

Yes, you must. Contrary to the spells created or discovered spontaneously, as is usual to you two, spells you learn in arcane tomes must be memorized, since you're not creating but learning them, and any knowledge not memorized gets lost. It's a rule of magic, but also of many other aspects of life."

"I see. Learn and memorize in order to retain the spell in my mind and be able to use it."

Eicewald nodded, smiling, pleased.

"Let's see if I'm capable of memorizing it," said Lasgol and read what the tome said carefully. As he was reading the text, he was able to visualize what he had to create more easily. The spell he was learning was to create a Guiding Light. He had to create a point of light that would move in front of the conjurer, lighting the way. It was extremely useful in the darkness of night, in caves, storms, dark areas, and the like. At the end of the two pages, there was a sentence that was the spell itself. That was the only thing that was not translated.

"I'm not going to be able to utter this sentence," Lasgol said to

Eicewald, pointing at it.

"Don't worry, try it—the tome and its magic will help you."

Lasgol concentrated and searched for his inner energy. He visualized the point of light before him, as the tome indicated, and read the sentence he could not read. To his surprise, even though he did not understand what he had said, he read the sentence with the ease of one who understands it.

There was a faint flash but not intense enough, and it went out.

"I couldn't do it…" he said ruefully.

"Don't worry. It's not that simple. It will take time, as does everything in magic," the Mage told him, patting him on the back encouragingly.

You try more, you do, Camu expressed his encouragement too.

Lasgol tried several times without success. Eicewald suggested he pause in between attempts and concentrate hard on each one. Lasgol did as the mage said but he managed nothing.

Lasgol spent almost all morning and afternoon trying, without success. Night would soon fall and they would have to stop for the day. He was extremely frustrated, since he was eager to begin learning spells from a magic tome and was not having success. He was beginning to doubt whether he would ever be capable, whether he really had what was needed to be a mage. Perhaps he would always be a person with the Gift but without advanced magic. If this was the case it would not be the end for him either, he could always be a great Ranger Specialist with the Gift, and he was happy with that because that already was a big success in itself. But something inside him pushed him to keep trying to become a high-grade mage who could master his power with great skills.

He clenched his jaw and did not give in to discouragement. He tried again, and would continue doing so even if it took him weeks, months, or years. At that moment there was a whitish flash, and before Lasgol, a handspan from his head, there was a tiny ball of light.

"A point of Guiding Light. Well done!" Eicewald congratulated him.

Very impressive, Camu messaged admiringly.

"Thanks." Lasgol stood and slowly moved to the bottom of the tent, towards Ona who was lying there. The point of Guiding Light went before him, lighting up the tent. Ona was frightened and leapt to get away from the point of light.

Ona, easy, only light, Camu messaged to her.

The snow panther was not convinced, and she ran out of the tent.

"It's amazing…" said Lasgol, surprised by the light as much as by the fact he had finally been able to conjure it. The latter more than the former.

"Now you have to memorize it so you don't lose it," said Eicewald.

"How do I do that?"

"You have to cast the same spell over and over again until you run out of inner energy."

"But if I do that, I'll be exhausted… I'll faint."

"That's exactly the point. You should end up exhausted. Sleep to recover. In doing so, you'll memorize the spell. When you wake up it'll be as if you had created it yourself. You'll never forget it and will be able to use it whenever you wish."

Very fantastic!

"Okay, I'll keep doing it as soon as we finish today's lesson," said Lasgol.

"Good. Now let's see whether Camu can do it too," Eicewald said, looking at the creature with interest.

I do too, Camu messaged, sure of himself.

"How do we do this?" Lasgol asked; because Camu could not read it was going to be complicated.

"That's a good question. I've never found myself in a situation like this. My students have always been able to read. Well, they've always been human. I've never instructed a magical creature like Camu." The mage remained thoughtful for a long moment. Then he finally spoke. "The only thing I can think of is that you read out loud and he repeats it," he said.

I repeat. Easy.

"That could work, yes," Lasgol said cheerfully.

"Well then, let's try it," Eicewald said, nodding.

Lasgol read the first sentence of the arcane text out loud. Camu repeated it exactly as Lasgol had read it. He continued reading all the text on the two pages while Camu repeated it until they reached the last words of power. He repeated them slowly after Lasgol and the three waited for the spell to activate.

It did not.

"It doesn't seem to have worked," Eicewald commented.

Very NOT happy, Camu messaged, along with a feeling of frustration.

"He repeated the text just as I read it, without any alterations or mistakes."

"Perhaps it's because Camu hasn't created a link with the tome," Eicewald muttered thoughtfully.

I try, Camu messaged, and he put his head close to the tome on the floor. He shut his eyes, and there was a silver flash around Camu's head. The tome seemed to respond with another flash, a whitish gleam.

"That looks promising," Lasgol said.

"Okay, let's try again," said Eicewald.

They tried again. Lasgol read the text out loud using the lens and Camu repeated the words one by one until the end.

Unfortunately, the point of light did not appear.

I very NOT encouraged, Camu messaged.

Eicewald and Lasgol were silent, wondering how to solve the problem

"We could try using Mental Communication, maybe that will be more direct and maintain the link," Lasgol suggested.

"That's a good idea, there's nothing to lose in trying," Eicewald nodded.

Lasgol read the spell in the tome again. He transmitted the text in mental messages to Camu's mind, and his friend recited them out loud as they reached him.

When he finished reciting the last arcane sentence, the point of Guiding Light appeared over Camu's head. It was much bigger and more powerful than the one created by Lasgol.

Very fantastic! Camu messaged excitedly as he started flexing his legs in his weird happy dance.

"That link of yours is really interesting. It never ceases to amaze me. It's quite rare."

"It surprises me too," Lasgol admitted, nodding.

I not surprised, Camu messaged, appearing to smile as he went on dancing joyfully.

"One thing I want you to keep in mind is that as long as you have the Guiding Light active, it will keep using up your magic energy."

I feel, use up little.

"Indeed, but if you become careless and keep it active for a long time, it might end up using your entire magical pool, and you wouldn't be able to use your other skills when you need them. You'll have to rest in order to recover all the energy you've used."

"Understood," Lasgol nodded. "It could also exhaust us by distraction, using up all our energy without realizing it, and then we'd be defenseless."

"Indeed. You should always be aware of your energy usage with spells or skills you may be actively maintaining and not lose sight of your energy level, or you could have serious problems. It's more common than you'd think, to keep a spell active and have it consume all your energy."

I remember.

"Yeah, we will."

"Now, in order to memorize the spell, I want you to repeat it until you've used up all your energy and fall asleep."

"That could take a while... especially in Camu's case."

"I can believe it, but so it must be."

"Okay, then we'll do that."

It took them until dawn to use up all of Camu's well of energy. Lasgol collapsed long before, and Camu went on alone. He created the spell, discarded it, and started all over again until he exhausted all his energy.

Eicewald stayed with them to watch over their rest, although in the middle of the Green Ogre Forest there was no danger. He did so out of a sense of responsibility—he had to look after his pupils.

When they woke up, well past noon, they had both memorized the spell. Eicewald proclaimed the lesson a success and the results excellent.

Encouraged by their success, they continued with the next simple spell, Making Fire, which consisted of creating a small flame to light a candle, bonfire, or something similar. They both started learning it at once, full of enthusiasm.

Chapter 25

Lasgol and Camu decided to practice alone that day, since Eicewald had obligations in the capital which prevented him from giving them one of his lessons in magic which they appreciated so much. Apparently, King Thoran had summoned him, so it could not be good news. They would have to wait to see the Mage again at the capital or here in the Green Ogre Forest to find out what His Majesty had ordered him.

They practiced the Principles of Magical Amplification and Magical Power for half the morning. They were not very successful, so by the afternoon they focused on the Principle of Magical Creation, which was the one they liked best. The weather was not bad, it was not even snowing, so they could stay outside the tent if they chose.

I want create new skill, Camu messaged, along with a feeling of excitement.

You're not the only one, Lasgol transmitted back, using mental communication, following Eicewald's recommendation to practice magic whenever they could to develop the skill being used and also increase their own magical level. *Me too, what are you trying to create?*

Dragon fire, Camu messaged back confidently.

You mean breathe fire like the great dragons were supposed to do, the most powerful ones?

Yes. I want be like dragon.

I'm not sure that's even possible. On the one hand, you're not a dragon, and on the other hand you're not so powerful either, no matter what you believe.

I more than dragon. I much powerful.

Lasgol snorted. Who was going to get that idea out of his head? Arguing with him was not going to have any effect whatsoever.

Ona growled twice and threw herself on a mound of snow on one side of the tent.

Well, try it and see what you can do, Lasgol said.

I try. I do sure.

If you don't manage to do that, try something else, don't be stubborn.

I not stubborn. I know.

Well, we'll see what happens.

What you create?

Lasgol thought for a moment—he did not quite know what skill to develop.

I think I'd like to develop a skill to create Elemental Arrows out of regular ones, since we often find that we've run out of them when we need them most.

Be much good idea.

The two friends spent the afternoon trying to create their new skills. At nightfall they stopped without success. There had not been much luck that day, but there were many days ahead of them in life, and they both knew they had to keep working hard until their efforts produced results.

They were both confident that they would get there. The important thing was that they were making progress, and that since they were two of them, they could help one another. That made everything less frustrating, even if the day ended in failure. They knew that success would come eventually, so they encouraged one another when they were overcome by frustration and exhaustion, which happened more often than they would have liked.

The following day they continue trying. Eicewald would not be able to join them that day, so he had given Lasgol a tome of magical knowledge so he could study and help Camu understand it. But Camu preferred the practice and wanted to continue creating spells.

"Eicewald told us to study from this tome," Lasgol told Camu, showing it to him.

I create skill.

"We were doing that all day yesterday and weren't lucky."

Today lucky.

"Oh yeah, just because you say so."

I sure.

"You're always so sure of everything, and then things don't turn out the way you want them to."

Many yes.

"And many don't."

Camu lifted his head as if he were annoyed and left the tent. It was raining outside and it was quite chilly, but that did not affect Camu in the least, and he set down to work on his spell.

Lasgol shook his head.

Don't be like Camu, he transmitted to Ona, who watched him out of her feline eyes from the back of the tent.

The panther growled twice. Lasgol smiled. Ona was good and obedient, not like stubborn Camu, who did whatever he wanted.

He put the tome on the floor and opened it. He began to study it with great interest and a will to learn. He could see Camu outside trying to create his skill without success while the rain kept falling on his scale-covered body.

I hope you do it, he transmitted to Camu, not wanting to remain at odds with the creature.

I manage, you see, was the reply, which did not surprise him in the least.

The tome Eicewald had given them was titled *Magical Principles of the North* by Morgan Andersen, and Lasgol began to pour over it. Following what Eicewald had recommended, he focused on the Principle of Magical Cost.

It took him a while to read and understand everything Morgan Andersen explained about this principle, but at last he started to visualize it in his mind, with examples, which meant he had understood it. He was very pleased.

What study? Camu messaged. He was still trying to create his Dragon Breath.

Principle of Magical Cost.

I know. Magic costs energy.

Yes, but it's a little more complex than that.

Not complex. Many spells, use up much energy.

Yeah, we all know that. And what is the difference between a basic spell and one with more power regarding their magical cost?

Camu was thoughtful for a moment.

Powerful spell uses up more energy, he messaged, nodding repeatedly. *Dragon Wings use up much energy. Animal Communication, much little.*

Very little…

But I right.

Yes, it's correct, Lasgol had to admit with a sigh.

I know much.

You still have a lot left to learn.

Camu did not message back but continued trying to get his dragon breath.

Lasgol returned to the study of that principle. Camu was right—the more basic the spell or skill summoned, the less cost in energy needed, and the more powerful the spell, the more energy necessary. Considering that as you climbed levels and reached new grades the magic and spells achieved were more powerful, meaning they required a greater use of energy. That was a problem, because as the mage became more powerful, he consumed more energy, and the energy a mage was born with was supposed to be finite, in most cases, as far as Lasgol had understood.

He checked the tome to see whether his assumption was correct and found that it was. The tome also indicated that there were spells whose cost on energy was such that most magi could not manage them. Only those with enormous reserves of energy were able to, and those were few.

Lasgol thought at once of his inner pool of energy. His was larger than he had initially thought, and that was thanks to Izotza, the Lady of the Glaciers. Now he could perceive it, and he was sure he would manage to get the most out of it once he repaired the bridge between his mind and the pool, something he worked on every single day and which was going pretty well. Lasgol credited it to the study of magic he was undertaking with Eicewald. Ever since he had started learning everything the Ice Mage was teaching them, he found it easier to repair the bridge. It was still a frustratingly slow and tough task, but less than before. That was in itself an achievement for Lasgol.

What had caught his attention in particular was the fact that the tome mentioned that most people who had the Gift possessed an innate amount of energy. You were born with it, and upon reaching adulthood it was fully developed and available for the person to use. But it never increased. This Lasgol knew, and seeing it written reiterated it. And yet it contradicted what Izotza had told him. The Lady of the Glaciers had explained that both him and his mother had a source of energy that grew, it was not static and innate.

This puzzled him, and he went on checking the tome. The only thing he was able to find of help was a paragraph that speculated, on the basis of rumor, about the possibility in the case of specific great magi that their inner energy had grown with time and the achievement of higher grades.

Was Izotza right? Was he like one of those rare magi, who as time passed and they achieved higher grades made their inner pool of energy grow? This intrigued him, and he kept going over Izotza's words in his head. If this was the case he could become a mage with great power, which was a wonderful dream. He wondered how he might know if it was true or not. For now, he needed to repair that bridge and see his whole pool clearly. Then he could analyze whether it was growing in size or not.

Frustrating much, he received Camu's message.

You're not getting it?

Not yet.

Well, I'd tell you to stop for a while, but knowing you that's not going to happen, is it?

Not stop, Camu messaged, shaking his head and lifting his chin.

I thought so, Lasgol waved him off; he was impossible to convince.

Ona moaned twice.

Lasgol went on with his study. This was a subject he found fascinating. According to the principle all magic had a cost, and as a rule was based on the energy the person with the Gift or Talent possessed, but that source of energy was not always used. It could be obtained from Objects of Power, or even from other people and beings. He had to read this last paragraph several times to make sure he had understood properly. On the one hand he was fascinated, but on the other he was concerned.

He remembered hearing something about this before, which had left him uncomfortable. He had half-buried it in his subconscious, but now seeing it written in a tome of magical knowledge made it different, since it confirmed his fears. There were really magi capable of doing something like that.

The book said you could obtain the magical energy needed for a spell from an object, and that in this case since it was not your own energy, the cost was higher. There was a drawing of a mage with his hands on a jewel similar to a diamond extracting energy from it, and this entered his body at chest level. The energy was depicted as blue waves, which represented it very well.

Lasgol scratched his head, that made sense, because if you were getting the energy from an external source, it would be more costly. After all, you had to extract it from the object, and that used up energy.

What made him uneasy was that it mentioned that a person could be used as a source. That meant that somehow you could use the inner energy of another mage to cast a spell. This sounded dangerous to Lasgol. You might hurt the person you were extracting energy from. The tome did not explain how it could be done, it only mentioned it was possible.

Lasgol snorted. He did not like that. If it were done with the permission of the person, it might be dangerous, but what if it were done without the person's permission? What if someone took that energy by force? That seemed even worse to him. It was morally unacceptable and absolutely dangerous, since the other person would be against it. Unfortunately, the tome did not delve deeper into the matter which Lasgol was sure, even with his lack of knowledge, was suspicious.

Not finding more information about this, he went on reading. He felt better not learning more about a subject which gave him goosebumps. Just imagining that someone might steal his inner energy by force, the invasion of his privacy... his body... his magic... he felt a chill down his spine and tried to shake it off.

He then came to an interesting part: 'Means and ways to reduce the cost of energy when using magic.' He found it interesting and something which probably most magi would study and use, since reducing the cost of each spell would mean being able to do more magic. This might mean the difference between life and death on the battlefield.

The text came with several drawings. In one of them two sorcerers were casting spells at one another. A second drawing showed the pool of energy of each of them more or less at the same level, halfway full of energy which had been colored blue, like the ocean.

Lasgol looked at the next drawings and read the accompanying text. He understood that the drawings represented two magi in a magical duel. The first mage was wearing a red robe and he did not have a 'magical-cost reducer,' so with every spell he cast trying to finish the other mage he consumed a considerable amount of energy from his pool of power. But the second mage who was wearing a green robe was using a cost reducer, and his spells consumed one third less than those of his opponent.

"How interesting..." Lasgol muttered under his breath as he kept turning the pages of the book, pouring over its contents. The result of the duel was that the first mage died when he used up all his energy. The second mage survived with one third of his energy left and available for use. The book's illustrations showed this clearly—

there was no space for doubt.

Ona yawned at the far end of the tent and shifted in her slumber.

Ona good, you rest, he transmitted to her. He knew the good panther got bored when they studied, but she would not leave them alone under any circumstance. Ona always wanted to be with them.

He concentrated on the book again and arrived at a most interesting paragraph—ways to reduce energy usage. Once again, he found detailed explanations and drawings. To Lasgol's surprise, there were several ways to reduce energy cost.

The first one described advanced spells summoned to that end. They did not belong to one type of magic but were cast by the mage before beginning to call upon the skills or spells they wanted to use. Once a mage was enchanted with a reducer spell, any magic performed would have a reduced the cost of energy. The amount depended on the power of the spell, which in turn depended on the power and grade of the mage and the spell used, since the cost reduction could be different for each spell.

He had to read it a couple of times to understand it properly. He reasoned it out and reached the conclusion that the more powerful the mage, the more powerful the cost reduction spell and the more energy saved in every spell or summons.

"Egil's going to love this when I explain it to him," he smiled to himself.

The next thing he found out was that there were certain potions you could take to reduce the cost of spells or to replenish part of your energy, or even accelerate the rhythm at which a person with the Gift regenerated energy. This fascinated Lasgol but did not surprise him. Eicewald had already explained to him that, in the world of magi, potions were widely used for all kinds of ends. The fact that they were used to reduce the cost of casting a spell or replenish energy at once or over time seemed like a wonderful idea.

He continued reading about potions and how to prepare them, but the tome did not delve into the matter since they were too advanced and required specific tomes to deal with each subject. He would have to find other tomes about energy-replenishing potions and study them. Perhaps he or Egil would be able to make them. It was likely Egil could.

The next pages were about objects charmed with the purpose of helping to save energy. The enchantment provided anyone who had the object with a reduction in any magic used. The illustrations showed elaborate necklaces, precious rings, elegant robes and cloaks in gold and silver, and various objects, from daggers and swords to mage staves. Lasgol noticed that the object itself was not important—what mattered was that it had been enchanted with a powerful spell which would reduce the cost of doing magic for whoever had it.

The more he read, the more engrossed he became. This world was new to him and he found fascinating. The last concept that affected the cost of energy was the mage's own grade, according to the tome, which included a drawing of three magi of different grades. The higher the mage's grade, the less energy lost. The grades not only provided more power but also greater efficiency. Magi of higher grades were capable of doing more with less energy.

Lasgol nodded to himself. This would help with the great spells that cost a lot of energy. Magi with advanced grades were capable of casting spells using less energy, which was of great value, since otherwise they would not fend off powerful spells.

He continued staring at the illustration of the mage with the highest grade and was overcome by envy. Would he ever be a mage like the one in the tome? A powerful mage capable of casting great spells and minimizing the energy cost? He highly doubted it, but he was free to dream, and for a moment he allowed himself to be carried away by that dream.

Chapter 26

Astrid and Nilsa were watching the fort in the distance, hiding among snow-covered trees and bushes. The snow had fallen the day before and it looked as if they would have favorable weather since there was no wind, which would make releasing easier. One of the worst enemies of an Archer was always the wind, and in Norghana the breath of the Ice Gods always made its presence felt day and night, especially in the mountains.

Several armed men were guarding the building of wood and rock. It was not very large but big enough to be considered a fort. It must have been able to hold about fifty armed men. It was in the middle of a clearing, on a hill that was now snow-covered with a mountain to the west. Two high towers gave advantage to the archers posted in them. A winding path made its way from the main road in the plain up to the building.

From what they had been able to find out about the fort, it had been used by the Norghanian army back in the day but had been abandoned a few years ago. The fact that it was rebuilt, in good shape and with armed men inside, indicated that someone had restored it for their own personal aims. From the information Egil had managed to obtain from his contacts, Viggen was among those who had financed the rehabilitation of the fort. As he said, 'if you follow the gold, it will lead you to the treasure.' In this case, the trail of the money had led them to a fort on the west coast, south of Copenghen and near the mouth of the river Utla.

"How many do you count?" Astrid asked from the second line of trees where she was hiding behind some snow-covered bushes.

"A dozen on the walls and four on each tower, the latter most likely archers," Nilsa replied beside her, also hiding and watching.

"Yeah, I got the same. At night there will be half as many most likely," Astrid said with a nod. Beside her, on a white blanket on the ground she had her impressive Forest Sniper bow all ready.

"We'll have to wait until the wind slackens," said Nilsa as she watched how it was shaking the bushes.

Astrid nodded, "Right now I don't have a shot, or a target, since I can't see him."

"No, he's not in the fort. I only see Visionaries inside, and Defenders of the True Blood on the battlements," Nilsa confirmed as she watched the military fortress with eager eyes.

"Don't you find it odd seeing them working together?" Astrid asked, wrinkling her nose.

"I find it dangerous. I don't like it at all that they've joined forces. But that's what the Dragon Orb ordered them to do, and it looks like they'll obey any order that comes from that object."

"You mean Dergha-Sho-Blaska's order."

"Well, yes. I'd rather deal with the Visionaries and Defenders separately, but it doesn't look like that'll be an option from here on out," Nilsa said ruefully.

"I wonder what they're plotting in there. Why have they taken over this old abandoned fort? What for?" Astrid said, frowning.

"That's a good question. There has to be a reason or they wouldn't have bothered fixing it. And that's what we're here to find out."

"And to stop or hinder their operations, whatever those are. That's what Egil wants us to achieve," Astrid said.

"We have to prevent them from accomplishing whatever it is they're doing here."

"The problem is we don't know what they're doing, and that makes the job difficult. When you don't know what you're up against, making a plan of action gets complicated."

"I think they must be indoctrinating new forced preachers to send out into the world," Nilsa said, shaking her head.

"It might be that, and if it is we'll free those poor wretches before they've brainwashed them," Astrid said firmly.

"But first we'll have to deal with the warlock who's turning them into preachers, I guess with that hateful dragon head. It must be that Vingar, or perhaps Xoltran."

"Or some other warlock. We have no idea how many Drugan has."

"That's not good... in any case, he can't have more than a handful at best. There are very few with the Talent. Drugan won't have been able to find and recruit many for his sect," Nilsa reasoned, wiping the snow off her red eyebrows.

"Let's hope so. But it doesn't matter whether we face one, two, or three warlocks and their minions, we'll deal with them," Astrid said confidently.

Nilsa nodded, although her eyes did not show the same level of confidence. She knew the warlocks would make things difficult for them.

"The one I'm hoping to see is Viggen, that's what I'm looking forward to," Astrid said.

"Your uncle? Why?"

"There are Defenders in there. They must be doing what my uncle has ordered them to do. I want to have a conversation with him, one that won't end well I'm afraid."

"We'll have to wait and see. The information Egil was given is that this fort, with one of the targets we're seeking is coming here. It might be your uncle Viggen, or Drugan, or one of his warlocks."

"And when they arrive, we'll deal with him and take apart this operation they've built, whatever that is."

"Distance to the target?" Nilsa asked.

"About four hundred and twenty-five paces," Astrid replied as she calculated again, squinting.

"Can you hit him at this distance?"

Astrid nodded. "If the wind doesn't play tricks on me, I can reach him."

"Fantastic. After three hundred and fifty paces I can't guarantee the shot."

"That's why you're a Mage Hunter and I'm a Sniper," Astrid replied with a wink.

"Besides Assassin of Nature and Stealthy Spy," Nilsa said, smiling.

"A rather strange combination, I know, but it's what I got," she replied with a shrug.

"What you got? Don't you believe you were born for it?"

"I'm not sure about that... although the tests at the Camp and Shelter led me down this path of Specializations, I'm not sure that if I started anew, if I'd follow the same path."

"You think you'd get other specialties if you had to do it all over again?"

"Well, I don't know whether I'd do it all over again," Astrid smiled. "It was very hard. But I do wonder whether, if we started all over, we'd get the same specializations or others. I wonder about that sometimes. Is our destiny written in stone, or can we change it?"

"I like to think that we can change it, that with our actions we create a new destiny every day. Otherwise, life would be pretty sad since it would imply that whatever we did would not make a difference because the final result would always be the same."

"The same, or one very similar," Astrid noted.

"Yeah… I believe that if you repeated the entire Camp and Shelter experience, if you wanted, you could obtain other specialties in the end."

"If I didn't know all of you, maybe."

"We've influenced your choices?"

"I think so. Not directly, but in an indirect manner, definitely. Your influence on me and my decisions are obvious."

"Especially Lasgol's," Nilsa chuckled.

"Apart from that," Astrid said with a big smile.

"I guess we'll never know," Nilsa said with a shrug.

"Unless we reincarnate—then we could do everything over again," Astrid said, her eyes widening.

"Do you believe reincarnation is possible?" Nilsa asked with a troubled look.

"I believe that we all believe that some type of reincarnation exists, even if we don't know what or how it happens. Otherwise, we wouldn't be here trying to stop the immortal dragon."

"That's true… but I find it hard to believe that a person might reincarnate into another being, whether animal or some part of nature, like a river, mountains, lakes, or trees… or something similar. I don't see how it could be possible…"

"You might not be as spiritual as you thought you were," Astrid replied, making a face.

"Yes, it's possible, it would have to be through powerful magic. I can't see it working any other way."

"Then you don't think that a poor human without magic might reincarnate as an eagle and fly through the skies?"

"No, I don't think so," Nilsa shook her head. "I don't think it's possible, no matter how much I go over it in my head trying to picture it."

"It's complicated. For now, let's say that the dragon has magic that will allow him to do it and we're going to stop him."

"That I can see, and we will stop it," Nilsa nodded.

"We'd better leave philosophical and religious matters to Egil, who loves to study them and lecture us about them."

"Because they're fantastic," Nilsa joked.

Astrid grinned and said, "Indubitably."

"Getting back to your specialties, I think they're a sensational combination. It makes you a double threat. You can finish off the enemy from near and far."

Astrid looked at her friend and smiled.

"I think you're right. I like that about being a double threat."

"As long as it doesn't go to your head, like it has with our smartass."

"Don't worry, there's no risk of that happening. I don't like fame and notoriety."

"I know, but just in case it does go to your head with the passing of time."

"No, it should really be the other way round. With the passing of time, you should become more prudent—what you should look for is to go unnoticed."

"Well, someone should tell Viggo that."

"He knows, but he'd rather ignore it."

"If he's not careful, it might cost him his life."

"That's true. But I believe that danger stimulates Viggo rather than to dissuade him."

"If he doesn't stop being so reckless, he's going to end up badly. And I don't care so much for him as I do for Ingrid, her heart would break if he got killed."

"Don't worry, Viggo is what he is, but he does know what he's doing when he takes action. He's not going to take risks."

"In any case, I've never understood what Ingrid sees in Viggo."

"You know what they say, opposites attract, especially on long, cold winter nights."

"Me, I wouldn't find Viggo attractive if all Norghana froze up!" Nilsa said, making a face.

"That's because you look for other qualities in a man," Astrid smiled.

"You can put that down on parchment, and I'll sign and seal it."

"Yet, we must admit that he's very special," Astrid said.

"Yeah, so special that there's no way of putting up with him," Nilsa said, giggling.

"Watch out, I see movement," Astrid warned.

They both looked toward the road and could make out a group of six riders coming up the narrow path to the fort. They had two dozen men in chains who looked pretty bad, as if they had been prisoners for some time. It looked as if they were being moved from one prison to another.

"I see them. Are they the target we're expecting?" Nilsa asked as she tried to identify them with narrowed eyes.

"It's hard to tell with the little information Egil has given us, but they should be," Astrid said.

"Egil gave us what little he got from his contacts, which is a lot, although he never mentioned prisoners, only the target moving toward the fortress that your uncle had financed with his gold."

"Now we know the reason for the movement. They're moving those poor wretches from some dungeon to this fort, which tells us that this fort also has dungeons, most likely under the main tower structure," Astrid guessed as she watched the prisoners with interest.

"The worst thing is not how they look but the fact that they're going to end up as messengers of terror. Poor men, they have no idea what awaits them."

"Yeah, I was thinking the same thing, but let's not get ahead of ourselves, we have to find out what they're going to do with them here. It might be even worse…"

"Oh no, not something worse…" Nilsa shivered just at the thought.

They followed the group with their eyes until they reached the entrance to the fortress.

"Which one of them is the target?" Nilsa asked. "I can't decide myself out of the six."

"I was wondering the same thing. I couldn't tell you. They're all dressed   the   same. None looks like the leader, so I can't make sure of the shot."

"And if you kill all six?" Nilsa suggested.

"Not possible. I could kill one or two, no more. The rest would escape and shelter inside the fortress. Using a sniper's bow is slow work, and securing the shot at this distance even more."

"I see… besides, we don't know who we're shooting at."

"One shot, one hit. That's the first rule of a good sniper. Trying to take more shots leads to failure and the death of the sniper."

"And we don't want that," Nilsa winked.

The riders conferred for a moment with the guards posted on the battlement above the gate. The gates opened and several Visionaries with swords and whips came out to lead the prisoners inside. The riders went in afterward and vanished from their sight.

"We'll have to wait until we have some clue as to who might be the target."

Fine. I'll keep my eyes open."

"One of them will go up to the main tower, to the good rooms," Astrid reasoned. "We'll wait and see who it is."

"That'll be the leader," Nilsa guessed.

"Almost certainly. That's what Egil has explained on some occasion."

"I can't believe that nowadays there are still people who use slaves. I think it's contemptible, unforgivable. Slavery has to be abolished completely," Nilsa said with rage.

"From what I've heard Egil say, there are some kingdoms and tribes who still use slaves in Tremia. Slavery hasn't been entirely eradicated."

"They can't be modern kingdoms then!"

"Kingdoms like ours, Rogdon, Zangria, Erenal, and Irinel don't practice slavery anymore. But the Nocean Empire still has slaves."

"That's unacceptable."

"It is, but I don't think the Nocean Empire cares about being too ethical or not. Slaves contribute to making it an economic and military power in Tremia. A much feared one."

"We should show them what's correct and dignified, by force if necessary," Nilsa said, making a fist, enraged.

"You're an idealist, and that's good, but be careful it doesn't kill you. Ideals will drive you to the grave."

"But we have to fight evil wherever we find it," Nilsa replied.

"We have enough evil to fight against here, don't you think?"

"Well, yeah... and seeing this besides..."

"Then let's leave it to others to teach morality and ethics to the Nocean Empire."

"Okay, but when we're not so...."

"We're always going to be busy, Nilsa, one way or another. That's why we're Rangers."

"You're right, it's just that the injustices of the world get to me."

"Let's focus on this one for now. We'll deal with the rest later on."

"You're absolutely right. And thinking about injustices, another has come to mind. I hope Egil and Gerd are all right," Nilsa said in a concerned tone.

"I'm sure they will be. Gerd will make sure Egil's safe, and Egil will help Gerd. Head and muscle, a great combination," Astrid said, smiling.

"Only in two different people."

"You very seldom find everything in one."

"Very true," Nilsa chuckled. "Anyway, I'm worried about Gerd not being fully recovered. This could be a serious problem in a critical situation."

"He seemed pretty recovered to me. He'll manage as long as he's not at the front line."

"You think so?" Nilsa asked, hopefully.

"I'm sure. As long as he stays with Egil, protecting him, staying at the back and not at the front line of the attack, everything will be fine."

"You make me feel more at ease. I don't want anything bad to happen to the giant. He has a huge heart and doesn't deserve what he's been through."

"As a rule, good people don't deserve the bad that happens to them. We're Rangers, we put our lives in danger every day to protect the kingdom and its people. We know the risks and what can happen to us."

Nilsa nodded.

"We all know, and yes, life isn't fair at all."

"Exactly. Watch out, there's more movement," Astrid warned.

They both focused on the tower. At the top a figure appeared at a window.

"There's our target," said Nilsa.

"That's not my uncle… pity," Astrid said ruefully, and her tone betrayed the anger she felt.

"That's Vingar, I recognize him now that he's pushed his hood back," said Nilsa.

"You have good sight. That is Vingar, yes."

"What's the plan?"

"Easy, we'll wait for night and go into the fort to find out what

Vingar's doing here with those prisoners. We'll eliminate him and stop this operation."

"Understood, very easy," Nilsa said with a horrified look on her face.

Chapter 27

Nilsa was crawling along the snow-covered grass. Night had fallen, and luckily for her it was quite dark. The light of the moon did not fully come through the gray clouds that covered the sky, so the darkness covered her incursion.

She was moving with bow and quiver on her back and wearing her winter gear which allowed her to melt into the snow around her. She was nearing the western wall of the fortress, the one that looked partially on the mountain and where the wall was lower.

She stopped for an instant to check the fortress. There were two men on guard at the southern wall and one on each of the two towers. There was also a watchman on each of the eastern, northern, and western walls. The night was quiet and the guards were beginning their rounds carrying torches to light up the battlements and the lower part of the fort's wall.

She was fifteen paces from the wall, and the light that came down from it was about to reach her. She would have to take extreme precautions, she was not an Assassin like Astrid or Viggo, but a Mage Hunter. The one she was after was inside the tower. Egil had assigned her this mission knowing it was very likely there would be a mage, a warlock in this case, at the fort. She was not going to disappoint Egil. He had sent her to take care of the warlock, and that was just what she was going to do.

She crawled to where the light was beginning to pose a serious problem and imitated the hoot of an owl toward her back, only it had a slight variation, one that only an expert Ranger would be able to distinguish. She waited a moment, watching the guard on the western tower. She strained her ears and was able to catch a whistling sound over her head. The watchman received Astrid's arrow in the heart. He fell backward in the tower.

Nilsa got into position to attack the western wall and imitated the hoot of an owl once again. A new, practically imperceptible whistling at great height warned her of Astrid's arrow. It buried itself into the western guard's heart. He vanished from sight with the impact.

"Astrid has incredible marksmanship," Nilsa muttered to herself and checked the battlement to see where the western wall guard was posted. Right then he was passing above her position. He did not see her and continued his round of the battlement. Nilsa jumped to her feet and ran to the foot of the wall.

She uncoiled the rope she was carrying round her torso with a hook at its end. She looked up and saw no danger. Very carefully so as not to make any noise, she threw the rope with the hook up onto the battlement so it would grip it and she could climb up the wall. Her first throw was not successful, and Nilsa worried she had made a lot of noise. But she must not have, because no one came to check what was going on.

She tried again carefully, and this time the hook did grip the battlement. Nilsa gave a few pulls on the rope to see if the hook would hold. It did. So, without second thoughts, she started climbing up the wall. Since it was built on the slope of the mountain, the wall was not very high and she did not have much trouble reaching the top of the battlement.

She arrived at the top and lay there on the floor. Then she got to her knees and was beginning to gather her bow when the guard saw her. Nilsa hurried to nock an arrow to kill the guard, who was a Defender of the True Blood by his clothes, but she had no time to release.

A whistling sound went over her head and the Defender was hit by a large arrow in the middle of his torso. He fell over the battlement and died.

"Those long-distance shots from Astrid are awesome..." she muttered under her breath.

She looked to both sides for signs of any other Defender or Visionary who might give warning, but she did not see anyone on the western wall. She crouched and followed the battlement to the southern wall, where the great entrance gate was. Two Defenders were on guard there. They were unmistakable even at night because of their attire. They looked like some kind of clergymen with their long gray robes with the two silver circles embroidered in the center of the chest, one inside the other.

Nilsa watched them for a moment. She did not know the meaning, but she was sure there was one and it would have to do with dragons, or their descendants of the true blood. If fighting a sect was already a problem, fighting two—one of them with warlocks in their ranks—would make it even more so. She did not flinch. She was here to stop them, and that's what she would do. She did not know whether she would stop them completely, but at least she would delay them in whatever it was they were planning. That was what Egil had told them to do, and they would succeed.

One of the Defenders of the southern wall started toward Nilsa, who remained hidden in the corner among the shadows. The watchman seemed to find her, because he stopped and looked in her direction, trying to make her out more clearly. Nilsa nocked an arrow and raised it in front of her. She pulled the string back to her cheek, aligning it with her eye, and aimed.

The Defender saw her at last and cried out. Nilsa released. The arrow caught him in the neck. The Defender took a step backward and then fell on his knees. Drowning in his own blood, he fell over the battlement and died. The other Defender saw his partner fall and looked up at the towers, seeking the help of the other two archers posted on them. Unfortunately for him, they were dead too. Nilsa nocked another arrow and was ready to aim when another whistling sound above her head told her it was unnecessary. Astrid hit the guard full in the head, piercing it through with one of her long sniper arrows. The guard died on impact before knowing what had happened. Nilsa snorted: there was nothing better than having a sniper like Astrid to protect her.

She took a look around the battlements and saw there were still two more guards. She headed to the one on the eastern wall, running at a crouch as she looked down into the fort. There was no one in the courtyard or the stables. They all appeared to be sleeping, and there were no suspicious sounds. But then she saw a light in the upper floor. She stopped to watch it and saw it going down along the floors of the main tower until it vanished on the ground floor.

No one would go downstairs at night with a lamp and then put it out, unless she had been found out and the person was hiding from her. This made her hesitate. Had she been found out, or was something else going on? Since she had no answer, she remained still, and alert. They would soon come for her if she had been discovered.

She waited for a long moment, but no one sounded the alarm and she did not see any suspicious movement that indicated she was in danger. No, she had not been found out. That had to have been Vingar, who had gone down to the cellars or dungeons since the light had suddenly disappeared on the ground floor. That could not be good. She had better go and find out what he was up to.

Before going any closer, she had to finish off the last two guards so they could not give any warning. She reached the corner and hid. She waited for the guard on the eastern wall to turn around and walk toward her before she released. The closer he was, the better the shot and the less risk of missing. The Defender on guard did not even see the arrow that killed him coming. Neither did the northern guard her friend Astrid brought down with another master shot in the head. Nilsa wondered whether her friend was becoming a little too fond of these efficient shots.

She went over to one of the torches above the entrance door so Astrid could easily see her. She signaled to her that there were no more guards. An arrow buried itself in the door—it was Astrid's, she had understood the message and was telling her to open the door.

Nilsa went down some wooden stairs to the door. Outside it looked strong and well-repaired, but inside it was quite battered. The repairs had been done with bad wood, pine and still green, hastily done and quite recently. She ran to the door and dragged off the huge crossbar as far as she could. It was pretty heavy, usually a job for two soldiers, but she finally managed to open the door enough for Astrid to slip through.

After opening the door, she did not wait for her friend but ran to the main building. She wanted to find out what Vingar was planning. She arrived at the door and found it locked from inside, so she looked for a service door, which was usually at the back and never shut. In this case it was watched by a Visionary who had fallen asleep. Nilsa finished him off with a powerful knife thrust, and the man died without waking up.

She went into the building and found it dark, no light, so she waited until her eyes got used to the darkness and then kept searching for the stairs down to the dungeons. It took her a moment to find them in the reigning gloom.

She began to go downstairs with her bow raised and an arrow nocked, sure of some unpleasant encounter. She went down warily, stepping carefully, and arrived at what looked like a well-lit large cellar. They had left the chains and shackles of the prisoners in here; Nilsa noticed there were three piles of chains along a wall. In front of the other wall there were large barrels with water and several cauldrons hanging over dead fires containing something that looked like food but smelled terrible.

She was surprised to find all this down here. They must have quite a few prisoners if they needed all that water, food, and especially the chains. The sight of it all and what it meant made Nilsa's stomach turn. She was going to find a horror here, so she shielded herself mentally so it would not affect her and distract her if she needed to fight. The target was below, and she had to finish him off. That was what she had to do, and he was not getting away.

All of a sudden, a Visionary appeared at the far end of the cellar. Where had he come from?

"What the...? How...?" the man asked, confused. He reached for his short sword with a dragon pommel.

Nilsa released swiftly, almost without aiming. She hit him in the torso.

"Where...?" he muttered before dying.

Nilsa nocked another arrow and went on. At the end of the cellar, she found another set of stairs, which was where the Visionary had come from. She waited for an instant in case anyone else came up, but no one did. With careful and measured steps, she started going down some wide stairs. They went down quite deep.

She arrived at a place she recognized at once: the dungeons. There were about fifty prisoners in them. She had to blink hard. She hid behind a weapons rack that held whips, clubs, and other tools to inflict pain. The prisoners were locked up in six large cells with metal bars—they looked more like cages than cells. They were guarded by several Visionaries.

Nilsa found a new hiding place behind some crates with debris near the door and watched the scene. At the far end, past the prisoner cells, she saw Vingar with another group of Visionaries. Forming a line were a dozen prisoners kneeling before him, surrounded by the Visionaries watching them. The scene gave Nilsa chills. Vingar took out an object which Nilsa thought would be the dragon head he used to turn the prisoners into preachers.

She froze. Were they really going to turn all those poor wretches into preachers of the terrible message of the end of the era of men? Did they want to spread their message of destruction throughout the world? If that was so, their message was going to be widely heard, and that was not a good thing. It would bring terror to the hearts of good people, and what was worse, it would recruit new adepts for his sect.

Although that seemed to be what was going to happen, she was mistaken. Vingar took out another object he had in a large black velvet bag resting on a stone pedestal. It was a huge claw, translucent, made of crystal shards inside with a thousand facets which shone as if it were made of diamonds. It looked like a priceless jewel, only it was shaped like the claw of a great bird or perhaps a dragon. Vingar was holding it with both hands. It was no jewel, because its sight caused terror and it was too big for someone to wear it as an ornament.

Nilsa was puzzled. What was this object, and what was Vingar going to do with it? More specifically, what was that object going to do to those poor people who were kneeling before him? It certainly could not be anything good.

Vingar started to cast a spell. When he finished, he shouted orders at the wretches with a furious voice.

"Everyone, look at this object!"

One of the Visionaries delivered a whiplash to one of the prisoners who was not looking at the claw. Another Visionary clubbed another man on the side. The moans of pain and fear filled the hall.

"Whoever shuts his eyes or looks away will suffer!" the warlock cried.

The rest of the locked-up prisoners kept silent. They appeared to have suffered intense punishment at the hands of the Visionaries. They did not dare say anything because of the terror they felt.

Nilsa could not understand what was happening here, but she knew it was not good. She readied her bow—she was definitely going to need it. She reached back to her quiver with her right hand and felt the nocks of her arrows. She had them marked and knew what they each were just by brushing them with the tips of her fingers. It was important to be able to choose the kind of arrow to use on each occasion quickly.

So far, she had used regular arrows with a steel tip. They were good for most occasions when it was a question of delivering a quick death to the enemy by piercing some vital organ. But these arrows did not always work, particularly when you did not want to kill the victim but render them unconscious or stunned. They were no good either when facing a mage or warlock, as was the present case.

She took a deep breath and devised her plan of attack and the arrow she would use. Mage Hunters used a variety of arrows to bring down the mage or warlock they were up against. She had also brought some arrows of her own design as well. She was going to have to use a combination of these to bring down Vingar.

All of a sudden, the diamond claw began to shine with great brightness. Vingar went on conjuring. Incomprehensible words came out of his mouth in an arcane language. The Visionaries kept hitting and whipping the prisoners so they would not stop staring at the claw. The flashes were rhythmical, as if they followed a predetermined beat matching the words of power the warlock was intoning.

"Look at the light, the power of the dragon will set you free!" Vingar proclaimed with arms spread.

The object, which Nilsa had no doubt was one of power and was likely related to the immortal dragon, increased the flashes it emitted, both in rhythm and power. They were coming faster, and the beams of light, bright like diamonds, hit the walls, floor, and ceiling of the hall and bounced off in different directions. The prisoners in the cells threw themselves on the floor and covered their heads with their hands and shut their eyes. No one was looking toward Vingar—they were all terrified at the beams of diamond light that bounced all over the hall.

Nilsa watched blankly. The beams of light bounced to where she was hiding at the entrance of the hall and, following the prisoners' example, she shut her eyes just in case something might happen to her or she was blinded by the beams of light. Her eyes were not particularly sensitive to the light because they were dark, but even so she did not want to risk it. She shut them and let the diamond rays go by.

She did not feel any pain, although she was sure they had hit her even with her eyes shut. She waited for a moment while she listened to Vingar conjuring with a voice that seemed to come from an even deeper floor, although there did not seem to be more levels in the dungeons. The flashes coming from the crystal claw increased their rhythm as the warlock uttered more arcane words.

Suddenly Vingar stopped conjuring, and at that same instant, as if he had given one last order to the dragon claw, it stopped emitting flashes. There was a moment of tense silence and then the warlock spoke.

"All rise, servants of the immortal dragon!"

The prisoners who had been kneeling and staring at the flashes rose, obeying the order.

"You will obey the designs of your all-powerful lord from me, as his representative before you!"

Nilsa was beginning to understand what was going on here. Vingar was dominating these people so they would do whatever he ordered them with some kind of arcane magic and the help of the Object of Power shaped like a dragon claw.

"Turn around and go back to your cell!" he ordered.

The prisoners turned, and when they did Nilsa's heart skipped a beat. Their eyes were shining with a diamond gleam that seemed caught in their irises. The image was dreadful, inhuman. She saw them walk to an empty cell and go in like meek lambs. They were under a spell and now would do whatever the warlock told them to.

Nilsa felt her skin prick and shivered. Those poor wretches with eyes possessed by the diamond light no longer looked human. She felt deep sorrow for them. They had not done anything to deserve ending up as servants of a cult against their will. She did not want to think what he would use them for. Was Drugan forming an army of pariahs? Could those men even fight? Another thing that puzzled her was that there were no women among the prisoners. Yes, it had to be to arm them and use them as fodder to defend that sect of dragon lovers.

"Sit and await my orders!" the warlock told them, and they all at once sat expectantly.

With great sadness for them, Nilsa wondered whether it would be possible to revert them into normal people again. Probably yes, they only had to break the spell that bound them. From what she had learned during her specialization as Mage Hunter, once the mage was dead the spell died too. But in some cases, when the mage was powerful and the spell created was also great, even after death the spell might remain in force for a long period of time.

"Bring me another lot!" Vingar told his Visionaries, and they went to another cell. With whips and clubs, they got another dozen prisoners out and made them kneel before Vingar. The warlock had left the claw on a granite pedestal beside him with great care. It must be heavier than it looked. It was big, but because of its crystal look it did not appear to weigh that much.

Vingar began at once to repeat the process with the new group of prisoners. The whipping and blows were also repeated. The terror the prisoners reached Nilsa and she felt it in her throat, she could not even swallow.

The warlock started to conjure with the claw of power in his hands and the flashes started again. They all cowered before the diamond light beams. Except the prisoners, already bewitched with their gazes bright and lost, they did not seem to notice what was happening.

Nilsa's narrowed eyes did not allow the beams of light to reach them. She decided it was time to act—she could not let Vingar bewitch these poor men. She had to free them all.

She took a deep breath and commended herself to the Ice Gods. The moment of truth had arrived.

Chapter 28

Nilsa was determined to stop the mage's designs, no matter the cost to herself. She aimed carefully at one of the Visionaries, the closest to the cells. The distance was short enough to safely shoot with her short bow, which was the one she had chosen to bring on this incursion. It was her least favorite one though, since she preferred to release from afar, quite a distance, with a composite bow or even a long one. But those bows were not useful in enclosed spaces where there was not enough distance to release.

She did not think twice and let the arrow fly. It buried itself in the Visionary's neck. Caught by surprise, he reached for the arrow without a cry and fell to his knees. Between Vingar's deep voice and the flashes bouncing everywhere, not even the other Visionaries or the warlock himself noticed that the watchman had fallen to the floor.

Nilsa quickly nocked another steel-tipped arrow, pulled the string back, and aimed. She waited an instant and released. The arrow flew through the dungeons and hit another of the Visionaries watching the cells, opposite the one she had already killed. She caught him in the heart from a sideways angle and the man fell forward, dead.

This time another watchman saw his comrade fall and gave the alarm.

"We're under attack! My lord, intruders!"

Vingar stopped his spell and looked at the end of the hall. Nilsa had hidden, hoping to create confusion among the Visionaries if they did not see her.

"She's here, at the entrance!" cried a voice at her back.

She turned around and saw another Visionary coming down the stairs with his sword in his hand.

"Bad moment to come down..." Nilsa said ruefully.

"Kill the intruder!" Vingar ordered, leaving the claw on its altar and unsheathing his long sword with the dragon-head pommel.

The Visionaries drew their swords and ran to attack the intruder.

Nilsa found herself in a tight spot. About ten Visionaries were running toward her and another one was coming down the stairs. She aimed at the one on the stairs.

"I'll deal with this one," said a voice Nilsa recognized at once.

Forgetting about the man on the stairs, she aimed at the first one running toward her from the other side of the hall and killed him with an arrow to the heart.

Behind her, the man on the stairs fell to the floor with his throat slit.

"I seem to have arrived in the nick of time," Astrid said as she leapt to her friend's side.

"Exactly in the nick of time" Nilsa said as she killed another Visionary.

"You shouldn't start the dance without your partner," Astrid said with a wink as she leaped to knock down the enemy arriving on her left.

"You're right about that," Nilsa replied. "The next time I'll wait for you," she agreed, releasing another arrow that finished off another Visionary.

Astrid buried her knife in the heart of the one she had knocked down and faced two others. She blocked one's sword thrust that sought to spear her stomach and avoided the fleeting thrust of the other's sword.

Nilsa had no shot and two men were coming at her. She decided to retreat and ran up the stairs fast. One of the Visionaries followed her and the other hesitated on the first step. Nilsa arrived upstairs, and with great speed and balance she spun around, aimed, and released all in the same movement. She hit the man in the torso. As he fell at Nilsa's feet, he tried to bring her down with him, but the redhead kept her balance, stepped back, and delivered a tremendous kick at the dying man's head.

"Wow," she muttered to herself, pleased, "I seem to be getting less clumsy in combat."

The other Visionary decided then to go upstairs too. Nilsa calculated she had no time to release again so she changed her tactics. Cheered by her skill, she jumped with both feet forward downstairs. She hit the Visionary's face as he was coming up, brandishing his sword to deliver a powerful stroke. The man flew backwards and ended up on the floor of the dungeons with a big blow on the head that rendered him unconscious.

Nilsa tried to land properly and almost succeeded. She set one foot on the stairs and bounced forward, hitting one of the crates and bouncing again. She managed to stop her fall with her hands on the opposite wall. She was standing. It had not been one of Astrid's or Viggo's glorious attack leaps, since they always managed to land delicately on their feet, but it was pretty good for her. At least she had not ended up hitting her head on the floor.

While Nilsa was turning and nocking another arrow, Astrid was already done with four of the Visionaries who were lying dead at her feet and was confronting the remaining foes. The amazing skill she had with her knives was awesome; the way she finished off her enemies in close combat without a single scratch from their weapons astonished Nilsa.

Suddenly, something went wrong. There was some kind of roar and Astrid flew backward and crashed against one of the prisoners' cells.

Nilsa realized Vingar had cast a spell at Astrid.

"Free the dragon's slaves!" Vingar ordered the two remaining men left standing.

Astrid moaned on the floor. Nilsa ran to help her. The brunette was trying to stand but she looked beaten up. The blow had been hard. Nilsa reached her friend and helped her to her feet.

"He took me... by surprise..." Astrid admitted.

Vingar cast another spell, pointing his sword at them and moving it up and down. He opened his mouth wide and this time the roar was shrill. The wave of force that followed the roar arched and then fell on Astrid just like a long shot.

Astrid fell down on her face and was flattened on the floor by the impact. She put her hands to her head.

"Stop him... conjuring ..." she begged Nilsa.

Her friend nodded.

"Slaves of the dragon, kill them!" Vingar ordered, pointing his sword at both Rangers.

The slaves came out of their cells with a slow and heavy but steady step and headed to Nilsa and Astrid as ordered.

Nilsa ignored the slaves coming slowly at her and nocked an Earth Arrow. She raised her bow and aimed. The shot had to avoid the slaves, so she had to readjust her aim a couple times.

Vingar had Astrid flattened on the floor as if an invisible anvil had fallen on her head. He now pointed at Nilsa, and he was going to attack her now. She knew she would suffer her friend's fate, but she was not going to let that happen. She released at once and the Earth Arrow brushed between two slaves and hit Vingar in the torso when he was opening his mouth to give one of his roars that hammered both body and mind.

There was a burst of earth and smoke, as well as blinding and stunning compounds. The warlock took a step back, shaking his head—it had affected him. He put the sleeve of his dull silver robe to his eyes to wipe the noxious substances that had gotten into them.

Nilsa saw she had a chance, nocked an Air Arrow, and released. The arrow went between two slaves just when Vingar was starting to cast again. This time she hit him in the stomach, and there was an electrical charge that ran throughout the warlock's body as if he had been hit by a lightning bolt in a storm.

Vingar doubled up in pain while his arms shook uncontrollably without him being able to do anything to stop it.

It was her chance to finish him off, so Nilsa switched to a regular steel-tipped arrow.

Two bewitched slaves came at her, trying to seize her. She had to avoid them and lost the shot. She hit one of the slaves and pushed the other one to get free, losing some precious time.

"You won't be able to stop me with your arrow for long," Vingar said, taking cover behind the pedestal the claw was resting on.

"We'll see about that," Nilsa replied as she released at the warlock again with one of her regular arrows, trying to hit him in the head. The arrow hit the crystal claw and bounced off to one side.

"You'll pay for that, you heretic!" Vingar cried, enraged.

Nilsa nocked another arrow while she stepped back in order to put distance between herself and the slaves that were coming at her.

"What are you doing here?" Nilsa asked Vingar now that he was hiding behind the pedestal and not coming out to attack her.

"Can't you see? We're creating servants of the immortal dragon!"

"Why do you need more servants?"

"So they can worship their new god!" Vingar cried.

"That doesn't sound like the whole truth. What's happening here?"

"I won't tell you anything, you unclean Rangers!"

"You should, or you can give up your life right here and now," Nilsa threatened him, and she released at the pedestal with a Fire

Arrow, which burst into flame upon impact. Vingar was taken aback but did not leave his shelter. Unfortunately, his cloak did not catch fire, which was what Nilsa had intended.

Three slaves tried to grab Nilsa, who stepped aside and withdrew swiftly to nock a new Earth Arrow. She released and hit one of the slaves in the torso. The burst of earth and smoke left him stunned and confused as the brightness in his eyes dimmed a little, although not completely. The second one tried to reach her, but Nilsa caught him with an Air Arrow and the charge left him unconscious. She delivered a kick in the stomach to the third, which made him double over in pain.

Nilsa was sorry to have to attack the slaves, but she had no choice. They were not going to see reason, and if she was grabbed by several she would be lost.

Astrid got up from the floor.

"Are you alright?" Nilsa asked in a whisper.

"Well enough..." Astrid replied, feeling better. She shook her head.

"We have work to do," Nilsa said, indicating the slaves that continued coming toward them.

"Ok," Astrid nodded, and stretching her back and shoulders, she lunged to finish off the last two Visionaries and the bewitched slaves.

"Hurry up or they'll overcome us!"

"I'll deal with these, you watch the warlock so he doesn't cast any more spells," Astrid told Nilsa.

"Don't kill the slaves!" Nilsa said.

Astrid stopped to look at her.

"They're coming to kill us."

"Just listen to me and don't kill them," Nilsa insisted.

"Fine, whatever you say," Astrid said and lunged to attack. She knocked down the slaves who were almost upon them with blows to the back of their necks, temples, or chins with the pommels of her knives.

"Come to me, protect me!" Vingar said.

The last two Visionaries and three slaves still standing went back to Vingar.

"Form a line in front of me!"

Nilsa understood the move. Vingar wanted to protect himself behind his minions so the Elemental Arrows could not reach him.

That was a good strategy, and she would have to counter it.

"Heretics, your end is nigh!" Vingar cried as he started to cast a spell behind his human barrier. If he managed to finish the spell and deliver one of his roars, they would be in serious trouble. This time the warlock was pointing at Nilsa with his sword.

An arrow left Nilsa's bow toward Vingar, but she hit the Visionary directly in front of him in the head. It was one of her new arrows, the anti-magic ones Nilsa was developing. There was a big bang and then a tremendous noise, and the man's head whipped backward from the shock. The loud noise distracted Vingar in the middle of his spell, interrupting it.

"What? How? No!" he cried.

Nilsa nocked another arrow of the same kind.

Vingar cowered behind a slave and started casting again.

Nilsa's anti-magic arrow flew swiftly and hit the slave in the torso. Once again there was a bang, followed by a noise so loud that the whole protective line in front of the warlock was startled. The sound, loud and annoying, distracted Vingar again, and he was unable to finish his spell.

"Dirty Ranger tricks!" he cried in frustration and rage.

Astrid reached Vingar's defensive line, and he knew he was lost. Nilsa was already nocking another anti-magic arrow and preparing to release.

Vingar grasped the crystal dragon claw and turned, running to the far wall of the dungeons. Nilsa's arrow hit above Vingar's head with another tremendous blast, which startled him and made him crouch.

The last two Visionaries attacked Astrid, who had already knocked out the slaves, and she defeated them in a fight of sword against knives. They both ended up unconscious on the floor.

"Vingar's escaping!" Nilsa warned her as she nocked another arrow.

Astrid ran to the end of the dungeons.

"I can't believe it!" she cried.

"What's wrong?" Nilsa asked.

"Come and see."

Nilsa arrived where Astrid was, indicating the rock wall at the end of the hall.

"He's not here," Nilsa said blankly.

"He's like an eel, he slipped away."

"How?"

"There must be a secret passage here. I can't find out how to open it," Astrid replied, feeling and pushing the rocks in case any gave way.

"We've lost him…" Nilsa said, annoyed.

"I think so."

"That's bad…"

"Look on the bright side, we've stopped whatever he was trying to do here."

"That's right. I think he was trying to make an army of preachers," Nilsa said.

"That sounds awful," Astrid said as she turned to look at the remaining slaves in the cells.

"Let's free the others," Nilsa said.

"Yeah, and let's hope the effect wears off the bewitched ones when they wake up."

"I'm not so sure that's going to happen. We haven't killed the warlock. The spell will remain," Nilsa said, remembering what she had learned during her specialization.

"That's not good." Astrid shook her head. She had found the keys and was opening one of the cells.

"We'll have to take them to the capital so Egil can take a look at them," said Nilsa.

"Yeah, but also as proof of what's going on for Gondabar. Our leaders have to realize that what's happening is very serious."

Nilsa nodded and started freeing the other prisoners. At least they had saved them.

Chapter 29

"We've missed you these past few days," Lasgol said to Eicewald when they met in the forest.

I better, much, Camu messaged at once to the Mage.

Ona countered him with two clear growls.

"Let's go into the tent and I'll explain, there seems to be a winter storm brewing," the Mage said, pointing at some ugly black clouds that were fast approaching. It was raining hard, a freezing rain, and the winds were beginning to be strong.

Storm come strong, Camu messaged in warning.

"I'd better check the tent's anchoring and secure it to those trees behind it," said Lasgol, who knew that if the storm was intense, it would blow the tent away, and them with it.

Ona could not help, but she followed Lasgol wherever he went, like a huge mountain cat after its master.

I create spell against storm one day, Camu messaged to Eicewald while Lasgol was working.

"That would be a high-grade spell. It has never been done, as far as I know."

Water Magic?

"Water and Air magic. Storms are affected by both, but in order to stop a storm it would require a lot of power. Nature and her creations are far more powerful than man or beast."

I do one day.

"That's the spirit, Camu. Never give up and always look forward to attaining new goals. That's how you get far in this life."

"Is Camu giving you any of his bigheaded nonsense?" Lasgol asked, entering the tent.

I normal head, came the instant message.

"He has big ideas. I'm encouraging him to follow them. Important things will come from those attempts, I'm sure."

"I'm not sure grandiloquence is a seed that bears good fruit…"

"Better that than not having any spirit and being resigned to get little out of life," Eicewald said in the tone of one imparting a lesson. "Only the brave, the daring, achieve unthinkable landmarks."

"In Camu's case the landmark might be to go through a wall with his head for being 'maximus stubbornious,'" Lasgol joked.

I fly. No go through with head, Camu messaged defensively, not having understood the joke.

Eicewald burst out laughing.

"So tell us, what's kept you so busy in the capital?"

"A pretty unpleasant business…" the mage replied in a resentful tone.

"Can you tell us about it?" Lasgol said curiously.

"A non-grata person has been reinstated by King Thoran and I must allow him back into the fold of the Ice Magi."

Lasgol sat down, cross-legged, and wondered who Eicewald might be referring to.

Who be? Camu was also curious.

"Someone who betrayed me, who stole something precious and caused a serious situation, one you were all involved in."

"It wouldn't be…" Lasgol began—he thought he knew who Eicewald was talking about, who the mage in question was.

I not know.

"The last time you saw him he was heading downriver," Eicewald said, "and I was leaving for Irinel because of him."

Camu blinked hard.

Still not know.

"He means the Ice Mage Maldreck," said Lasgol who had already guessed.

"Exactly. I mean the traitor and thief who stole the Star of Sea and Life and caused so much trouble."

Oh, mage thief. I remember.

"Why has Orten forgiven him? I'm surprised, since he's not usually the forgiving kind when someone fails him."

Eicewald nodded.

"Orten hasn't forgiven him, it's Thoran who's done it. The kingdom only has a handful of Ice Magi and the youngest aren't very powerful yet. Maldreck might be a treacherous weasel, but he's powerful. King Thoran has opened the doors of the Tower of the Ice Magi for him, and I couldn't say no."

"The King is looking to have more Ice Magi? Any particular reason?" Lasgol asked, wondering about such a suspicious move.

"The King is always looking to increase the kingdom's magical power to be superior to the magical prowess of other kingdoms."

"Because it's well-known that magi can settle battles, or is there another reason?" Lasgol asked, raising an eyebrow.

Eicewald smiled.

"Both. Magi not only settle battles, they can also decide wars. More than one kingdom has had to surrender to the superiority of another's magical power, although a great army is usually more powerful than a handful of magi. As to the other reason, I think it's because of the Princess of Irinel."

"The Princess of Irinel?" Lasgol said blankly.

Eicewald nodded.

"Well, we do know the kind of character the Princess has, we've experienced it ourselves. And it would seem the Princess doesn't always curb her temper with the King…"

"I knew she had become way too conciliatory," said Lasgol.

Princess not fun, Camu messaged.

"There are quite a few raised arguments between the King and Princess. From what I've found out, one of the arguments has been about the magic of both kingdoms. It seems that King Thoran believes his Ice Magi are much more powerful than Irinel's Druids. As I've been told, the Princess, who has Druid blood, didn't like the comment at all, and there was a heated argument about the matter. In the end the Princess left the Throne-hall in a huff, screaming that for every Ice Mage of Norghana there were a hundred Druids and that the magical power of her people could sweep all of Norghana."

"Ooooo, and our King can't have liked that much," Lasgol said, chuckling.

"Indeed. And he's ordered me to look for and train more Ice Magi at once. He's called several who had fallen into disgrace in the past to come back. One of them, unfortunately, is Maldreck."

"Wow… that's not good for us at all."

"Indeed. It means I have to leave in search of new potential pupils and stop your training for a while. I'm very sorry."

I much upset, Camu messaged, along with a feeling of sadness.

"Perhaps we should teach Camu how to use 'very' and 'much' properly, he seems to mix them up quite a bit," Eicewald said.

"I think what he does is improvise sentences including some term he's heard and doesn't know the meaning of, and, of course, he utters these wonders."

I know upset.

"But it's 'very upset,' not 'much upset,'" Lasgol told him.

I prefer much upset. More powerful.

Eicewald laughed and Lasgol slapped his forehead.

"It's not about what you prefer, you need to speak correctly," Lasgol tried to make him understand.

You understand well.

"We understand, yes," Eicewald confirmed.

"Don't tell him…"

So, if understand, be well. Much upset is.

Eicewald laughed again. Lasgol cursed the ice gods for charging him with this stubborn creature.

The storm's winds lashed the tent, and for a moment it seemed like they were going to blow it off the ground, but it held.

Ona shifted restlessly. She did not like being inside a tent when the winds blew. She wanted to go out to find shelter in the forest, but she was stalling. Lasgol knew it was because she wanted to be with her friends, even if she didn't like the situation.

"It's as if a great Ice Mage had gotten angry with us," Lasgol said joking. "He's created a pretty strong storm, let's hope it's not too strong."

"That leads me to the lesson I wanted to teach today," Eicewald said.

"Go ahead, we're ready," Lasgol said.

"There's a universal principle of Magic you need to learn. It's the Principle of Magic Limitation."

I want know, Camu messaged as he stared at Eicewald with his large eyes wide open.

The Mage nodded.

"You need to know and remember, always, that magic has a cost and some limits."

"We've been studying about cost of magic in the tome you left me with the Principle of Magical Cost. Well, it's really me who's studying it and then I explain it to Camu, who's busy trying to create new skills."

I understand. Magic cost energy. Be problem, Camu messaged.

"There's much more regarding the cost of magic than that, but for now, as long as you learn what the tome says, I'm happy," Eicewald said. "We'll leave the more advanced subjects for later on."

"There are things in this tome that require more study…" Lasgol commented in a tone that implied they needed more help and, of course, more time.

Eicewald bowed his head.

"In every tome of knowledge that you study, you'll find more advanced concepts and areas of study. It's natural, since the tomes I'm bringing you are about general principals. If later on you want to go deeper in new areas, you'll have to do that in the future and with another instructor. There are specialists in each subject."

"There are?" Lasgol asked, awed.

"There are indeed. The difficulty lies in finding them. Some are in nearby kingdoms, but others are far away in distant realms. Also, they don't usually take on pupils since they're focused on their own studies."

No good.

"Unfortunately, there isn't one great school of unified magic where you can study all the facets of magic in depth," Eicewald explained, spreading his arms.

"So, if we want to learn about one type of magic or a particular concept in order to improve on it, we'll have to find an erudite in that subject, and said erudite might be at the end of the Nocean Empire?"

"I'm afraid so, although you still have a lot to work on before you can progress further in the study of advanced matters. So don't worry and keep learning. Before you run you must learn how to crawl," the Mage told them.

Very little good, Camu protested.

"There are few things in life that you can obtain easily," Eicewald said.

"The Principle of Magical Limitation, continue explaining that, please," asked Lasgol, who was watching Eicewald with interest.

"As I was saying, all magic has its limits. It's a universal principle."

"All magic? Regardless of type?" Lasgol asked.

"Indeed. All magic, no matter how trivial or powerful it might be, has a cost and a limit," Eicewald said in a serious tone.

Not want limits, Camu messaged, shaking his head.

"Otherwise, those of us blessed with the Gift or Talent would be like gods. The universe doesn't allow it," Eicewald said, smiling.

"And that's a good thing," said Lasgol. "No one should be as powerful as a god."

"There are many who pursue exactly that," the Mage commented disapprovingly.

"Magi?" Lasgol asked.

"Magi, sorcerers, warlocks, shamans, erudites, and others with the Talent. They all have one thing in common: they seek to rise."

"Rise? What does that mean?"

"They seek to progress in the grades of magic to the point where they transcend mortality and become demigods," Eicewald explained.

Transcend? Camu did not know what that meant.

"I'm not sure I get it either," Lasgol admitted, wrinkling his nose. He was not familiar with those concepts and their meaning.

"Don't worry about that for now. You'll understand in time. What I want you to understand is that there are people with the Gift who devote their whole being to improve their gift and be able to reach the final grade and go beyond. They call it transcending, reaching a level higher than the highest grade. Their goal in life is to become demigods through magic."

"I'll keep that in mind…"

"I doubt we'll come across one of them, but they do exist," Eicewald told them in a warning tone.

Very powerful? Camu wanted to know.

"They are. They think they're improving their Gift and that what they're doing is nothing less than art. They call themselves Arcane Virtuosi," Eicewald explained.

"Arcane Virtuosi? Sounds weird… almost mystical…" Lasgol commented, wondering what they would be like.

"It is, in a certain way," the Mage confirmed. "They consider themselves as artisans of the magical. They've reached such a level that they are virtuosi in the arcane realm."

I want meet.

"I doubt we'll meet any here in Norghana, but it's good that you know they exist, in case you come across any."

"Are they dangerous?" Lasgol asked, thinking the mage's explanation sounded like a warning.

"They are, very dangerous. They can kill a person merely to show their power or because you've interfered in some way, regardless of how small, in their progress or path toward the ascension they thrive for."

No good, Camu messaged.

"No, they're not as a rule, no. That's not to say that there aren't any kind ones, but my advice is to get as far away from them as you can."

"Advice we'll be sure to follow," Lasgol promised.

Eicewald nodded repeatedly.

"That would be wise."

Chapter 30

"Let me explain the concept of Magic Limitation," he said, putting a tome about the principle on the floor of the tent. He opened it at the beginning and turned some pages until he found what he wanted.

"What are those limitations?" Lasgol asked impatiently.

"Well, you see, my dear pupils, magic has limitations regarding the physical as well as the temporal, since these are two variables that define our universe. These are unbreakable boundaries. No-one has ever been able to break them, although many have tried, and it is said that some magi, the most powerful, have managed to bend them."

"What are the physical limits?" Lasgol asked, puzzled. He was a little lost.

Physical? Camu was blinking hard. He did not understand the concept.

Eicewald gestured with his hand to take it easy.

"I mean the physical laws of nature," he explained in a calm tone. "For instance, if I wanted to move that mountain you see to the east of the forest, I couldn't do it no matter how powerful I became."

"Because the weight and foundation of the mountain are fathomless," reasoned Lasgol.

Mountain very big. Too much.

"Exactly. You yourselves may sense that no mage could move that mountain because magic is limited to nature's physical limitations. You can manage great things, like, say, wrench the top off of it, but not the whole mountain. Do you understand the concept?"

Move tip of mountain, yes. All mountain, no, Camu messaged.

"Correct, but do you understand the reasoning? Why it's not possible to do it?"

Too much weight, much big.

"That's right. If our own logic tells us that it's too much, it likely is," Eicewald said.

"But you could uproot a tree, even half a forest if you wanted to," Lasgol replied.

"How do you know it's possible for me to do that?"

"I've witnessed your winter storms—they're strong and can freeze any being they reach. Their winds are also extremely strong, capable of pulling out trees no matter how deep their roots are," said Lasgol, pointing at the roof of the tent that was shaking under the storm above them.

Be true, Camu messaged.

Eicewald nodded slowly and repeatedly.

"Indeed. I can do it because a winter storm is nature-based—nature can do it. I'm not breaking any physical laws of nature, what I'm doing is imitating her. I create a winter storm that is magical but that's just an imitation of a natural one and therefore has the same limitations. A storm cannot uproot a mountain, but it can uproot half a forest or knock up houses in the air, particularly if they're wood. What I conjure is within the limits that nature establishes, and therefore I can create magic within those same limits."

"I think I understand…" said Lasgol.

What limits me?

"That's a good question. It's difficult to know beforehand, you'll have to keep trying and seeing how far you can go."

I fly. No limit?

"That's a singular skill which nevertheless is within the limits of nature, since there are great birds larger than you in Tremia that can fly."

I want see! Fly with them! Camu messaged excitedly.

"I'm not sure that's a good idea. Some of the great birds are harmless, but others not so much. There are huge raptors that live on the highest peaks of Tremia which are carnivorous and will eat anything that has flesh, and the more the better. Their size and wingspan is such that they can pick up an ox or elephant and fly up to the top. Having first killed it, of course. They drop it from a height and take it away when it's dead."

Now not want see, Camu messaged, not looking forward to it after the Mage's explanation.

"Then can a mage create a tree, like the ones in this wood for example…?"

"Good, I see we're beginning to see the limitations. A real tree, like the ones in the forest, no. But the mage can use Illusion Magic to make you believe you're seeing one; you can create something that looks like a tree but not create one directly, because that goes against the limits of nature."

Food? Camu messaged, interested.

"Yeah, that, can a mage make a whole meal appear out of nothing?"

"Is that possible in nature?" the Mage asked, raising his eyebrows.

"No… I don't think so. Well, not just like that, out of nothing. You'd have to hunt, gather, cook, and prepare the whole thing," Lasgol said.

"In their ignorance, many believe magi can create food, drink, gold, jewels, and riches out of nothing, out of thin air. Let me assure you that's not true. If one day you find a mage who says he's capable of doing that, it is almost guaranteed he'll be trying to fool you."

"Well, that's a real pity, we could feed and help the poor and underprivileged," Lasgol said ruefully.

"But consider that if such a thing were possible, it would also be possible to make a man, or an army, appear out of thin air. That would entail death and destruction, not only of the poor and underprivileged, but of whole kingdoms."

No good, Camu messaged, shaking his head.

"Indeed, it's not good. That's why, at least in this universe we live in, nature always limits what we can do with magic," Eicewald explained.

"Always? Or almost always?" Lasgol was curious. "Is there a way of breaking these limitations?"

Eicewald remained thoughtful for a moment, his chin in his hand.

"There are magi, even erudites, who seek to break those limits, some to attain more power, others for more knowledge. Some have managed to bend these limitations but not break them, at least as far as I know."

"Bend them? How?"

"By driving the limitations to their breaking points or looking for a way to overcome them, since they haven't managed to break them. It's a complex and arcane matter, dark even, because in many cases what they seek is to break reality itself. There are magi who haven't managed to break the limits but have curved them, extended them… a little."

"Egil told me there are Elemental Fire Magi who are capable of creating a small volcano that spews lava and fireballs, obliterating everything around them."

I want see.

"No, no, that's not what I mean. And yes, there are Fire Magi who can do that. It's a powerful spell which only a few know how to cast. The thing is it's not a real volcano, it's a creation of a Fire Mage imitating reality. Therefore, it's not real, it's a limited imitation."

"I think I understand…"

"We magi imitate nature, her elements. We find inspiration in her and try to create spells that imitate her. But they're never real, they almost always fall short in comparison with what nature can do."

"And the other limitation, the temporal one you mentioned earlier?" Lasgol asked, keen on understanding the limitations he and Camu would have to face when it came to using their magic.

Eicewald nodded.

"The temporal limitation is essential. All magic is limited by time. Any spell, charm, or enchantment has a temporal limit."

Magic not last forever, Camu messaged.

"Indeed. Spells always have a specific duration. It might be a bit longer or a bit shorter, depending on the type of spell and the mage's grade of power, but it will always be limited by time."

"We're already experiencing that now. Our skills last for a while and then vanish."

Not fly forever, Camu messaged, annoyed.

"That's because it's a magical skill."

Birds fly forever.

"That's not entirely true. Birds have to rest, since flying tires them. Some can fly very far, others not, but in the end they all have to stop to rest because their bodies can't bear such a continued effort. Magic is similar—it doesn't last forever."

I want fly forever.

"I'm sure, I would too," Eicewald said, smiling.

"The temporal nature of a spell can be worked on, right?" Lasgol asked.

"Indeed. But only up to a point, and it's one of the amplifications that's most difficult to achieve."

"You mean that making a spell last longer is difficult?"

"Indeed."

I do.

"Of course," Eicewald chuckled. "I encourage you to try and extend your skills in time."

"I'm not sure encouraging him to do something difficult is such a good idea, he's always going to be sure he can succeed."

"Life will teach him that not everything can be done, no matter how much we set our mind to it," Eicewald said without looking at Camu.

"Anything else we should know about the temporal limitations?"

"Yes, and it's important. You must never try to manipulate time. Many magi have tried, and most have ended up very badly. Time—yesterday, today, and tomorrow—must be left intact."

Lasgol was scratching his head.

"Because we could go to the past and change things?"

I go future. I be old.

"You mustn't go to the past or the future. Run away from any person with the Gift who tries to do so. Time must not be altered under any circumstance. It would destroy our world if it were tampered with. The implications would be catastrophic," Eicewald warned them sternly.

"Not even to correct a great tragedy?"

"Not even for that. The consequences of altering the past or the future would bring about a greater tragedy. Listen to me carefully. It's forbidden to alter time. Never get involved in its study. Don't give in to the temptation of trying to go to the past and change things."

"If you think we shouldn't, then we won't," Lasgol promised.

"I swear it's for your own good, and for that of all Tremia," Eicewald said in a fearful tone.

We behave.

Eicewald looked at Camu, who blinked once and tilted his head to one side.

"Not sure why, but I don't feel completely at ease."

Chapter 31

Several weeks had gone by since Lasgol and Camu had seen Eicewald for the last time. They took it for granted that they would not see him for a good while because of the situation with the King and his request for more Ice Magi.

So, on this afternoon they were both trying to make progress with their magic, which as usual was not being at all easy.

From what Eicewald told us about the Principle of Magical Power and what we've studied in the tomes, in order to achieve more power, we must reach a new grade of magic, Lasgol transmitted to Camu. *I wonder if it's something we'll feel when it happens.*

Feel magical grade? Camu messaged, blinking hard.

Yeah, I wonder whether we'll feel it somehow or if once we reach a new grade, it will manifest somehow. It's a little hard to grasp this concept since it's not intuitive.

Intuitive? Camu messaged, tilting his head.

Something that's easy to understand without thinking too much about it, Lasgol transmitted, trying to explain.

I feel grade.

You've felt it, or do you believe that because now you know grades exist, you'll feel it when it happens?

I feel when it happen.

I knew you'd say that. Let's hope it happens in a way we can notice.

I shine, you see.

Well, if you're going to start shining, I won't be left behind.

I shine more. I shine silver.

So, I'll shine green, which is warmer.

I get new grade before.

No way. I intend to beat you. I'm going to put all of my willpower into passing level before you.

You not do. I win, Camu messaged, lifting his head very dignified.

Ona, who was inside the tent snoozing, came out to see what was going on. The day was mild and it did not look like there was going to be a storm, which was a novelty, because autumn was turning out very hard.

Let's get started.

I practice Dragon Fire, Camu messaged to Lasgol and moved away toward the pond to practice. He still had not managed to create the skill, but Lasgol thought he might be close to it. For his part, he had not managed the skill to create elemental arrows, which left him feeling frustrated.

Let's see if you succeed. If you do, it will help you rise to another level.

I feel it near. I practice much.

I hope you get your dragon fire breath. That would be a fabulous skill.

I much fabulous.

Of course, Lasgol transmitted to him, and he was not being sarcastic, he wished Camu the best of luck in advancing his magic, both in skill creation and reaching a new level, and afterward a new grade. That would be good for the group. The more powerful Camu became, the better for the Snow Panthers. Besides, it made him strive even harder so as not to be left behind. He could not let Camu get ahead of him, at least not too far ahead.

As he helped Camu with the magic tomes and understanding the concepts explained in them, Lasgol felt like Camu's older brother again. A feeling he had missed during the recent past as Camu grew up and needed him less. Now that Camu needed him again, Lasgol was happy to perform this function and help him. It produced a joy in him that encouraged him, and there was also a bit of personal satisfaction, although it was often difficult to fight Camu's stubbornness.

You no practice? Camu messaged, seeing that Lasgol was watching him without starting himself.

Of course I am, right away. I'm not going to let you beat me, no way, he transmitted back with a smile.

I win, you can't help, Camu messaged, looking toward the pond, and he started to try to create the skill in a hurry, as if he had to beat Lasgol.

Lasgol smiled and fetched his bow, quiver, and satchel from inside the tent and went to stand not too far from Camu, also looking toward the pond. Following what he had learned from Eicewald, Lasgol proceeded to do his new set of skills progression. He called it that because before attempting any progress, as a warm-up and also as a means to continue advancing in his magical level, he called on all his skills, one after the other, activating each several times.

He started. At first when he had begun to use this system it was quite messy; he had often gotten mixed up with the skills and order. Sometimes he forgot a couple of skills, and others he repeated too many times, which had been dreadful. Egil had helped him. Between the two of them, they had created a table of skills and the number of repetitions to do with each one. They had listed them in an order that would be easy for Lasgol to remember and follow. Of course, Egil had lent him one of his notebooks to write down the table of skills and how to proceed.

He started with the easiest one, *Animal Communication,* and since he did not want to distract Camu, he sent it to Ona.

Ona, Lasgol practicing.

Ona chirped once. She was used to this by now and knew that Lasgol was going to do his usual exercises. The first few days the poor panther would look at Lasgol's eyes, not knowing what was wanted of her. It had taken him several days to make Ona understand that he was only practicing and that he did not want her to do anything.

He called upon his *Animal Presence* and then *Aura Presence* upon Ona. The good panther could not perceive these skills.

He went on with the list of skills, and after seeking his inner energy, he concentrated and called on *Cat-like Reflexes, Improved Agility, Hawk's Eye,* and *Owl Hearing* five times in a row, each one as fast as he could. With each skill a green flash left his body and he felt a certain tingling letting him know they had been properly activated.

Once he finished this group of skills, he took a deep breath and exhaled. Then he bent over and called on *Dirt Throwing, Trap Hiding* (using one he carried in his satchel), and *Trail Erasing,* which hid his own footprints. He did that, three times each.

Straightening up again, he took out his mother's medallion and called on *Arcane Communication* to interact with the object. A blue flash coming from the jewel told him he had been successful.

He continued with the Archery skills. He held the bow with his left hand, nocked an arrow, pulled the string back to his nose, aimed, and called on *True Shot, Blind Shot, Fast Shot,* and *Multiple Shot.* He called them three times each.

Finally, he called on the last skills he had learned: *Woodland Protection, Guiding Light,* and *Fire Creating.*

Once the whole table of skills had been revised, he felt much better. It gave him a feeling of serenity and confidence being able to call them up, repeatedly and without mistakes. He had used up quite a bit of his inner energy, but he still had a pretty large supply to draw from. There were a couple other skills he did not use in this table because they were more complex.

Lasgol inhaled and exhaled the cold air of the pond once again and felt ready to try to create the skill he was looking for. To his left, a few paces away, Camu was trying over and over, sure he was going to make it, even if he continued to fail time and time again. He stood staring at the creature and all of a sudden something came to his mind.

Camu, I have an idea, he transmitted.

Camu turned his large bulging eyes toward him.

Idea good?

I think so, although I'm not sure it'll work.

Good, we try.

Lasgol nodded with a smile. Good thing Camu had his unsinkable optimism and courage to try anything. Nothing was too outrageous or too small. He was always willing to try new things, whatever they were.

All right. We're going to do the following. A competition between the two of us.

Competition?

Yup, to see who's capable of creating a skill first. Whoever does, wins the competition.

Prize?

You need a prize? Isn't the satisfaction of beating me enough?

Camu shook his head.

I want prize.

That's odd, but okay. What do you want for a prize?

Silver

What do you want that for?

Me know

Lasgol snorted and then cursed the heavens.

Whatever, I'm not even going to try and understand that. If you win, I'll get it for you, but if you lose and I win, you'll do whatever I say without deviation for a whole month.

Camu thought for a moment.

Okay.

What I thought of is that we do it as if it were some kind of a duel. We stand facing one another, and the first one to create the skill beats the other.

Duel fun.

I guessed you'd see it that way, Lasgol smiled. He knew his friend would love anything that was a game.

They both stood in position, leaving about fifteen paces of separation between them. The pond was on their right and seemed to be watching, half-frozen, the latest idea of those annoying visitors who came so often to disturb the peace, reigning over the landscape.

Very well, let's begin, said Lasgol.

I count.

Okay, go ahead and count.

Three, two, one, start!

Lasgol concentrated and sought his inner energy. He gathered a good supply and imagined in his mind as clearly and concretely as he could what he wanted to achieve. He visualized his right hand taking an arrow from his quiver. He focused on the arrow and imagined the final result of the skill: a handful of elemental arrows of the four main types to use with the bow he was holding in his other hand. That was what he wanted.

At the other end, his opponent was trying to create his Dragon Fire skill in the same way. Camu gathered energy, concentrated, and imagined what the powerful jet of fire that would come out of his mouth would be like, capable of burning everything in its path up to a hundred paces. It would burn it all, reducing everything to ashes in an instant. He would even incinerate rock.

Ona was watching both, aware they were practicing their magic, which the panther was not too enthusiastic about. Resigned, she went into the forest to hunt something to keep entertained and stay in shape.

Lasgol wanted to beat Camu in this singular duel. If he lost, apart from having to pay the prize, he would have to cope with the creature's comments and vanity for a long time. Yet, he was aware that the creature's magical capacity was far superior to his own, so it was going to be difficult for him to win this competition.

He concentrated as hard as he could to visualize the skill activating and wished with all his being for it. Suddenly there was a tiny flash, a weak one, that started blinking. Lasgol felt he had it, that he was going to make it. The blinking would become a green flash or would fade into a weak one. Now he could better perceive the creative process of the skill and when it was really going to work or fail. He even felt a tingling in his neck and arms when he was successful. Everything he had been studying and practicing was beginning to bear fruit. If he beat Camu and managed to create this skill, the reward would be double.

The intermittent flash stopped and Lasgol did not feel any tingling. He could not make the skill happen. He sighed. Camu was taking the lead. He opened his eyes and saw his friend flashing intermittently silver. If there was a final strong flash, he would have done it. He waited a moment, watching the creature. All of a sudden, the intermittent silver flash vanished.

Camu opened his eyes and looked at Lasgol. They exchanged a taunting look, both knowing the other had not made it. They challenged one another, glaring with half-closed eyes as if they were enemies. There was no real enmity in their eyes, but they did have a touch of challenge. Healthy rivalry might get out of hand if they were not careful.

A moment later they both concentrated and tried again, forgetting their rival, focusing all their attention and effort on creating the skill they were thriving for. One of them would succeed, they were both sure of it. Yet magic was a tough teacher to please, and perhaps she would not grant them what they were seeking.

They both kept trying, and with every failure they observed one another and tried again. Neither wanted to lose. Neither would give up before the other. They would go on until they ran out of their last drop of inner energy. Only then, when it was impossible to continue, would they admit defeat. Not a moment before.

Suddenly from Camu's mouth there came, not a roar as he expected, but a shrill hiss. The sound, which made Lasgol cover his ears, was followed by a tremendous jet of something like water and steam, only freezing, extremely cold. Lasgol reacted when he saw it coming directly at him. He leapt to one side to avoid it. Camu's freezing breath brushed past Lasgol as he rolled to one side and stared at the creature in surprise. He had not managed his Dragon Fire skill, but he had created another one.

Camu was left with his jaw hanging open for a moment. The frozen jet kept coming and reaching a greater distance. Lasgol noticed it froze the ground where it touched it, leaving a mark.

Considering that the ground was already snow-covered and very cold, this meant the jet had a very low temperature. Camu shut his mouth and stopped the frozen jet.

Wow... Lasgol transmitted, very impressed.

I manage skill! Camu messaged excitedly.

Yeah, you did it, and it's most spectacular.

I powerful. I freeze everything.

Yeah, but let me remind you that it wasn't the skill you were going to develop.

Not matter. I new skill.

I'm not sure I can concede victory... Lasgol was teasing Camu. Of course, the new skill counted, but he was not going to admit it so readily. He would let the creature fight for it a little.

Be good!

That was ice instead of fire...

No matter. I Ice Breath now. I win bet.

Hmm.... I don't know about that...

Camu leapt in place and planted his four legs firmly in the snow.

I win!

Seeing that Camu was getting really angry, Lasgol decided to concede victory.

Fine. You won the bet.

Yes! I winner! He messaged gleefully and began to do his happy dance, flexing his legs, moving his body up and down, and wagging his long tail.

No need to rub it in my face so.

Little yes, Camu messaged, smiling broadly as he continued dancing.

Lasgol had to be patient and let Camu do his dance. To make that moment even more endearing, sleet began to fall, driven by a most annoying wind.

Great... just what I needed...

Camu took his sweet time since the winter weather did not affect him, and he danced and laughed for quite a while. Luckily Ona had not yet returned from the forest, or else she would have joined Camu to add insult to injury.

When he finally finished celebrating his victory, Camu looked at Lasgol with his bulging eyes.

Now you do, he messaged encouragingly.

Lasgol concentrated and tried again. He did it with a cheerful will, leaning on the good feelings that Camu's success had brought up in him. He was happy for him, and it gave him hope that he could succeed too. He was filled with optimism. The blinking flashes came at once—he had it. He was going to do it. He was sure. The flashes died out.

Failure, he transmitted to Camu, very frustrated.

Try again. If I do you do too, Camu said with his usual optimism and stubbornness.

Lasgol was furious and frustrated for failing. For having been beaten by Camu, and most of all, for not being as good at magic as he wished to be. Those feelings, strong and rooted, caused something to ignite inside Lasgol, as if the breath of the wind stoked the embers of a fire.

Using these feelings, the spark inside him acting as a trigger, Lasgol tried once again. Without knowing why, he nocked the arrow and aimed at Camu as if he were the enemy. The blinking flash finally became a strong one and the skill was created at last.

The green flash ran through the bow and arrow and Lasgol released. The arrow flew toward Camu and suddenly, halfway along, it turned into a Fire Arrow. A different one from those the Rangers used. The arrow was literally on fire as it flew toward Camu. It was surrounded by a flame which, although it looked as if it were going to consume the arrow, did not burn it.

The arrow hit Camu's right leg and there was a small flare. The flames climbed up Camu's leg, who shook them off, and then he buried it in the snow to put the fire out.

Did I hurt you? Lasgol was concerned as he watched, surprised and fearful at what had just happened.

No, not worry. Arrow not through scales.

And the fire?

Heat little but not much. I bear.

Lasgol snorted. He had been scared when he saw the flame on Camu's leg.

Arrow turn Fire Arrow.

Yeah, not exactly what I was looking for, but close enough.

What want?

To create a bunch of elemental arrows to have at hand to use later, not in the moment and only one.

Me like. You shoot with Fire Arrow now when want.

242

Yeah… not a bad skill, Lasgol had to admit.

Only Fire Arrows?

Hmmmm, that's a good question. Let me see.

Lasgol nocked another arrow, pulled the string back to his nose, aimed, and released. This time he did not aim at Camu but at a tree, and instead of a Fire Arrow he thought of creating one of air. He called on the skill and the green flash came, accompanied by the tingling sensation. The skill activated.

The arrow turned into one of air as it flew to the tree. The electric charge could be clearly seen sparkling all along the arrow. It looked as if a small bolt of lightning were riding the arrow. When it reached the tree, a charge ran along the trunk as if lightning had just struck it. The smell of burning wood reached them, carried by the wind.

Much fantastic! Camu messaged excitedly as he started doing his happy dance again.

It really is!

Lasgol smiled. He could not believe they had both done it. He had created Elemental Arrows and, although the skill did not work exactly as he had planned it to, it was a good start. Now he could turn a regular arrow into one of the four elemental ones. That would come in handy, since it would allow him to choose the right arrow for each situation he found himself in. He wondered whether he could create another type of arrow like the ones Nilsa was making, although it was not likely. Anyway, he would try in the future. For now, he was happy with this success. He was tired, with little inner magic energy left, but he was very happy.

What call skill?

Lasgol scratched his head.

Elemental Arrows, he said.

Sound good. Like.

And you, what are you going to call your skill? because it can't be Dragon Fire….

I call Icy Breath.

I like it. It fits and is very descriptive.

I know.

Lasgol watched Camu and realized that the healthy competition he and Camu had, now that they knew of the existence of levels and grades in magic were measurable, was very good for both of them. It was a friendly rivalry which forced them both to excel beyond what they would normally do if they studied and practiced each on their own. Witnessing how Camu practiced creating new skills or amplifying the ones he already had pushed Lasgol to do the same and try to do better. That was where the idea had come from to have a direct competition, and it had turned out a lot better than he had imagined.

He wished his ideas and plans would work as well. Unfortunately, in most plans something always went wrong, or some unexpected event changed everything. That was life, at least theirs. He wondered what Egil and the others might be doing. He should go back and find out. He had a strange feeling that things were going to go awry, once again.

Chapter 32

Egil summoned the Panthers to the Tower room that morning. The different parties had already returned from their operations, and it was time to study the possible repercussions of all they had learned, as well as plan their next steps.

The group was happy to be back and pleased with what they had achieved, even if they had not defeated the enemy completely, which is what they had been after. All their operations had ended well too, which was an added bonus. They were each in their bunk and had been chatting about everything that had happened for a good while.

"It's wonderful to see all of you back safe and sound," Gerd told them with a big smile.

"Same here, big guy!" Nilsa replied cheerfully, clapping her hands.

"I don't know why you worry so much. It's all been as easy as pie," Viggo said with his usual air of having absolutely everything under control.

"Oh sure, piece of cake, so much so that if I hadn't been there the warlock Zirken would have fled," said Ingrid.

"He wouldn't have fled. I was about to catch him."

"From a second floor?"

"I wouldn't have broken anything, I'm very flexible," Viggo stretched his legs.

Ingrid rolled her eyes and did not say anything else, since she knew it was useless. Viggo was never going to admit he had needed help in front of his friends.

"Have you managed to get any information out of Zirken?" Ingrid asked Egil.

"Not a word. He's an obstinate warlock," Egil said, shaking his head. "I've tried several interrogation techniques but I haven't been able to make him talk, beyond telling me that the immortal dragon will rise and destroy us all."

"Yeah, they all have that message down pat," Astrid said ironically.

"Or imbued with magic," Nilsa said.

"The warlocks like Zirken, who serve Drugan and the immortal dragon, aren't bewitched by any magic," Egil corrected. "They truly believe what they preach, that's why they're so dangerous. Whoever believes blindly in their destiny will kill whoever gets in the way without stopping to see who it is."

"Well, they bewitch others to use as preachers or an army or whatever," said Nilsa.

"That's deplorable. It's inhuman," Lasgol said, disgusted.

Astrid nodded. "It is. Nilsa and I have seen it up close, and it makes your stomach turn."

"Haven't you used your two friends, Ginger and Fred, to elicit the information?" Viggo asked, raising an eyebrow.

"I have, and even so he resisted. His fanaticism is greater than the terror my two little dear friends can cause him. It's most impressive—I'd have never thought there were stronger feelings than the terror and panic Ginger and Fred cause, but it seems there are. Fanaticism is one, from what I've seen. I find it absolutely fascinating, albeit not fantastic at all."

"I'm sure love is another," Nilsa said with a smile.

"You think?" Gerd asked with a doubtful look on his face. "When panic overcomes you it's difficult to shake it off, and in my case nearly impossible."

"Love conquers all," said Astrid and looked at Lasgol with eyes filled with tenderness, something not usually seen in the Assassin's gaze.

"Love conquers all," Lasgol nodded.

"I had to turn him over to Gondabar so the Royal Rangers could question him. I don't think they'll get any answers, but it'll serve so that Gondabar and the Rangers themselves take this matter seriously."

"And not think we're insane," said Ingrid.

"We've also delivered Vingar's bewitched slaves, and seeing the state they're in, together with the Visionaries, I have no doubt that Gondabar and the rest of leaders will take us seriously."

"Let's hope so," Lasgol nodded.

"Have you found out where the slaves came from?" Egil asked.

Astrid nodded. "They're mostly Norghanian, from the lower status. They recruited them by offering easy money at taverns and other ill-reputed establishments. Almost half of them are sailors looking for an easy job. Visionaries with bags of gold approached them."

"Interesting. Were they good with weapons?" Egil asked.

"Yes, they were. Not in great physical condition, but they weren't starving paupers," Astrid told him.

"That's interesting. It indicates the Visionaries didn't want to use them for spreading the message but for something else…"

"The spell was different from the one with the dragon head we witnessed before. Here they were bewitched with eyes as bright as diamonds. It was horrible," Nilsa said. "I think the Visionaries want to create an army of slaves."

"Vingar called them servants of the immortal dragon."

"I've asked Gondabar for permission to see them," Egil said. "I'll go this afternoon, they intrigue me."

"The Visionaries won't tell you anything. And I doubt they really know their superiors' plans," Astrid said.

Egil nodded with resignation. "I guessed as much. But even so, I'd like to question them. Sometimes fate smiles on those who don't give up."

"Or not," Viggo said with an ironic grin.

"That too," replied Egil.

"Try to find out anything you can, Egil. We still don't know where the immortal dragon is or how he's going to reincarnate," Lasgol said in a troubled tone.

"Exactly. Is it just me, or did we achieve nothing with these operations?" Viggo asked.

"I wouldn't say that," said Egil. "We've managed to interrupt and upset operations of both the Visionaries and the Defenders. We have one of their deputies in the dungeons and their plans have been affected, without a doubt. We've achieved something, even if it's simply delaying them."

"Yeah, but delaying what?" Ingrid said.

"Reincarnation, no doubt. That's why the Visionaries and the Defenders are being so active and we've been able to find them. If they had been hiding it would've been a lot more difficult."

"But we still don't know what that reincarnation's going to be like," Lasgol said. "That has me puzzled and worried."

"We lack important information to find out how they're going to do that. But everything we've achieved has to be related to the reincarnation. We still don't have the full picture, but I swear we have relevant information about parts of Drugan's and Viggen's plan."

"Well, I don't see much," said Viggo.

"Because you're too busy looking at your own belly button," Nilsa said. "Open your eyes wider and look forward."

Ingrid smiled, "That's a good one."

Viggo blinked hard and pretended to lift his gaze from his stomach to look straight to the far end of the room.

Gerd burst out laughing.

"Don't get discouraged, we've made progress, I promise," Egil told them.

"Is the Quill of the True Blood still not working?" Astrid asked.

Egil nodded. "I'm afraid the Dragon Orb is still too far for the quill to feel it and locate it. Most likely they've realized that was how we found them the last time and won't make the same mistake twice."

"That would be too lucky for us," Nilsa said.

"The Orb is too far away, and yet the Visionaries and Defenders continue working in Norghana. Isn't that funny?" Lasgol asked.

"Maybe it's because what they need is easier to get here," Ingrid said.

"My uncle Viggen also has gold and contacts here."

"And both sects are rooted here," added Nilsa.

"All good guesses," smiled Egil.

"Let's see how you explain that these lunatics believe themselves to be descendants of dragons... they're fanatics!" Viggo said.

"Hence their true blood," added Nilsa.

"Their kind of power is very peculiar, there's no record of such a magic."

"You mean the roars and subsequent blows of force?" Astrid asked. "Because I can tell you it's like being hit on the head with a huge hammer."

"Yeah, that's very rare. Lasgol, what do you think?" Egil asked his friend.

"That type of magic that affects the body as well as the mind, although it may seem the head, is very uncommon. In everything I've been studying I've never read about something like this."

"We should ask Eicewald about this," Egil told Lasgol.

"They can't be descendants of dragons," said Nilsa, shaking her head. "How could they be?"

"It's hard to believe. Dragons and men never lived at the same time, as far as we know, or if they did, it was sporadically. According to what we saw in the desert caves," said Astrid.

"True. Dragons existed long before the time of men," Egil commented. "I don't see how they could've had descendants among men even if there had been a dragon living during the time of men."

"Not to mention that it would be physically impossible, right?" Ingrid said with her arms folded and a look of distaste on her face.

"Physically perhaps, but what about magically?" Gerd said.

"I find that unlikely too," said Lasgol.

"Another question for Eicewald, perhaps he can shed some light on the matter," said Egil.

"In any case, now we know why they're such fanatics," said Astrid. "They believe that dragon blood runs through their veins and the warlocks believe it's that blood that gives them their magic power."

"That seems to be the case," Nilsa said, looking distraught.

"We need to stay focused on the goal," said Egil. "We have to stop this immortal dragon from reincarnating. That's what we have to achieve."

"And what if it's already reincarnated?" Gerd asked in a fearful tone.

"I couldn't say why for certain, big guy, but I don't think that's happened yet. We would know."

"More than any other reason because he'd want to eat us alive," Viggo said.

"Yeah, that's for sure, with all the trouble we're causing him," Astrid added,

"Not only us. If the dragon is such, and immortal, he will destroy all Norghana. That's what his fanatic followers say," Nilsa added.

"Camu says that if the dragon reincarnates, he should be able to feel it, to feel his power, since it'll be enormous and Drakonian in nature," Lasgol commented.

"That's interesting," Egil intervened. "Camu believes he'll be able to feel the Drakonian power of the dragon?"

"From what he's told me, and you know what he's like, of course. The truth will be more restricted, I guess. Camu's always overly confident he's going to achieve everything and then it turns out not to be so. I still believe however, that Camu will be capable of feeling the dragon. They've already established a link: the Orb communicated with him. If we add that to the fact that powerful magi and creatures with powerful magic are capable of sensing other magi and creatures with great magic, I don't see why Camu wouldn't be able to feel Dergha-Sho-Blaska when he leaves the Orb."

"That's an interesting theory," Egil said thoughtfully.

"Definitely not interesting!" Viggo said. "The only thing the bug does, just like the weirdo, is get us into trouble. I don't believe he's going to sense the dragon when it comes out of the orb and gets into someone's body."

"Someone's? Whose?" asked Ingrid.

"Well… I don't know… but if it does reincarnate, it's not going to do so in a rock, is it?"

"That's another angle of the problem we must study. We're chasing after the Orb and its minions, but perhaps we should be chasing after the final destination of the dragon's spirit," Egil said thoughtfully.

"I still think that all of this, about the spirit of the dragon leaving the orb and reincarnating in someone's body… well, I just don't see it…" Nilsa said.

"I'm finding it hard to believe that's possible. It sounds unnatural, almost an aberration," Gerd joined in, looking repelled.

"I already find everything we come across as weird, so I'm not fazed by anything," Viggo said mockingly.

"There's literature on the subject," Egil said. "Which doesn't necessarily have to be true. The fact that something is written about, or that thinkers and erudites discuss mystical themes such as reincarnation is normal. That their derivations and conclusions are accurate… that's something completely different. Besides, we're talking about mythical beings here, dragons, which adds complexity to the matter."

"So, unless you've drunk about four large beers, you don't believe anything," Viggo summed up.

"I think that what Egil means is that we shouldn't believe everything we read or hear, but that we shouldn't brush it aside completely either," Lasgol said.

"Irrefutable, my dear friend."

Lasgol and Gerd smiled at Egil.

"I'm with Egil," said Ingrid. "Let's stay focused on the goal and stop the dragon. He won't reincarnate."

"You can count on me," Viggo said with a wink.

The others firmly agreed.

But the enemy had other plans. Plans the Panthers had not fully fathomed.

Chapter 33

The following morning, Gondabar summoned the Panthers. They were informed that they were expected at the dungeons under the Rangers' Tower. They attended the summons at once. The dungeons were big enough to hold about fifty enemies of the realm.

Gondabar was standing before one of the cells. There was someone they did not know next to him, but they guessed who he was by his clothes.

"Royal Eagles," Gondabar greeted them with a nod.

They all replied with a small bow.

"I don't know if you've met First Ranger Raner Olsen," he said with a wave at the man beside him. They all watched him, intrigued. He was not very tall or strong, but at the same time he was enough of both so as to be intimidating. His features were sharp and his eyes were an intense blue. He was a Norghanian blond and wore his hair short. They could tell he was wiry and had to be quite nimble. He looked back at the Panthers and they saw in his cold, deep gaze that he was a dangerous man, the kind who could slit your throat without batting an eye.

"I haven't met him but I was looking forward to meeting him. I'm Viggo, Natural Assassin, Forest Assassin, and Stealthy Poisoner," he introduced himself.

Raner examined Viggo from head to toe.

"I see you've spent a lot of time studying specializations. I, on the other hand, have been kept busy on missions to save the kingdom and its monarch."

The reply did not please Viggo at all, and he was about to answer when Ingrid beat him to it.

"It's an honor to meet the First Ranger," she said.

"Yes it is," said Nilsa who had already seen Raner in the castle but always in passing, and she had never had the chance to speak to him.

"Sir," the others said respectfully.

"The pleasure is all mine. The Royal Eagles are the pride of the Rangers. The King speaks highly of you and, as you know, the King isn't the kind of person who speaks well of anyone," Raner said.

"We are happy to serve the King as His Majesty deserves," Egil said obligingly.

Raner looked at Egil with more interest than the rest. Lasgol noticed as well that Egil's comment had a double meaning.

"I've summoned you because we've been studying and interrogating the subjects you apprehended," Gondabar told them and indicated Zirken first, who was sitting on a long bench. Then he indicated two Visionaries who were in another cell, and finally he waved at a dozen dragon slaves who shared another cell and still had their glittering, diamond-like eyes.

"Have you gained any relevant information?" Lasgol asked.

"Not relevant as such," Gondabar replied, "but information that has left me quite uneasy nonetheless. In fact, I've had trouble sleeping ever since you brought them in. The message they preach and their fanaticism are most troubling."

"That's how we feel about it as well," Egil said.

"That's why we brought them, so they could serve as evidence of everything we had shared with you."

Gondabar nodded several times.

"I'm not at all sure that everything is true though. I refuse to believe it, especially their belief in that immortal dragon that's going to reincarnate, the said Dergha-Sho-Blaska. I find it hard to believe that in particular. But I do believe that their sect," he said, indicating another cell where they were holding two Defenders of the True Blood, "does represent a threat to the kingdom."

"We believe so too, and we think it's a serious problem we have to take out at the roots," Lasgol said.

"What these wretches have done is deserving of hanging from a tree," Gondabar said, pointing at the dragon slaves.

"I would prefer a more painful death," Raner intervened. "These men are Norghanian. They're under the King's protection, under our protection. What has been done to them is intolerable witchcraft. I'd opt for hot irons before piercing these fanatics' hearts with a blunt knife."

"We can't use such barbaric methods. The Path forbids it," Gondabar said, "although I understand your rage."

Raner nodded.

"They'll be judged and sentenced to death, have no doubts about that."

"Yes, but first they'll be our dungeons' guests for a while. I want to see whether we can elicit some more information that might help us eradicate them," Gondabar said.

"We have to get to their leaders. You cut the head off and the snake dies, no matter how long it is," said Raner.

"Yes, I am of the same mind. That's why I've summoned you," he told the Panthers. "The First Ranger and I have been discussing the matter, and we've decided to give it the attention it deserves."

"We'll send more Rangers to look for their leaders," Raner told them. "I myself will choose the ones to be sent, since they must be skilled for this type of mission."

"Assassins?" Lasgol asked.

"Yes, and also Stealthy Spies," Raner told them.

"All the help our leaders can give us will be most welcome," Lasgol said.

"I want you to continue investigating this problem until you find the leaders. I want them here to be held accountable for what they've done."

"We'll do that, sir," Ingrid said.

"And what about the dragon...?" Lasgol asked.

"I'm sorry. It's not that I don't trust your word, but I can't believe that's going to happen. It's too unlikely and incredible. I've meditated on it a lot, and I must admit that this possibility has no place in my mind. I need unequivocal evidence that my hands can touch to even consider it. We're speaking of a dragon, which is a mythological creature we have no record of having ever existed really. It's part of the folklore and mythology of many kingdoms in Tremia, but it's just that, fantastic legends about powerful creatures. Added to this is the fact that it's going to reincarnate. That's another mystical or spiritual concept that isn't rooted in our culture and that I can't conceive of either. I find it difficult to accept those two concepts, even with the evidence you've brought me and after hearing it from their mouths," he said, eying the prisoners.

"Our leader is forgetting the fact that he's immortal," Viggo noted with a little sarcasm.

"I don't even want to think about that. The only immortals are the Ice Gods," Gondabar snapped.

"By the time we gather convincing evidence it might be too late, sir," Lasgol replied.

"I also can't accept that something like that could even be possible," the First Ranger said. "As our leader says, we must have certainty before letting ourselves be fooled by what might be nothing more than the beliefs of several fanatical groups."

"Whether it's the fanatics' folly or a reality to come, we have to stop the sect of the Visionaries and the Congregation of Defenders of the True Blood," said Egil.

"We'll do that," Gondabar promised. "The rest of what they preach about the end of the era of men, we'll leave aside until we have more evidence."

At the refusal of both leaders, Lasgol did not insist.

"We'll get started on that at once," Raner said.

"Know that I've communicated what's going on to the leaders of the Shelter and the Camp so they're informed and also on alert in case significant information reaches them," Gondabar explained.

"We appreciate our leader's efforts," Egil said courteously, "the help of our Masters and Elders is always welcome and appreciated."

"Has the King been told?" Ingrid asked.

Gondabar and Raner exchanged a look that showed concern.

"His Majesty has been informed of the existence of these two secret organizations," Gondabar said.

"He's charged us with ridding the kingdom of them," Raner added.

"He hasn't been told the rest, has he?" Egil asked.

Gondabar shook his head.

"There are things you can't tell a king unless you have rock-hard evidence," Gondabar said.

"The King would throw us out of the Throne Hall if we came to him with stories of immortal dragons that are planning on coming back to life," Raner said, bowing his head in shame.

"Very understanding, our monarch," Viggo said with irony.

Gondabar glanced at him sternly.

"The King has many concerns, including a Royal Wedding. He's not open to listening to anything that's not of the greatest importance," he replied, looking at Viggo.

"We understand," Ingrid said quickly before Viggo could say anything improper.

"You can count on my help, and by extension that of all the

Rangers. It's the least I can do. Having two sects infiltrating Norghana, attracting followers and bewitching poor helpless Norghanians, is something I can't tolerate."

"Those responsible will be apprehended and will pay for it," Raner said determinedly.

"Let's hope so," Gondabar said wishfully.

The Panthers decided they would not gain anything if they continued to press the matter and took their leave respectfully, leaving the two leaders to discuss the actions to take.

They went outside to breathe in the fresh air and comment on what had happened, moving away from the Tower, since Rangers were coming in and out and they did not want to be overheard.

"Well, if you want my opinion, that Raner, the First Ranger, isn't much to talk about," said Viggo, who could not hold his tongue any longer.

"I found him very much in his place, supporting Gondabar, and you can tell he's one who follows the Path. He'll protect the realm and the throne," Ingrid said.

"I agree with what you say about the people of the realm, I think he's good for that. But as to the latter, I'm not so sure," said Nilsa.

"I've watched him and he seems very capable," said Astrid. "You'd better not mess with him, Viggo, you might be in for a surprise. His gaze is that of an expert Assassin, the kind that doesn't make mistakes. Besides, he looks very fit."

"Thanks for your concern about me, brunette, but there's no need. I can defeat him any day of the week, day or night, and with one hand tied behind my back."

"Here we go boasting, don't be foolish," Ingrid chided. "And don't you dare taunt him or seek out a fight, because you could hang for it. He's the First Ranger, and we have to respect him and follow his orders."

"I'm speaking in the case of a tournament, or an exhibition for instance," Viggo corrected himself as he smiled innocently.

"Not even then. Don't you even get close to him," Ingrid said in a stern tone.

"Yeah, he looks competent enough and lethal," said Lasgol. "Besides, we have enough problems already without making an enemy out of the First Ranger. It's better to have him on our side in this matter. We shouldn't be surprised that they're not convinced about the dragon. We all find it hard to swallow, and we know about the Orb and have witnessed Dergha-Sho-Blaska's power and spirit."

"Let's be cautious, that's the best approach in almost all of life's situations," Egil advised them.

Suddenly they saw Eicewald with several of the Ice Magi coming out of their Tower to the middle of the bailey. They were talking in whispers, something usual for magi. It could also be because there were several groups of soldiers practicing with axes and shields nearby.

"Am I going senile, or do I recognize the Mage beside Eicewald? Isn't it that rat…" Viggo asked.

"You're not going senile. That's Maldreck," Lasgol confirmed.

"Isn't he the one who stole the Star of Sea and Life?" Ingrid asked, unable to believe her eyes.

"The one and only," Lasgol confirmed.

"But didn't he fall in the river?" Gerd asked.

"Yes, he did, when we stole the Star back," said Ingrid.

"Then why on earth is he here, alive and kicking? Hadn't he fallen in disgrace with Orten for losing the Star?" Viggo said.

"It seems Thoran has brought him back. He wants to increase the number of Ice Magi he has in his service," Lasgol told them.

"Even if they're thieves and creeping human snakes?" Ingrid said.

"Kings tolerate such deficiencies in their servants if that serves their own purpose and convenience," Egil recited as if it had poured out of a tome of knowledge.

"So, all his errors have been forgiven because he's valuable as a Mage for the King and his dear little brother," Viggo translated.

"Irrefutable, my Assassin friend," Egil replied with a smile.

"Well, I find it gross. What little honor and integrity!" Ingrid said, frowning and wrinkling her nose and looking very unpleased with it all.

"Well, we've already noticed that trait in our King, his brother and most of the Court. It's nothing new," Nilsa said.

"I know, but witnessing it makes me sick," Ingrid said, making a fist.

"I wish one day we could have honorable, fair leaders," Gerd said, looking askance at Egil.

"Perhaps one day we will," Lasgol joined him as he laid a hand on the giant's shoulder.

"Eicewald had better tread carefully with that viper beside him," Ingrid muttered.

"He knows the danger he's in," Lasgol told them. "He'll be alert to any strange moves."

"He'd better check his back at all times, or he'll find a dagger buried in it," said Astrid.

Eicewald saw them and took his leave from the other Magi to come and greet the Panthers with a big smile.

"I'm glad to see you all together again, you've been missed."

"We're all back safe and sound," Ingrid said.

"While you were away, we've been studying and working on the difficult discipline of magic. Once you delve into the books, you lose yourself and time flies," he said, nodding at Lasgol, who smiled, also nodding.

"That's a great truth," Egil nodded as well. "Nothing like a good book for the day to go by in a flash."

"We've seen that *your friend* Maldreck's back…" Viggo said.

"Yes, that's why I'm going for a ride today. I need you to watch him so he doesn't follow me."

"You can count on us," said Lasgol.

"Wouldn't you rather I killed him and end the problem?" Viggo offered.

Eicewald heaved a deep sigh.

"A problem he certainly is, and he's going to give me real headaches. But if we kill him, I'll have to answer to the King for it. The cure is worse than the illness, in this case."

"It might be so, but that illness in particular might end up killing you," Viggo told him.

The Mage nodded.

"You're right. If I see that the illness is beginning to be dangerous for my health, I'll let you know," he told Viggo with a wink.

"I'll cure it without any trouble," Viggo said, winking back.

"Can I ask the reason for that ride?" Lasgol asked, concerned for the Mage and wanting to help him if possible.

"Of course. It's none other than to hide a precious object I'm studying and which I don't want falling into Maldreck's hands."

"Oh… the Silver Pearl, the one you found in Irinel," Lasgol whispered so no one other than them would hear.

"Indeed. I'm going to hide it where Camu and Ona are now…"

Eicewald replied with another wink.

Lasgol nodded. Eicewald was going to hide the Silver Pearl in the Green Ogre Forest.

"It'll be safe there. Maldreck won't be able to steal it."

"A wary man lives a long life," Egil recited with a smile.

"Very true," Eicewald nodded.

"Have you heard about what's happened and the prisoners we've brought in?" Ingrid asked him.

"Yes indeed. Gondabar asked for my help, and of course I lent it to him. I've been with the prisoners, examining them from the magical perspective and also seeing if there was anything I could do for the dragon slaves."

"And could you help them?" Nilsa asked with interest.

The Ice Mage shook his head sorrowfully.

"I'm afraid that, although my magical knowledge is quite extensive, I don't have the power to help them."

"Couldn't you use your magic to counter Vingar's?" Astrid asked.

"Unfortunately, magic doesn't work that way. My magic can't counter magic that is such a different type. If it were elemental magic, maybe, but the magic used on them is one I know nothing about."

"But you're a powerful mage…" Gerd said.

"I can't undo a spell of such magnitude. The warlock who cast it is powerful, and the object used to cast the spell even more so."

"Isn't there anything you can do for them?" Nilsa pleaded.

"No, the only thing I can think of is that a Healer from the Temple of Tirsar could see them."

"Edwina?"

"She might be able to help them."

"Let's hope so. She's at the Shelter now," said Lasgol.

"We'll have to call her," said Gerd.

"We have another doubt you can help clear up," Egil said.

"Good, if it's within my power I'd be pleased to do it."

"It's about the warlocks and Visionaries and their belief that they have dragon blood in their veins," Egil explained. "Do you think that's possible?"

Eicewald looked up and was thoughtful for a moment, his gaze lost in the gray sky.

"I find it difficult, although not impossible. This isn't the first time I've heard that someone was descended from dragons. That it is true is something that can't be proved, like many things that have to do with magic."

"What we're wondering is how it could happen..." Egil said. "Through magic? Or in any physical way?"

The Mage pondered his reply.

"According to some myths, the most powerful dragons, because of their magic, were able to take on the shape of certain beings— among them, men. This of course is pure fable and therefore impossible to prove. But it's a belief that exists among some peoples and tribes of Tremia."

"If that's the case, it would explain the fact that they had human descendants..." said Ingrid.

"That's an aberration," Nilsa said.

"More than that I'd say," Gerd said, looking horrified.

"I don't see anything weird about it," Viggo said with a shrug.

"Which brings us to the magic they attacked us with," Astrid told him. "I was hit with some type of power both physical and mental, as if a wave of force attacked me. I couldn't see it, but I felt the blow."

Eicewald nodded. "In any case, I can tell you that the type of magic you're describing, and that I felt from the warlock in custody is extremely rare. I've heard of some magi who could directly attack people's minds with waves of magical energy, but it's an anomaly in the magical world. Or at least there are very few, and that's why we don't have any information about their type of power and obviously it hasn't been studied, at least as far as I know."

"That's interesting, because we've come across three warlocks and their leader who have that type of magic," Astrid told him.

"That is surprising and strange. That there are four, and that they've united is very significant," Eicewald said, looking quite puzzled.

"Indeed, and they want to bring an immortal dragon back to life," said Viggo.

"Hence the significance. They must have united for an important cause," the Ice Mage guessed, "one you already know."

"Do you really believe it's possible they have dragon blood in their veins and are bringing an immortal dragon back to life?" Astrid asked.

"Well, that's stretching it... it's possible they descend from a lineage with dragon blood, if we really want to accept the possibility.

But I see them bringing an immortal dragon back to life highly unlikely, even for a mage like me who's open to all magical possibilities."

"Our leaders think the same thing, they don't believe it's possible either," Ingrid said.

"It's only natural. People of good judgment can't make decisions based on myths and legends," Eicewald told them, "Not even mages do that."

"Yet, you still think it's possible they're descended from dragons," Lasgol said.

"Rather that, in some way, there's dragon power in them, not necessarily that they're descended from them."

"Magic passes from parents to children through blood, from one generation to the next, you taught me that yourself," Lasgol told him.

"Indeed, but we're talking about dragons here, creatures of mythological power. It's not the same," Eicewald said, opening his arms wide in an apology.

"We'll have to remain open to the possibility that, somehow, we don't know how, Drugan and his warlocks have dragon power in them that allows them to perform a powerful unknown magic," Egil concluded, sounding more as if he were thinking out loud than making a statement.

"You've summed it up perfectly," Eicewald agreed. "In any case, I'm going to keep digging into this matter, it intrigues me a lot. I want to get to the bottom of this mystery and understand where the magic these warlocks are using comes from. And also, whether it's true that they really have some relation with dragons or if it's all an elaborate fantasy of a sect that believes in fictional mythological beings."

"As soon as you find out, which I believe will be easy for you, make sure to tell us," Viggo said with sarcasm.

Eicewald smiled.

"You'll be the first to know."

"We appreciate all the help you're giving us. We know this is beyond your duties," Lasgol said gratefully.

"It's a pleasure to be of help," the Mage told them. "Now, if you'll excuse me, I'm going to hide a certain artifact..." he looked out of the corner of his eye to see whether Maldreck was close, and when he did not see him, Eicewald headed to the stables.

That evening the Panthers were resting in the room they shared in the Rangers' Tower. The events of the day had them all thinking. There had been good news and not so good news.

Egil and Gerd came into the room last. They had vanished at mid-afternoon and had just come back.

"Everything all right?" Lasgol asked Egil when he saw the thoughtful look on his face.

"Everything's fine, but I have news to tell you. It's important."

"Tell us, what's the matter?" Ingrid asked, and they all paid attention from their respective bunks.

"It'd better be important, I was busy with my own things," Viggo told Egil.

"Working on reducing your immense ego?" Nilsa said, making a comical face.

Lasgol smiled and Ingrid couldn't help chuckling.

"If you weren't so clumsy, I might feel offended, but since you are…"

"That doesn't make much sense," Gerd said.

"It makes as much sense as he does," Ingrid replied.

"Will you please stop messing with me and listen to Egil? It's bound to be important!"

Egil, who had been thinking beside one of his notebooks, finally spoke.

"The gold I paid the Guild of Collectors has gotten me some important information."

"Trustworthy?" Viggo asked, raising an eyebrow.

"It has been so far," Egil replied. "I trust this will be too."

"What information is that?" Ingrid asked with an eager look.

"I managed to get information on one of the leaders we're looking for," Egil said, unable to suppress a small cry of success.

"If you know where he is, we'll leave immediately to capture him," Astrid said, jumping to her feet.

Egil raised his hand.

"Easy now. We're all anxious to stop the immortal dragon from coming back, but acting hastily will only lead us to failure. Remember that we're up against two strong organizations, with many members who are now working together and collaborating."

"We'll deal with them, I'm not worried," Viggo said with an air of superiority.

"Sure, you always believe we can deal with everything, and that's not usually the case," Ingrid told him. "Let Egil explain the situation and what's come up."

"Fine… I'm only saying that you always worry too much."

"Very well. This lead is important. It might take us to one of the leaders and the dragon orb besides. We can't fail. Now listen to me carefully."

Chapter 34

Viggo was moving among the shadows and gloom of the forest. He felt comfortable in that environment. This was his favorite—well, his and that of all the Rangers—to be surrounded by bushes, trees, and thick vegetation. Viggo felt at home, especially now that snow covered everything and he was wearing his white winter gear which allowed him to melt into the surroundings.

He moved forward among the snow-covered chestnut trees and went to the river that was running full with white water. He was approaching his target from the west. Astrid was making her way like him, but from the east. He stopped for a moment to see if he spotted her and saw the Assassin a distance off in the forest. She was there one moment and gone the next. Viggo knew she had done it on purpose so he could see her.

Perfect. Everything was going according to Egil's plan. Astrid and him were leading the way, one on each flank. Ingrid and Nilsa would follow, covering the Assassins' backs in case they were surprised in their advance. Finally Lasgol, Egil, and Gerd would approach to take their positions once the watchmen were dealt with. Camu and Ona were coming from the north, camouflaged. Their mission was to stop the leader of the sect from escaping in that direction. If everything went as expected, it would be a great day, and if it did not, at least they would have some fun. Well, Viggo would have fun, the rest not so much.

He focused his gaze and discovered one of the watchmen posted on the other side of the river under a fir tree. Unfortunately for the watchman he did not know how to hide well enough and he was going to regret it, or rather he was going to regret it only for a moment—his final moment. The world was filled with simpletons; it was not their fault if many of them crossed the Panthers' path and had to be sent to the kingdom of the Ice Gods.

Viggo stealthily crawled along the snow to the river like an albino viper, camouflaging in with the surroundings. He reached the water and went in slowly. He swam strongly under the surface to the other side without coming up to breathe and without the current taking him.

He appeared on the other side and dragged himself along until he was covered in snow. He stayed very still, all his senses on the alert, but he did not hear any sound that signified danger. He had to admit that the Assassin winter gear they were wearing was magnificent: it protected them from the cold and the water. Besides, the hooded cloak they wore was one of Enduald's special objects and was imbued with enchantments that protected them from the elements and increased their strength and stamina.

A little magical help was always welcome. Viggo was one who seized every advantage, even the slightest, because it might mean the difference between life and death in critical situations. His equipment provided him with several advantages he was not going to let pass unused.

He lifted his head a bit and watched. He saw a second watchman a little more to the east, sitting on a fallen tree trunk. For the trained eye of an Assassin like him, spotting the watch was easy. Besides, as soon as he spotted them, the plan to attack and take them down began taking shape in his mind. It was something that came to him without even thinking, like a reflex.

He snaked along until he reached the trees and hid behind them. He inspected the area again to check for any other watchmen who might pose a problem, and behind a large boulder he discovered a third one.

"Where there are two there's always a third one," he muttered under his breath.

He waited for a moment to make sure there were no more watchmen that might surprise him but did not see any. So, he decided to act.

The first watchman died a moment later with his throat slit. Viggo had surprised him while he was snoozing. The man did not even know what happened to him.

Viggo moved forward at a crouch through the underbrush until he reached the position of the second watchman sitting in the tree. Viggo continued his advance, crawling straight toward him through the snow. The man noticed something was off and stretched his neck to see.

Right then, Viggo jumped up and threw his knife, catching him in the neck. The man fell backwards, dead, and was hidden by the trunk he had been sitting on.

Viggo continued snaking his way through the snow until he reached some snow-covered bushes. Night and stealth were his allies. He recovered his knife and went on.

He reached the third watchman after going around to get at his back, which was covered since he was leaning against the boulder. Viggo leapt onto the rock—it was not the most orthodox approach, but he liked to improvise and look for unusual ways to finish off his enemies.

He climbed to the top of the boulder, put his head out, and looked down. The watchman was leaning against the rock.

Viggo whistled at him.

The man looked up, surprised.

Viggo dropped down with his knives in his hands.

The man opened his eyes wide in panic. An instant later he was dead.

Viggo dropped onto the snow to muffle his fall. Then he got up nonchalantly, as if nothing had happened there, and looked at the dead man.

"Every day that passes I become a better Assassin," he congratulated himself.

He waited for a moment until he heard the hoot of an owl to the east. It was Astrid letting him know she had finished her job. Viggo smiled and replied by hooting that he had also finished. He continued his way to the target.

Ingrid was following Viggo's trail, which was not difficult in the middle of the snow. One of the things snow was always good for was that it made it easier to follow trails. At a crouch and in snow-white gear so as to blend in with the landscape, Ingrid moved toward the target, following the path Viggo had opened for her. The trail was visible in the snow.

They had debated about how to handle that part of the operation, and Egil had told them it would be better if Viggo and Astrid led the way since they were the best at cleaning the area of watchmen and preventing them from sounding the alarm. He did not want the prey to discover the hunters and run away.

Ingrid believed she could have dealt with the watch just as well as Viggo. She would have finished them off with mid-distance shots while remaining hidden in the snow. But according to Egil, it was better that an Assassin finished off the watch because there was less risk of the alarm being raised.

She was not so sure of that, but she had not wanted to argue with Egil. The plan was his, and they would follow it as Egil had planned it. She snorted and crouched behind some trees.

Egil was probably right, but she did not want to admit it because that would mean she was not capable of carrying out that part of the operation as well as Viggo, and she did not like that idea at all.

She continued advancing, following the trail, and she reached the position of the first dead watch. Viggo had covered the man up with snow and he could not be seen from afar, but Ingrid could read the signs of what had happened.

She went on crouching and, following the trail, found the second watchman behind a tree trunk also covered with snow. Although unwillingly, she had to admit that Viggo had done a great job.

A little farther ahead she found the third watchman dead in front of the great boulder. She looked around and was able to guess that Viggo had dropped onto the man by climbing onto the boulder from behind. She shook her head. Now he was showing off. There was no reason to kill the watchman in that way. He could have used a safer approach.

That made her feel a little better. Viggo was an exceptional Assassin, but he liked to perform risky and dangerous actions, something she would never do. As soon as she could, she was going to have a chat with Viggo about his risky maneuvers. He would most likely not listen to her, but they would have one of their special fights the two of them enjoyed so much.

Ingrid knew that the rest of the group did not understand the special relationship she and Viggo had, but she did not care. They understood one another perfectly. Ingrid put Viggo in his place and made him behave. Viggo brought her out of her comfort zone and made her laugh and enjoy life. Besides, he had a vision of the world and life which was a lot more fun than hers. Viggo might be a numbskull, but he was charming and hilarious.

Just thinking about Viggo made her heart feel tender. Then she thought of what he had just done and the moment passed. With Viggo, it was always a pinch of tenderness and joy, and another of annoyance for what he did. The attraction she felt for Viggo was inexplicable, but she could not help it and she had tried for a long time. One roguish glance from Viggo and Ingrid's icy armor melted.

She went forward, making sure there was not any danger stalking Viggo from behind. She saw no enemy trail nearby. So, still crouching and doing her best to hide among the foliage, she moved until she glimpsed Viggo's position. She could not see him, but she could see the signal he had left for her marked on a tree. He had carved a target on the bark—Viggo was ahead of her hiding in the snow.

Ingrid stopped beside a fir tree and hid behind it. It was time to wait for the Panthers' return.

Lasgol was moving in from the south, heading north. He had his bow in his hand and an arrow nocked in case of trouble. Egil was coming behind him, also with his bow ready. Gerd brought up the rear, and every now and then he checked behind them. So far, they had not found any opposition, something that did not surprise him, since Astrid and Viggo had cleared the path ahead of them.

For an instant Lasgol was worried for Astrid's fate, but the moment soon passed. Astrid was an exceptional Assassin and very experienced. In that environment, in a snow-covered forest, he doubted any enemy could surpass Astrid. In fact, whoever dared confront her would die. Besides, Nilsa had her back, so she was well protected.

He looked around while he advanced along the forest covered by the recent snowfall and thought about his group, the Snow Panthers. They were veteran Norghanian Rangers, Specialists, and they were in their element here, in the forest and mountains, while the Visionaries and Defenders were not. If they fought, their enemies would be at a severe disadvantage and have high odds of losing. This reasoning brought him peace, he had to trust in who they were and that they would come out victorious.

They were nearing the point where the camp of the Visionaries was supposed to be located, according to the information the Guild had given Egil. They had delivered a rudimentary map to Egil with an X marking the spot where the person of interest was that Egil had asked them to find. It was none other than Drugan.

Lasgol was hoping the information was good and the camp would be there, where the X indicated. He also hoped they were not heading straight into a trap, which could be the case as easily as not. In any case, they would be fine. In this environment the odds of winning were stacked highly in their favor, against sectarians or the Zangrian army.

They came to the last trees before the plain, where there was a sawmill. Lasgol raised one hand and the three crouched down. He signaled to them to come and take a look. Several large cabins used in that type of operation were in the middle of the clearing. Three large piles of cut logs were piled not too far from the river.

Beside the river, there was a dock and large tree logs were floating, tethered to it. Lasgol remembered that the logs used to be transported by water since it was easier and faster. He also noticed a pen with strong draft mares and other riding horses. This was strange. Why did they need riding horses in a sawmill? The answer was soon obvious.

He saw Drugan coming out of one of the cabins, along with Xoltran and Vingar, and they were talking. Several Visionaries accompanied them, apparently as an escort. They arrived at one of the cabins and Drugan pointed at it while he seemed to be giving orders to his deputies.

"Drugan and his warlocks are there, the information was correct," Lasgol whispered to Egil.

"Gold is an important motivator. It gets great results," his friend smiled at him.

"Should we attack them?" Gerd asked eagerly.

"Not yet, I want to know whether the Dragon Orb is here too," Egil said. He took out the Quill and handed it to Lasgol.

"Give me a moment," Lasgol said.

He lifted the Quill and spun around. The Quill did not react. The vibration and whistling he had been expecting that indicated the Orb was close did not happen.

"It seems like the Dragon Orb isn't here," he said. "At this distance the Quill should be able to detect it."

"It's weird that it's not with them," Lasgol said, indicating the group.

"That's what I was thinking, it should be. Something's not right..." Egil said with a troubled look on his face.

"Maybe Viggen and the Defenders of the True Blood have it," Gerd suggested.

"That could be the case..." Egil said, nodding.

"Don't you find it odd that they need so many cabins for a sawmill this size?" Gerd asked.

"What do you mean?" Lasgol asked him, not knowing what his friend was referring to.

"A sawmill this size usually has a couple of cabins for the workers. I count eight here, and most of them are quite large, with a capacity for over twenty loggers. If you look closely, I'd say that at least six of them have been recently built."

"True, only two, the ones closest to the river, look like the original ones," Egil confirmed, looking at them more closely.

"But if there are workers in them it must be to fell large numbers of trees. Why does Drugan want so much wood?" Lasgol asked. "What does he want to build?"

"The only thing I can think of is that he wants to build some kind of structure..." said Gerd.

"But there are no workers visible, nor the foundations for any structure..." said Egil, scratching his head thoughtfully.

"We don't know where Viggen and his Defenders are either."

"There's something about all this that doesn't fit," said Egil. "The fort where Astrid and Nilsa found Vingar and his people is a little further north from this position, not too far away."

"That's true, about three leagues give or take," said Gerd.

"There has to be a connection," said Egil, thinking. "Two Visionary camps so close to one another."

"But there's nothing here but mountains and the sea a little to the west," said Lasgol. "There's not any important city in this area, not even villages of any mentionable size."

"Icelbag and Denmik are a lot more to the east, south of the capital," said Gerd.

"That's right. There are no cities, mines, or places of any importance in this area, and to the north is Copenghen, a port city but quite far. And yet they're in this area. What for?" Egil wondered out loud.

Suddenly they saw Xoltran heading to one of the large cabins with several Visionaries. Vingar did the same and went to another. Drugan himself went to the largest cabin. They opened the doors and shouted orders inside.

A large number of slaves started to exit the cabins. Some had the diamond light in their eyes but most had still not been turned into dragon slaves. They were chained by the waist in groups of about six. The Visionaries made them line up in the center of the southern plain of the sawmill, not far from where Egil, Gerd, and Lasgol were watching.

"There are almost three hundred slaves..." Lasgol said in a surprised tone.

"They must've had them piled inside the cabins, most inhumanly," Gerd said with pity in his eyes. "Otherwise, they couldn't make so many fit in there."

"This discovery is very interesting," Egil muttered. "We're beginning to unravel the skein, now we have to follow the thread and see what we find at the end, once it's fully unraveled."

"Why are they bringing them outside and making them line up there in the middle?" Lasgol asked, more to himself than to his friends.

"To go somewhere else?" Gerd said, not convinced.

"That's not a bad idea... elaborate a little, please," Egil told Gerd.

"Well... we're in the middle of the mountains and there's not much around apart from trees. They've gathered here, and there are a lot of them, almost three hundred. If they're not going to stay here, I guess they'll go someplace else... it's just a thought."

"Not a bad one at all," Egil told him.

"You think this is only a regrouping point?" Lasgol asked.

"That's exactly what I think," Egil nodded. "Here we have Visionaries and slaves gathered from different areas. There are too many for them to have all been attracted in one or two cities, they would've drawn too much attention. The fact that there are also dragon slaves, tells us they've been bewitching them here and at the fort we dismantled. There's also Drugan and his deputies—they're not here to do something, what they're doing is gathering here to march somewhere else as a group."

"It makes sense, yeah, now that I see them all together," Lasgol said, beginning to see what Egil and Gerd saw. This place was not a base of operations, or the place where the dragon was going to reincarnate, but a meeting point to continue their plans.

"And where are they going?" Gerd asked.

"I think I have an idea," Egil said.

"North? to Copenghen?" Lasgol ventured.

"No, not north."

"To the east? The capital?" Gerd said.

"No, not the capital either."

"Then where?" Lasgol and Gerd asked in unison.

"They're going west," Egil said with the certainty of someone who has cracked a riddle.

"They can't go west, the sea is west," Gerd said.

"And that's precisely where they're headed."

Chapter 35

Egil was not mistaken. Drugan gave the order and his minions set out to the west, taking all the slaves with them. They formed a long line with Drugan in the lead, Xoltran riding in the middle of the line of slaves and Vingar bringing up the rear on a black stallion. The Visionaries marched on both sides of the miserable parade, urging the slaves forward with clubs and whips.

Drugan and his warlocks were watching the forest attentively; apparently, they feared being attacked. Egil had given the order to the other Panthers to follow the caravan without attacking it. He wanted to know their destination and whether or not the Dragon Orb was there. Drugan and his people, on the other hand, already knew they were being watched, since their own watchmen had not returned from their posts when they were ready to leave.

They were playing the dangerous game of cat and mouse. The Panthers had the advantage of the land, and the fact that Drugan and his men did not know how many Panthers were watching, or from where. The truth was that Ingrid and Viggo were following the caravan from the left, hiding in the mountains. On the right, in the woods, Astrid and Nilsa were following the caravan. Camu and Ona had joined Lasgol's group and were following behind.

Although Egil had given the order not to attack, there was always the question of what Viggo would do. They were hoping he would hold back, but with Viggo, you never knew what would happen in the end. Following such a caravan was not so simple. Trails so wide were hard to hide. Even a blind man would see them, since they were walking on snow, crossing a large forest. Their pace was slow.

Drugan was expecting to be followed—Egil was sure of that, and perhaps he was leading them to a trap. The mouse could turn into the cat and vice versa in an instant if they were not careful. The advance was tense, with both parties watching in case there was an attack to respond to.

They went up a high mountain, along a well-known path, and down the other side, heading west to the sea. Yet there were no cities there, or villages or piers. The closest thing that had a dock was the mouth of the river Utla, more to the southwest.

The tense march took the entire day, and when night fell the caravan was crossing the last mountain and facing a clearing that led to the sea. The Panthers, hiding around the caravan, followed in silence expectantly.

"They're approaching the sea," Lasgol whispered to Egil.

"Yes, the coast is very close now," Egil nodded.

"There are no villages there, the coast is deserted so far south," Gerd said, wrinkling his nose.

"Very true. Let's see what they're planning. They might be trying to throw us off. I'm also not ruling out a strategy to lead us into a trap," Egil told them.

"That doesn't sound good at all," said Lasgol, "we'd better be on the alert."

I always alert, Camu messaged.

Ona growled once to indicate she was too.

The caravan continued its slow advance and at last they arrived at the coast. The Panthers had to retreat a little because the plain that led to the shore had no hiding places. Viggo and Astrid did go forward, along with Ona and Camu, but the others had to remain hidden at a prudent distance to avoid being spotted.

Camu's warning reached them a moment before the Panthers could see them.

Ships, four, he messaged.

Astrid and Viggo ran to make sure. Indeed, four cargo ships were coming in toward the point where the caravan had stopped. They were sailing dark, without a single light that might identify them. The Panthers had not made them out until they were already upon them. They were ships with deep holds for animals and cargo.

Astrid recognized her uncle Viggen at the bow of the first ship. His deputies of the Congregation of the Defenders of the True Blood were on the other three ships. Astrid felt the need to jump on board the ship that was already anchoring in front of a stony beach but forced herself to hold back. If she jumped aboard, she would jeopardize her friends, and it was not a good idea to reveal themselves until they had a good plan of attack, no matter how much she wanted to attack her uncle.

The four ships anchored one after the other before the beach. Astrid saw several barges ready on the beach itself to get to the ships.

This was a grand operation, and she was starting to think her uncle had financed and prepared it. The question was for what final purpose.

The slaves started climbing onto the barges, urged by the Visionaries, following the orders Drugan, Xoltran, and Vingar were yelling out. Astrid was sure the slaves were going to be taken to the ships. The question was what they were going to do with them. She knew Viggo was not far from her, even if she could not see him. The night was dark and the sky was covered.

She decided it would be best to retreat to inform Egil and the rest. But right at that moment she received a mental message.

Warn this?

Astrid nodded. She could not see him, but she was sure Camu was close to her.

I go. Come back soon, he messaged, and Astrid was able to hear the light sound Camu and Ona made as they moved away.

Camu reached the others' position.

Defenders in ships.

"Is Viggen in command of the fleet?" Egil asked.

Yes. First ship.

"Are there Defenders on the other ships?" Lasgol asked Camu.

Yes. Have shields of silver.

"Then they're coming to fetch them," Nilsa said.

Boats in beach.

"That confirms it," Lasgol said, nodding.

"What should we do, Egil? Do we attack before they escape?" Ingrid asked.

"Did you feel the Orb, Camu? Is it on the ships?" Egil asked.

I not feel.

"Lasgol, check with the Quill, please," Egil said.

Lasgol took the Quill out and held it in his hand, pointing it to the ships. It did not vibrate or give off any whistling sound.

"The Orb doesn't seem to be here."

"In any case, we could board the ships and make sure the Orb goes down to the bottom of the sea," said Nilsa.

"I don't think fire would destroy it, and we already know it can hibernate for thousands of years. If it falls in the sea it won't perish," Egil said.

"We lose nothing if we try," said Ingrid.

"The Orb isn't on board those ships. It makes no sense to risk it simply to fetch some slaves. It must be somewhere else," Egil said.

"And where would that be?" Gerd asked.

"They'll lead us to it," Egil said, waving toward the ships, whose masts could be glimpsed in the distance when the occasional moon ray managed to pierce through the autumnal clouds that covered the sky.

"So we're not attacking then," said Ingrid.

"No, we're not. I have another plan," Egil said.

They all looked at him.

"Go on, we're listening," Lasgol encouraged him.

The last of the barges on the shore cast off toward the fourth ship waiting, anchored. The other three ships had already left with their cargo of slaves on board, and only the last ship was left weighing anchor and getting ready to set sail as soon as the last barge arrived.

Drugan and Viggen were in the first ship. As soon as they had greeted one another they both cast looks toward the shore and exchanged comments. Drugan must have told Viggen they were being followed, but he would not have been able to tell him by whom or how many. The Panthers had made sure they were not seen.

Viggen had loaded the slaves into the ships as quickly as possible, and he had set a watch in each of the ships' masts to see if anyone was approaching to attack. Armed men stood on both rails of the vessels, prepared for a possible attack.

But there was none. The first ship set sail as soon as the cargo of slaves was on board. After that, the second ship, captained by Xoltran, set sail. The third one sailed shortly after, captained by Vingar. Only the fourth one was still being loaded. They seemed to be in a hurry to do so, which was not surprising, since they knew they were being watched.

The last barge arrived and the slaves started climbing ladders made of rope and wood to get aboard. The ascent was not fast, since they were in chains. Besides, the barge was moving quite a bit so the ladder was shaking with the waves.

While the crew was helping the slaves climb up, something else was going on that they were not aware of. Camu, Lasgol, and Egil were climbing the stern of the ship. Camu had used his Extended Invisibility Camouflage skill and was covering Lasgol and Egil with it. They did not have much trouble because Norghanian ships did not have much draft, even cargo ones. Lasgol and Egil managed to climb up with Camu's help, since he could cling to any surface with his feet.

We need to hide in the hold along with the slaves, Lasgol transmitted to Camu.

I take. Not go away of me. Skill not much big.

Yeah, don't worry, we'll stay close to you.

Lasgol and Egil, one on either side of Camu, with a hand on his body, moved toward the hold. Luckily, all the crew were by the rail helping the slaves aboard as fast as they could, amid the orders of two of Viggen's silver-shielded Defenders shouting at the top of their lungs.

Lasgol and his friends waited for the right moment and went down into the hold. There were slaves there already, resigned to their fate, sitting on the floor and trying to rest.

There are crates of supplies and barrels of drinking water at the far end, we'll hide behind them, Lasgol transmitted to Camu.

They had to go past the slaves on one side, and with Camu's size that was quite complicated. Luckily, most of the slaves were still getting on board or else they would never have made it through to the back, where they got as comfortable as they could. Lasgol and Egil moved some crates unobtrusively to form a small wall to hide behind. That way the slaves would not see them when Camu's protection wore off, revealing them.

On land, Viggo was voicing his disagreement.

"I can't believe they persuaded us to let them do this!"

"It's a good plan," Ingrid said.

"It's Astrid and I who should've gone with the bug. We're a lot better at this kind of thing than the weirdo and the bookworm."

"That kind of thing usually ends with casualties if you're involved," Nilsa told him. Egil doesn't want casualties, he wants to find out where the Orb is."

"I can go without killing anyone for quite a while if I really set my

277

mind to it," Viggo replied.

"Yeah sure, that's why you're staying on land," Nilsa said.

"I'm not happy about it either," Astrid said, also annoyed.

"Egil knows very well what he's planning, and Lasgol had to go because of Camu," Ingrid told them, trying to make them see reason.

"And who'll take care of the panther?" Viggo said, seeing her moan as she looked out at sea.

"I will. I'm delighted to do so, I love panthers and any other animal," Gerd said, petting Ona. The good panther was grateful for the giant's affection.

"I want to go after them," Astrid said out loud, although it sounded more like a feeling than a purpose.

"Why don't we go up to Copenghen and take a ship to go after them?" Gerd suggested.

"That's a good idea. We could take a war ship, which is a lot faster than cargo ones, and we'd be able to catch up with them," Nilsa said.

"Only we don't know where they're going," Ingrid said.

"They're heading west," Nilsa replied, watching the ships disappearing in the horizon.

"They could change course at any moment, in fact they'll have to, or they'll go straight to the Wasted Island."

"Isn't that the desolate island to the west of here?" Gerd asked.

"It's uninhabited, which isn't the same as saying it's desolate," Ingrid told him. "In fact, there's a military fort and an old port that's used during times of war."

"You mean our glorious army?" Viggo wanted to be clear.

"Yeah, that one, of course. Wasted Island doesn't strictly belong to Norghana, but we have it as a defensive post in case the Rogdonians decide to come with their fleet."

"Well, if that's where they're heading, we could follow them," Nilsa said.

"But we don't know for sure, and we can't anticipate events," said Ingrid.

"They're already lost on the horizon," Gerd commented, looking out at sea.

"So what can we do now?" Nilsa asked.

"What Egil told us to. We wait for news from him." Ingrid ended the discussion.

Astrid was thoughtful for a moment.

"My uncle must've got those ships in Copenghen. They were coming from the north hugging the coast."

"Most likely," said Nilsa.

"Then I'm going up there to investigate. I want to know what else he's planning," Astrid told them.

"It doesn't make much sense to wait here in the middle of nowhere…" Gerd agreed.

"Fine. You go to Copenghen, Viggo and I will watch this area in case there's more movement from the Visionaries or Defenders."

"The whole area?" Viggo asked her, frowning.

"Coast, sawmill, and fortress, wherever we've spotted them," Ingrid said.

Viggo gave a loud snort.

"Well, that's going to be fun…"

"Well… think of it this way, you'll have me for company."

Viggo smiled from ear to ear.

"Come on, go now, don't waste any more time," he told the others, shooing them off with his hands.

Chapter 36

Egil hoped that Viggen's fleet was heading to the Wasted Island, since it was near the Norghanian coastline. But it did not. The ships went by the island and kept their course north, which puzzled the scholar.

"Are you sure we're going north?" Lasgol asked him after a few days of voyage.

"If my calculations are right, we are."

"Northwest?"

"That's right," Egil nodded.

"There's nothing that far north, unless it's…"

"The Reborn Continent," Egil said.

Reborn Continent? Camu messaged.

"They also call it the Melted Continent. It's a continent, although it's not very large. Some people don't even grant it that status and treat it only as a large island that stretches from the northwest of our continent to the west. It's about the size of the Masig Steppes and the kingdom of Rogdon put together."

Why melted?

"Scholars believe that thousands of years ago, that continent and Norghana were joined, and in turn, that our Norghana was connected to the Frozen Continent. As you've experienced, the Frozen Continent is still frozen with large glaciers. The northern part of Norghana is also quite freezing, although not as much. And then we have the Reborn Continent which, no one knows why, went through an era of warm periods and went from being as icy as the Frozen Continent to a much warmer climate, albeit still cold."

Not know why ice melt?

"No, it's still very cold to the north, but in the south the weather is similar to ours here in Norghana."

I understand.

Egil smiled, "I'm glad you do, Camu."

"Well, I hope we're not heading there, the voyage will take longer."

"Let's hope," Egil nodded.

But as it often happens, fate, destiny, or the Gods decided to deal them a bad hand, and they were indeed headed to the Reborn Continent. Lasgol could not believe it. They had no choice but to stay in hiding until they got there. The slaves were no trouble, they were desolate and barely paid attention to anything that went on. They could not move and did not discover them either.

What did pose a problem was that several times, members of the crew came to fetch supplies and water from the back of the hold where they were hiding. Luckily, Camu slept at night like the crew, and by dawn his energy was restored so he could hide them again when dangerous situations came up.

The end of the voyage was tense. Camu wanted to go out and stretch his legs and tail; they had been boxed in the hold for days, and although they had water and food, it was tight in there and they could not walk, so they needed to stretch their backs and legs. They seized any commotion to stretch without leaving their hiding place.

They reached land at last. The crew announced it and the slaves started to get nervous, but only the ones who were not dragon slaves, because those who had been bewitched, seemed to simply vegetate. They had been ordered to sit and rest, and that was what they had done the whole voyage. The crew did not take long getting the slaves out, which meant they were anchored close to the shore.

Lasgol, Egil, and Camu had to wait for everyone to leave the ship. Once they were sure there was no danger, they went up on deck. Two Defenders had been left on watch duty. They never noticed the three stowaways slipping down the stern and swimming underwater to the shore. They came out onto a beach of half-frozen sand. Camu was actively maintaining his camouflage, so they managed to cross the beach and hide behind a small hill.

The refreshing dip had been very invigorating and they had been able to stretch their legs at last. They watched the landscape around them. It was as Egil had told them. They could see a still-frozen environment, snow-covered, icy tundra, especially to the north. But in the southern part, where they had landed, they could see grass growing and plants and flowers in the green areas.

On a beach more to the east they saw over a hundred seals and walruses. They were resting quietly without paying attention to the four ships that had anchored nearby. Drugan quickly lined up the slaves and did not take a moment longer than necessary to set the group in motion toward the northwest.

"Whereabouts in the Reborn Continent coast do you think we are?" Lasgol asked Egil.

"Given the days we've been at sea, the appearance of this place, and the sun's position at this time of year, I'd say we're not far from the coast of Norghana. If we sailed east from here, we'd arrive at Oslenbag, in the north of Norghana. That's a rough estimation, I'll be able to tell for sure when night comes and I can see the position of the stars."

"Your rough estimations are good enough for me," Lasgol said, smiling.

"We'd better follow them," said Egil. "They're not wasting any time."

Lasgol nodded.

They followed the caravan and remained hidden as they watched it. They followed it for two days in a northwestern direction. This land seemed uninhabited—they saw no trace of anyone. They did see wildlife, from reindeer to wolves prowling around them, but no sign of any humans, no ethnic groups of any kind.

Finally, they saw the peak of a high mountain ahead of them. Lasgol felt they were coming to a destination at last. The caravan was heading to the top of a frozen mountain that was not too high. The climb was difficult and the prisoners went slowly under the weight of their chains. The distance from the foot of the mountain was not great, and they could see a path that had been made to reach the top more easily

Leading the long line of over two hundred men was Drugan, accompanied by his two warlocks. In between went the slaves with the Visionaries and Defenders controlling them. Bringing up the rear were Viggen and his most trusted Defenders. Every now and then they looked back to see whether they were being followed. They were uneasy.

Viggen's Defenders and Drugan's Visionaries whipped and pushed the prisoners so they kept moving along the path that led to the top of the mountain. They did it carefully though, so their cargo would not leave the path and fall down the hillside. Every prisoner was chained to five others. If one fell, all six would be lost.

What was most surprising in that strange caravan of slaves was that the first two in each group were dragon slaves. Their eyes shone with that diamond light, unmistakable even from a distance. They obeyed their lords' orders at once, orders the rest of the prisoners did not want to follow, although the regular slave prisoners did not dare resist, which was understandable, since they were closely watched and the whip or club was upon them as soon as they opposed the smallest command from their lords.

The slaves were receiving a clear message. They had to reach the top of the mountain, and fast. Those who lagged behind would suffer. Those who resisted would suffer doubly. Besides, the dragon slaves pulled on the groups as if they were draft beasts. They did not feel the cold in their bodies, or the ice under their feet, or the exhaustion of walking up such a steep path. They seemed immune to the conditions around them. Undoubtedly that made them precious to their masters.

Lasgol, Egil, and Camu watched the ascent impatiently. They wanted to go after them and find out their destination. Lasgol felt troubled, not only because of everything this meant but also for Egil and Camu. He had the feeling, just like Egil, that something serious was going on here, something they were not going to like at all. He could not tell why he felt that way, but he could not shake off the feeling.

"They seem to be getting to the top," said Egil as he squinted to see better.

"Yes, the head of the caravan has reached the top," Lasgol nodded. "They seem to be going on to the other side of the mountain."

Follow them?

"Yes, Camu, we're going after them. Is your skill still working? Can you camouflage us?"

Use much, but a while I can.

"Then we'd better wait for everyone in the caravan to get to the top. Then we'll follow them so Camu doesn't have to camouflage us for now. Let him save his energy for later," Lasgol said.

Egil nodded, "Good idea."

They went after the caravan a moment after the last members of the group had reached the top. They followed the same path at a good pace without overdoing it. The mountain was higher and more slippery than it looked, so it took them a while to reach the summit.

From above, camouflaged, they looked down on the valley

behind the mountain. They saw the caravan about five hundred paces down below, on a second, larger peak guarded by the mountain where they were now. They were surrounding something that stunned Lasgol.

"Life is full of surprises, some of them fascinating," said Egil.

"Is that what I think it is?" Lasgol asked.

"It is, my dear friend, it is," Egil replied.

"I wasn't expecting this…"

"Fascinating. A White Pearl, like the one at the Shelter," Egil confirmed.

"And the portal it generates is active," Lasgol said.

Indeed, a large spherical-looking portal with a sea of silver inside had formed above the White Pearl. In front of the portal were all the slaves, and around them the Visionaries and Defenders. Drugan, Xoltran, and Vingar were watching the portal closely. Viggen and his Defenders with silver shields stood to the side, also watching the portal.

Portal open, feel power.

"Can you tell who opened it?" Egil asked.

"It must have been Drugan or his warlocks Xoltran or Vingar. They're the only ones in this group who have the Gift. To open the portal, you need magic. It has to be one of them."

No see who open portal.

"Have you seen or felt the Dragon Orb?" Lasgol asked Camu.

No, no feel.

"This is most fascinating," said Egil, who had taken out the Quill to check whether the Orb was nearby. The result was negative.

"Is it?" Lasgol did not find it fascinating at all but an enormous problem. Drugan and his people had found a White Pearl and somehow had opened a portal.

"Yes, because if the Orb isn't here, and so it seems, then it didn't open the portal, which means the warlocks did. And if that's the case, the Orb must've taught them how, so there's a way to do it. One we might be able to learn," Egil said.

"Well, that's saying too much," Lasgol said, doubt in his eyes.

"I'm not saying it'll be easy, only that it's feasible," said Egil.

"What I don't understand is what this Pearl is doing in the middle of nowhere," Lasgol wondered, looking at the spread of tundra to the north.

Yes, here be nothing.

"We don't know whether this continent is nothing," Egil said. "Let me remind you that it hasn't really been studied. We don't even know that it's not inhabited for sure. It might be further north. Or perhaps the people here became extinct when the ice began to melt."

"True, I was hasty in my conclusions," Lasgol apologized. He remembered having the same feeling the first time he set foot on the Frozen Continent. He had been greatly surprised to see all the life its glaciers were hiding.

"It's likely the Pearl has always been there," Egil reasoned, "just like the other three we've found."

"The one at the Shelter, the one in the Usik forests, and the one in the desert," Lasgol counted.

"Exactly. It looks like the other Pearls. Its function is to open a portal to transport whoever crosses it to somewhere else," Egil said. "If it's open, it's because they're going to take the slaves someplace else."

"I wonder how they found it," Lasgol said.

"It must have been the Dragon Orb, I can't think of any other explanation," said Egil. "If you remember, the Orb was looking for something and wanted to reach that something using the portals."

Yes, I feel that.

"Maybe it was its servants who found it, either the Defenders or the Visionaries," Lasgol said. "Following its orders, I guess."

"Yes, the Dragon Orb must've guided them here. It was looking for something but couldn't find it..." Egil was thoughtful.

Not find with me.

"Perhaps it did find it by itself with the help of its servants," said Lasgol.

"That's what I was thinking," said Egil. "If that's the case, we have an added problem, since whatever it was looking for has to be to help Dergha-Sho-Blaska reincarnate."

Need power, I feel.

"Yes, it could be searching for an ancient source of power."

"Look! They're starting to go into the portal," Lasgol warned.

The three watched the scene. Drugan and Viggen were throwing orders at their minions and they in turn were yelling at the slaves. They were going to make them enter the portal. The slaves did not know what that great sphere was above the white rock, but they were terrified and did not want to go in. The dragon slaves were walking toward the portal following orders, but the rest were resisting.

The Defenders had placed some wooden ramps for the slaves to go up to the Pearl and enter the portal which was emitting silver waves, indicating it was active. The first slaves finally went in and vanished. The rest of the slaves, seeing their comrades disappear, became even more terrified and began to scream and resist. Whips cracked and the Visionaries started pushing them into the portal with clubs.

"Those poor wretches. I wish we could help them…" Lasgol said, frustrated.

"Now isn't the time. We have to find out where they're sending them, since I'm sure it's where the Orb's waiting."

"They wouldn't be taking them somewhere to sacrifice them, would they?" Lasgol asked suddenly, horrified by the idea.

"I really don't know… I hope not. A ritual of reincarnation might require sacrifices, it wouldn't be so farfetched. I hope that's not the case, but I can't assure you it's not."

Sacrifices much bad.

"I hope there's some way we can save those wretched people," Lasgol said wishfully.

"Me too. Let's not lose hope. We don't know what's happening on the other side of the portal. Speculating with the worse scenarios is necessary, but it doesn't mean that this is what's happening."

The groups of slaves went into the portal, one after the other, pushed, beaten, and even thrown in by force. When the last group vanished inside the portal, something odd happened, neither Drugan, his warlocks, the Visionaries, Viggen, or his Defenders went into the portal.

"That's interesting… I wasn't expecting that…" Egil said thoughtfully.

"Why aren't they going with them?" Lasgol asked.

Camu had the answer.

Bring more.

"Irrefutable, my dear Camu. They're going to bring another cargo of slaves, that's why they're not crossing yet."

Viggen and Drugan talked for a moment. Then they gave instructions to their deputies. The caravan formed again, this time without slaves, and began making their way back up the mountain path.

"They're going back to the ships," said Lasgol.

"It would appear so. That's not a bad thing."

"It isn't? Why do you say that?" Lasgol asked Egil, since things were looking pretty grim to him.

"Because it means they haven't finished whatever it is they're doing. And if they're not done, it means we still have time to stop it."

"Oh, I see. When you put it like that…"

We time. We win.

"That's the spirit, Camu," Egil told him.

"Let's keep our spirits up," Lasgol joined them, "even if the situation isn't too favorable for our goals."

"There's still time, we can stop this horror," Egil told them, trying to persuade himself and his friends.

"Ingrid does that better," Lasgol said and winked at him.

"I know, but I had to try," Egil replied with a smile.

"So, what do we do now?" Lasgol asked in a concerned tone.

"Seeing what we've discovered, I think the best thing to do is go back for our comrades and bring them here."

"And how are we supposed to do that?" Lasgol asked blankly.

"Easy, we'll use the Pearl's portal."

I not know how use Portal, Camu messaged, along with a feeling of worry.

"I think the time has come for you to learn," Egil said, smiling.

Chapter 37

Egil, Lasgol, and Camu waited in hiding until Drugan and Viggen's caravan had made their way back to the ships. They could see the White Pearl on top of the small hill and the portal, which remained open for a while before fading until it completely vanished.

Lasgol was not confident of the plan. He loved Camu very much and he knew his magic was powerful, but Camu had already tried opening the portal before without success. He had only managed to do it with the help of the Orb's magic.

"Are you sure it wouldn't be better to sneak back on one of the ships as stowaways?" he asked Egil.

"That would delay us for days. Besides, we're going to need Camu to learn to use the portals."

Need to learn I?

"I'm afraid so, my magical friend. The Orb can use the portals, so it has a lead on us. We're never going to catch up with it unless we can get to it using the same means."

"It's very risky... if Camu can't open the portal we'll be stranded here in the Reborn Continent without any way to get back."

"Is a risk, yes. But I'm sure Drugan and Viggen will be coming back soon with another shipment. If by then we haven't succeeded, we'll have their ships to carry us home again."

"And what about bringing the rest of the group?"

"They already know what's happened. If we don't give any signs of life, they'll come for us."

How know where?

"The same way we did—they'll follow Viggen and his ships. Astrid will guess that her uncle got the ships in Copenghen. They'll go there to see what they can find out, I know it."

"You've got it all figured out, don't you?" Lasgol said, still not convinced with the plan.

"If you think about it, you'll realize that going back with the ships now makes no sense. We won't gain anything and we'd lose an obvious opportunity."

Obvious opportunity?

"I'm wondering what he means too," Lasgol joined him.

Egil smiled. "Let me explain. Drugan and his warlocks have used this portal, and it must've been with the Orb's help. We have the chance to see whether we can learn from it. We might, you know."

"Rather than an obvious opportunity, I think it's a very distant one…"

I try. Learn sure, Camu messaged with his usual optimism.

Lasgol was not so optimistic, but he did not want to say anything.

They waited until Drugan, Viggen, and his people were well on their way to the ships before they started toward the Pearl. They saw them disappear in the distance, but even so they waited in case for some odd reason they decided to return. They did not. Once they were sure the men were not coming back, they went down to the White Pearl.

"It's just like the one at the Shelter," Lasgol said after going around it a couple times.

"It is," Egil agreed as he studied it carefully.

Feel energy, Camu messaged.

"It must be because there's still a remnant of magic from the portal," said Egil. "Try to see if you can catch the remaining energy before it fades completely. It has to be from the portal, and it might tell you something."

I try.

Lasgol used the time to wander around the small summit the Pearl was standing on and also the immediate surroundings in case he saw anything of interest. He was beginning to like the Reborn Continent. It was mostly like Norghana in autumn. He could see the tundra to the north and large mountain peaks covered with ice. He did not see glaciers, which he found strange, but perhaps they were further north or had melted   when the continent came out of its ice age and was reborn.

"How are you doing, Camu?" Lasgol asked him after a while. His friend had been concentrating with his eyes shut and without saying a word for quite a while now, so Lasgol decided to see if everything was okay.

Feeling energy of portal. Feel other energy too…

"Do you know what energy it is? Do you recognize it?" Egil asked.

Feel far. Not know who.

"Most likely the Orb's," Egil commented.

"Do you think it opened the portal from the other side? From another place?" Lasgol asked.

"It could be that, or perhaps it traveled here and opened the portal when it saw its followers arriving."

"And didn't wait for them? Weird, isn't it?"

"Yeah, that is weird…. There must be a reason for it, or if not, it opened it from wherever it is."

"We don't know how many Pearls there are in Tremia. It could be anywhere on the continent," Lasgol said.

"That's true. It might even be on some other continent we don't know anything about," Egil said, staring at the horizon thoughtfully.

"Are there continents we don't know about?" Lasgol said, surprised.

Egil smiled.

"It's a trick statement. If the continents are unknown, we can't know whether they exist or not."

"Ugh, I fell into the trap," Lasgol blushed. "But there could be more continents that haven't been found yet? Do you think so?"

"I don't see why not. We don't even know all the lands and peoples of Tremia, let alone all the creatures that hide away from men. Look at the sea in the horizon—it's vast. Of course, it's possible that there are more continents we still haven't discovered in the midst of the infinite blue ocean. Maybe because they're too far or because they're hidden to our senses."

"Like the Turquoise Realm."

"Exactly. Or it might be that a powerful magic keeps them hidden. There might be whole continents to be discovered still in this world," Egil stated with enthusiasm. "Wouldn't it be fantastic if there were?"

"As long as they're not filled with aggressive savages wanting to cut off our heads, or military kingdoms wanting to conquer the whole world…"

"We always tend to believe the worst. There might be peaceful civilizations in beautiful lands. More advanced even than ours that could teach us medicine, philosophy, how to reach happiness," Egil went on wishfully.

"You're a dreamer and well-intentioned. If there are other continents, I'm sure they'll send troops to conquer this one. You'll see."

"Your pessimistic view of humanity makes me sad."

"It's not pessimistic, it's realistic," Lasgol said.

"Let's hope that the future brings us great discoveries and happiness," Egil said.

"You're forgetting that we're trying to stop a thousand-year-old immortal dragon from reincarnating and destroying mankind," Lasgol reminded him bitterly.

Egil nodded and his optimism vanished.

"We'll do it, and then we can go and discover new and fantastic continents," he joked.

"I'll hold you to that," Lasgol replied with a smile.

Camu continued perceiving the residual energy the portal had left behind when it had activated, as well as the energy he had identified as the Orb's.

I learn energies, he messaged.

"Yes, try to memorize them so you remember them," Lasgol suggested.

"Why don't you try to open the portal? Go ahead," Egil told Camu. "Let's see what happens. If you don't try, we'll never know whether you can do it or not."

"Everything we've been studying and learning with Eicewald—about magic, its laws, how to improve and reach new grades—might help you now, and maybe you'll succeed. I should think so."

I learn much with Eicewald. I improve.

"That's what I think," Lasgol said. "Come on, give it a try."

Camu shut his eyes and concentrated. After a moment there was a silver flash that ran though his body, and Lasgol knew his friend was using his power. He hoped he would succeed, for all of their sakes.

Two more flashes ran through Camu's body and then he started sending pulses to the great spherical object, searching for the right frequency. The silver waves issued from him and crashed against the Pearl without causing a reaction.

Egil and Lasgol watched. They had already witnessed this before and remembered it had not ended well before.

All of a sudden, by surprise, there was a flash from the Pearl. A silver one, as if it were awaking from a deep slumber and responding.

"A flash!" Lasgol said excitedly.

"Fantastic!" Egil joined him, delighted.

Camu opened his eyes and caught a glimpse of the dying flash. He shut his eyes again and continued trying. He had made the Pearl react. It was a start. Now he needed to find a way to open the portal.

He tried over and over again until he almost ran out of energy and was exhausted. He finally had to give up.

Not have more energy. Need rest.

"Don't force yourself. We'll continue tomorrow. Rest now and we'll try again in the morning."

I get flash. Be something.

"Of course it's something," Lasgol told him. "Tomorrow you'll get two."

"I'm sure. It'll be fascinating!" Egil joined in.

But, on the next day, Camu got nothing but another flash. He did not improve. Nor did he do so on the following day or the next. Lasgol had to improvise a shed between some rocks north of the Pearl. More than a shed, it was a roof and two wooden walls with boulders making up the rest of it. They were sheltered from the cold during the night, which was almost freezing. If there was a storm it would not hold up, but it was better than nothing.

They soon ran out of supplies and Lasgol had to go out in search of food. Camu and Egil stayed by the Pearl and tried new approaches to see if they could make any progress. So far, they were not having much luck, but Camu refused to give up. His stubbornness was a strong point at times like these.

Finding something to eat was not difficult for Lasgol. He went down to the beaches and fished or gathered shellfish, or else went into the plains and sought some reindeer to kill. He found forests to the east that looked young compared with the Norghanian ones, and in them he found game. He found it harder to find food for Camu, but the forests offered an abundance of berries, roots, and other plants which were not very savory to humans but which Camu ate, delighted.

Thanks to the simple spells they had learned, making a fire or creating light was now very easy for them and quite useful. They had also learned how to generate heat without fire to keep themselves warm, which helped during the nights. They called it Blue Fire, since it created a blue flame which gave off warmth without smoke. Lasgol found this useful spell wonderful, but unfortunately when they fell asleep the fire died out because they were not imbuing it with magical energy. Eicewald had told them that a Blue Fire could be generated that would last all night without needing to feed it, but that was no longer a basic spell but an advanced one, and they had not yet learned it.

Every day at dawn Camu tried again, and once again he got no result other than one single flash in response from the Pearl. The days went by, and everything he could think of and tried failed. Egil wrote down all the failed attempts and called out new variations or new combinations of elements.

Camu, in turn, applied everything they had learned about the principles of magic. But the days were passing by, and the only thing he had managed to do was exhaust himself faster. There were days when he had to stop by mid-morning because he had used up all his energy in three or four attempts to power his spell.

Lasgol decided to try and help Camu, even if he was convinced, he would not achieve much. In order to interact with the Pearl, you needed to have some Drakonian magic, like that of Camu or the Orb, and not Nature magic like Lasgol's. In any case he decided to help him, because even Camu had a limit, and he was reaching it. He would quit soon if they did not achieve something.

Camu began to send his silver pulses rhythmically to the White Pearl, and it responded with a whitish flash. Lasgol placed the palm of his hand on the surface of the Pearl and called upon his *Arcane Communication* skill which allowed him to communicate and interact with Objects of Power or magical objects on some occasions. It was one of the skills he used less often because he was not that good at it. But they were desperate and he thought it might help somehow.

Lasgol's head shone with a green flash, and suddenly he felt the Pearl and the pulses Camu was sending to it. He shut his eyes and concentrated on sending a lot of energy to strengthen his skill. The more energy he sent, the clearer he felt the pulses Camu was hitting the Pearl with.

Then something unexpected happened: Lasgol started to feel the Pearl's magic. He could pick up an internal aura of great intensity inside the Pearl. He was shocked—he did not understand how it was possible for him to pick up the Pearl's aura of power. He sent more of his energy to amplify his skill, and the more he sent, the clearer he could feel the enormous power the Pearl held within like a treasure.

It was like thousands of auras of different magi all together inside the Pearl.

He tried to communicate with the Pearl to see if he might interact with it. That was the aim of the *Arcane Communication* skill, after all, and perhaps he might achieve it. He focused on establishing some type of communication with the Pearl but was unsuccessful. The Pearl did not respond to his attempts; it was as if it was not listening to him or perhaps did not want to listen to him.

No matter how hard he tried to interact, with the Pearl or make it react, he could not do it. He found it most frustrating, because he was able to feel the power, the essence of the Pearl, and yet he could not make it react.

"I can pick up the Pearl's aura of power," he announced without opening his eyes or losing concentration on his skill, "but I can't make it communicate with me."

You feel?

"Yes, the power it has within is enormous, although I think I'm incapable of feeling it all and am only admiring a part of all its power."

I only feel, no catch aura.

"I do, but I can't interact with it," Lasgol said ruefully.

"Perhaps Lasgol can help you pick it up," Egil ventured. "Try it, Lasgol, see if you can help Camu."

"Fine. Although I'm not sure how I can make Camu pick up the aura," Lasgol thought about it, and then he remembered his *Aura Presence* skill. He knew Camu's auras well: his body's, that of his mind, and his power. Perhaps he could make him feel what his *Arcane Communication* skill was showing him if he transmitted it to Camu's mind with a combination of his *Aura Presence* and *Animal Communication* skills.

Try, he received Camu's message.

Lasgol snorted—it was not going to be easy, if at all possible, which he really doubted. Keeping his *Arcane Communication* skill active, he called on his *Aura Presence* skill. At once there was the green flash that ran through his head, and he picked up Camu's and Egil's auras. He ignored Egil's and focused on Camu's. As he did so he began to lose his *Arcane Communication* skill, as if by losing his concentration it had escaped his control.

So he had to concentrate harder and focus on both skills so as not to lose them. Now the complication began—calling on his *Animal Communication* skill, Lasgol sent to Camu's mind what he was picking up from the White Pearl through his *Arcane Communication* skill.

I… pick up… Camu messaged.

"What are you picking up, Camu?" Egil asked him.

I see Pearl, see inner aura.

Lasgol was relieved, because he was finding it increasingly hard not to lose the skills. He felt that at any moment they were going to escape his control and vanish. He tried to focus even harder on them.

I try reach aura of pearl, Camu messaged.

After a moment, the Pearl gave off a silver flash in response to the pulses Camu was sending it.

Pearl answer, Camu messaged.

Suddenly, the portal they had been hoping would form began to appear above the Pearl.

"Keep going, you're doing it!" Egil said.

Lasgol did not want to open his eyes so as not to break his concentration. He could feel the portal opening, but if he opened his eyes, he would lose control.

Above the Pearl three silver round shapes began to form. First the circle the same size as the Pearl right above it, then a second circle, egg-shaped and bigger, as if the circle had turned into an oval, and then, at last, it all became a great silver sphere.

Portal almost open. Little more, Camu messaged.

Lasgol continued sending all the energy he had left to potentiate his skills and, through it, to help Camu. He was not sure it was doing any good, but he did not care, he had to do it. So he continued sending all his energy.

Portal open, Camu messaged.

Above the White Pearl, the great spherical silver Portal had finished forming. Lasgol opened his eyes and looked into the great sphere, which seemed filled with liquid silver. It looked like a sea made of silver with waves moving inside the sphere. The enormous sphere hovered above the Pearl in complete silence. It did not give off any flashes or reflection. The underside of the circumference was a few hand-spans from touching the top of the Pearl. Seeing the two spheres, one above the other, amazed Lasgol once again. Then, all of a sudden, he lost control of his skills, which vanished, and fell to his knees from exhaustion.

"You did it!" Egil cried, hopping around gleefully.

Camu lowered his head, bent his legs, and dropped down on his side.

Very tired ... was all he could message.

A moment later Lasgol and Camu were fast asleep from sheer exhaustion.

Egil was left standing in front of the open portal.

"It's fantastic!" he cried.

Chapter 38

Now that Camu had managed to learn how to open the Portal, they focused on trying to solve the next big problem: determining their destination. They had decided to enter the portal and see where it took them. Perhaps it would take them to the Pearl at the Shelter, or maybe not. Egil argued there were more odds that they would appear in any place other than the Shelter, simply because there were multiple Pearls in Tremia and therefore the chances were they would appear anywhere else.

Camu and Lasgol were trying to pick up some mechanism in the Pearl's aura that would let them select a destination, specifically that of the Shelter. But they were not having much luck. They were not surprised though. Nothing was simple in the magical world, and least of all a given. They would just have to suffer in order to solve this enigma.

What they did discover was that the Portal always formed in the same way, so they figured the destination had to be set once the Portal was open. It was just an idea, but they were working with it in mind. Camu was trying to determine what Pearl the portal might be aiming for.

Lasgol helped him in trying to pick up the destination of every portal Camu opened, but he was having no luck. Egil reached the conclusion that the portal led to some other Pearl by default when it formed, since it was a portal and had been created with that purpose; what they could not find out was which other Pearl the portal had selected. It might be the closest one, based on proximity, which would be the most efficient method. But once again, these were only guesses.

They tried for days and then, one morning, Lasgol had an idea.

"Camu, remember when we got here that you picked up the Orb's energy?"

Remember.

"Do you feel it still?"

No, but remember.

"Wonderful. I want you to search for it in the Portal's aura once it's formed, not in the Pearl itself."

Look for energy of orb in portal?

"That's right, see if there are any traces of that energy in the Portal."

Okay.

Egil came over and raised an eyebrow.

"Interesting…" he told Lasgol.

Camu concentrated and opened a Portal. He could now do it without Lasgol's help since he had found the right rhythm in the pulses he sent to activate it. Once the portal formed, he searched for traces of the Orb's energy in its silvery interior.

He was at it for a long time.

Pick up traces.

"You do?" Lasgol was thrilled.

Yes. Concentrate traces.

"Is anything happening?" Egil asked him after a moment.

"Give him time," Lasgol whispered to Egil.

Now see white sphere on top other silver sphere.

Where are you seeing that?" Lasgol asked.

Center of portal.

"That must be the representation of a specific Pearl," said Egil. "It must be the destination it's aiming at."

"Is there anything that indicates what Pearl it is? Any symbol? Number? Rune?" Lasgol asked.

Rune, same in two circles.

"Wonderful! Do you know that rune?"

Not know… familiar…

"That's a great advancement," Egil said. "Even if you don't know it, if it's at all familiar, we can assume it has to be a dragon rune, or a Drakonian one…"

"That's what I was thinking too…" said Lasgol.

"We know, or to be precise, we're guessing that dragons used these portals to travel all over Tremia quickly," said Egil. "Therefore, that rune has to be one they can understand, and therefore so would Drakonians."

I not understand… Camu messaged, disappointed.

"Don't worry. For now, just memorize it," Egil told him. "You can do that, right?"

Yes, I memorize.

298

"Fantastic," Egil said encouragingly.

"Can you see any other runes like it? Try to see whether there are other similar ones."

Camu was silent for a good while. Egil and Lasgol waited patiently, feeling a little excited—this was a big step.

Find other rune.

"Different from the first one? Above two spheres, one white and one silver like before?" Lasgol asked him.

Yes. See two spheres in center of portal. Rune different.

"This is most fascinating!" Egil cried.

"How did you manage to see it?" Lasgol said, curious.

I think of Pearl Shelter.

"Fantastic! Very clever, Camu!" Egil told him.

"It must be the mechanism to change destinations," Lasgol reasoned. "He found it. Camu, think about the Pearl in the desert and see if the rune changes," he asked.

I think.

"I'll ask Camu to describe those runes and I'll draw them in my notebook, that way we'll have visual depictions of the destinations in the language of dragons."

Done, rune change.

"Great. That corroborates it," said Egil. "Memorize those runes, because I'll need to draw them."

Okay.

"Can you see if it shows any other runes?" Lasgol asked hm.

I try.

Egil was very excited with what they were discovering. Lasgol was more uneasy than excited because of the repercussions of the discovery.

Appear symbol. Two spheres, no rune.

"It must be that it's showing him the Pearls he already knows, that he's visited, with runes, and this last rune must be by default."

"We know three pearls. Why doesn't he see the third one? Because we're in it?" Lasgol wondered out loud.

"That must be it. It shows him destinations. This Pearl can't be a destination because we're already here."

Camu opened his eyes. *Tired,* he messaged.

"Rest, champ, you did wonderfully well!" Egil congratulated him.

"You did really well!" Lasgol told him too.

I much unbelievable.

Egil and Lasgol laughed out loud, and Camu lay down to rest, exhausted from the magical effort he had just made.

Three days later, Lasgol and Egil were watching the caravan moving while they stayed hidden at a prudent distance behind some boulders. They seemed to be experiencing déjà vu. With Drugan and Viggen in the lead, the caravan of slaves were climbing the mountain that led them to the Pearl in the Reborn Continent. They had about two hundred more prisoners with them, guarded by about thirty Visionaries and Defenders.

What was different this time was who they were being followed by. Lasgol and Egil, watching the caravan closely, had detected that a small group was following the caravan at a distance that allowed them not to be seen. But Lasgol and Egil had seen them from their vantage point.

If was, of course, the rest of the Panthers.

"It seems that, as always, you were right," Lasgol whispered to Egil.

"You can always make an educated guess as to your friends' most logical behavior," Egil replied.

"As you would say: irrefutable."

"Exactly," Egil said, beaming.

Ingrid, Astrid, Nilsa, Viggo, Gerd and Ona were following the caravan without going into the open. Viggen and his Defenders would see them if they did. They could not let that happen, or they would lose the element of surprise. They stopped, hiding in the snow.

"If we release now, we can still surprise them," Nilsa said in a whisper from where she was flat on the snow.

"Don't kill my uncle, I'll handle him," Astrid told her as she took her Sniper's bow and laid it down beside her on the snow.

"Isn't it odd that they should come all the way here across the sea?" Gerd asked.

"I think so," Astrid replied. "As far as I know, people abandoned this land a long time ago. There's only cold in this wasteland, isn't that right, Ingrid?"

"In the first place, we're not going to release or attack them in any way. We have to find out what they intend to do here," Ingrid said. "Attacking without seeing our comrades or the Dragon Orb would be a serious mistake. We should only attack if we can get hold of the Orb or if our friends are in danger."

"Otherwise the Orb might fulfill its purpose," Gerd added.

"That's right. We don't know what they're planning, and it's important we find out," said Ingrid. "I want to attack Drugan and Viggen too, don't get me wrong. I want to free those slaves, but I know that if we do, we might lose the Orb and put Lasgol, Egil, and Camu in danger, and that would be catastrophic. We can't allow it."

"Do you believe they're close to getting the dragon out of the orb and reincarnated?" Gerd asked.

"Unfortunately, these last events we're witnessing lead me to believe so. This whole operation of coming to the Reborn Continent, bringing all these slaves, has to be for that," Astrid said.

"I feel the same way. Otherwise, they wouldn't have organized such a voyage," said Nilsa.

"Let's not get ahead of ourselves," said Ingrid. "We don't actually know what's going on. So far, we know they're transporting slaves here by ship, nothing more."

"And what do they want all those slaves for?" Gerd asked.

"I'd want them to serve me as their king," Viggo said, smiling.

"I'm convinced it's to form an army," said Nilsa.

"Yeah, I'm also leaning in that direction," Astrid joined in. "If they get hundreds of dragon slaves to protect their master, things will get very complicated."

"If we have to kill hundreds of those shiny eyes, I'll do it," Viggo said nonchalantly, as if it were no trouble at all.

"They're wretched human beings who've been enslaved with evil magic, they don't deserve to die," Nilsa chided him.

"If they attack me, they'll die, and if they get in my way they'll die too. Whichever way it happens is irrelevant," Viggo said firmly.

"We're not going to attack anyone until we find our friends," Ingrid told him, "and show some compassion, for heaven's sake."

"I show it for this singular group every day," Viggo replied ironically, glancing at his comrades.

"Whatever it is they're planning, this is turning into something we hadn't anticipated," Astrid admitted. "I don't like what we're witnessing."

"You have a bad feeling?" Nilsa asked her.

"It's more than a feeling. Something's wrong, very wrong, and it's troubling me," Astrid admitted.

"I don't understand why you're so worried," Viggo said.

"Whatever it is they're planning, we won't let them succeed. We have them ahead of us, we can finish them off if necessary," said Ingrid. "If only we knew where Lasgol, Egil, and Camu are."

I be here, Camu messaged to them.

"By all the Ice Gods!" Viggo cried as he turned on the ground with his knives in his hands.

"Camu!" Gerd cried.

Ona moaned.

"Camu, are you here?" Astrid said too, looking behind them.

Yes, I let see, Camu messaged as he became visible.

"You really scared us, you bug!"

I no bug. You scare easy.

"The things one has to hear!"

"Lower your voice, Viggo, or they'll hear you from the caravan," Ingrid snapped.

"Where are Egil and Lasgol, are they okay?" Astrid asked Camu with a worried look on her face.

Yes, well. Hiding.

"Thank goodness," Gerd grunted.

"Yeah, they had me worried," said Nilsa.

"The weirdo and the bookworm can take care of themselves, there's nothing to worry about," Viggo stated.

"Hiding where?" Ingrid wanted to know.

Behind big summit, east.

"Let's go to them," Gerd urged.

"We'd better wait for the caravan to reach the top, then we'll move. If we do it before then they'll be able to spot us. There's nowhere to hide on that hillside," said Astrid.

"True. As soon as Viggen and his people disappear behind that peak we can go after them," said Ingrid.

"Action awaits us behind that hill. I can smell it," Viggo said, preparing his knives for the fight.

Get ready to climb," Ingrid told them.

Drugan, Viggen, and the rest of the caravan reached the summit and vanished from sight down the other side. The group looked at Ingrid, waiting for her signal to go after them. She waited a short while that seemed to last forever, then she gave a curt nod.

"Let's move" she said, and they began the chase.

Ingrid led the group, with Nilsa and Astrid behind her. Then came Viggo and Gerd, and Camu and Ona brought the rear. They were not following the path the caravan had taken but were going up across the hillside. It was a lot more dangerous because of how slippery the ice was, but it was much faster than following a path that wound its way up.

Their legs were beginning to feel the effort of the climb. The mountain was high and steep, but for Rangers like them, it posed no problem. Ingrid was setting a fast pace and the others followed her, careful where they set their feet, since the greatest risk was a fall, which would mean a long tumble and maybe broken bones.

They made their way up the mountain quickly, their weapons ready, alert to the terrain and the wind, which was blowing hard, especially as they neared the summit. Ingrid increased their pace for the last stretch. When she reached the top, she noticed it was flat and walked over to the other side to see what was at the back of the mountain. She reached the edge and flattened herself on the ground. The others, coming right behind her, also dropped to the ground and lay flat to watch.

They saw the caravan further below on a second lower peak hidden by the mountain they were on. Drugan and Viggen were talking in front of something that froze them all. Ingrid's hard gaze changed into one of utter surprise, and for a moment no one spoke. They all stared in surprise, feeling uneasy.

"Is that what I think it is?" Gerd asked after a moment

"You can bet your huge body it is," Viggo said.

"It's a White Pearl like the one at the Shelter," Nilsa confirmed.

"And the portal it can create is activated," said Astrid.

Indeed, a great spherical-looking, silver Portal has formed above the White Pearl.

Portal open, Camu messaged in warning.

"What's this Pearl doing here in the middle of nowhere?" Nilsa asked.

"Have they come here to take a ride through a portal?" Ingrid asked as if to herself.

"It looks that way," Astrid said. "It's certainly more discreet than going to the Shelter."

"This is getting most interesting," Viggo commented.

"I think it's becoming incredibly ugly," said Gerd.

"Where are Lasgol and Egil hiding? I want to talk to them," Ingrid told Camu.

I take. Careful not be seen.

"Good. Let's go with Camu and stay low so we're not spotted."

They took a detour to the east and Camu led them to where their two friends were hiding. It was a hollow protected by several large boulders from where they could watch the portal clearly.

"Welcome," Lasgol greeted them with a big smile.

"Good hiding place," Ingrid said, and they all dropped into the hollow.

Astrid threw Lasgol a kiss, which he received with delight.

"We've been waiting for you," Egil told them.

"How did you know we would come?" Gerd asked.

"I guessed you'd follow the ships' trail."

"You guessed correctly," Astrid told him. "We discovered Viggen's operation in Copenghen, so we decided to wait for him and follow him on his next transport."

"You have a ship?" Lasgol asked.

"A war ship, with crew and all. It's anchored at a bay further east," said Ingrid.

"We asked Gondabar and he got it for us," Astrid said. "We followed Viggen's ships from a distance."

"To this wasteland of a continent," Viggo added with certain disdain as he looked around.

"We don't know whether this continent is a wasteland," Egil said. "It hasn't been studied in depth."

"There's nothing here," Viggo protested. "It's like a copy of the Frozen Continent, only less frozen."

"What's that Pearl doing here, and with its portal open?" Gerd asked Egil and Lasgol.

"I think the question we should be asking is what Drugan and Viggen are doing with that Pearl," Egil corrected him.

"It's likely the Pearl has always been here," Lasgol said. "Just like the other three we've found."

"The one at the Shelter, the one in the Usik Forest, and the one in the desert," Nilsa said.

"How did they find it I wonder," said Ingrid.

"It must've been the Dragon Orb," Lasgol said.

"Their servants might have found it for them," Nilsa ventured.

"It could've been the Defenders—my uncle's been traveling throughout Tremia for years on his famous quest," said Astrid. "I'm sure he found this Pearl on one of his travels."

"Even if he had found it, he wouldn't know what it was or what it was for," Viggo said.

Astrid was thoughtful for a moment.

"He might not have known and even so, taken notice of its importance for his quest."

"In any case, we're in front of a Pearl with an open portal. If they didn't know what it was when they found it, they surely know what it is now," said Ingrid.

"Look! They're starting to enter the portal," Nilsa said, pointing.

The Panthers watched the scene. Drugan and Viggen were shouting orders to their men, and they in turn were yelling at the slaves. They were going to make them enter the Portal. The slaves did not know what that great sphere of white rock was, and they were terrified and did not want to go in. The dragon slaves were walking to the Portal, following orders, but the rest were pulling back.

"What should we do, are we going to attack?" Viggo asked, sounding eager to fight.

Egil watched the slaves entering the Portal, whipped and pushed by the Visionaries.

"No, we're not going to attack."

"We aren't? And why not?" Viggo asked.

"They don't have the Dragon Orb," Egil replied calmly. "We've checked with the Quill."

"Camu, do you pick anything up? The power of the orb?" Lasgol asked him out loud so everyone could hear.

Camu strained his neck and closed his eyes.

Not feel power of orb.

"But they're taking the slaves," Nilsa joined Viggo. "We have to free them."

"If we attack them, the Orb will know we're coming for it and we'll lose the only advantage we have surprise," Egil told them.

"If Drugan and Viggen and their men go into that portal too, we'll lose them all," said Gerd.

"No, we won't lose them," Egil assured them.

"We won't?" Ingrid asked.

Lasgol had already guessed Egil's next move and said nothing.

"No, because we're going in after them," Egil said.

"No way! We kill them now and we don't have to enter the portal!" Viggo cried.

"That would get us nothing," Egil told him.

"What do you mean nothing? They'd be dead."

"They're going to lead us to the Orb. That's what matters, not killing them," Lasgol joined him.

They saw all the slaves go in, and with them the Visionaries and the Defenders. Once they had all entered the portal, Xoltran and Vingar did too. Only Drugan and Viggen remained in front of the Pearl. Drugan took out what looked like a silver scepter and cast a spell with it.

Drakonian power, Camu messaged.

"What are they doing?" Ingrid asked.

"They're keeping the portal open," said Egil.

"That scepter must be an Object of Power the Orb got for Drugan so he can operate the portal," Lasgol explained.

"Did Drugan open it?" Astrid asked blankly.

"That's right," Egil replied.

Drugan and Viggen waited a good while, and finally they both entered the portal, which stayed open.

"They've all crossed over," Nilsa said. "What do we do now?"

"We go and inspect the portal," said Egil.

They all got to their feet and went to the great white sphere.

Camu went over to the still-open portal with Lasgol beside him as Egil watched, right behind them.

Study portal, Camu messaged.

"Good idea, let's do that."

Camu concentrated and sent a rhythmic pulse to the Pearl. Lasgol placed his hand on its surface and called on his *Arcane Communication* skill.

"Do those two know what they're doing?" Viggo asked.

"They're not in danger, are they?" Astrid sounded worried.

Ona was moaning, also worried.

"Everything'll be all right. We've made great progress with the portals," Egil said with a smile.

Ingrid, Nilsa, Astrid, Gerd, and Viggo exchanged puzzled looks.

"What do you mean great progress with the portals?" Ingrid wanted to know.

"While you were on your way here, we've been studying them. They're most fascinating."

"What do you mean by studying them? Can you open them?" Nilsa asked, opening her eyes wide in awe.

"Oh yes, and we've learned many things about how they work."

"Unbelievable! and he says it so calmly!" Viggo put his hands to his head.

"You know how to use them?" Gerd asked with fear on his face.

"We're learning," Egil smiled at him and showed him one of his logbooks where he had been writing down everything regarding portals. Camu and Lasgol continued using their skills until the portal began to fade away. At that moment they stopped, waiting until the portal finished fading.

"Do you have the location of their destination?" Egil asked.

We do, Camu messaged.

"We've located their destination," Lasgol replied.

"Wonderful, tomorrow we'll go after them," said Egil.

"Go after them?" Ingrid questioned.

"Irrefutable—we'll open our own portal to their destination," Egil said as if it were the most natural thing in the world.

Chapter 39

Around mid-morning the following day, the Panthers were ready to continue. Or as ready as they could be, considering that Camu and Lasgol were going to open a portal. Lasgol was sure Camu could do it on his own, but since his friend had insisted, given the importance of the moment and Egil thought it was a good idea, he had agreed to help. They had to open a portal to wherever Drugan, Viggen, and the slaves had gone—there they would find the Orb and stop the reincarnation.

Or that was Egil's plan at least.

Camu and Lasgol stood in front of the White Pearl and summoned their skills. The rest of the Panthers watched closely. The White Pearl responded with a great silver flash, and soon after the portal began to form above the Pearl.

"Amazing…" Gerd muttered.

"Impressive," said Astrid when the portal finished forming.

"This is going to be a pain in the…" Viggo started to say.

Portal open, Camu messaged.

Lasgol stopped using his skills.

"Everything's ready," he told his comrades.

"It's time to go in," Egil told them. "Remember the negative effects it will cause. That's why we've given Drugan and Viggen some time, so they don't capture us when we enter after them and we're still unconscious. But, there's no way of knowing whether any other danger awaits us on the other side."

"You haven't seen what's on the other side?" Nilsa asked.

"It doesn't work that way," Lasgol said. "It's not like a door you open a little and you can see what's on the other side. It's as if you ceased to exist on this side of the portal to exist again on the other."

"That sounds bad. I don't like the idea of ceasing to exist," Viggo protested.

"Don't worry, we're going in together," Ingrid said with a wink.

"Not even that puts me at ease," he replied. "Although, well, I go in happier." He smiled.

"In any case, Camu and Ona don't suffer the effects of the portal, so they'll protect us if any watchmen have been posted," Egil said soothingly.

We protect, Camu messaged.

Ona growled once.

"Very well, let's do this," Ingrid said.

Camu and Ona were the first to jump onto the catwalk the Visionaries had placed to help the slaves climb onto the Pearl. Camu arrived at the top and waited for Ona. When they were both ready, they leapt into the portal. Then the whole group climbed onto the catwalk and went into the sphere, blending into the liquid silver that made up the portal. They fainted at once.

Lasgol came to with a terrible headache, a feeling he remembered well. A clear light and the sounds of birds he did not know assaulted his eyes and ears. He felt awful, as if he had been run over by a stampede of wild horses. An unpleasant smell told him he had vomited to his right. From his prior experiences he knew it would take a moment to fully recover. Well, several moments—he did not try to open his eyes, because he knew he would feel nauseous again.

Camu, is there any danger? He managed to transmit with great effort.

No danger. We watch.

Ona growled near where Lasgol was lying, which relaxed him a little. He turned onto his back, trying to recover. He noticed that the ground he was lying on was some type of grass with an exotic aroma. He felt very hot, and the air was heavy with humidity. After a while he managed to open his eyes and realized he was in some kind of jungle. He managed to keep his eyes open while shocking greens and deep reds and oranges filled his senses.

He looked around and saw his friends on the ground, slowly recovering and getting on their feet. Lasgol went over to help Gerd, who was unable to stand and kept falling back down. Gradually, they all got up. Astrid helped Lasgol, Nilsa and Ingrid helped one another, and Viggo pulled Egil up by his arm.

"The ride's been great," Viggo commented sarcastically.

Behind them they saw a White Pearl. The portal had shut down as they had expected, since they had been unconscious for quite a while.

"Are you all well?" Lasgol asked.

"We appear to be, but these two not so much," Ingrid said, indicating two Visionaries lying on the ground. One was dead with half his body completely frozen and the other one had his throat opened by a vicious bite.

"What happened?" Egil asked Camu.

Two Visionaries watch. We appear, they attack.

"And in all cases, they die," Viggo said with a big smile.

I use Ice Breath. Ona bite.

"Yeah, yeah, we can see that. Good work," Ingrid congratulated them as she examined the two dead Visionaries.

"They left them behind in case we followed them. They would've killed us all when we crossed," Astrid said.

"I owe you two a dinner," Lasgol told Camu and Ona.

We protect. Want dinner too.

Ona chirped once.

"Great work!" Lasgol said.

"Are we in a jungle?" Nilsa asked.

"I would say so, yes, and a very exotic one. I don't recognize most of the flowers and plants. Gerd, do you recognize those colorful birds?" Egil said, indicating some flying over what looked like large palm trees.

"It would be nice to know where we are, you know, to give us a sense of direction," said Viggo.

They all looked at the landscape around them. They were on a hillock in the middle of a large clearing. Behind them was the White Pearl, and before them they saw a great lake with three enormous waterfalls pouring down from several highlands around them.

"We've already seen this place before," said Nilsa, looking frightened.

"This is the place the Orb wanted Camu to bring it to. It showed it to him and we saw it," Egil said.

"We're on that faraway island we saw from a bird's perspective," Lasgol guessed.

"It looks that way, yeah, this is the place we saw," said Ingrid, looking around warily.

"From what we saw it seemed deserted, didn't it?" Astrid asked.

"We don't know if that's actually the case. Remember what happened to us in the Usiks' forest," Ingrid said. "The fact that it looks deserted doesn't mean it is. It could be full of indigenous tribes who know how to hide, blending in with the jungle vegetation, and that's why we didn't see them."

"Egil, do you have any idea what island this might be? You were looking for it after we had the vision."

Egil nodded. "From its size and the climate and vegetation and wildlife we saw, I guessed it was Cinders Island."

"Cinders Island? Isn't that the great island south of Tremia?" Astrid asked.

"Yeah, it does ring a bell, a large island below the deserts and which, unlike those, has jungles," said Nilsa.

"That's the one," Egil confirmed. "I need to make sure, but if that's the case, we're at the southernmost point from Tremia."

"And how are you going to ascertain that?" Viggo asked, raising both eyebrows.

"The island has a volcano, still active. We have to locate it. If we do, we'll know if I'm right."

"An active volcano?" That's all we needed!" Viggo said, raising his arms in the air.

"The volcano is known as the Sizzling Wrath, and it's on the northeast of the island. There's a high range of mountains called the Sierra of the Gods. They named it that because of its height, and because it looks like a saw," Egil explained.

"It makes all the sense in the world that the portal brought us to the island the Orb wanted to get to," Lasgol reasoned. "That means it's here somewhere."

"And if we consider that Drugan and Viggen are also here with a large number of slaves, I think the final moment of reincarnation might be getting close," Astrid said.

"Yeah, that's what I think too," Egil confirmed.

"In that case, we have to stop it," said Ingrid. "No matter what island we're on or whether there's an active volcano or not. We're here, and we're going to stop this immortal dragon from reincarnating."

"That all sounds wonderful, but how do we do that?" Viggo asked.

"We follow the gold—it always leads to the target," said Egil with a light smile.

"What gold?" Viggo said blankly.

"He means the cargo, the slaves—they'll lead us to the Orb," Astrid told him.

"Oh, sure. I knew that already," Viggo tried to pretend.

Lasgol got up and looked at the ground.

"The trail is clear. We can follow it without any trouble. They're one day ahead of us," he said.

"Very well. Everyone get ready, we're going to pursue them," Ingrid ordered.

A moment later the Panthers began the chase through the jungle. Lasgol was in the lead as a tracker. Ingrid and Nilsa followed as archers, Astrid and Viggo came after in case there was trouble both ahead or in the rear, which was brought up by Egil and Gerd. Camu was moving through the vegetation a few paces left of the group and Ona a few paces to the right. They were in charge of the flanks.

Lasgol went forward, clearing the way with his knife. He had to cut through exuberant flowers and plants that surrounded them. The tall, thin trees were covered in lianas and hanging plants of all kinds. Wherever they looked they met lively colors, mostly greens with spatters of red, orange, and yellow flowers they did not recognize. They continued going deeper into the close, unknown jungle.

They felt a damp heat like they had never experienced before. They were not dressed for this climate and were sweating profusely. Every now and then they had to stop to wipe off the perspiration that got into their eyes from their foreheads and hair. They eventually had to stop to take off their cloaks and put them away in their rucksacks. They rolled their Ranger scarves and tied them around their foreheads to keep the sweat out of their eyes.

The sun fell on them unmercifully, and it was soon clear that they were indeed south of Tremia. Only there did the sun shine so strong, and only in the deep south was it so hot. It was easy enough to follow the trail through the jungle, but putting up with those temperatures and the humidity was a lot harder. They were not used to such a climate. Their clothes clung to their bodies and were already soaked because of the insufferable humidity, which also made it difficult to breathe.

They came to a stream and stopped to freshen up and fill their water-skins. They were going to need a lot of water in this jungle.

"You have no idea how much I'm enjoying this stroll through the jungle," Viggo said as he dipped his head in the water over and over.

"This climate is bad for us," said Ingrid. "We're used to extreme cold, snow, ice, and frost. This is torture," she said, looking at the vegetation that surrounded them and seemed to want to swallow them.

Suddenly, Astrid took out her knives and with two dull blows nailed the head of a huge snake to the trunk of a tree on her right.

"The wildlife doesn't seem very friendly either," Nilsa commented.

"That's a man-swallowing snake," Gerd told them. "I'd never seen one with such vivid colors, but it belongs to the same family."

"The wildlife here can be dangerous, especially snakes and spiders whose venoms we don't know and aren't used to," Egil said.

"I just glimpsed a hairy spider the size of a Norghanian rat," Nilsa said, making a face and shivering.

"And don't eat any fruit or berries. Although they look tasty, they might be poisonous," Egil added.

"If anything tries to sting or bite me, I'll pierce it through," Viggo said, his knives ready.

Jaguar, they received Camu's warning message.

"Well, in the worst-case scenario, if a jaguar or tiger attack us, at least we'll see it coming, and they're not venomous," said Ingrid.

"That's true," Astrid said with a broad grin.

They continued following the trail and soon realized they were heading northeast where the volcano was supposed to be, if Egil was not mistaken and they were indeed on Cinders Island. The vegetation was so close that even though they tried to see what was ahead, it was impossible.

They moved through the jungle all day, and when it started getting dark, they reached an area with several tall trees which allowed them to see over the jungle canopy. Astrid and Viggo climbed to the top of two of these trees, avoiding snakes, spiders, and other native venomous species to scan the horizon and get their bearings once they climbed back down.

"What did you see?" Lasgol asked the moment they touched the ground again.

"What did we see? A bloody smoking volcano, that's what!"

"We're heading straight to it across the jungle," said Astrid. "There are a few clearings and other open areas, but we're heading to the volcano diagonally."

"In that case, I was right. We're on Cinders Island," Egil said.

"The fact that the trail goes through the most difficult terrain, straight to the volcano, suggests that's the final destination of the caravan," said Lasgol.

"It couldn't be any other way, of course!" Viggo cried. "If there's a volcano on the island, where would we go? Straight to it, of course!"

"Let's not get ahead of ourselves," Ingrid tried to calm him. "So far we're heading there, but that doesn't mean we're going into it."

Viggo raised his arms to the sky and uttered a number of curses.

"We'd better look for a place to spend the night. The volcano is still several days away," Astrid told them.

"Fine. Let's find a place to shelter for the night," said Egil.

They found a pond with a group of boulders on the north side. It was a good place to rest. They climbed the boulders and slept there. They set watch shifts and spent the night without any major incidents, beyond the biting mosquitoes. It appeared they were attracted to their pale white skin, and the bites were spectacular.

The following day they found two of the caravan prisoners dead. Egil determined that they had died from illness and weakness during the long march. It made the Panthers feel bad. Viggo wanted to go and kill Drugan and Viggen and all their minions. Ingrid managed to calm him down, but he would not stay that way for long.

They increased their pace, and by the third day they caught up with the caravan. They could hear them trudging ahead of them, about five hundred paces. Ingrid ordered complete silence and they followed the caravan to a wide lake in a clearing. The imposing volcano could be seen in the horizon, its smoking crater threatening to burst with lava and fire.

"Let's attack as soon as night falls," Viggo suggested.

"Wait, we're very close—if we're hasty we could lose our chance to get to the Orb," Ingrid told him.

"If we let them go on, more prisoners will die…" said Nilsa.

"We find ourselves in a difficult situation," Egil said. "We all want to save the prisoners, free them from the slavery they're doomed to, but I believe we're very near the Orb. If we attack, we might lose it. It'll know we're here and that we've come for it. It might escape."

"Or come to kill us," said Gerd.

314

"That too," Egil agreed.

Lasgol was watching Astrid, trying to guess what she was thinking. As if she could read his thoughts, she spoke.

"I'd like to slit all their throats, especially my uncle's, but I agree with Egil. We've come this far and we're so close. Let's get to the end and do it properly."

Lasgol said nothing, but he felt the same, though it pained him not to be able to help the prisoners.

"We'll follow the caravan to the Orb and then we'll make them pay dearly," Ingrid sentenced.

Egil nodded, Viggo protested, and Nilsa agreed.

Two days of marching later, they were almost at the foot of the great volcano. They stopped to let the caravan start up the side of it. While they were waiting to get going they heard a threatening growl.

Lasgol recognized it at once. It was Ona.

"Watch out, danger!" he warned his friends.

They all readied their weapons and stared in the direction where Ona was watching.

All of a sudden, the jungle plants began to move, shaking as if something were approaching.

A native appeared through the vegetation. He was the most bizarre being they had ever encountered. He was wearing only a loincloth and his feet were bare. He was not very tall or brawny. His eyes were yellowish, like his hair, which he wore shorn on the sides, leaving a crest in the middle. Yet most curious was the color of his skin, a deep orange, and his body was all painted with depictions of scales. He was armed with a knife at his waist and a very strange weapon in his right hand, like some kind of flute.

Egil recognized the weapon—it was a blowpipe.

"Beware! Poisonous dart!" he warned.

Chapter 40

The Panthers stayed calm. They had their weapons ready for whatever might happen. The first native was followed by two more who appeared on either side of him, also out of the jungle. These two were followed by half a dozen who appeared behind them. They all dressed the same and had similar, exotic features. They carried blowpipes or small bows with close-range arrows.

The first one to appear was looking at the Panthers closely. He put his head to one side and then to the other. He was examining them. From the puzzled look on his face, he did not seem to know what to make of them.

Suddenly, he did something odd with both hands, as if he were grasping a round object, and spoke to them in a strange language.

They all looked at Egil out of the corner of their eyes. He noticed and prepared to try and communicate with the native.

"We…" he said, pointing at each one of the Panthers, "are friends…"

The native made a face. He did not seem to like Egil's response. He repeated the same gesture, as if he were grasping the object, and muttered strange words in his jungle language.

Egil raised his hands, palms up.

"We come in peace…"

The native leader barked out a couple sentences, and it was clear he was upset.

Egil bowed slightly in homage, trying to appease his anger.

The leader repeated his gesture a third time and pronounced words they did not understand once again. He stared at Egil as if he expected a specific answer. The problem was that Egil did not understand what he was being asked. He imitated the native's gesture with his own hands.

"Friends," he said.

The native leader turned to his men and shouted an order.

It was absolutely clear it was not a friendly one.

The natives raised their blowpipes and bows, aiming at the Panthers.

"Watch out! They're attacking!" Ingrid warned.

Before Ingrid's warning, Astrid and Viggo had already reacted and were moving to flank the natives. Gerd grabbed Egil by his shoulder and pushed him backward. Lasgol and Nilsa aimed at the natives.

A number of darts flew in search of Egil's body, but he had been pushed back by Gerd. The darts brushed past but did not touch him. Ingrid and Nilsa released against two of the men with bows, hitting them before they could release. Lasgol saw one of the natives ready to jump on him, and he had no choice but to bring him down with an arrow to his naked torso.

More darts sought Astrid and Viggo, who were advancing toward the natives, but they avoided them with swift moves. A moment later they lunged at the attackers and finished off two of them.

Ingrid moved aside and released again with lightning speed, killing another attacker   aiming at her with his blowpipe. Nilsa was slower, and the native she wanted to hit crouched and vanished from her sight. A moment later, a dart flew out of the vegetation straight at Nilsa, who saw it coming toward her face. She put her bow in the dart's way and it hit the wooden frame, bouncing off course.

The leader of the natives blew his pipe at Lasgol, and Camu, in his camouflaged state, leaped in front and the dart hit him but could not penetrate his scales. From one side Ona jumped on the native leader and knocked him down. She clawed him in the shoulder, giving him a deep wound. The leader turned on the ground and ran off into the jungle.

A moment later they heard a powerful shout and the remaining natives withdrew, vanishing into the jungle as if it had swallowed them.

"Everyone all right?" Lasgol asked.

"Yeah… by a hair's breadth…" said Egil, getting back on his feet.

"These little orange men have bad tempers," said Viggo who, bending over the man he had killed, was studying the color of his skin and the scales he had drawn all over his body.

"Quite aggressive indeed," Ingrid said, looking among the plants with her bow ready in case another native appeared with war-like intentions.

"I did all I could to avoid a confrontation…" Egil said ruefully.

"It's not your fault," said Lasgol. "You can't always establish a dialogue."

"Especially when you don't know the language or signals they use," said Gerd.

"I think he was looking for a specific answer, a gesture and a reply, and since you didn't give them to him he took us for enemies," Astrid guessed.

"Yeah, that could've been it," Egil nodded. "By the way, thank you, Gerd, you saved my life."

"You're welcome. I realized you weren't going to have time to move away, although I might have pushed you a little too hard," the giant said.

"No, not at all," Egil replied with a look on his face that meant the opposite.

Lasgol and Nilsa smiled.

"Thank you too, Camu."

I happy help.

"Check that you haven't been hit by any darts or arrows, even if they simply brushed you," Egil said as he examined one of the darts used in the attack. It had a greenish substance on the tip.

Gerd checked his legs and arms. "I haven't been hit."

"They wished they could graze me, but no way," Viggo said, sure of himself.

"Everything's fine here," Nilsa said, and Ingrid nodded too.

The others checked their bodies but luckily found nothing.

"These darts are poisoned, as I had guessed," Egil said, studying them. "I've read of tribes that use blowpipes with poisoned darts in tomes about ancient civilizations of Tremia, but I'd never encountered one."

"Well, think of our luck, now we know one," Viggo protested.

"This complicates things a lot," said Lasgol. "Now we're not only facing the Orb, Drugan, Viggen, and their followers, but also the aggressive natives of this jungle."

"Yeah, things are getting very ugly," Gerd said as he watched the impenetrable jungle that surrounded them.

"Don't worry, the caravan's not too far ahead of us. Let's follow it to wherever it leads us and end all this," Ingrid said cheerfully.

Nilsa nodded. "I agree."

"Let's go carefully, we might encounter more of these savages," Astrid said.

"D'you think they're cannibals?" Viggo asked all of a sudden.

"Why would you ask that?" Gerd said with a distressed look.

"Because they're weird, and there are cannibals in some lost regions of Tremia," Viggo replied.

"I don't believe they are. From their teeth and the fact that they weren't wearing any bones as decoration, I'd say they aren't," Egil said.

"Thank goodness," Nilsa snorted in relief.

"Anyway, if I were you, I'd be alert big guy, you look very tasty," Viggo joked.

"Don't be a dumbass, things are already pretty tense," Ingrid chided him.

"Camu, you and Ona had better lead the way in case more natives appear," Lasgol suggested.

We go, Camu messaged.

Ona joined him, and they both vanished ahead of them to clear the way.

They continued their pursuit of the caravan. Now they had their weapons in hand and were alert to the jungle around them in case another orange native appeared or they saw arrows and poisonous darts flying in their direction. They were all alert and tense, since the thickness of the jungle did not let them see more than two hand-spans ahead.

They were crossing the jungle at a slow pace, suffering from the humidity, the heat, the mosquitoes, and alert to the dangerous wildlife and savages. The march was tough, and it seemed it was never going to end. The caravan was moving in the same direction, northwest through the jungle, and it did not seem like it was going to stop any time soon. Night came and the caravan stopped, which allowed the Panthers to stop and rest as well. They set up watch shifts to pass the night, and it was a long and tense night since that environment was too hostile to allow them any rest.

The following morning, they continued their march. Nothing of notice had happened during the night, and they gave thanks to the Ice Gods for that. By dusk they arrived at an area with less plant life and they all felt somewhat relieved. From the clearing they could make out the great smoking volcano. It was really impressive, of a similar height to one of the great Norghanian mountains. It looked inaccessible, at least the upper part of the crater. And to make it even more fearsome, the smoke it spewed made it look as if it might erupt at any moment.

They were watching that wonder of nature when they received Camu's message.

Caravan foot of volcano.

Can you get closer to see where they're heading next? Lasgol transmitted to Camu. His *Animal Communication* skill now reached much further since he had amplified and powered it.

I investigate.

"I bet they're going to sacrifice the slaves to the volcano, d'you want to bet?" said Viggo.

"Don't be ruthless," Nilsa said.

"And a numskull," added Ingrid.

"Why? It's the most logical option, and you all know it."

"Regardless, shut up," Nilsa told him.

"Isn't that...?" Viggo started to say, then he crouched with almost inhuman speed.

All of a sudden, they heard several dull whistles.

"They're attacking, get down!" Lasgol said, having heard the sound and thrown himself to one side, dodging two darts that sought to hit him.

They all reacted at once and dropped to the ground.

A dart brushed Nilsa's head, but she managed to avoid it. Astrid had thrown herself on the ground and was crawling like a snake in search of her prey.

Egil felt the impact of a dart in his stomach. He was frightened—he had been hit. He dropped down and checked the wound. It did not hurt, which surprised him. He found the dart had hit his Healer's belt, striking a container and not reaching his flesh.

"That was close," he snorted, relieved.

Lasgol, Nilsa, and Ingrid were releasing against the natives coming out of the thicket to attack them with their blowpipes and short bows. Astrid and Viggo crawled along the ground and entered the jungle to deliver death.

"I'm hit!" Gerd warned.

Lasgol retreated to help him while he continued releasing, using his archery skills to finish off several savages and helped Gerd. He made a tourniquet on Gerd's arm in case the arrow was poisoned. Then Lasgol opened the wound with his knife and sucked Gerd's blood, spitting it out, trying to get all the poison.

Ingrid moved to cover Egil, who was trying to get on one knee to release and defend himself.

"It looks like the native leader went to get reinforcements," said Nilsa as she released whenever she saw movement in the vegetation.

"Don't hit me!" she heard Viggo's warning as he was hunting for natives in the jungle thicket.

They continued fighting, and suddenly there was silence. Ingrid, Nilsa, and Lasgol were aiming their bows, although they had no target to release at. Astrid and Viggo were among the vegetation, but they could not see the enemies and the bushes were not moving now. Gerd and Egil were crawling towards a tree to hide behind it.

Lasgol used his *Animal Presence* skill and powered it to amplify his area of action. He picked up his friends, several jungle animals, and two humans who had to be natives a little to the south. He made a sign at Ingrid to let her know where they were and she nodded. Lasgol used his new *Elemental Arrows* skill and created an Air Arrow, which flew away, seeking the spot among the plants which he had identified as one of the native's hiding places.

The arrow hit the native and upon detonation released a charge that made him stand. Ingrid finished him off with a shot to the head. The other native rose to release at Ingrid, but she had already moved to a new position. By the time the native started to correct his blowpipe shot, he had another of Ingrid's arrows buried in his torso.

With his *Hawk's Eye* skill, Lasgol saw the last native fleeing south.

"Clear, there's no-one left," Lasgol told the others as he used all his hearing and seeing skills again to see, hear, or detect any enemies.

Egil ran to check on Gerd's wound.

"Don't remove the tourniquet. Lasgol saved your life with that hasty cure. Let me give you a couple antidotes I carry with me. I'm not sure they'll work against the poison these natives use, but we lose nothing for trying."

Gerd nodded, "Thanks, pal," he said to Lasgol, who smiled at the giant.

"You're welcome."

"These natives are a pain," said Viggo, coming out of the vegetation.

Astrid rose a little to his right.

"They're dangerous indeed."

"We can't fight them here in their own environment, they'll gradually get us all one by one," Ingrid said.

"I agree," Lasgol said, nodding.

Camu and Ona appeared right then.

Natives attack? Camu messaged.

"Yup, it was quite close," Nilsa said.

We follow caravan, know where is.

"Where have they gone?" Lasgol asked.

They go in volcano through cave.

"See? I was right!" Viggo said.

"We have to follow them. They're going to the Orb," Egil said as he finished curing Gerd's wound.

"Do we want to go into a volcano?" the giant asked.

"Would you rather stay here and have these savages riddle us with darts so we die from poison?" Viggo said.

"No... not really..."

"We have to go into the volcano," said Ingrid. "There at least we'll see those devilish natives coming, unlike here."

"They won't have the advantage the jungle grants them," said Lasgol.

"Very well then, to the volcano it is," Ingrid said.

"How nice, I've always wanted to take a dip in hot lava," Viggo said, smiling.

"Shut up, or I'll bury one of these poisoned darts in your butt myself," Ingrid said, pulling one out of a tree beside her.

Viggo smiled and did not say another word.

Lasgol heard movement in the jungle to the south.

"I think more savages are coming!" he cried.

"Let's get out of here!" Ingrid ordered.

"Camu, Ona, guide us!" Lasgol told them.

Follow, quick, the creature messaged, and they all ran off.

They reached the end of the jungle and ran to the southern slope of the volcano. As they ran, they kept looking back in case the natives were following, sprinting as if they were being chased by a pack of hungry lions.

They arrived at the first ledges of the volcano and the terrain became a waste. There was no vegetation growing here. There were only layers of solidified lava, one on top of another. They leapt over the rocks and faced a cave that looked like an ancient lava outlet of the volcano. Going into the cave did not particularly appeal to them, since where there had been lava once, there could be lava again.

"They're chasing us!" Lasgol cried. He had seen a group of about a dozen savages leaving the jungle and coming at them.

"We'll deal with them!" Astrid said, stopping to release. Nilsa and Ingrid stopped with her.

Lasgol was helping Gerd climb, and Egil was with them. Viggo was already at the entrance of the cave with Camu and Ona, clearing the way.

The savages were running now along the plain, without the cover of the jungle. They were easy targets no matter how fast they ran, and they did so like wild horses.

"Don't let them get to us," Astrid told Nilsa and Ingrid.

"They won't," Ingrid promised.

Arrows flew, one and then in threes.

Lasgol, Egil, and Gerd arrived at the entrance to the cave.

"All clear!" Viggo told them, indicating two Visionaries dead on the floor inside the great cave.

"Watchmen?" Lasgol asked.

"It would seem so. They were running to sound the alarm, but I stopped them."

We help. Camu messaged.

"True, the bug kept me and Ona invisible. By the time these two ran off, we were already up here."

"Then they haven't sounded the alarm," said Egil.

Viggo shook his head.

Astrid, Ingrid, and Nilsa arrived.

"The savages are no longer chasing us," Ingrid announced.

"Wonderful. I believe it's time we dealt with the Orb and its sects," Egil said and pointed at the tunnel on the far end of the great cave.

"And nothing better than going into the belly of a volcano to do it," Viggo said.

"Didn't you want a bit of action?" Ingrid asked him with irony.

"True, and entering an active volcano to finish off two sects and an immortal dragon that wants to reincarnate is what I call a bit of action," he smiled.

"Everyone, be very careful. Great danger awaits us in there," Egil warned them, and his tone was of great concern.

Lasgol looked at Gerd and saw fear in his eyes—fear of the unknown they would have to face. Lasgol felt it too. Luckily, he was surrounded by his friends. He looked at Astrid, Ingrid, Nilsa, Viggo, Egil, Camu, and Ona. In their eyes he saw concern, but also courage. This comforted him. Whatever they had to face, they would do it together.

"Let's go, Panthers!" he cried, leading the way into the volcano.

Chapter 41

They went down the long tunnel of rock and solidified lava. The walls were black and porous, giving the corridor a grim look, as if they were entering the lair of a creature of fire and rock that was going to burn them through and swallow them all. They would end up being a part of those walls of scorched rock.

No-one spoke as they went along, going down the grim tunnel that seemed to descend into the depths of the volcano. The tension and the feeling that they were going into a hell from which there was no return grew with every step. If that tunnel kept going down, it was likely they would reach the molten heart of the volcano.

Luckily, that was not the case. The tunnel opened onto another deeper cavern. They felt a scorching heat coming from yet another cavern to their left. They knew at once it was there they had to go. It was an intense, dry, burning heat. They went toward it without flinching—if they had to go to the belly of the volcano itself, they would, as long as they could prevent the immortal dragon from rising.

They continued descending along two more tunnels and caverns. In the last one they found some lit torches, so they decided to be extremely cautious. Camu would use his invisibility to move forward with Astrid and Viggo. The rest would wait until they were told the way was clear.

Can go on, Camu's message reached them.

With Lasgol in the lead, the group kept walking. They entered another tunnel that also went down and found two Visionaries dead. Astrid and Viggo were clearing the way. If the two Assassins were already difficult to make out in dark environments like this one, with Camu's invisibility cloak they were able to go much faster.

They came out into a still deeper cave, and their fears started to become real. Through one of the cracks in the floor they could see a river of molten lava flowing past. The fumes coming out of the cracks were toxic, and they had to cover their mouth and nose with their scarves. The heat was now unbearable, the rock was aflame in the areas close to the lava.

"This is getting uglier," Nilsa said.

"I'd say hotter," Ingrid said, making a face.

"Let's keep going, we must be getting close now," said Egil.

They went into another cavern that was difficult to access. They climbed and jumped over a series of colossal boulders that were broken, raised, and facing other boulders, as if they had once been a floor and had broken with the pressure coming from below. They were left speechless by what they saw through the cracks: deep down, there was a sea of lava.

They were reaching the core of the volcano.

"If we keep going down, we won't survive the heat and the fumes," Ingrid told Egil.

"I know. We must be close now. The Visionaries and the Defenders won't be able to go down much further."

"No-one can," said Lasgol.

Come quick! Camu's message reached them, along with a sense of urgency.

They ran to the end of the cavern and found a passage with two more dead guards. They walked to the end of the passage, which ended in a lookout of black rock.

Lie low. Not see, Camu messaged in warning.

They threw themselves on the floor at once. The lookout was large, and it went up toward the giant dome of a volcanic cavern. The cave was colossal regarding its height and width at the base. They crawled to the edge of the lookout and carefully watched what was going on down below.

And what they saw froze them on the spot.

They would never forget it.

On an irregular, blackened floor under which they could glimpse streams of molten lava, they saw over fifty slaves working without pause. They were controlled by Visionaries with whips and swords. One third of the slaves were working in a huge rectangular pit they had excavated along the northern wall of the cave. It must have been about a hundred and fifty feet long and ninety feet wide. The depth was over fifteen feet.

The slaves were covering the walls of the huge pit with blocks of what looked like steel and silver. Those of silver were being placed over the steel ones. The depth and width of the pit were such that it occupied two thirds of the base of the colossal cavern. From what they could see, the slaves had very little left to finish.

The blocks were so big and heavy that they were lowered with dozens of pulley cranes placed all along the edge of the pit and which another number of slaves were operating under the supervision of the Defenders. The banging of hammers and chisels echoing on the lofty walls of the cave was deafening. The walls were dark, and there was only light at the base where everyone was working.

Another third of the slaves were finishing setting up what looked like four steel pipes that came out of four holes on the eastern wall of the cave and went to the huge pit inside which the slaves were striving to finish their work. The shouts of the guards and the cracking of whips mixed with the hammering, and the noise went in crescendo.

The last third of the slaves were lying exhausted right below the lookout where the Panthers were, more than forty-five feet down. They must be working in shifts, and now it was their turn to rest until they had to take over their work-mates' turn.

A winding path chiseled on the wall of rock went from the lookout at the entrance all around the perimeter of the cave to the floor below where the slaves were working.

"What on earth are they doing?" Ingrid asked, frowning.

"The pit they've dug out is immense!" Nilsa cried, and her jaw dropped.

"This is overwhelming... they have all those slaves working on... on what?" Lasgol asked, unable to understand the purpose of it all.

"We've already seen something similar... on a smaller scale..." Gerd said.

"Have you? Where?" Astrid asked as she became visible once Camu stopped using his camouflage and withdrew to the passage so as not to be seen.

"At the forges in the northern side of Bilboson, we saw them building one like this but on a much smaller scale," Egil explained. "What didn't occur to us is that they were just practicing... we thought they were doing something there... we were mistaken..." Egil said thoughtfully.

"Practicing for what, if I may ask? Why all this mining operation?" Viggo asked, making a face.

"It doesn't look like mining..." Lasgol said.

At that moment they heard loud voices. Several figures appeared in a tunnel at the western side of the cave, at floor level. First, they saw five orange-skinned natives with yellow hair, only they did not wear the sides shorn, but had long hair all over their heads. They must be tribal leaders, and with them were a dozen natives.

Then Drugan walked in with his two warlocks, Xoltran and Vingar. After them, came Viggen and his Defenders with their silver shields.

At last, there came the one they had been after for so long: the Dragon Orb.

The Panthers watched in silence, holding their breaths to avoid being found out, although they were high up and should not be either seen or heard with all that deafening noise.

"There it is, finally," said Ingrid.

"For a moment I thought we'd never find it," Nilsa admitted.

"They're in league with the savages," Astrid commented.

"That explains their confusion when they saw us—they thought we were Drugan's or Viggen's people," Lasgol reasoned.

The Orb was hovering and went to the center of the great pit.

Let there be light, the Orb demanded in its deep, dominant, mental voice, giving off a silver flash.

All of a sudden, the whole northern wall lit up. Hundreds of torches had been placed around something embedded in the rock, and they all lit at once. What the light revealed left the Panthers speechless.

Perfectly fossilized and preserved in the rock in what looked like amber or some type of similar resin, they saw a monstrous dragon over forty-five feet long. Its huge lethal mouth was open, and they could perfectly appreciate the reptilian yellow eyes, the horns above them, the crest that ran down its back to the tip of the tail, and its whole scale-covered body. Its powerful claws seemed to hold it to the wall. Its wings were folded against its body, but they could tell they were formidable.

"It... can't be..." Viggo muttered.

"It's a real dragon," Nilsa could not believe her eyes.

"It's preserved in that substance..." Ingrid said. "How is that possible? Why hasn't it rotten?"

"It must've been here for thousands of years, it should be nothing more than bones and dust," said Astrid.

"It's a fossil... or rather the dragon's been preserved inside fossilized resin. You know it as amber. I'm afraid this was no accident," Egil said.

"The Orb has found what it was looking for, the body it needs to reincarnate," Lasgol said, finding it hard to believe what they were witnessing.

The dragon's body appeared to be amber-orange and its head was ochre-yellow. It was no doubt the effect of the resin it was fossilized in. That explained, up to a point, the strange appearance of the natives, who also had orange bodies and yellow hair. The hair was undoubtedly painted, as were the scales on their bodies. The orange pigmentation, though, was something else.

"The natives knew of the existence of the dragon," Egil said.

Suddenly the Orb spoke again, and all those present heard it powerfully in their minds.

Let the fire come forth, it ordered.

The Defenders who were by the wall opened the four floodgates to the pipes that came out of the wall, and molten lava started pouring down them. The slaves had just finished securing the last stretch and moved away so as not to be reached by the lava.

"What are they doing?" Ingrid asked Egil.

"They're going to fill the pit with molten lava," he replied.

"What for?" Nilsa asked.

"I'm not sure…" said Egil.

The lava was coming out of the wall through the four openings and flowed down the big pipes into the pit.

"What are we going to do? Something's happening, and I'm sure it's not good," Ingrid said.

"Whatever they're doing, we have to stop it," said Astrid.

All of a sudden, the Orb communicated mentally again.

The moment has come. All kneel before my power, it called.

"Our master's wishes will always be honored," Drugan replied as he knelt. An instant later Xoltran and Vingar knelt as well.

"We serve our all-powerful lord," said Viggen, also kneeling. The Defenders knelt with him.

The native leaders also knelt and paid homage.

I am Dergha-Sho-Blaska, the Immortal Dragon, he who sleeps and does not die. King among the dragons.

"Our lord is the Immortal Dragon," Drugan recited like a creed.

"King among dragons, lord of dragons," said Viggen like a

dogma.

The moment of reincarnation has arrived.

"We are at your service. We are awaiting your reincarnation," said Drugan.

This is the body I have been searching for. Where my spirit can revive.

"The body of a dragon king," said Drugan.

"Unaltered by the passing of time, waiting to be summoned," said Viggen.

With this new body, I shall reign over this whole world.

"It's time we acted," said Egil. "We can't let him complete the reincarnation."

"We have to take action!" Viggo cried.

"Let's end this!" said Ingrid.

Chapter 42

"Archers, we have the advantage of the higher position, use it well," Egil said.

"Very well, everyone ready to release," said Ingrid.

"I'll use my Sniper bow," said Astrid.

"Viggo, Ona, Camu, cover the ramp, don't let them get to us," Egil said.

"Not one will pass," Viggo promised, showing him his knives.

We defend. Not pass.

Ona growled twice.

"At my signal, shoot the leaders," said Ingrid.

The Panthers prepared for the attack. They nocked arrows in their bows, pulled back to their cheeks, and aimed.

Suddenly, the Dragon Orb flashed silver.

Orb sending wave energy, Camu messaged in warning.

The Panthers did not know what to do.

"What's that wave the Orb is sending?" Gerd asked.

Not know. Expansive wave, fill all cave.

Lasgol guessed what the wave was. It was similar to his *Animal Presence* skill.

He was not wrong.

Intruders! Above! the Orb sent to the minds of its followers, who turned to gaze up to the lookout.

"Release! He's detected us!" Lasgol shouted.

"Finish them off, let our arrows be accurate and find their rotten hearts!" cried Astrid.

The arrows flew from the Panther's bows toward the enemy leaders, who were hastily getting ready to defend themselves.

Each of the Panthers' arrows sought a different target.

Ingrid's was seeking Drugan's heart as he unsheathed his short swords with dragon pommels. The arrow headed straight toward the heart of the warlock leader. With a swift crossing of swords, Drugan managed to stop the arrow and break it before it hit him.

Lasgol's arrow sought to kill Xoltran. It was heading straight to the center of his torso. He thought he had him, that he had surprised him. Suddenly, Xoltran's bracelets shone with a silver flash and produced a defensive wave that deflected Lasgol's arrow.

Nilsa's arrow sought to kill Vingar. He had already got away from her once, but he would not do so a second time. The warlock cast a quick spell and, opening his mouth wide, let out a great roar. Nilsa's arrow met with a wave of force that followed the roar and bounced to one side without reaching the warlock.

Egil's arrow flew at one of the native leaders. A good shot, with the advantage that releasing from a height like that gave him. He caught him in the torso and the leader fell dead on the floor. The other leaders ran up the ramp to get Egil.

Astrid's arrow sought to get her uncle Viggen. It was a large arrow, launched by her Sniper's bow.

"Sorry, Uncle, you chose the wrong quest," she muttered as the arrow flew down swiftly. Viggen saw it coming and raised his silver shield. The arrow hit it hard and made Viggen step back, but it could not pierce the shield.

"Defenders, bunch of sacred shields!" Viggen called, and at once seven Defenders with their silver shields that had been behind Viggen surrounded him and formed a curved shell that covered Viggen and his men from the floor to their heads.

Astrid cursed under her breath while she nocked another arrow.

"Dragon slaves, form a defensive line before us!" Drugan ordered. The slaves with shining eyes dropped what they were doing and moved in unison at their lord's order. They stood in front of the warlocks and the Orb. If the Panthers released, they would hit the slaves instead of the warlocks.

Go up and finish them off! Nothing must stop my reincarnation! Dergha-Sho-Blaska ordered. He did it so forcefully that it reached the minds of all, including the Panthers'. The mental blow the message produced numbed them for a moment. An instant later, once the effect was over, all the Visionaries and Defenders grabbed their weapons and started up the ramp toward the platform. They ran, brandishing their weapons, shouting as if possessed by the words of their lord.

Death to the heretics!" the Visionaries were shouting.

"The heretics will die!" cried the Defenders.

Drugan, Xoltran, and Vingar, protected behind the dragon slaves, started to attack the archers, sending roars of mental force. The three warlocks roared, and the waves that issued from them hit the ledge where the Panthers were shooting from. Part of the impact was broken by the ledge, but another part reached Ingrid, Nilsa, and Astrid, who fell backward from the tremendous physical and mental blow. It did not reach Lasgol or Egil though, who were more to the side.

While the fight was going on, the great pit was filling up with molten lava coming from the heart of the volcano. The slaves, free of the surveillance of the Visionaries and Defenders, were looking for some way to escape the chamber where the fighting was taking place. They could not go up the ramp, since the Visionaries were on it. They were terrified and running here and there not knowing what to do, panic-stricken.

The Orb began to flash with great force. It seemed to ignore the fighting, which it had left to its servants. Dergha-Sho-Blaska began to send strong silver waves against the northern wall, where the giant dragon was resting like a terrible picture of a horrendous evil.

The Orb's waves of power reached the fossilized dragon and the substance appeared to respond to the power sent by the Orb. Little by little it began to shine a bright amber-yellow color.

Egil noticed and warned Lasgol.

"He's imbuing the resin with power—he intends to free the dragon's body."

"I see it. That resin isn't just amber, it must have some magical component to shine like that," Lasgol said.

Egil nodded, "Most likely."

The Orb sent more and more power to the bubble of resin the dragon's body was in. The magical amber started to shine as if it were pure gold reflecting the sun's rays.

Servants, your lord commands you to kill those intruders. I cannot be disturbed, the process of reincarnation has begun, Dergha-Sho-Blaska ordered his minions.

While the Panthers were still trying to reach the enemy leaders, with the added difficulty of not wanting to kill the dragon slaves, the Visionaries and the Defenders were arriving at the final stretch of the ramp. Viggo, Camu, and Ona waited, camouflaged, and as the enemies reached their position, they killed them or threw them to the void to crash down below. The Visionaries and Defenders did not know what was going on—an invisible force was killing them and sending them to the bottom of the cave.

The three warlocks realized something was happening and attacked the area where Viggo, Camu, and Ona waited camouflaged with their roars of force. Camu foresaw the attacks and used his skill to cancel their magic. He flashed silver and created a protective anti-magic dome. The roars did not reach them, instead hitting the dome and dying out.

But the natives running up noticed something odd was happening and released at the area where the fighters they could not see were with their bows and blowpipes.

I shield, Camu messaged and stood in front of Viggo and Ona to receive the arrows and darts and prevent them from hitting his friends. He felt almost invincible going forward in camouflage and without the enemy attacks being able to penetrate his scales which were as hard as diamonds.

"Let's move forward and knock these natives off the cliff," Viggo told Camu.

I move, you follow, Camu messaged and headed to the natives, who were shooting at them from halfway up the ramp.

The Orb continued sending waves of energy to the fossilized dragon. It changed the pulses it was emitting to a long, sustained one over the whole surface of the fossilized amber, as if it wanted to light it up with its power.

"The Orb is sending more energy to the fossil, and now it's focused," Egil warned.

Lasgol looked out of the corner of his eye, worried. Then he sent a True Shot that went between the heads of two dragon slaves without touching them and almost hit Xoltran, but the magic of his bracelets deflected the shot.

"With the Visionaries in front of them we can't reach the warlocks!" Ingrid cried.

Astrid released directly at the Orb and hit it with a Sniper's arrow, but the arrow did not even make it quiver. It went on hovering and sending its beam of energy to the dragon in the rock.

The warlocks roared, defending their lord, and the archers had to flatten themselves on the floor of the ledge for protection so the waves of mental force would not reach them.

"I have an idea, cover me with Earth Arrows," Nilsa said.

Lasgol nodded and used his *Elemental Arrows* skill, releasing an arrow which, upon leaving the bow, became an Earth Arrow, one that hit the torso of one of the dragon slaves in front of Xoltran. The blinding-stunning explosion did not appear to affect the slaves, who did not move, but Xoltran had to take a step back.

Ingrid released another Earth Arrow and distracted Drugan enough to make him crouch to protect himself from the effects of the explosion. Egil released at Vingar, who hid behind the legs of the slaves to save himself from the Arrow's effects.

An instant later Nilsa released an arrow marked purple. When the arrow reached one of the dragon slaves it burst, freeing a purplish-blue gas. Two of the slaves fell down, unconscious.

"Summer Slumber! Great idea!" Egil congratulated her.

Nilsa smiled and released another Summer Slumber arrow, and three other slaves fell unconscious to the floor.

The warlocks realized the ruse and withdrew so the gas would not reach them. While they retreated, they sent more mental roaring attacks against the archers, who once again had to throw themselves on the floor to avoid being hit.

Camu, Ona, and Viggo reached the natives and finished them off in the blink of an eye. Camu had been hit by a number of darts and arrows, but they could not pierce his scaly armor so he was unharmed. One of the darts almost hit him in the eye, and he had the feeling that if he had been hit in the eye, it would have hurt him. His scales protected his body but not his eyes if he had them open. He also thought about his mouth and tongue—if he opened his mouth he could be hit and poisoned. All of a sudden, he did not feel so invincible; he felt the Orb was using an immense amount of Drakonian power. This troubled him, and he warned his friends.

Orb much great power now.

Suddenly there was a great blast. It seemed as though the northern wall was splitting. The fighting stopped for an instant, and all the fighters looked at the wall. The Orb, with its power focused on the fossilized dragon, had started to extract it from the wall. There was another blast of splitting rocks at the far end of the wall, behind the fossil. The Orb started extracting all the fossilized amber with the body of the dragon inside it. The colossal piece of amber, which was over forty-five feet long by sixty feet wide, came out of the wall it was contained in with all the force of the Orb's power.

"By the Ice Gods!" Ingrid cried.

"He pulled it out from the wall!" Gerd cried, eyes popping in disbelief.

"And he's carrying it as if it were nothing. It has to weigh as much as a castle," Nilsa cried.

"If he spends his power he'll be weakened, won't he?" Astrid asked.

"According to the laws of magic, that's correct," Lasgol replied.

Those laws, do they apply to a Dragon Orb?" Ingrid asked.

Lasgol nodded. "They're universal. They apply to all magic, including the Orb's."

"Then we can attack him when he's weak," Ingrid suggested.

"The thing is, we don't know how much magic he has available," Egil said.

The Orb continued making the great dragon fossil levitate with its beam of sustained silver light. It brought the dragon over to itself and moved it slowly toward the pit, which was already filled with molten lava.

Spend much power, Camu's message reached them, warning them that the Orb was using a lot of its energy.

And then something unexpected happened. Slowly, while they were all watching as if hypnotized, the Orb placed the colossal piece of fossilized amber in the lava pit. It submerged it until it was completely covered. A golden-orange smoke came out of the pit that had been specifically made for it. The lava began to melt all the amber that surrounded and contained the body of the great dragon while the silver walls and power of the Orb helped in this strange process.

"Now we know what it intended," Egil said. "We have to stop it from taking the dragon's body."

They all came out of the hypnotic moment and the fighting continued. The slaves who feared for their lives were running here and then, seeking an escape. One group went into the adjacent cavern the Orb and his minions had come out of but it had no exit, so they came out again and chaos took over them.

The Panthers continued attacking Drugan and his warlocks and Viggen and his Defenders. They had no more slaves to hide behind, so they were forced to defend themselves with magic and shields.

Nilsa started to use her thundering arrows. She released against Vingar, and when he used his roar to protect himself, the arrow burst, distracting Xoltran with the blast and keeping him from using his power. Astrid, Ingrid, and Lasgol saw this and released against Xoltran while Egil shot at Vingar. The two warlocks managed to stop the attacks, but by the skin of their teeth.

Nilsa released again with her anti-magic arrows and Lasgol joined her with an Earth Arrow he created with his skill. Both arrows were stopped by the silver bracelets' defense, but when the bracelets blocked the shots the two arrows detonated at once, uniting their effect. Vingar and Xoltran were struck dumb and could not cast spells. Gerd and Egil hit Vingar in the torso with two arrows. The warlock took two steps back and fell dead.

Astrid and Ingrid released at Drugan now that Nilsa's and Lasgol's combined attack had stunned him. The warlock tried to roar but could not. He deflected Astrid's arrow with one sword and tried to deflect Ingrid's arrow, which he managed to deviate slightly, although not enough for it to not hit him. It buried itself into his shoulder and he took a step back to try and compose himself.

Camu, Ona, and Viggo arrived below and went for Viggen and the Defenders, who were running toward the ramp to go up and finish off the archers. They crossed halfway up.

No can hold extended camouflage much time more. Cost much energy, Camu messaged Viggo and Ona.

"Don't worry, I don't need it anymore," Viggo said.

I stop skill, need little energy.

"No problem," Viggo assured him.

Camu stopped his skill, and Viggen and his Defenders saw them appear to their left.

"Attack them! Defend our lord!" Viggen ordered his men.

"Death!" the seven cried and lunged into attack.

Viggo hurled himself in a great leap onto two assailants, the ones on the outer left. Ona did the same with the two on the right. The three who were left went for Camu. Viggen stayed back, watching the Orb as it continued the weird ritual.

Nilsa and Lasgol released again in unison against Xoltran, who was left dazzled and struck numb and was stepping backward toward Gerd. Egil and Astrid released at him, but his bracelets saved him, once again deflecting the arrows.

"Do you have any Summer Slumber arrows left?" Lasgol asked Nilsa.

"No, I've used them all. And I don't have many anti-magic arrows left either. We do nothing but release."

"Those bracelets protect him from physical attacks… we should try magical attacks," Egil reasoned.

Lasgol nodded.

Camu, attack Xoltran with your magic, Lasgol transmitted to his friend.

Little energy, Camu messaged back as he was being attacked by three Defenders who were unable to hurt him. The sword thrusts and cuts they delivered did not penetrate his scales.

One attack will be enough, Lasgol transmitted, *I'll help you from here.*

Okay.

"Focus on Drugan, Camu and I will deal with Xoltran."

"Consider it done," Ingrid replied.

Five arrows sought to kill Drugan as he was retreating without turning his back on them. He roared to avoid them. One of them was Nilsa's, the last anti-magic arrow she had left, and the blast of the detonation distracted him. For a moment he would be unable to cast a spell. The five archers released again. Drugan defended himself with his swords, but Astrid's arrow hit him in his right side. The mage doubled up in pain and fell to one side.

Viggo and Ona finished off the Defenders before they could get up from the floor. Viggen attacked Viggo, who defended himself with his knives. Ona ran to help Camu, who had the three Defenders on top of him but was still heading toward Xoltran.

Lasgol used a *Multiple Shot* and caught the three Defenders before Ona could even reach her brother to help him. Camu reached Xoltran, who turned when he saw him coming and raised his two-handed sword to attack him.

I use Ice Breath, Camu told Lasgol.

Perfect, Lasgol replied, already aiming at Xoltran.

Lasgol released at the same moment that Camu opened his mouth and released his Ice Breath. Xoltran's bracelets shone and deflected Lasgol's arrow, but the Ice Breath hit Xoltran fully and he died frozen on the spot.

Viggo had Viggen against the wall. The leader of the Defenders used his sword and shield skillfully, but he was no rival for an Assassin like Viggo. The Ranger Specialist cut him in the shield arm and then in his support leg, using swift combinations which Viggen

338

was unable to block completely.

"This is the end, this impure one's going to pierce your heart," Viggo said with a malicious grin.

"You might kill me, but you and your friends won't be able to stop my lord," Viggen replied and nodded toward the Orb, which was fixed at the edge of the pit.

Viggo looked at the Orb.

A powerful flash came out of the fossilized dragon inside the pit of lava. All of a sudden, they were able to see how the body of the dragon, free from the resin, surged from the lava and floated above it. The heat and the fire of the lava had freed the dragon from the amber, and now the body of the great magic reptile was lying, perfectly preserved, on the lava, which did not affect him.

"You will all die here. My lord will reincarnate. He will rise and conquer Tremia," Viggen assured him.

An arrow from Astrid caught Viggen in the shoulder and knocked him down.

"You seemed to have angered your niece," Viggo told him with a smile.

Five arrows hit the Orb, but it did not waver and it sustained no harm.

Viggo approached the object and struck it with his knives.

He could not even leave a mark on it.

Ona tried clawing at it and could not even scratch it.

Finally, Camu came over, and with the last of his energy he used his Magic Tail Whiplash followed by his Frozen Claw Slash. The Orb received both magic attacks and quivered. It seemed to have been somewhat affected. But unfortunately, Camu had no more energy left.

The Orb began to shine with flashes that were becoming more powerful and at a greater rhythm. The brightness was so intense, they had to cover their eyes to protect them. It began to spin on itself at a devilish speed while it emitted flashes, and suddenly the Orb's crystal cracked. An intense light came out of the crack, as if the Orb had broken from the inside.

And from the crack, an ethereal being, like a translucent shadow, came out and moved to the body of the dragon resting in the lava. The Orb stopped spinning and flashing, and fell to the floor with a hollow bump. The eyes of the dragon opened and shone silver. Then the whole dragon shone silver too.

Before the Panthers' terrified stare, the great dragon stood up on its legs in the middle of the lava pit. He spread his immense wings and roared a thundering bellow that made everyone cower. He beat his wings, and the force of the wind it caused pushed Viggo and Ona against one of the walls.

With a leap, the dragon began to fly, flapping his wings and rising from the pit.

"Release! We have to kill it!" Ingrid cried.

"Everyone, shoot!" said Nilsa.

"He can't escape!" Astrid cried.

The Panthers released at the dragon, and their arrows flew and bounced on his body. They could not pierce his scales.

I am Dergha-Sho-Blaska, the Immortal Dragon, King among dragons, and I am reborn, he proclaimed.

He rose and headed to the ceiling of the cavern. He gave a tremendous roar, accompanied by magic, and part of the ceiling collapsed.

The Panthers were still releasing but could not hurt him.

The slaves, scared to death, were running, seeking to escape while large pieces of rock fell on them. The rocks that fell in the pit splattered lava in every direction.

"Get out of there!" Nilsa told them.

"The rocks and lava will kill them all!" Gerd shouted.

"Viggo, get the slaves out of there!" Ingrid called out to him. Viggo nodded and sent Camu and Ona to the ramp. Then he grabbed several slaves and pushed them onto the ramp too, motioning them to run up.

There was another roar and more rocks fell from the upper levels. Part of the volcano was crumbling while Dergha-Sho-Blaska made his way outside.

"Come on, everyone out! Quick!" Viggo was shouting while huge pieces of rock kept falling.

The slaves followed Viggo's indications and went up the ramp. He was the last one to come out while great boulders continued falling from the upper levels that covered the cave.

They heard one last thundering roar.

Dergha-Sho-Blaska emerged in the outer sky.

The immortal dragon had awakened.

Chapter 43

The Panthers were sitting on the rocky beach half covered by solid lava, not far from the volcano, watching the Norghanian ships come to the rescue. Behind them in an improvised camp the surviving slaves were waiting, guarded by Norghanian soldiers. The Panthers had managed to get them out of the volcano alive and had reached a nearby beach without encountering the natives. Because there were so many of them, they had had to ask for more ships to transport them, and at last they were arriving. Luckily the natives had not attacked them. They did not seem to want to leave the jungle to come out into the open.

Several days had gone by since the awakening, and the Panthers' spirits were very low. They had tried with all their might, but they had failed. Dergha-Sho-Blaska, the immortal dragon, had reincarnated. It was a big failure for them. The feeling went deep, and it was troubling that no one spoke about it, not even Viggo. The dragon king had awakened, and they had not been able to stop him, despite their best efforts.

The Snow Panthers were not used to failing. They always found the way to solve great problems, one way or another, but this time it had not been so. The feeling of failure, concern, and great frustration had them all feeling downhearted. Even Camu, who was lying beside Ona, barely said a word, and his usual self-confidence and stubbornness had faded with the latest events.

"It's my fault," Ingrid said. "I should've done things better."

"No, it's not your fault, Ingrid. You did everything you could, and you did well," Astrid told her.

"Even so, I feel responsible…" Ingrid admitted, bowing her head, something very rare for her, who was always determined and strong.

"We all did our best. It's no one's fault," said Lasgol.

"For once I'm not going to blame the weirdo or the bug or the know-it-all," said Viggo. "You were all good, and we still didn't achieve our goal. Life's tough, it's not fair, and the good ones don't always win. That's how things are, and we must accept them."

"That's a good thought," Egil joined in. "After analyzing everything that's happened, I've reached the same conclusion as Viggo. No matter how hard we tried, perhaps it was inevitable after all. The Orb was too powerful for us."

"There will always be more powerful enemies than us, from kings, to mythological beings or sorcerers of immense power," Lasgol said. "We will fight them if Norghana or her people are in danger, but there's no guarantee we'll come out victorious, I can swear to that. Remember what happened to my parents. They both died trying to do something they believed in, something better for Norghana. Maybe that's the destiny awaiting us…"

"Let's not be fatalist," said Viggo. "We're still alive and kicking, and we've got a lot of fight still in us."

"That's for sure," Ingrid joined him. "No-one will be able to say we didn't fight and give our all for the cause, no matter how unlikely our victory might have been."

"That Orb was indestructible," said Nilsa "We hit it with everything we had and we didn't even scratch it."

"Well, it broke from the inside, so it wasn't indestructible," Astrid said.

"Only it wasn't us who broke it," Gerd said, annoyed.

"Destroying the Orb was going to be a tough task anyways. It wasn't only powerful, but highly intelligent. Remember, it used us to try and come to this island, which is the one it was looking for, because it knew there was a body here it could use."

"Yeah, it was smart, but it didn't know how to get here at first. It got the place wrong and took us to the never-ending forests of the Usik," Nilsa commented.

Orb not know rune island, Camu messaged.

"Is that what you think?" Egil asked, intrigued.

I not know, orb either if not be here before.

"Oh, that's true, in order to know the rune that directs the destination in the portal of a White Pearl, the Orb needed to have used it before, and perhaps it never had."

"Then how come it showed us the image of the island if it had never been here?" Nilsa asked.

"It hadn't used the Pearl, but it had flown over it when it was a living dragon," Egil guessed.

"That's what I was thinking too," Lasgol told him.

"Then we think the Orb knew where the body was, on this island, but it had never used a portal," Gerd summed up.

"It would seem that way," Lasgol replied, "So it wanted us to bring it here."

"And perhaps that's why it didn't attack us at first," said Ingrid.

"Yeah, but when it found fanatical followers it changed us for them," said Viggo.

"They wanted to serve it, we didn't," Astrid said. "It's natural that it went with its own people, particularly considering the colossal work they needed to do to revive the fossilized dragon."

"I was convinced we were going to make it," Gerd said sadly.

"Me too. It never even occurred to me that we wouldn't stop the awakening of the immortal dragon," Astrid admitted.

"I feel the same as you do. Whenever we set out to do something, we manage to accomplish it, one way or another…. This has been a hard blow…" Nilsa said.

"I already predicted that someday the weirdo, the bug, and the know-it-all would get us into such a tremendous mess that we wouldn't be able to get out of it. And it's happened. I told you so."

"Are you happier now? Because you're not helping at all," Ingrid snapped at him.

"I believe I am a little happier," Viggo smiled.

"There's always a first time for everything, even for a great failure," said Egil. "We can do nothing but accept that we failed and move on."

"You think we've run out of luck? That things are going to start going wrong for us?" Nilsa asked, worried.

"Let's hope not," Gerd said, looking horrified.

"Luck had little to do with what happened," said Egil.

"We did have some luck—we're not dead and we've confronted an immortal dragon and his fanatical followers," said Astrid.

"I wonder why he didn't turn to face us and kill us all," Viggo wondered aloud, more to himself than to the group.

Not have energy, I feel.

"He had no power left?" Ingrid asked.

No. Almost not escape. Exhausted.

"The process of reincarnation must've consumed all the Orb's power. Once the spirit of the dragon passed into the body it must've been left with almost no energy," said Egil.

"He used what little he had left to escape," said Lasgol.

"Perhaps that's why he hasn't come back to kill us," Astrid reasoned, "because he still hasn't recovered all his power."

"It's very likely, I guess that recovering all the power he spent in the reincarnation will take the dragon quite a while," Egil mused.

"What do you think, Camu? How long do you think it'll take him to recover?" Lasgol asked him.

Many days. Maybe need sleep long sleep.

"Sleep a long sleep? What does that mean?" Viggo asked, raising an eyebrow.

"I think what Camu means is hibernation," Egil clarified.

"It might be, although he could appear right now and try to kill us all."

"It makes me so angry we weren't able to stop the reincarnation," Ingrid said, greatly frustrated.

"At least we managed to save those poor wretches," said Nilsa as she watched the slaves at the camp.

"Yeah, we did that. It would've been a terrible tragedy if they had perished in the volcano," Gerd nodded, also watching the prisoners.

"Do you think anyone else survived?" Astrid asked.

"I doubt it, several levels of rock fell in the cavern, burying it. We were lucky to get out of there alive," Lasgol said.

"So, what do we do now?" Nilsa asked in a sad tone.

"Yeah, we're in a terrible situation," Gerd said. "The dragon will raze Norghana, bringing death and destruction to our people."

"Well, it's easy. We find out how to kill a dragon, find him, and kill him. Case closed," Viggo said nonchalantly.

"Of course, because that sounds so easy to do," Nilsa told him.

"Look here, for once I think it's a fantastic plan," Ingrid said to Viggo with a wink.

Viggo beamed happily from ear to ear.

"I think it'll be a little more complex than Viggo has calculated in his plan, but without a doubt it's the plan we have to follow," Egil said, nodding.

Plan good. Much difficult, Camu messaged.

Ona growled once.

"In that case, that's the plan we'll follow," Lasgol said too.

"Speak no more, death to the dragon!" Astrid cried.

"Death to Dergha-Sho-Blaska!" Viggo cried, punching the sky

345

with his fist.

"Death to Dergha-Sho-Blaska!" they all joined in the same gesture.

The adventure continues in the next book of the saga:

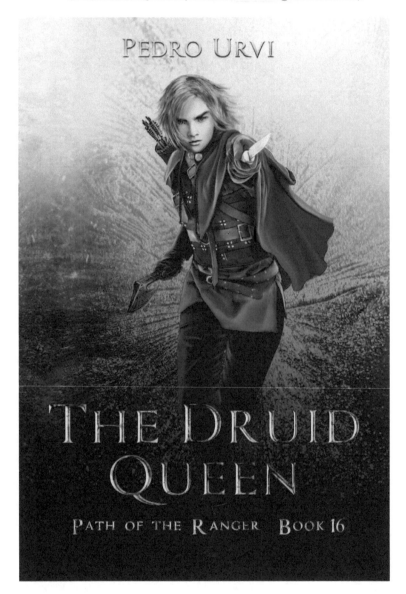

Note from the author:
I really hope you enjoyed my book. If you did, I would appreciate it if you could write a quick review. It helps me tremendously as it is one of the main factors readers consider when buying a book. As an Indie author I really need of your support.
Just go to Amazon end enter a review
Thank you so very much.
Pedro.

Author

Pedro Urvi

I would love to hear from you.
You can find me at:
Mail: pedrourvi@hotmail.com
Twitter: https://twitter.com/PedroUrvi
Facebook: https://www.facebook.com/PedroUrviAuthor/
My Website: http://pedrourvi.com

Join my mailing list to receive the latest news about my books:

Mailing List:
http://pedrourvi.com/mailing-list/

Thank you for reading my books!

Other Series by Pedro Urvi

THE ILENIAN ENIGMA

This series takes place several years after the Path of the Ranger Series. It has different protagonists. Lasgol joins the adventure in the second book of the series. He is a secondary character in this one, but he plays an important role, and he is alone…

THE SECRET OF THE GOLDEN GODS

This series takes place three thousand years before the Path of the Ranger Series

Different protagonists, same world, one destiny.

You can find all my books at Amazon.
Enjoy the adventure!

See you in:

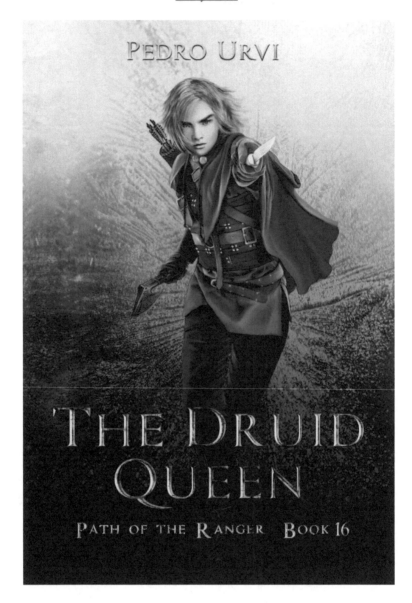

PEDRO URVI

THE DRUID QUEEN

PATH OF THE RANGER BOOK 16

Made in United States
Troutdale, OR
02/25/2024

17951591R00199